Terminal Justice

Terminal Justice

Lyle Howard

Terminal Justice/Lyle Howard

Contact Information: Lylehoward1@aol.com

ISBN-13: 978-1511508957
ISBN-10: 1511508957

For Riva,
My one true love, inspiration and the reason I persevere.

For Tali, Nave, Eric and Jeff
Who make dreams come true.

1

Las Vegas, Nevada
12:10 A.M.

One hour to live

Isaac Berger stood in front of the mirror and tried to admire himself in the uniform. It wasn't easy: he thought he looked like a scarecrow. His hair had fallen out months ago, and all that remained were a few valiant strands here and there, sticking out like weeds on a sidewalk. He'd thought about shaving his head, but that would have been like giving into his affliction. He wanted the hair to grow back ... prayed that it would. He longed for the feeling of his wife's fingers running through it. *Oh, that seemed like such a long time ago...*

The photograph on the security badge made him laugh. The face was his, but the hair was thick and dark. He hated wearing the toupee, but it would only be for an hour.

They had even given him a name tag. Jerry. Jerry the waiter. Thirty years at the head of a successful hosiery factory on the lower east side, and this is what his life had boiled down to—Jerry the waiter! Berger squinted to read the full name printed on the security badge. Jerry Smith.

"Smith? Just look at this face," he muttered as he manipulated his sagging jowls in the mirror. "Does this look like the puss of a Smith? Maybe a Shapiro, or even a Blume, but a Smith?"

Two years ago, they would have needed an extra-wide lens to fit his entire face on the badge, but now, with his body withered down to a measly 110 pounds, it fit with plenty of room to spare. He shrugged sadly at that thought, and clipped the identification badge onto his jacket's breast pocket as he had been instructed.

He had pleaded for slip-on loafers, but they told him that all the waiters working the room would be wearing the same style laced shoes. They wanted him to be just another nameless face in the crowd. Security would be tight they had told him, and even something as unpretentious as shoelaces could jeopardize his cover. But he could barely cut his steak, let alone tie a shoelace. It had taken him what seemed like an eternity to accomplish this elementary task, and, as he stared down at his shoes, he felt as proud as a climber who had just scaled Everest without a Sherpa.

The belt was last, but before that he had two more things to do. The manila envelope containing all of his instructions lay next to the phone. On the bed, a week-old newspaper lay scattered across the tussled sheets. The large bold headline that read "Salvatore Mangione Found Not Guilty" was all he could decipher without his trifocals. He knew the details of the article by heart.

He took the folder and a pack of matches with him into the bathroom. Lifting the lid of the toilet, he tried over and over again to set the envelope ablaze. His hands were so bloated and his knuckles so gnarled by arthritis, it took him nearly the entire pack to ignite a single match. His hands trembled as the corner of the envelope turned grey and then to black as the fire finally engulfed it. Once he was secure in the knowledge that the information was destroyed, he flushed the toilet and watched as the embers circled out of sight.

What else was left? Ah, yes … he couldn't forget this!

Berger chose to store his dreaded toupee in a plastic bag. Every time he slipped it over his scalp, it made his skin crawl. Tipping his head from side to side in the bathroom mirror, he thought he looked ridiculous, like one of those old farts who strutted across the casino floor with a big-breasted chippie on each arm. *Who were they kidding? This wasn't hair. It was a beaver pelt!*

The belt was stretched across the foot of the bed. Size 28, black leather with a fancy square brass buckle. The disease had shrunk him to a mere size 28 from a heftier size 36. As he stared down at the short strip of leather, he tried not to think about being half the man he once was.

Ignoring his hopelessly crippled hands, he lifted the belt cautiously off the bed and carried it to the mirror like a surgeon transferring a heart from a donor to its recipient. One loop at a time, he intently slid the belt around his waist, careful not to touch the bottom of the buckle as instructed. He didn't realize it until he had finally secured the buckle, but he had been holding his breath the entire time.

One last glance in the mirror, an adjustment to the toupee, and he was as ready as he would ever be. He checked his pocket for the six quarters he would need for bus fare and the $78 cash they'd given him to pay for the room. Still there. He folded the old newspaper, and tucked it away under his arm. He would find a trash bin to toss it in later.

Out of habit, he patted down the rest of his pockets. Why was he bothering? Money no longer had any meaning to him. His identification was a sham. Isaac Berger no longer existed.

He took one last hard look around the room. Everything seemed in order. He took a deep breath and flipped off the lights. The darkened room turned into a carnival of blinking colors reflected from the street below. As his eyes welled up from the awe-inspiring kaleidoscope of lights dancing across the walls, he heard his father's disembodied voice whispering something to him from his distant childhood:

Happiness is the only good.
The place to be happy is here.
The time to be happy is now.

Twenty-five minutes to live

Standing outside the employee's entrance to the Stratosphere Tower, Isaac Berger craned his head back and gaped up at the endless spire of concrete. Standing 1,149 feet high, the Stratosphere Observation Tower is the tallest free standing structure in the United States. A futuristic needle stretching skyward from the desert floor, it boasts the world's highest roller coaster encircling its roof, a daunting amusement ride, some 100 stories above the ground. Against the starless void, the base seemed to rise into oblivion, the blinking red antenna atop the observation rotunda piercing the night like the tip of a bloody needle.

According to the information Berger had been supplied with, the ride as well as the 360° viewing deck should have been closed to tourists for more than an hour now, and only one restaurant up there would still be serving food, a very special catered affair.

The doors before him opened as a Mexican-looking fellow wearing a stained apron and cook's cap carried out two bags full of garbage. "Señor?" he asked, as he courteously held one of the doors open by leaning his back against it.

Berger patted the worker on the shoulder cordially, and stepped inside. A cleanup crew was busy mopping down the dimly lit hallway leading to the service elevators. Watch your step, he warned himself: all you need to do is lose your footing and fall! What a catastrophe that would be!

Like a child learning to ice skate, he plodded along the slippery corridor, one hand continually glued to the wall for support. The closer he drew to the elevators, the more he began to sweat. Was it suddenly hot in here, or was it just him?

The lift was being guarded by one of Mangione's bodyguards. Everything was exactly as they told him it would be, except for the enormous size of this man! Berger reached to press the "up" button, but the guard immediately grabbed him by the wrist. "Just where do you think you're going?"

Isaac kept his eye on the elevator switch, preferring not to make eye contact with the no-necked gorilla. "Top of the World."

The guard unbuttoned his coat so Berger could clearly see his shoulder holster. "The Top of the World Restaurant and the observation deck are closed tonight for a private party."

Berger didn't know how his legs were still supporting him. "I ... know all about it," he stuttered. "I'm ... supposed to be working the room."

The flat-nosed brute perused the peculiar-looking waiter skeptically. "But the whole kitchen staff was checked in over two hours ago."

"Yeah, I had some problems ..." the old man quickly interrupted.

The guard reached into his coat ... and Berger was sure it was all over. It wasn't until the huge hand came out holding a walkie-talkie that Berger regained the ability to swallow. "What kinda problems?"

They had told him not to use illness as an excuse! Mangione was a well-known hypochondriac. *They'll never let you up...*

"First, I ... couldn't find the jacket to my uniform, and then I had to hunt all over my apartment for my security badge, which by the way, my dog ended up hiding under the couch with some of his chew-toys. Then, I missed my bus—"

The goon shook his head that he had heard enough. "Alright already. Lemme have your badge."

"Excuse me?"

The security badge was yanked from Berger's uniform. "Hey Pauly, you there?" the guard said into the handset. "Come in, Pauly."

"This is Pauly," the radio crackled. "What'dya need Tony?"

Tony held the badge up in the indistinct light. "You got a Jimmy Smith on your list of cleared employees up there?"

Berger closed his eyes and prayed. *Nothing counted unless he was upstairs.*

"He's a no-show," crackled the reply.

"Not no more, Pauly. He's down here. Had some problems getting here. You still need him up there?"

"Yeah, it's okay. We can always use the hands. Send him on up."

Berger didn't know how his heart was holding up under all of this stress. One more incident like this, and someone would have to scrape him off the floor with a putty knife! "Everything okey-dokey?" he asked.

Tony nodded as he handed Berger back his security badge. "Yeah, you can go, but I gotta pat you down first."

"Excuse me?"

"Up against the wall. Mr. Mangione can't be too careful these days. There's a lotta crackpots who'd like to see him dead."

Berger put his palms flat against the cold concrete wall. "Do I look like a crackpot to you?"

The bodyguard raised a bushy eyebrow. "Rules is rules, pal. You could look like the Pope, but I'd still have to pat you down."

Tony began frisking Berger head to toe, but paused at his chest. "Your heart is really racing. You feeling okay?"

Isaac stared straight ahead at the bleak gray wall. "All this rushing around takes its toll on someone my age."

Tony's hands crept slowly downward, further exacerbating Berger's sudden palpitations. The old man could almost hear his own heart trying to burst through the wall of his chest. The bodyguard was just about to check around the old man's waist when they were both distracted by a voice echoing from somewhere down the musty corridor.

"Excuse me." She was trying to balance herself against the damp wall, a cloud of steam partially obscuring her. She held a broken shoe in one hand, a stiletto heel in the other. "I seem to have lost my way, and now I've broken my shoe as well."

Berger recognized her instantly. Like the cavalry, she had come because she knew he would need her help. He wondered how she could have gotten there ahead of him, but he didn't dwell on it for long. He knew nothing about her, not even her name. She was a shadow, an apparition, and something told him this wouldn't be pretty.

Tony stood up stiffly and straightened his tie. He had never seen such humongous breasts before. She looked like she had been poured into her outfit. "You need some help, sweetheart?"

Berger instinctively took a few steps away from the guard.

"Can you please give me a hand?" she said in her soft, enticing accent. "This is my first day on the job, and I got lost trying to find the casino. And now I've gone and shattered my heel as well!"

Tony brusquely palmed Berger against the wall. His fragile body hit the wet concrete with a soggy smack. "You wait here, old man. I got me a damsel to save."

Berger nodded and watched as Tony followed the buxom cocktail waitress back into the cloud of steam and out of sight. There was a clattering of dishes from somewhere down the corridor as Berger waited. Steam hissed from beneath the door of the laundry room, and dryers and presses slammed and whirled. Isaac Berger seemed to be soaking up every sight, every sound, every sensation, like a dry sponge. But even over the cacophony of grinding machinery, there came an unfamiliar sound. A horrifying sound.

Coughing. Gagging. Someone struggling for breath. Wheezing. Gurgling. A heavy thud, as though a bag of laundry had been slammed to the ground. Then eerie silence.

Berger looked around. The corridor was gray and seemingly endless in both directions. He wasn't sure of what to do. Sweat streamed down from beneath his ragged hairpiece. He took two steps in the direction Tony had gone ... and then stopped.

She came around the corner in her stocking feet. As she approached, she was slipping her shoes into her shoulder bag. From the purse she withdrew a handkerchief and blotted away a few speckles of blood from her cheek and neck. With the same piece of linen, she lovingly wiped down her trusted switchblade, holding the gleaming edge up to the light to make sure the blade was pristine once again. With a flip of her wrist, the knife retracted and she lifted the hem of her dress, slipping the slim weapon into a leather scabbard strapped to her thigh.

Berger stared at her as she walked by, barely acknowledging that he was standing there, gawking at her. She had almost vanished down the long, dark hallway when she nonchalantly turned to him and smiled indifferently. "Elevator's free, love."

Fifteen minutes to live

Riding an express elevator over 100 stories in less than 20 seconds is like being shot out of a cannon. For a robust person, the quick ascent might be described as exhilarating or perhaps even terrifying, but for Isaac Berger, the only word that came to mind was excruciating.

The pressure inside his head was unbearable! His skull felt like a helium balloon that some unseen sadist was inflating beyond the bursting point. He forced his hands over his ears to fight the torture, but the higher the elevator climbed, the deeper the invisible hand drove the spike into his brain. He wanted to scream ... anything to relieve the pounding! Forty ... fifty ... sixty stories the lift rocketed upward. Staring at his distorted reflection in the elevator doors, the normally white sclera of his eyes were now a road map of crimson variegations.

Ninety ... ninety-five ... Top of the World. He didn't think he was going to make it!

When the elevator finally jerked to a stop, Berger was so queasy he thought he might lose what little of his dinner he had managed to keep down. With his eyes still unable to focus and his vision blurry at best, he grabbed for the handrail inside the compartment to steady himself. As the doors slid open, harsh kitchen light rushed into the elevator compartment assaulting his incapacitated eyes with its glaring intensity. *Just hang in there a little longer; it'll all be over soon!*

"Hey, Smith. What's the matter with you?" The voice came from an indistinct silhouette standing between the opened doors. Berger assumed that this was the Pauly that Tony had been speaking to on his two-way radio.

"I just got so sick all of a sudden." It was all Berger could think to answer.

An arm cinched around the old man's waist and helped him into a chair. "Lemme have a look at you here." He felt a finger under his chin, lifting his head up. "Whoa! Look at them peepers! They look like a pair of three-balls from a pool table! I ain't never seen nothing like that before! Can you even see me?"

He wondered how he was supposed to get close enough to Mangione if he couldn't differentiate someone standing two feet in front of his face? "I ... I just need to rest a minute. That elevator ride takes it out of me every time!"

Pauly scanned his clipboard. "Yeah, I can see that you're not a regular here. You usually work down in the hotel?"

Berger nodded in the affirmative. The fictitious Jimmy Smith supposedly waited tables in the casino's coffee shop. "Can you wet a dish rag for me?"

The activity in the kitchen was calamitous. Waiters and cooks were running all over the place, screaming orders and directions at the tops of their lungs. The malignant odor of overcooked broccoli filled his nostrils. He would have known that stench anywhere. It was a foul odor he had smelled every Friday night of his entire married life. Why was it that he never had the heart to tell Sara how much he despised that vegetable?

Weaving his way through the tumult, Pauly managed to return promptly with a dampened towel. "Here, put this over your eyes," he advised. "Let 'em cool off for a minute. Jeez, old man, you're sweatin' like a pig!"

Berger let the cool compress do its work. For the first time in the past two weeks, the pain was so terrible, his mind could think of nothing else.

A few minutes passed and, thankfully, the nausea began to subside.

"You gonna be able to work?" Pauly asked, as he gnawed on a celery stick he had snatched off a passing tray of table garnish.

Berger rubbed the wet rag on the back of his neck. It felt refreshing against his clammy skin. "Sure, I can work. I'm feeling a bit better."

Pauly pointed the half-eaten celery stalk at the old man. "You're lookin' much better. The color's coming back to your face, and your eyes don't look nearly as bad as they did a few minutes ago."

"The towel did the trick," Berger said. "Just point me to my station."

Pauly shrugged. "Hey, I'm just security around here. You're gonna have to find out from the caterer where you're supposed to go."

Berger held out his hand. "Well, thanks for all your help. You're a nice young man."

Pauly dried off his hand on his pants before shaking the waiter's hand. "Anytime. I'm glad to see that you're feeling better."

Berger was about to walk away, when he paused. "Oh, by the way..."

"Yeah?"

"Tony asked me to tell you that he was hungry and he wanted a sandwich."

Pauly shook his head. "That guy must have a hollow leg or something. He just ate!"

Berger shrugged. "Well, if I make him a sandwich, will you take it down to him? I can't face that ride again."

Pauly looked around and shrugged. "Yeah, okay. I guess I'll do it."

Berger smiled, as he remembered the words of Robert Frost etched on the wooden plaque that had hung behind his desk at the hosiery factory for over 30 years: "In three words I can sum up everything I have learned about life: It goes on." "Okay then," he said, knowing full well that by sending him back down, he just might have returned Pauly's kindness a million-fold. "Wait right here. I'll be right back."

Seven minutes to live

The party had been well underway for over two hours. Congratulatory banners, colorful streamers, and cigar smoke as thick as British fog filled the ceiling of the rotating room. Every hour, the Top of the World restaurant made one full revolution, affording diners, and in this case party-goers, a breathtaking vista of the undisputed gambling Mecca of the United States.

Chivalry was not a neglected custom in this circle of organized crime bosses, but one would have never known it from surveying this room. The women stood off to one side, sipping their martinis or stirring their gin fizzes, each trying to upstage the next with their exaggerations of wealth and power. What any one of them might have spent on their finery and jewels could have bought the average teenager a decent college education.

Unlike the women, whose voices grew louder in direct proportion to the amount of alcohol they imbibed, the men conversed in whispers. Through the choking haze of $25 illegally-imported Cuban cigars, new contacts were being made, old relationships were being cemented, and life-ending decrees were being deliberated.

And at the center of it all sat Salvatore Mangione.

Berger could see him through the diamond-shaped windows in the doors that swung out from the kitchen into the dining area. Mangione was holding court, like some sleazy pontiff accepting devotions from his faithful parishioners. Spinning his cigar between his lips until it bordered on the obscene, the stocky little man with the Julius Caesar haircut was enjoying every last minute of the party being thrown in his honor. *Every last minute...*

Five minutes

The cápos of nearly every major crime family were present. Berger hadn't memorized all of their names, but he recognized them from their pictures. They stood huddled together like football players on a gridiron, with Mangione, the quarterback, in the middle of the pack. The scene was set, the timing was perfect. Berger couldn't have asked for anything more.

"Hey! You by the door!" Berger turned to see the caterer, a tall, thin fagela scowling at him. "You come here to work, or to watch?"

"Sorry; you caught me daydreaming."

The caterer waggled his finger in Berger's face. "Well rise and shine, Mister Sleepyhead! You've got an entire plate of hors d'oeuvres to pass out before they turn to mush!"

Berger accepted his reprimand, grabbed a tray of stuffed mushroom caps, and headed out to meet his destiny.

Four minutes
A quartet from one of the casino lounges had been hired to play nothing but old Italian ballads. This style of music was obviously not an integral part of their normal repertoire—and it showed—but no one cared.

The invited guests attacked Berger's tray of food like a flock of hungry vultures. He hadn't made it 50 feet from the kitchen before his tray was emptied and he had to return for another. As he moved around the room passing out napkins and lukewarm egg rolls, he feigned a gratuitous smile and tried to focus on what they had told him. His instructions were specific: keep them between you and the windows.

That was easier said than done.

Three minutes
There was an unequivocal hierarchy to the way the other men were positioned around Mangione. Like the rings inside a severed tree bark, the further away you stood from the core, the newer you were to the organization, and the less power and respect you commanded. Getting close would be no simple task. At least a dozen foot soldiers stood protectively around their cápos, only allowing the waiters bearing beverages to pass through their imposing perimeter. It was time for him to make a switch.

Two minutes
Berger stepped quickly over to the bar and took his place in line behind another server waiting for a tray of drinks.

"I've never seen you here before. You new?" the other waiter asked.

Berger pointed to the man's bowtie implying that it was crooked. "Filling in for someone."

The waiter set his tray down on the bar top, handed the bartender a list of drink orders, and straightened his tie while the tray was being filled. "So, you making any money here?"

Berger shook his head.

"Yeah, me neither. All the friggin' money in the world, and the cheap bastards got nothing but lint in their pockets! Hey, I got a wife and two kids to support for God's sake! Cheap bastards!"

Berger grabbed the waiter by the sleeve and spun him around. "I want you to listen to me and listen closely."

The waiter jerked his arm away. "Are you crazy, old man?"

"You've got to do exactly what I say."

"Why should I?"

Berger pulled the waiter's head close to his, and whispered in his ear. Without a moment's hesitation, the waiter walked quickly but nonchalantly from the dining room and headed for the elevator. Berger picked up the abandoned tray of drinks. *It goes on.*

One minute

His hands were trembling so hard, the ice in the drinks was rattling. Through the panorama of windows, Berger could see the glitter of the city sparkling below, and in stark contrast, the foreboding darkness of the desert on the horizon. The short trek from the bar to where Mangione was ruling his roost seemed interminable. *Coming through ... dead man walking!* He remembered hearing that in a prison film somewhere.

"Where you goin' with those?" one of the underlings gruffly asked him.

Berger stared down at his belt buckle. "Somebody ordered drinks?"

"What happened to the other guy?"

Berger took a deep breath. Even in this stale atmosphere, the air suddenly tasted wonderfully sweet. "Somebody beeped him from home. You want these drinks or not?"

The bodyguard scanned the tray suspiciously. "Yeah, go ahead."
The rest seemed to happen in slow motion.

Salvatore Mangione was in Berger's eyes, but not in his mind or heart. His wife Sara—he remembered her the way she looked on the day they first met. His three children, five grandchildren ... their security was all that mattered. Happiness makes up for in height what it lacks in length.

Three seconds
Isaac Berger held out the drink tray with one hand and recited the Kaddish to himself. Salvatore Mangione never even saw his executioner's face.

Zero hour ... 2:42 A.M.
Windows were blown out as far away as the Mirage Hotel from the thunderous concussion of the blast. Gamblers were thrown from their stools as the shock wave rumbled down the strip. In the bumper-to-bumper traffic, windshields imploded, sending shards of razor sharp glass through the air like shrapnel from a grenade. Sleeping tourists were hurled from their beds with the force of an earthquake. Flying glass turned faces into pin cushions. Unprotected arms and legs were flayed and slashed. Eardrums were burst, and eyes were blinded, as the tidal wave of sonic force steam-rolled over anything and anyone in its path.

Everyone inside the Top of the World Restaurant simply ceased to be. The explosion came as a blast of searing white light that disintegrated everything within a 200-foot radius. The family members who were unlucky enough to be standing near the windows at the moment of detonation were catapulted outward into empty space, only to plunge headlong through the breach and splash onto the merciless pavement below.

Hundreds of stunned bystanders found themselves frozen in terror, unable to run from the surreal vision of the cars from the rooftop roller coaster plummeting toward them. Like a 50,000 pound snake slithering its way down the side of the tower, the miniature train caterwauled all the way to the sidewalk below. Over 30 innocent bystanders were instantly pulverized by the falling cars. A smoking crater 60 feet wide and eight feet deep was left in the train's bloody wake.

As far away as Henderson, Nevada, the burning tower was clearly visible. It glowed brightly against the night sky like Lady Liberty's torch.

The cause of the explosion would be reported as a gas leak in one of the kitchen's ovens, but there would be no in-depth arson investigation. The gossip tabloids would do their best to pursue the idea of a conspiracy theory or perhaps even a vendetta against the mob families, but all of those stories would hit a brick wall after a few weeks.

* * * * * *

The obituary said Isaac Abraham Berger died of complications from cancer very early in the morning on February 16th, 1997. His widow was the only person present at the time of his death. The funeral services were held the next afternoon at the Mount Zion Cemetery with a closed coffin. It rained the entire day.

During the grave-side eulogy, Sara Berger told her family and friends the reason for the closed coffin was that she wanted her husband to be remembered for the way that he lived, not for the way he died.

Only Sara Berger and one mysterious red-haired woman standing alone in the downpour by the cemetery gates knew that they were lowering an empty casket into the ground.

2

Downtown Miami, Florida
8:55 P.M.

Rain pummeled the city for the fifth straight day. Outside of Strofsky's Deli, the downpour filtered through the amber streetlights creating an almost other-worldly vista to those who stared out through the restaurant's front window. The forecast called for clearing skies, but there was no sign of a let up. It was the kind of weather that chilled a person to the bone and made them want to stay inside where it was warm and toasty—unless your job description said otherwise.

Police detectives Gabe Mitchell and Joanne Hansen sat at their regular booth debating the same topic they always did. Gabe, dressed in blue jeans and a red flannel shirt, always faced the door, keeping one eye on the coat rack where both of their raincoats hung to dry. This neighborhood didn't have the best reputation, and losing two jackets in one year was a record Gabe didn't care to break.

Gabe, the 17-year veteran, scarfed down his usual double hamburger and a side of fries, while his younger partner grazed on her usual mixed greens with balsamic vinegar dressing eaten straight out of the Tupperware container she always brought from home. It was the same old thing, night after night. Rather than listening to her incessant lectures on eating healthy, Gabe would have much preferred dining by himself in the privacy of his own place, but he really needed the overtime.

"Don't you ever eat anything but salads?"

"You probably wouldn't be feeling so crappy all of the time if you tried eating something healthy instead of all that processed meat," Hansen chided. "Just look at yourself."

Gabe's partner was never one to mince words. Everyone on the force saw it. Gabe had simply lost his zest for life since his wife and daughter had died a few years earlier.

He let a french fry dangle limply from the corner of his mouth. "What's the matter with the way I look?"

He watched her stab at her lettuce and dip it into the dressing she always kept on the side. It was her only attribute he thought dainty.

"Don't you have a mirror in your apartment?" she asked. "For the last few weeks, you've looked like crap on a cracker."

Gabe molded his cheeks. "Crap on a what?"

"You're losing your good looks, my friend."

Gabe dipped another french fry in the massive puddle of ketchup that covered nearly half his plate. "Well, I have been feeling kinda crummy lately. You really think it's my diet?" He held up a french fry and examined the thin, golden strip as it fell limply between his fingers. "They're only potatoes."

Hansen snatched the potato from him and held it up to his face. "Not after they've been given a hot-oil Jacuzzi, for cryin' out loud."

"Aw, leave me alone. You're just a crazy vegan!"

Gabe watched her posture stiffen across from him. He could almost feel the temperature of the room suddenly drop.

"Someday after you've had a quadruple by-pass, my friend, I want you to remember everything I've warned you about! Mark my words," she growled, popping a cherry tomato into her mouth. "All of that garbage you're ingesting is going to be the death of you!"

Gabe took a long swig from his creme soda. "Hey, you don't know what you're missing!"

His partner took a sip of the bottled water that she always carried with her. "You're killing yourself."

Gabe lifted the top of his hamburger to reveal its ingredients to her. "Really? How? Just look at all these yummy veggies!"

Hansen forked a sliver of green pepper. "I'm telling you, I can hear your arteries clogging as we speak! You really have a death wish, don't you?"

Gabe let out a long exasperated sigh. "And you could walk out of here and get clobbered by a bus!"

"Your point being?"

"Well, when they're loading you into the ambulance, and the heart monitor is just about to flat line, you can say to yourself, *'Damn, Gabe was right! I knew I should have tried that delicious looking burger!'*"

"I'd bet you'd never let Casey eat that same kind of sludge, would you?"

Gabe took an extra big bite from the burger and, with his mouth near bursting, smiled. "The only good thing I'll say for my in-laws, is that they make sure my boy eats well. Marta the housekeeper sees to that."

A clap of thunder shook the building and the lights in the restaurant flickered. Gabe knew Hansen was right about everything, but now it was a contest of wills that Gabe refused to lose.

"A Cuban housekeeper that tips the scales at over 300 pounds from living on a diet of frijoles negros and plantains? That's some healthy diet for a 7-year-old."

Gabe pointed the last few bites of his burger at her. "Hey, don't you knock Marta! If it wasn't for her, I'd probably never get to see my kid."

"Well, you keep eating that shit, and the only place Casey's gonna see you is in intensive care!"

Gabe was just about to hit her with one of his patented zingers when the door to the restaurant suddenly burst open, catching him in mid-grouse. "Oh jeez, I'm not believing this…"

Dripping wet and looking like a famished rat, a young Latino stood in the doorway brandishing a pistol. "Everybody, down on the floor!" he yelled, as the cold and rain poured in through the door. He held the gun in a trembling hand and waved it like a Fourth of July sparkler. "Just get down on the floor and nobody will get hurt!"

There were only four other patrons besides Gabe and his partner, along with two waitresses, the cook in the back, and old man Strofsky who always tended the cash register. Instinctively, Hansen's hand went below the table, but Gabe widened his eyes, a signal for her to hold off.

"He's just a junkie," Gabe whispered through unmoving lips. "He's strung out. He could shoot someone by accident. Do what he says."

The sound of chair legs scraping against linoleum echoed through the restaurant as everyone went to their knees. Everyone except Gabe Mitchell who nonchalantly continued to stuff french fries into his mouth.

"Didn't you hear me, buddy?" The robber screamed, shaking his gun at Gabe. "You tryin' to be *un tipo duro?*"

Gabe took another sip from his soda and wiped his mouth. *Un tipo duro, a tough guy.* Gabe smirked, then he slid out of the booth. But when he stood, something was terribly wrong.

His head began to spin, and he felt disoriented. He had to grab the back of his chair to regain his equilibrium. Taking a second to fight off the feeling, he stepped around his table and moved closer to the junkie.

The bandit took a step backward and aimed the pistol at Gabe's forehead.

"You don't wanna do this, slick," Gabe warned.

It was obvious to Gabe from the thief's bloodshot eyes that he was hopped up on something. His nose was running and he was shivering, but not from the cold. "Shut the fuck up, man, and get down on the floor like everybody else!"

Gabe turned a bit to his side, revealing his own gun and gold shield. "This ain't your night, *compadre.* Now, you don't really wanna kill any of these nice people, do ya'?"

The robber took another step backward and wiped his nose on the sleeve of his ragged topcoat. "I don't give a fuck who you are, man! Come any closer, and I swear I'll shoot you!"

Gabe took *two* giant steps closer. "Go ahead and pull the trigger, slick. You'd be doing me a huge favor. The way I'm feeling right now, killing me would probably be a blessing in disguise."

Having found refuge behind the counter, Gabe's waitress grabbed a steak knife and was holding it with surprising proficiency.

"Hey, you think I won't shoot you, 'cause you're a cop? Bullet'll go through your head good as anyone else's."

Gabe held up his hands, showing that he had no intention of reaching for his firearm. "Then go ahead and pull the trigger, *amigo*. My life ain't worth two shits anyway."

Hansen used Gabe's distraction to free her gun.

Gabe caught her movement out of the corner of his eye and stepped between her and the robber.

The junkie held his gun with both hands. The weapon shook in front of him like a divining rod that had discovered water.

Gabe cocked his head. "Uh-oh. You hear that?"

The gunman fidgeted nervously and swung the gun around to where old man Strofsky was lying prone on the floor. "Man, all I wanna hear is the sound of that cash register opening up!"

"Come on," Gabe said. "You had to have heard it, right?"

"What are you talkin' about, man?"

Gabe gestured with a thumb over his shoulder. "Well, it was kinda faint."

The robber brought the gun back around toward Gabe, staring down the barrel at him. Snot was running freely from his nose no matter how hard he sniffled—and he sniffled a lot. Gabe could sense that everyone else in the restaurant was holding their breath.

"You're a crazy motherfucker, man." Spittle flew from the robber's mouth. "Now get down on the floor so I can get my cash!"

Gabe nodded over his left shoulder. "So you didn't hear my partner unsnapping her piece from its holster? You *sure?*"

One of the robber's bloodshot eyes peeked out from behind the gun.

"Listen to me, *amigo*," Gabe pleaded. "If you pull that trigger, you're gonna hit the floor a few seconds after I do."

The gunman looked longingly at the cash register.

Gabe's demeanor suddenly turned grim. "I'm guessing this night ain't quite workin' out the way you planned, right?"

The junkie scratched his face with the muzzle of his gun, as though it was infested with bugs that only he could feel. The moment of truth had come: his face knotted up in frustration. "Next time, *hijo de puta!*" he screamed as he bolted out the front door and disappeared into the camouflage of the pouring rain.

"What the fuck!" Hansen chided, standing up and holstering her gun. "I gotta give you points for originality, but why didn't you let me take the shot?"

Gabe just shrugged and helped old man Strofsky to his feet.

"Dinner's on me," the old man called out gratefully as Gabe slid back into the booth.

Joanne Hansen took a deep breath of relief and stared across at her partner who was once again eying his plate of food indignantly. Gabe looked up at her and frowned. "Now my fries are cold."

* * * * * *

Fifteen minutes later, after things had calmed down, the dispatch the two detectives had been waiting so long for finally came through. The dispatcher's voice crackled over the hand-held radio sitting on the table. Gabe quickly gobbled down the last mouthful of his burger as he listened. The 911 call to central receiving had been cut off. The caller's name was Jamal Wallace; the dispatcher had spelled the first name. The location was Seminole High School. Wallace thought the intruder was still present, so he had spoken in a whisper. Wallace claimed there was blood all over the third floor, which he worried might be that of his wife, a night custodian at the school. The dispatcher reported that there was the sound of a scuffle, after which the line went dead.

Seminole High School was 15 minutes away in the poor weather, but, if Gabe drove, they could make it in eight.

Their waitress came by the table and offered Gabe a refill on his creme soda. He threw a couple of singles onto the table for her. "This could be number six. I'm not letting him get away again."

Hansen stood up and grabbed her backpack from the booth. "Stop it, Gabe. He was a face in the crowd back then. If he's resurfaced, we'll stop him this time."

"Maybe another time, Gladys," Gabe said, noticing the waitress' name tag for the first time. "We've gotta run."

Suddenly, the room began to spin and the waitress had to catch Gabe before he lost his balance. "Detective?"

Hansen moved quickly to her partner's side. "Want someone else to take the call with me, Gabe?"

He braced himself on the back of the booth. "You reach for that radio and I swear I'll break your arm."

"They're getting more frequent," Hansen warned, scrutinizing his face with her fingers.

Gabe brushed her hand away as the dizziness subsided. "I'm fine."

"It's been over a year," his partner argued, "and you're still letting Renee and Kimmie's deaths rip you up. You need professional help."

"First things first," Gabe grunted as he headed out into the turbulent darkness.

* * * * * *

While old man Strofsky wiped down the detectives' dirty table, he glanced angrily over at Gladys who was staring out the front window into the street. "It wouldn't be too much to ask for you to bus your own table?" he asked in his thick Yiddish accent.

But the waitress wasn't listening. She was watching the tail lights of Gabe's car blink out around a corner. In a flurry of activity, she hustled toward the rear of the restaurant, untying her apron, kicking off her shoes as she went.

Strofsky followed her into the storage closet that doubled as a locker room. Once inside, pungent odors accosted their nostrils, coming from a shelf full of liquid cleaners and an opened box of toilet bowl deodorant blocks. The room was small, barely big enough for them both to squeeze into. A single 60-watt light bulb hung from a chain, scarcely illuminating the room. "And just where do you think you're going?" Strofsky demanded, his fists clenched at his hips. "I'm running a restaurant here!"

"I've got business elsewhere," Gladys said coolly.

"What is it with you? Do you think you can come and go whenever you want to? You haven't worked back to back days in the three months since I hired you!"

An amazing metamorphosis came over the old waitress as she quickly slipped her work shoes into a nylon tote bag and eased into a pair of comfortable running shoes. She pulled a dark track suit out of the same bag and proceeded to strip right in front of the old man. No longer hunched over, her eyes sparkled with the enthusiasm usually reserved for youth. She stood and squeezed Strofsky's jowly cheek hard enough to leave an imprint. "I'm leaving now," she said. "And I won't be back."

"And why is that?"

She shoved past him and threw her uniform across the room, missing the soiled linen bin on the far wall. "Come over here."

Strofsky approached her cautiously, but before he knew what hit him, she grabbed him by the scruff of the neck and pushed his face against a rust encrusted mirror that hung over the equally decrepit looking sink. She slammed him against the glass so unexpectedly hard that the old man thought she might have loosened a few of his capped teeth. "Your office is on the other side of this wall?" she whispered menacingly, her lips mere inches from his ear.

The side of his face was flattened against the glass, his eyes beginning to water from the pain.

She yanked him backward by his thinning gray hair. "Such a randy old man," she said, wagging her finger playfully in his face. "It's a one-way mirror. Do your female employees know about the private peep show you're running back here?"

She had him by the short hairs.

"Okay, you can work whenever you want," he stammered, massaging the swelling side of his face.

Her eyes narrowed and she shook her head. Her natural Irish brogue was menacing. "This behavior is inexcusable."

"You want money?" Strofsky pleaded. "Everybody wants money. Take what's in the register and go."

She rubbed her ample chest up against his back. "You think this is about money?"

"If it's not money, then what do you want from me?" The old man sounded puzzled.

The room went quiet as her eyes rolled up into her head in the same way a shark's does. The gleaming blade came out of nowhere. It drew a flawless arc through the air, only slowing momentarily to bisect the old man's throat.

"I want you to die."

3

Seminole High School was one of the oldest structures in the Dade County School System. High stucco arches over the exterior doorways harkened back to a simpler time in the school's history, when ice cream vendors, not crack dealers, waited to sell their wares on the nearby street corner after school. Wrought iron bars protected every window and a ten-foot chain link fence surrounded the perimeter of the campus. Fifty years after the first class bell sounded, the building now gave the appearance of a maximum security prison rather than an institution of higher learning.

Adrenaline pumped through his body as Gabe Mitchell brought the car to a screeching halt in front of the school. The storm that assaulted the car was growing in intensity. Water backing up from the overtaxed sewers nearly covered the wheel wells.

"This weather sucks," Hansen griped.

Gabe checked the clip in his gun. "You're not gonna let a little water bother you, are you?"

His partner took out a tissue and wiped the fog off the inside of the windshield. "A little water? We just drove past animals walking in pairs!"

Gabe reached for the door handle. "We go on three. Meet at the front door."

Hansen pulled a rubber band out of the glove box. "Hang on a minute. I need to tie up my hair."

Gabe waited impatiently while his partner tied her long blond hair into a pony tail.

"You ready now, princess?"

She nodded.

"Make a bee line for that big arch!"

On three, both detectives threw open their respective doors and bolted for the school's main entrance. It was less than a 100-yard dash for both of them, but with lightning bursting all around them and thunder slamming at their bodies, it was like running through a war zone.

They reached their destination, but the overhead archway didn't offer very much protection from the elements. "Cover me," Gabe ordered as he warily opened the front door.

Hansen drew her weapon and did as she was told. They inched their way slowly down the dark main corridor past the school offices. Their soggy shoes squeaked on the tiled floor, giving away their position and any opportunity for surprise. Gabe pointed down at their feet, and they both quickly removed their shoes and socks. The floor proved shockingly cold.

"Wallace said the third floor," Hansen whispered, her back to a wall of metal lockers.

Gabe wiped the water off his face that kept dripping down from his hair. "That was fifteen minutes ago," he whispered back, pointing up at the hallway clock. "If he's still here, he could be anywhere!"

Methodically, the two detectives leapfrogged past each other checking out every square inch of both the first and second floors. Their quest turned up empty.

Hansen pointed her pistol toward the stairwell. "Only one floor left!"

Gabe ducked his head out of the protective cover and glanced up the stairs. "Don't forget there's the roof too!"

Hansen looked skeptical. "In this storm? I doubt it."

The school's central air-conditioner was on a programmed timer and had been off for more than two hours now. Even though it was cold outside, the lack of circulating air made the humid hallways feel like a sauna. Gabe's leather coat was already sticking to his arms like a second skin. "You think some guy that's going around raping and killing women is going to mind the rain as much as you do?"

He motioned toward the stairwell. Hansen gestured back that she had him covered. "You're just never gonna let me live this rain thing down, are you?" she snarled as he wormed past her.

Gabe took two steps and paused.

"What's the matter?"

He rubbed his forehead and his hand came away soaked, not from rainwater, but from sweat. "I feel a little woozy again ... like the whole place is spinning around me."

Gabe felt his partner's hand on his sleeve. "Are you gonna be alright? You want me to go ahead?"

Pain shot through him like someone had jabbed an ice pick into the base of his neck, but he was sure it would pass. He had had this same strange sensation three times over the past week or so, and each time the discomfort dissipated after a few minutes. It was probably another one of those quirky little aches and pains that creep up with age. "Just give me a second to get my bearings."

Hansen stepped ahead of Gabe on the stairs. "I'll go. You cover me."

"I'm right behind you!" As he raised his gun to track her ascent up the stairwell, Gabe discerned a vile taste rising in the back of his mouth. His hamburger was about to make a return appearance. He wanted to call out to his partner, but the words choked off in his throat.

* * * * * *

Reaching the third floor landing, Hansen looked down over the railing, but saw nothing in the spiraling darkness. "Gabe?" she whispered. "Get your ass up here!"

When no response came, she called over her shoulder. "I'm moving out into the hallway. Stay close!"

Always believing that she had to constantly prove herself to the rest of her male colleagues, Joanne Hansen occasionally crossed the fine line between aggressiveness and recklessness.

Hansen stepped into the hallway with the firm belief that her partner was following not far behind her. The third floor was dark like the previous two, but smelled from an odor that she couldn't quite put her finger on. With her gun raised to her sight line, she tip-toed toward the first classroom door. Thunder rattled the metal locks that hung on the lockers lining the corridor. She was less than a yard from the first door when she suddenly stopped.

Beneath her feet, Hansen felt something sharp and knelt down to retrieve it. It was a splinter of wood about two inches long. She groped in the darkness with her free hand to see if there was more. There was. She turned to show the evidence to Gabe, but he wasn't there! She was alone!

This wasn't good! Everything Hansen had ever been taught about correct police procedures told her that, before she took another step, she needed to find out where her partner was.

But suddenly, there was a noise coming from a few feet away ... from inside the doorway where she had discovered the slivers of wood.

Kneeling as low as she could and with her back pressed against the wall, she began feeling her way toward the door. Sweat glistened on her face as she tried to keep her gun poised and ready. She advanced her way cautiously down the shadowy corridor. Keeping her eyes fixed on the door, she never saw the three-inch splinter that had wedged itself into the baseboard only a few inches ahead of her. Like a skewer piercing a chunk of beef, it impaled the small toe of her bare right foot! Covering her mouth, she had to command every ounce of willpower she had not to scream in pain! As she bit into her lower lip to hold back the tears, she yanked the sliver free. The shard of wood tore out of her tender flesh with a grisly sucking sound.

There it was again ... that sound ... like thumping. There was definitely someone moving around behind that door!

The pain in her foot was so intense! Warm blood oozed from both sides of her toe. She found a mangled tissue in her pants pocket and haphazardly bandaged the wound with trembling hands.

Don't pass out, girl! You're so close, you can hear him!

Hansen pulled herself up into a standing position as thunder once again rattled the lockers and flashes of lightning silhouetted the hallway. She worked her way to the doorway with both hands wrapped around the butt of her raised pistol. Silently, she began counting down.

Three ... stop shaking!

Two ... shoot only if you're compromised!

One ... only the good die young, right?

Jamal Wallace was dead, hanging from a rafter in the teacher's lounge. A telephone cord had been used as a noose and cut a deep red gash into the unshaven skin beneath his chin. Wind and rain rushing in from a broken window caused his lifeless legs to rhythmically bump into a coffee table in the center of the room. That must have been the noise she had been hearing! His bloodshot eyes were bulging from their sockets, frozen in a ghoulish gaze. Even in the murky moonlight and occasional lightning flashes that filtered into the room through the broken window, she could see that the man's tongue had been removed. A steady cascade of blood dripped down his chin, forming a sticky puddle on the floor beneath his swaying boots.

Hansen felt sick to her stomach. The person who did this would have to be awfully strong to overpower someone this big, let alone lynch him.

There was no longer any doubt that she had to get back to Gabe. This situation was spiraling out of control. Too much to handle herself.

She had only lowered her gun for a split second when, out of the corner of her eye, she glimpsed a fleeting movement in the shadows. Before she knew it, he was upon her. Like a linebacker charging a ball carrier, he barreled toward her, his head down, shoulder aimed at her mid-section. The collision jarred the pistol from her hand and knocked the wind from her lungs, hurling her backward over the coffee table like a circus acrobat, but with far less grace. Dazed and barely able to catch her breath, she felt the assailant hoist her off the floor by the collar of her coat, as easily as someone would lift a can of beer. He was brutally strong. He held her up by one gigantic hand and shook her sadistically. Her head snapped back and forth so hard she heard the bones cracking in her neck.

In the chalky light, it wasn't easy to make out his features, but what stood out through the gloom were his eyes: two black pearls burning with evil intent. He carried her toward the window, her arms beating against his shoulders to no effect, her legs flailing helplessly. She scratched at his face, gouged at his eyes, but he continually blocked her awkward blows with his free hand. There was no stopping him! What was this monster planning to do? Ram her into the window?

He twisted her around until she was facing the broken window. Through the busted panes, she spotted the brass ball atop of the flag pole outside, the cord used for raising the colors clanging wildly in the gale. Hansen lifted her legs to stop her forward motion, but knew she was only delaying the inevitable. Her bare feet hit the glass kicking. She could feel her attacker's torrid breath on the back of her neck as he grunted angrily.

"Put ... her ... down ... you ... motherfucker!"

Wait! That was Gabe's voice!

Hansen was spun around so fast she thought she was going to be ripped in half. Her assailant still held her around the waist and positioned her to partially shield his body.

"Don't make me tell you again, asshole!"

Gabe Mitchell had his gun aimed right at them as he held the door frame with his free hand for support. "You alright, partner?"

Before she could answer, the behemoth had his hand over her mouth, his massive fingers probing for her tongue. She tried to bite him, but his digits were so thick she couldn't shut her jaws.

"Don't you know how unsanitary that is?" Gabe grunted, as he pulled the trigger.

* * * * * *

With no clear target, Gabe shot out a second window. A deluge of rain and freezing air came rushing into the room as the devastating squall unleashed its hellish fury upon everything in sight.

The primal wrath of nature was demolishing the teacher's lounge as nearly every book in the room was blown off the shelves. A normally harmless cup of pencils turned into a quiver of deadly projectiles that shot across the room and impaled themselves inches from Gabe's face like darts in a cork board. The unbridled wind reverberated inside the room like an approaching freight train.

In a rather disgusting display, Jamal Wallace's dangling body thrashed around in the gale like a child's piñata. Reams of loose paper were caught up in the swirling wind and flew round the room making it nearly impossible for Gabe to pick a clean line of sight to target another shot. He took another shot anyway, this time firing upward into the acoustic ceiling tiles.

With surprising agility, the goliath dropped Hansen, spun, and dove head-first through the missing window.

Gabe fired one more shot blindly into the storm as he stumbled across the room, swatting away flying debris and paper. When he finally reached the window, he had to protect his eyes from the onslaught of water. After he managed to clear his vision, he couldn't believe what he saw. Hansen's attacker had caught the flag pole, slid down it like a fireman, and was making his escape across the school's front lawn.

"Can you make it?" Gabe yelled to his partner over the driving rain.

Hansen stared out at the metal pole that couldn't have been more than eight inches in diameter and probably 20 feet away. "Are you out of your mind? I'm not jumping!" she screamed back.

Gabe was drenched to the skin, but thankfully his nausea and headache had passed. Shivering in the icy air, the cleansing rain had already washed away most of the vomit from the front of his clothing. "Then let's get moving," he shouted, pulling Hansen away from the window. "If it's the last thing either of us does tonight, this son-of-a-bitch is going down!"

* * * * * *

Gabe Mitchell always thought of himself as invulnerable. Or perhaps *lucky* might have been a more apt description. During his 15 years on the force, he had finagled his way through some incredibly tense situations, but nothing in recent memory could compare with what was going down tonight. He was normally the embodiment of levelheadedness, but now, crouching in his bare feet, gun drawn, at the entrance to a pitch dark alley nearly three miles from the school, his knees were actually knocking!

The weather refused to let up. It was easily the coldest night of the year—cold enough to see each exhalation as Gabe strained to catch his breath. The rain was unmerciful. It was coming down in sheets so thick, he could barely see Hansen positioned behind a dumpster ten feet across the alley.

"You okay?" he screamed at the top of his lungs.

The garbage dumpster she was squatting behind was beneath an overhang, but she too was soaked to the bone. "I didn't know you could run that fast!" she yelled back.

Gabe had his back against a brick wall. His sopping wet hair hung limply in his face. He was breathing in great gasps. Hansen laughed nervously at the sight of him. "How do you wanna do this?"

Gabe reached into the pocket of his leather jacket for a fresh clip and jammed it into his gun. "This asshole's raped and mutilated at least five women that we know of," he yelled, wiping the water from his eyes. "As far as I'm concerned, he's bagged his limit! I say we shoot first and ask questions later!"

"Are you sure you're up to this?" Hansen yelled back.

Gabe brushed his wet hair back with his free hand. "I'll be fine," he said, trying to sound convincing. But bile was once again rising in his throat.

"You had me worried back there!" Hansen shouted.

"That makes two of us," he mumbled under his breath, as he massaged a sudden numbness in his left arm through his coat sleeve

"I've called for back-up," Hansen yelled, wiping the rain out of her eyes. "They'll be here any minute. Maybe we should wait!"

Gabe's chest felt like an elephant was sitting on it. He wasn't used to walking three miles, let alone running the same distance, through backyards, over fences, and around speeding cars. "No way! This guy's going down now!"

Hansen nodded. "Go ahead then! I'll cover you!"

Gabe drew in a deep breath. The freezing air rushing down his throat felt like swallowing a mouthful of needles. "I'm ready."

Gabe stayed low as he entered the alley. The smell of rotten Chinese food hung heavy in the air, making his stomach even queasier. The narrow passageway appeared to span half the width of the block with no apparent exit: a dead end. Five-story buildings flanked each side of the alley, making the access where the two detectives were positioned the only way out. If the killer wanted to escape, he would have to get through them. Only this time, Gabe wouldn't be firing any warning shots.

Garbage dumpsters were scattered on each side of the alley. He and Hansen would move in tandem from cover to cover. In the distance, the faint sound of sirens could be heard between the unrelenting claps of thunder.

"Work your way up to the next dumpster. I've got you covered!" Gabe shouted.

Hansen nodded, and sprinted for the next oversized waste receptacle less than 50 feet away. With his gaze fixed on the insignia that read *Humpty Dumpster*, Gabe never saw his partner crash into the rubber trash can that had been blown into her path by the wind. She hit the obstacle running full speed and sprawled face first across the slick pavement. When her hand hit the asphalt, her gun flew out and skidded off somewhere into the darkness.

"Are you alright?" Gabe shouted.

There was no sound, aside from the unstoppable rain.

"Jo-Jo!"

Still no answer.

Gabe stepped out from behind the dumpster with his gun pointed straight ahead into the stinking emptiness. Thunder crashed off the high walls of the alley, making him feel like he was standing inside of a huge kettle drum. "Hansen? Answer me, goddamn it!"

Straining for any sound that would give him a clue to her exact location, Gabe suddenly began to feel that dreaded ice pick jabbing at the back of his neck. *This can't be happening again! Not so soon after the last one!*

Gabe's lightheadedness was back and attacking with a vengeance. The darkness that had been merely patrolling the perimeter of his head a few seconds before had now become frighteningly disorienting. "Joanne!" he screamed again. "Where are you?"

The sirens were growing louder by the second, but they seemed to be taking forever to arrive. On a normal evening, a helicopter unit would have had this alley already lit up like midday, but in this pea soup the choppers were still strapped down to their landing pads.

From out of the abyss came a piercing scream that Gabe would carry with him into eternity: "Gabe!"

Lightning exploded overhead briefly revealing his partner once again tangled in the giant mauler's clutches. He had her by the throat, her legs dangling a good three feet off the ground. A long, strawberry blemish was torn down the side of her face.

Gabe raised his gun, but his arms felt like boat anchors. "Put her down!"

The killer turned his head slowly, growling and grunting with a guttural savagery that could only be described as inhuman. His maniacal eyes seemed to open wide with vicious glee, penetrating the darkness like a pair of demonic headlights. Totally ignoring Gabe's warnings, he spun around, once again using Hansen's squirming body as his first line of defense.

"I said, put her down!"

He had no shot. It was too damned dark! He might hit Hansen!

The giant began to back into the shadows, taking Hansen along with him.

"Don't you take another step with her, or I swear—"

Gabe's admonition was greeted with low, throaty laughter that made his skin want to pack a suitcase and leave town. There was nothing worse than someone who didn't care whether they lived or died.

"Shoot him, Gabe!" Hansen demanded. "He'll kill me anyway. Just go ahead and sho—" Her selfless plea was cut off mid-sentence, as the murderer constricted his beefy hand around her throat.

What if he accidentally shot and killed his own partner? No matter how much Hansen begged, he couldn't just fire blindly into the dark!

Gabe didn't have to dwell over his dilemma for very long: before he had time to pull the trigger, his body was gripped once again by his paralyzing disorder. With the alleyway suddenly ablaze in flashing blue and red lights, Gabe's equilibrium went haywire and he lost complete control of his motor functions. As his legs gave way, he thought he heard a gunshot, but it must have been thunder.

Seconds later, he lay incapacitated at the mercy of a deranged madman.

Excerpt from the Arizona Republic Newspaper—

"Acquitted Televangelist Richard Hillard Set to Confess His Version of Scandal to Curious Red Rock Crowd"

SEDONA, AZ—"Champion of religion," "conniving showman," and "acquitted murderer" are all epithets that have been used at one time or another to describe the Reverend Richard Hillard.

In his first public appearance since his exoneration on murder charges stemming from the April 2005 beating death of 18-year-old Christina Malloy, Hillard will be preaching tomorrow night at the Red Rock Amphitheater.

The sensational trial, which grabbed national headlines and turned the local faith healer into a notorious celebrity, ended last Thursday with a controversial verdict of "not guilty." Hillard's acquittal sent immediate shock waves throughout the country, calling into question once again the validity of the American judicial system.

Hillard had been charged with the murder of Christina Mary Malloy when it was discovered the two had been having an illicit relationship for the six months leading up to her death.

Friends of the slain Tempe Junior College student testified during the two-month-long trial that Hillard physically threatened Malloy when she attempted to end the abusive affair. Malloy's body was found bludgeoned and bound three days after that alleged quarrel, in an alley behind a Tempe restaurant.

What the 45-year-old Reverend will reveal in this first public sermon is anyone's guess, but sources close to the flamboyant clergyman say he is most certain to address the events of the past year.

Hillard is scheduled to take the pulpit tomorrow night at 8:00 P.M. The Red Rock Amphitheater is already sold out, and security will be at an all-time high since Hillard claims that he has been receiving threatening phone calls from angry detractors whom he loathingly refers to as "promulgators of the lie."

Could all of this rhetoric be just another attempt by the Reverend Hillard to revive his once lucrative televangelist empire? One thing is for certain: we will all learn the answers tomorrow night.

4

In 2004, Cory O'Brien was going to the Olympics. To the average 15-year-old from Santa Barbara, California, Athens, Greece probably seemed as far away as the craters on the moon—and just as unreachable—but Cory had earned her way.

Pike, layout, tuck, cutaway, gainer: all terms that might seem foreign to the uninitiated, but Cory knew the meaning of these competitive diving terms before her fifth birthday. Her father Shaun was favored to win gold in the 17th Olympiad in Rome in 1960, but to his endless humiliation came home to America empty-handed. He was unrelenting in his persistence to make sure that his daughter would not repeat his failure, to the point where his determination actually backfired and became a self-fulfilling tragedy.

This moment of solitude during the last hours of her life made her contemplative once again. The decision to do this was never a very difficult one. In truth, it was probably better for everyone involved. Perhaps it was the sedatives talking, but the burden of her life was far too much for any family to endure. Her parents didn't know that she heard their conversations late at night. Her "electric chair," as Cory came to call it, could be pretty damned stealthy when she wanted it to be. She only needed eyes and ears to sense the decline in the family lifestyle since the accident. There was the van that hadn't been replaced in nearly ten years that was held together by spit and glue; she heard her father gripe every time it broke down again. There was the constant doting on her, even though she told them she didn't need anything. How quickly they both had aged, seemingly overnight. She thought that might have been the final straw, but it wasn't. That day came a week before Christmas. The phone was ringing so long, and so often, her father ended up tearing it out of the kitchen wall. "Just another creditor," he bristled under his breath, but Cory still heard him.

One fractional error in judgment on her part, and her father was about to declare bankruptcy. It was the family's only way out, or so she thought.

Cory was snapped out of her woeful daydream by the sound of Darrin Weber entering the room.

"It's time, Cory."

Out of the corner of her eye, she could see him in the mirror. His eyes seemed puffy, as though he might have been crying. She had only known him for a few hours, but he seemed as focused as she was to make this happen. "Has it really been an hour already?"

Weber came up behind her chair and unlocked the brakes. "Almost an hour and a half. We really need to get going."

Weber stepped behind her and began rolling her chair toward the door. "You are quite a remarkable young woman, Cory O'Brien. I would have really liked to have known you under different circumstances."

The specially-equipped van was as nondescript as any vehicle that had ever left a Detroit assembly line. Plain white, with an untraceable license plate, the van rumbled slowly toward the south with Cory secured in the back and Weber sitting next to her. Cory could see that the driver up front was a woman.

"Weber?" Cory whispered. The van glided to a stop at a busy intersection. "What's with the driver?"

Weber glanced at the chauffeur's eyes in the rear view mirror. The eyes that stared back at him were as green as the traffic light they were waiting for. "Don't worry. She's with us. Sort of a guardian angel, I'm told."

In the mirror, Cory saw the driver's attention shift to her. "Nice to meet you," Cory said innocently.

The driver nodded wordlessly, a tuft of bright red hair peeking out from beneath her L.A. Dodgers baseball cap.

It wasn't only her lack of conversation that told Cory this person was not someone to be messed with. This woman had that indescribable something, be it her mannerisms or just the way she carried herself, that warned you to stay clear.

"Are you coming in with us?" Cory asked politely, trying to prove that her instincts might be wrong.

Weber's finger shot up to his lips. He gestured that perhaps it would be better if Cory were to leave the driver alone.

"I'll be there if you need me," the driver replied, her native Irish inflection creeping through. "Otherwise, you won't even know I'm there."

Cory couldn't hide her apprehension. "Weber, can we go over the plan again?"

Weber fidgeted nervously in his seat. "We've already discussed it a thousand—"

"One more time ... please?"

5

Sedona, Arizona
Red Rock Amphitheater
7:40 PM

Cory's wheelchair was lowered to the sidewalk. She spun around in time to see that the driver had shed her top coat and was now wearing the blue-gray uniform of a private security company. The woman tossed her Dodgers cap onto the passenger's seat and checked herself out in the van's side-view mirror, adjusting a new official-looking uniform hat onto her head. "Official enough?"

Weber leaned in through the driver's window. "Looks like the real McCoy to me!"

The bogus security guard took one last look around to make sure she left nothing behind in the vehicle she would never be returning to. "You two had better get rolling."

The crowd already seated inside the amphitheater buzzed with anticipation. Already the Reverend's purple-robed minions combed the aisles, plates in hand, scavenging for donations, as if the unconscionable sum of $35 each follower had already plunked down for each admission ticket weren't alms enough.

What was it about the mystique of a scandal that could focus the attention of so many people, to attract them in droves to a stone stadium in the middle of the Arizona desert?

Virgil Dawson, head of security, watched the throng of people continue to fork over their $35 admission fees and pass single-file through the metal detector. As the crowd slowly moved through the gate, the warning light remained green and the German Shepherd tethered nearby seemed more interested in scratching his haunches than paying heed to anyone in line.

Anytime the buzzer sounded above the metal detector, Dawson moved in to supervise the inspection. One of the guards would pass his wand around the person in question and, as usual, their search would turn up a set of car keys or a surgical pin as the culprit.

"Virgil? Are you there? Over." Dawson recognized the voice belonging to Charlie Rumson, one of his sentries. "I think we've got a real situation over here, Virgil. Over."

Dawson looked on as one of the guards frisked yet another annoyed patron. An oversized tin belt buckle turned out to be the offender this time around. He was almost afraid to ask. "What've you got, Charlie?"

"Our sniffer is going crazy, Virgil. I think you should get over here! Over."

If Rumson hadn't mentioned the dog, Dawson would have just chalked his partner's hysteria up to his overzealous imagination. "Repeat, Charlie! Did you say your dog was picking up something?"

"At the East gate, Virgil. Like garlic in a pizzeria! You'd better get your butt over here—and I mean now! Over!"

Before he could even acknowledge his partner, Dawson was slashing his way through the crowd. "Out of my way!" he screamed, gruffly barreling his way across the periphery of the amphitheater grounds. "Look out! Coming through! Move it! Look out!"

"Where are you, Virgil? Over."

Dawson nearly dropped the radio as he tried to answer and keep up his blistering pace at the same time. "I'm almost there! I can already hear the dog barking!"

When Dawson finally reached the second entrance, he was startled by the scene that unfolded before him.

"You can't take away my wheelchair!" the pretty young woman sitting before a very agitated and barking German Shepherd was saying as her frustrated, older male companion looked on.

Bent over, with his hands on his knees, Dawson fought to catch his breath. "What the hell ... is ... this all about ... Charlie?"

Rumson was standing over him, as nervous as he sounded over the radio. "I told you the dog was going crazy, Virgil!"

Dawson looked up to see the Shepherd showing his fangs and growling at the young woman. Dawson pulled off his gloves and slipped them in his coat pocket. He waved to the dog's handler, observing curiously that he needed both hands to restrain his animal. The dog was up on his hind legs, barking and snapping as the wheelchair rolled past. This was not the behavior of a flustered canine; no, this animal was performing as he was trained to do!

Dawson turned to Rumson. "Did you check their ID?"

Rumson nodded. "I was just about to explain to Ms. Flannery and Mr. Whitlock that our dog is trained to detect explosives, and is acting mighty strange around this wheelchair."

"Explosives!" the young woman exclaimed incredulously. "Why would you think we had explosives? Because your dog gets a flea up his nose, all of a sudden I'm a mad bomber in a wheelchair? Do you think that this chair is some kind of elaborate ruse? Do you want to jab your penknife into my thigh and see if I scream? This is an insult! I want your name and your supervisor's phone number!"

Dawson couldn't argue with Rumson but he heard the crowd behind the woman muttering and bore their glares as impatience and irritation grew around him. "I don't think *that* will be necessary, Ms. Flannery, but we *are* going to have to check out your chair." He flagged over the dog handler again.

"This is an outrage!" the girl in the wheelchair protested. "Just you wait until my lawyer hears about this! You won't be able get work as a school crossing guard. This is discrimination!"

Her male companion stepped forward. "Just let them check out the chair again, so we can be done with this already. The show is about to start any minute!"

"But—"

"Everything will be fine, Carla," the companion said, trying to defuse the situation. "Just let them examine the darned chair!"

Every inch of the wheelchair was given a thorough going-over with Dawson's watchful supervision and the dog's energetic nose. Rumson ripped open every storage pocket, unlocked the battery case, and removed the battery. The Shepherd sniffed at the energy cell, but quickly returned his attention to the chair itself.

"How much longer is this going to take?" the young woman asked, impatiently. "I think I saw the houselights starting to flash!"

Rumson, who was down on his knees examining beneath the leather seat, looked up over his shoulder at Dawson with a baffled expression. "There's nothing down here either, Virgil!"

The dog was relentless.

"We're going to need to frisk you both," Dawson said.

The young woman's eyes narrowed. "I don't mean to make this third degree any more humiliating for you jokers, but you'll understand if I don't get up!"

The guard pulled back the dog and Rumson gingerly began to feel his way around the young woman's inanimate body. "Hey, your hands are like ice!" she yelled, which made Rumson draw back until he realized she couldn't feel a thing.

She smiled devilishly. "That'll teach you!"

A physical examination of the male companion came up empty as well. Even the Shepherd sniffed at him, huffed, and turned his attention back to the chair.

"Can we go now?" the companion griped.

Dawson stepped a few feet away and waved his partner over to join him. "I just don't understand this, Charlie. Why would the dog be acting like that?"

Rumson nodded. "It's got me baffled too, Virgil. I've examined every square inch of that damned chair! Which is why..."

"Why what?"

Rumson scratched his head thoughtfully. "I think there's something in the chair!"

Dawson eyed his partner skeptically. "You mean in the steel tubing itself?"

Rumson nodded. "I was going to confiscate it when you arrived. What else could it be?"

Dawson shook his head. "Charlie, do you know what you're suggesting?"

Rumson shrugged. "It's your show, Virgil. You gotta make the call."

Dawson rubbed his forehead in frustration. "You're suggesting that we cut into a paraplegic's wheelchair, Charlie? For God's sake, isn't there some other way?"

"Unless you happen to have an x-ray machine handy, I don't think so."

The houselights flashed again, signaling five minutes until the Reverend was to take the stage. This whole fiasco was turning into a comedy of errors. There had to be another way.

It is said that invention is born out of necessity, and this time the adage held true. It might have been degrading and perhaps it would open his firm up to one hell of a lawsuit, but Dawson saw no other choice. He tapped his partner on the shoulder and motioned for him to accompany him back to where the couple was waiting. "Ms. Flannery, I'm really very sorry for all this fuss and hassle, but because of our dog's unusual reaction to your wheelchair, I'm afraid I'm going to have to confiscate it until the event is over."

"You can't take away my wheelchair!" the young woman cried. "I've never been so insulted and ill-treated in my entire life!"

Dawson put up his hands defenselessly. "I'm sorry, Ms. Flannery, and I fully understand your indignation, but it's either take your chair until the show is over, or I will have to refuse you and Mr. Whitlock admission. It says right there on the reverse side of your tickets that it's management's prerogative to refuse admission to anyone at their sole discretion." If Virgil Dawson didn't feel like a banker who had foreclosed on a widow's farm, then he didn't know what he felt like. Taking away a paralyzed woman's lone means of independence, on the questionable nostrils of a rented German Shepherd? Surely he had just bought himself and his partner a couple of one-way tickets on the express train to hell.

6

The companion stepped forward. "How do you propose that my friend listen to the sermon that she has been looking forward to attending for so long?"

The temperature had plummeted to nearly 45 degrees, yet Dawson found himself sweating. It was time to do a little spin-doctoring. "For all of your understanding and inconvenience, we will be more than happy to set you both up in front row seats, directly in front of the pulpit. How's that?"

The girl's waterlogged eyes darted over to her escort.

Dawson looked at the other guard. "Do we have anything—"

Her companion put his hand on the girl's shoulder. "She can sit on my lap."

The lights in the arena slowly began to dim, and the buzz of the crowd that had been so pervasive suddenly drew hushed.

"You can't do that!" the girl argued.

The escort squeezed her shoulder. "You've come so far to hear this sermon. I can't let you miss it." He looked over at Dawson. "You said directly in front of the pulpit, right?"

The head of security nodded. "Charlie, go clear out two spots for Mr. Whitlock and Ms. Flannery. If the people in the seats give you a hard time, give them a freaking refund and send them packing."

The girl was speechless as her companion unbuckled her harness and lifted her out of the chair. "And we can come back for the chair when the lecture is done?"

The security chief pulled away the chair as the man cradled the girl's body in his arms. "It'll be right here waiting for you when it's over."

Dawson accompanied the two to the back row of the amphitheater and pointed down the aisle toward the stage. "My partner has already cleared the seats for you. As I promised, you'll be less than ten feet from Reverend Hillard! Again, I apologize for the trouble. I hope you both enjoy the sermon!"

The man toted the young woman down the dimly lit aisle like a newlywed groom carrying his wife over the threshold.

* * * * * *

"Why are you doing this?" Cory whispered. "I've failed as long as I don't have the chair! I need my family to get that money! Why are you doing this? You're not even supposed to be here with me!"

There was a female master of ceremonies making a brief introduction before the Reverend Hillard was scheduled to take the stage. Behind the pulpit, Hillard's name was spelled out in garish Las Vegas-style flashing lights, turning the normally tranquil venue into a surreal carnival sideshow.

Even at 82 pounds, Cory was quite a load for Weber. The cancer that ran rampant through his body had sapped most of his strength and dexterity. He walked slowly and deliberately down the aisle, not wanting to trip and mess everything up. He had come so far.

"I have something to tell you, Cory," he whispered.

Her eyes had fully adjusted to the darkness, and now she saw the same sadness and resignation on his face that she had noticed back at the motel. "What's going on, Weber? What haven't you told me?" She saw his Adams apple wobble in his throat.

"I have to admit that I haven't been entirely honest with you."

Cory wouldn't turn her head to see the people in the audience pointing at them, but she could feel their eyes like heavy air. "Tell me now! I want to know everything!"

Weber pulled his head away so that he could see her face. "I'll bet dollars to donuts, you've probably been under the assumption that I work for WDI."

Cory couldn't believe what he was telling her. "You don't?"

They had almost reached the stage, so Weber began to talk softer, but also faster. "No, Cory, I don't. I'm just another person with nothing left to live for … like you."

"What are you talking about? How can that be?"

In the soft purple light coming off the stage, Cory saw his lips quiver. "Eight months ago, I was diagnosed with an aggressive form of pancreatic cancer. So I guess … I'm kind of in the same boat you are. You and I are a team!"

"But everything is so messed up now! We can't do anything without the wheelchair!"

Weber carried her along the front of the stage, whispering to her out of the corner of his mouth. "They've thought out every detail, Cory. The wheelchair was only a distraction and a means to get us past the dog."

Weber took his seat directly in front of the pulpit and arranged Cory on his lap so that she was facing the stage. Around them, the unsuspecting crowd began to clap their hands in time to the choir singing "This Little Light of Mine," a raucous gospel tune that was the Reverend Richard Hillard's trademark opening number.

"So, you like your new outfit?"

Cory looked at him questioningly. "Excuse me?"

Weber smiled. "Very fashionable belt they've furnished you with."

Cory tried to glance down, but her waistband was out of view. "My belt?"

He nodded. "Exactly! That's why the dog was going berserk, but those security people naturally assumed it was because of something hidden in your wheelchair. You see, if I had come here alone, wearing a similar belt, the dog would have detected me immediately. I don't mean to sound indelicate, but they knew the guards wouldn't risk the bad publicity by denying a paraplegic her chance to be healed. No one would have the gall to cross-examine someone in your condition."

Once again, Cory was awed by the sheer brilliance of their cunning, and the depth of their foresight. "Why don't you leave me here, Weber? Go back out into the world and enjoy whatever time you have left! I can do this on my own!"

Weber ran his finger along the soft leather of her belt. "There's a trigger mechanism on the bottom of the buckle. Can you press it?"

Suddenly, Cory understood everything so clearly. "Of course. I can't."

Weber smiled warmly, and planted a gentle kiss on her forehead. "You see, Cory? I told you. We're a team."

The Reverend Richard Hillard strutted up to the pulpit, his eyes ablaze with renewed fervor—a vindicated man. But before he uttered one syllable of his highly anticipated comeback speech, two fingers held together as one pressed down on Cory's belt buckle. An instant later, the outdoor arena exploded in a firestorm worthy of hell itself.

Excerpt from the Arizona Republic Newspaper

Explosion rips through packed Red Rock Amphitheater

SEDONA, AZ — A massive explosion ripped through the canyon walls of the Red Rock Amphitheater last night, just outside this normally tranquil town. At the latest count, 15 people were killed, including the Reverend Richard Hillard, 12 of his choir members, and a young disabled woman and her escort who had taken their seats in front of the stage.

The explosion that shook shops and homes as far as 15 miles away erupted in the outdoor venue just as the Reverend Hillard's "comeback revival" was getting underway. Eighty-seven others were seriously injured by the mysterious blast and rushed to nearby St. Luke's Hospital for treatment.

An FBI spokesman says it could be weeks before an official determination is made as to the origin of the fiery explosion. Rescue workers are being hampered by the large amounts of debris and rubble scattered by the tremendous force of the detonation. An unnamed source said there had been numerous threats called in against the Reverend Hillard's life, but all were investigated by the FBI and none proved serious enough to cancel the event.

This revival was to be Hillard's first public appearance since his acquittal on murder charges in the beating death of Tempe Junior College Coed Christina Malloy. Hillard was reportedly planning to speak out for the first time about his romantic involvement with the young woman, and his part, if any, in the events leading to her tragic death.

Virgil Dawson, who runs a private security firm hired specifically for the event, was unable to be reached for comment, but sources claim Dawson was contracted because theater management felt an attempt on Hillard's life was imminent.

The FBI refused to comment until their inquiry is completed.

7

Downtown Miami, Florida
Offices of Worldwide Dispatch Incorporated
15th Floor - Tower of the Americas

Inside an office that would have done any Forbes 500 CEO proud, August Bock scrutinized the satellite linkups that filled his bank of television monitors. The fifteen 32-inch viewing screens that covered an entire wall of his office had become his eyes and ears to the outside world over the past few years. Murder, treason, rape, blackmail, arson, extortion—all on display for him, either through live feeds, or tape-recorded playbacks, like vegetables at a farmer's market, ripe for the picking. Bock made notes on each incident as he slowly maneuvered his wheelchair along the length of the wall, from one screen to the next.

Milan, Guangzhou, Oklahoma City, Los Angeles, Havana, Miami Beach—no quarter of the world was unscathed from its fair share of corruption and turmoil. Political unrest, famous athletes exonerated of murder, dictators who just wouldn't go away, crackpots seeking vengeance with a rented truck and two tons of fertilizer: Bock's laundry list detailing the deterioration of the human race grew longer with each passing day.

But it was the events unfolding on the eleventh screen that always seemed to catch the focus of his attention lately: a live, local court television feed from the City of Miami Beach Courthouse, just a few scant miles across Biscayne Bay from the WDI offices. Bock reached down to the pocket on the side of the wheelchair and withdrew his remote control. One by one, the scene on each monitor was replaced by the videotaped life and death drama that had recently played itself out in Courtroom CMB-206. Staring at the screens, his mind couldn't help but drift back to that day when everything changed…

8

Baltimore, Maryland
1998

This Tuesday afternoon had turned into a truly dark day in the jam-packed Federal Courtroom. With his knuckles blanched white and his face flushed red with anger, August Bock's hands strangled the corners of the prosecutor's dais.

Across the courtroom, defendant Earl Keely basked in the joy of seeing the arrogant lawyer squirm, but you wouldn't have known it by his demeanor. He always wore the same "cat who had just dined on the canary" smile. With his wiry gray hair pulled back in a shoulder-length ponytail, and dressed in a dark blue suit issued to him by the prison, Keely looked like the proverbial fish out of water. Uncomfortable in his binding new clothes, he fidgeted behind the defendant's table with his coat sleeves pulled up to his elbows, revealing a hideous tapestry of tattoos that ranged from the pornographically bizarre to the blatantly sacrilegious.

Between yawns, Keely folded a piece of yellow legal paper into 32nds and began picking his gold-capped teeth with its sharpest edges; all of this endless ranting by that melon-headed prosecutor had been going on way too long as far as he was concerned. *What was that Bock guy's problem, anyway? Hey Chief, you win some, you lose some, you know what I mean? Chalk this one up to your incompetence and move on! You think this is some kinda fucking personal vendetta? You want personal? I'll be more than happy to show you what personal is after this whole thing is over!*

He leaned his head back and stared blankly at the ornate woodwork overhead, his ponytail dangling over the back of the chair. On and on the tirade continued ... in one ear and out the other. *Yadda-yadda-yadda ... enough already!* He tried to focus his limited attention span by counting the ceiling tiles, but he kept losing track. His lawyer had told him this was nothing more than a formality, so how much longer was it gonna take? All that mattered to him now was getting the hell out of this place ... putting the pedal to the metal and basking in the freedom of the open highway ... feeling the sun warming his face once again ... and of course, last but never least ...

Gettin' laid!

* * * * * *

Slivers of daylight poured into the courtroom through the panoramic windows facing west. If you looked closely enough, you could see millions of dust particles floating aimlessly through these radiant beams of light. These tiny grains of debris were continually being swept up in the air currents caused by the prosecutor's flailing arms, before they eventually settled invisibly to rest somewhere on the cold marble floor.

August Bock was livid! Wiping a handkerchief over his cleanly-shaven head, he looked over at his associates who both looked away to avoid his Medusa-like glare. "But Your Honor, I must beg you to reconsider your position!"

"I understand your frustration, Counselor," Judge Althea Simmons consoled him from the bench, "but all of the evidence admitted must be regarded as tainted. Need I remind you of the textbook example of fruit from the poisoned tree?"

On a scale of one to ten, Bock's headache was an 82. He had expended so much time and effort on this case, and now, because of a rookie patrolman's inexperience, this piece of sleaze was going to walk!

"Your Honor," Bock pleaded, "the Government has already proven its case beyond all reasonable doubt! Earl Keely must be found responsible for the mass murder of these six innocent schoolchildren during the commission of capital counts of murder, not to mention kidnapping and extortion! Surely, Your Honor won't allow the naive oversight of one young officer to jeopardize that conviction by discrediting the entirety of the Government's testimony!"

Bock watched the judge fumble with a file folder in front of her. She couldn't look him in the eye.

"Mr. Bock," she addressed him, "I sit here in a very unenviable position. I've listened very carefully to the overwhelming body of evidence that the Government has presented, and I've had to counterbalance it with the testimony the defense has produced."

He stared at her incredulously as she rubbed her temples as though trying to suppress a whopping migraine of her own.

"I have a feeling that once my next comments go into the record, it will give the defense all the grounds they will need to file a motion for a mistrial, but I honestly feel it's gone way beyond that point already."

Almost in unison, the throng of reporters crowding the gallery all inched forward in their seats. Bock and everyone else in the courtroom waited impatiently as she contemplated the exact wording of what she would say next. All eyes were on her as she toyed with a miniature bronze sculpture of Lady Justice, blindly balancing her scales which graced the corner of her bench.

"This was a vile and contemptible act on the part of a vile and contemptible human being." She glared down at the defense table. Earl Keely pointed to himself and smiled maliciously. "Don't flatter yourself, Mr. Keely: I'm referring to your lawyer."

A murmur rolled through the crowd like a human wave at a sporting event. The judge slammed down her gavel to silence the gallery. Everyone flinched with the exception of August Bock.

"Over these last few weeks, the law in this courtroom has been so manipulated, bent, and distorted that it's no longer recognizable.

You should be very proud of yourself, Mr. Greenwood," she snarled at Keely's seedy legal practitioner. "You have served your client well. It pains me to see that the bottom line in this sad day and age is that it's your duty to see that your client is *set free*. Now, notice that I said 'set free,' and not '*found innocent*.'"

Now she gazed down at Bock, who had collapsed into his chair. "It sickens me to contemplate what I am about to do, Mr. Bock. I want you to know that I admire and commend you and your colleagues on the case you've presented, but unfortunately, the outcome of a trial does not hinge on its personalities: rather, it survives on the letter of the law. And I know, after almost a year and a half of heartache and delays, there are six families sitting out there who have every right to hate me, and whom I wouldn't blame if they introduced a petition for my impeachment. Quite honestly ... unless I have a drastic change of heart ... I just might make those impeachment proceedings a moot point." Tears welled up in her eyes. "I ... I don't know what else to say right here, except ... it is my finding that Officer Curtis performed an illegal search and seizure of the defendant's property, and for that reason, all evidence gained from said search and seizure must be deemed inadmissible. Unless the prosecution has any new evidence to offer—"

August Bock hung his head in disillusionment.

"—or until the Government can offer any new evidence on which to issue another indictment against Mr. Keely..." Althea Simmons' final ruling issued through trembling lips, "... I must grant the defense their motion for a mistrial."

You could have heard a pin drop in the stunned courtroom. Then the gavel slammed down and the place erupted like thunder.

Flashbulbs turned the ordinarily dignified courtroom into a Fourth of July fireworks spectacular. With their microphones and palm-sized tape recorders jockeying for the best position, the army of reporters and newscasters pleaded for the first words from both the defense and prosecution.

Earl Keely rolled down his sleeves and held up both arms in a Nixon-esque victory salute. "Y'all wanna hear what I got to say?"

August Bock chose to remain silent. He just stood up behind the prosecutor's table and methodically began filling his briefcase with the case files that were spread across the table's surface. The sadness on his face was easily explained, but the sorrow ran much deeper. Of course losing the case bothered him, but that was only the tip of the iceberg. Something was going terribly wrong. The legal system wasn't working anymore! He knew it, the judge knew it, and just about everybody who turned on the evening news or read a newspaper knew it.

Bock didn't hold Officer Curtis responsible for the outcome determined here. He was young; he would learn. Nor did he feel the judge was at fault. It was the law itself that no longer worked! The very rights and tenets that the American system of civilization was based upon, the rules that he'd sworn before God to defend, had become so diluted by loopholes and lawyer-created sleights of hand that they not only safeguarded the innocent, but protected the guilty as well!

Bock closed his briefcase and sat back down. There was no need to push his way through the herd blocking the entrance; they would catch up to him on the courthouse steps. They always did.

"Are you going to be alright, August?" Kathy Randolph, his closest aide, asked.

Bock fidgeted with the lock on his briefcase. "You'd better go out the side door, Katie. It's bound to get pretty messy out front."

She put her hand on his shoulder. "If you want me to walk out there with you, I'll be more than happy to do it."

He shook his head. "No, I'll be okay. I just wanna let Keely have his five minutes in the limelight before I head out there. He's been itching to tear into me, and I don't think my office would want to have our confrontation broadcast on the six o'clock news."

Randolph squeezed his shoulder. "You did your best, August. You have nothing to be ashamed of. We can go back to square one and start digging all over again. We won't let Earl Keely get away with this!"

"Tell that to the six families who would love to have my head mounted above their fireplaces right about now. Did you see their faces as they left the courtroom? If they had me in their mouths, they would have spit me into the river!"

"August, you're being much too hard on yourself!"

Bock slipped on his sunglasses and stood up. "No. Quite frankly, I don't think I'm being hard enough! Whatever happened to the good ol' days when justice was as simple as an eye for an eye?"

Kathy Randolph smiled. "Well, I for one am glad those days are long gone!"

* * * * * *

The media schooled around the bottom of the granite staircase like sharks in a feeding frenzy, waiting for him to make his appearance; like their aquatic kin, they smelled blood in the water. They had already picked apart Earl Keely and realized there was nothing much there to begin with. But victory was something that rated a 30 second tag following the sports. Defeat, on the other hand, was lead material!

August Bock stood inside the building, just beyond the revolving doors, watching them down there, salivating like a pack of hungry wolves.

"Why don't we go out one of the side doors?" Randolph suggested.

Bock shifted his briefcase into his other hand nervously. "What, and have them track me down at the office? Uh-uh, might as well do it here, and get it over with."

"I'll be standing right next to you. If you need a way out or someone to deflect some of the heat, give me a sign."

Bock took a deep breath and stepped into a space between the spinning doors. "Thanks, Katie, but I've gotta take responsibility."

The afternoon sun was blistering hot. Beads of sweat formed on his bald pate the instant he stepped outside. Even with his sunglasses on, he was momentarily blinded as his eyes adjusted to the glare, but he could still hear their frantic rush up the stairs.

Hundreds of voices all screaming his name at the same time. Such adulation, such notoriety, such a pain in the ass. He would have gladly traded it all for a solid conviction.

"Mr. Bock!"

He pointed at a woman he knew worked for one of the lesser networks. He had met her at a charity function, and they'd seemed to hit it off. *Start off with a nice softball before the big boys step up to the plate.* "Yes, Ms. Chandler?"

She stuck the microphone in his face like it was a wooden spoon covered with chocolate icing. "Would you care to explain to the taxpayers of this state how, after all of the time and money that you've wasted on this case, Earl Keely is a free man?"

So much for softballs!

Bock set his briefcase on the top stair, and one of the cameramen promptly knocked it over with a thump. "First of all, Ms. Chandler, Earl Keely is *not* a free man—"

The voice screamed out over the crowd noise like fingernails raking across a chalkboard, causing everyone to turn and look. "What do you mean, I ain't a free man? I'm standin' out here like you are, *Mister* Bock!"

Earl Keely stood defiantly on one of the lower stairs, his arm wrapped around a woman who looked like she was posing for the cover of *Easy Rider* magazine. Dressed from head to toe in black leather and studs, she had a ring piercing one of her nostrils and another in her ear, with a thin gold chain draped between the two. As she spoke, she jawed her gum the way a cow would gnaw its cud. "You tell him, lover!"

Bock thought better than to accept the verbal challenge. "As I was saying—"

"Hey, what's the matter, college boy?" Once again, the crowd of reporters turned and aimed their cameras and microphones up at Keely. "You just pissed off 'cause my lawyer's too smart for you?"

Looking at the heads of the reporters, you would have thought they were watching a tennis match. Now their attention shifted back to the federal prosecutor, waiting for his response.

"I really don't see a need to justify—"

It was clear Earl Keely wasn't going to let him talk. He enjoyed being the center of attention, and he was in no hurry to give up the spotlight. "Are you people writing down all that bullshit? He don't see a need."

Every man has his breaking point, and August Bock had been pushed so far beyond the limit of his tolerance he could no longer stand idly by. Despite Kathy Randolph's futile attempt to hold him back, the prosecutor shoved his way through the horde of media and stormed down the steps. Keely released his grip on his leather-clad girlfriend but steadfastly held his ground. August Bock was a perfectionist. He did his homework. He knew everything about the man perched at the top of the courthouse steps. Nothing or no one ever intimidated Earl Keely. He was born and raised in the backwoods of Jackson, Tennessee. By the age of 12, he was already classified by the State of Tennessee Corrections Department as a habitual offender. Dealing drugs, stealing cars, robbing liquor stores—Keely had done it all by the end of puberty. Murder and extortion wasn't much of a stretch for the long-haired Tennessean— it was more like a rite of passage.

Bock stopped when he was so close to Earl Keely's face he could smell the staleness of the biker's breath.

Keely inched closer until his chest was nearly touching Bock's. Without blinking, he put on his most ferocious facade, tipping his head slowly side to side, smiling like the deranged madman he was and letting his gold teeth glimmer in the afternoon sun. "You think you're such hot shit," the biker growled.

August Bock never flinched. He slowly removed his sunglasses and looked Keely square in the eyes. "Your time is coming, Earl. There's nowhere to hide. This was just round one."

Bock spied the nearly imperceptible tremble in Keely's lower lip. He knew which of Keely's buttons to push. Keely was all hat, no cattle.

"You ... you think you're hot shit," Keely stammered again.

Bock's steely gaze never wavered from the biker's pock-marked face. "You said that already."

Keely took his fingers and jabbed at the prosecutor's shoulder. "Well, tell me, Mr. Bock ... if you're so damned great at your job, then why are we holdin' this conversation out here in the sunshine, huh, smartass?"

Bock casually glanced down at Keely's encroaching hand and frowned. "If you ever lay a finger on me again, Earl," he said, in a voice soft, yet threatening at the same time, "I'll crush your nose so far into your face, you'll have to breathe through your ears."

Bock returned his sunglasses to his face and straightened his tie. "Enjoy the time that the court has graced you with, Earl. Go out and learn yourself a trade ... take up a hobby. Just make sure it's something that you'll be able to keep yourself occupied with while you're enjoying your life-long stay at Cumberland, because the next time we meet—and mark my words, there will definitely be a next time—you'll be going away for good. And I'll be the person slamming the door!"

Every camera and microphone was trained on the two men. Traffic bustled on the busy street not more than ten yards away, but no one appeared to notice. Pigeons fluttered overhead scavenging for their next meal, but no one was bothered by them. Trying to be heard over the commotion, a hot dog vendor screamed at the top of his lungs hawking his boiled sauerkraut on the sidewalk only a scant distance from the confrontation.

Keely pulled off his jacket and threw it at Bock's feet, then ripped the buttons off the front of the shirt the state had provided him. His chest was heavily matted with gray and black hair, but beneath it all, there was a tattoo of a skull with some sort of venomous-looking serpent curling from its empty eye sockets. The skull wore a helmet bearing a Nazi swastika, and peered out hatefully through the thicket of hair. "You see this face, baldy? Now, you mark *my* words: this is gonna be the last sight you'll ever see!"

Bock turned his head toward the cameras and then back to Keely. Always knowing how to pander to the jury was the prosecutor's strongest attribute. "Are you threatening me in front of all of these people, Earl?"

Keely grabbed his girlfriend by the arm and dragged her behind him down the remaining few granite steps. He was moving so fast, that twice she almost lost her balance. "No," he shouted, without ever bothering to turn around. "That ain't no threat. It's a fuckin' promise!"

* * * * *

Two terrible weeks after the showdown on the steps of the federal building, August Bock's life was in turmoil. After the fireworks with Keely, the district attorney had "politely" asked him to step down. Tired and deflated, he sipped on the last of a Diet Coke and stared out through the restaurant's panoramic window at the colorful pleasure boats gliding around the inner harbor. All of this sudden free time bothered him almost as much as being swamped with work. Everyone at some point in their life needs to reassess their values, and now it was August Bock's turn.

Since they had first found the six bodies of those poor children, Bock had given up nearly 18 months of his life, managed to take his marriage for granted, neglected his friendships, and spent less than a single day mourning the loss of his own mother! *His own mother for God's sake!* And for what? So Earl Keely could be out there somewhere, swilling Budweiser and laughing in the face of authority? An eye for an eye was sounding better and better by the minute. That's all there was to it; August Bock had simply been born in the wrong era!

Gwen Bock slid the dessert plate away and pressed her hand against her stomach. "Dinner was scrumptious. I'm stuffed. I shouldn't have eaten the cake."

Bock snapped back to reality. "It's your birthday. You can't have a birthday without a piece of cake!"

"Are you trying to fatten me up?"

The restaurant was crowded for a Thursday night, but Bock had eyes for no one else but his wife. "Have I told you how fabulous you look tonight?"

Gwen Bock stirred the rock sugar through the foam of her cappuccino and then daintily set it down on the rim of the saucer. "You haven't told me that I look fabulous in quite a while. I guess I'm glad I had a birthday!"

Her husband winced. "Ouch. That hurts."

"Am I wrong?"

August Bock gazed across the table at his wife of 11 years. Silhouetted against the sparkling lights of the inner harbor, she was a vision in sapphire blue. Her hair was swept back in a cascade of dark curls that accentuated her loving, honey-colored eyes. *What does she see in me? For the past two years I've all but neglected her, my reputation is in shambles, and yet, she sits here across from me, treating me like I'm the greatest thing since sliced bread! August, you idiot! What have you done?*

"No, you're not wrong, and to my eternal shame, I want to take this very special evening to apologize for my—"

She reached across the table and put her finger on his lips. "Don't say it, August. I knew the pressure cooker that you've been working in while trying to convict that vermin. No one was rooting for you as much as I was, and no one felt your heartache the way I did." She took his hand. "Go ahead and let them use you as a scapegoat if they need to. It doesn't matter one iota to me what other people think. I loved you as a first year law clerk, and I'll love you as an old man roaming the shoreline with a metal detector. Whatever road you chose from here on out, as long as we travel it together, nothing else matters. Always remember that!"

He lifted her hand to his mouth and kissed it, savoring its suppleness. "What could I have ever done so right, that the good Lord would bless me with you?"

The waiter came by to refill their water glasses, and Bock politely asked for the check.

"August?" She sounded as if she were afraid to broach a new subject.

He reached into his coat pocket for his wallet. "What is it, sweetheart?"

Her voice took on an unusually serious timbre. "Let's get out of here."

Bock patted her hand and smiled. "I'd love to, sweetie, as soon as the waiter returns with the check." He rolled his eyes. "I don't think they'd look too kindly on us if we left without paying."

"That's not what I mean."

He looked at her curiously. "I don't understand. What are you talking about?"

Nervously, she began folding her napkin, smoothing the edges into razor-sharp creases. "I mean, out of here..." She waved her hand indifferently in the air.

"You mean the hotel?"

She shook her head. "No. I mean Baltimore ... and Essex. Let's just get the hell out of here! There's nothing holding us back now! We can leave behind the awful winters that we both complain about so much, go somewhere tropical!"

Bock stared at his wife as though she had suddenly sprouted a second head. "Are you serious?"

She paused while the waiter placed the check on the table and cleared away the crumbs from her overpriced slice of birthday cake. "As a heart attack, August! There's nothing keeping you here anymore."

Bock glanced at the bill thoughtlessly and slipped one of his credit cards into the check's leather folder. "Are you talking about taking a vacation? You know what? Some sun and fun might be just what the doctor ordered!"

Gwendolyn Bock's jaw was clenched so hard, you could see it pulsing through the soft, pink flesh of her cheeks. "A week in Bermuda won't cut it this time, August. I was thinking along the lines of something a bit more permanent."

What have I done to this woman to make her so frustrated, that she would want to chuck everything they had struggled so long and hard to achieve? A fine house, good friends ... she's willing to give them up ... all because of what?

"Why are you saying this, Gwen? What's gotten into you? Is it all because of me?"

She stared at him as though he had just slapped her. "You can't honestly believe that I'd be that superficial?"

"Then what's really bothering you?"

Bock watched her pause and smile at the waiter when he came back for the check. When she was sure the waiter was no longer within earshot, she leaned forward and spoke in a very earnest whisper. "Have you taken a good look at yourself in the mirror lately, August? You're a 44-year-old man, going on 74! Your job ate you up and spit you out! Everything that happened in that courtroom, you've taken so damned personally!"

Bock fidgeted with his wallet, and glanced around the restaurant to make sure no one was eavesdropping on their conversation.

"I didn't mind you coming home at 11:00 every night ... I understood that. I managed to come to terms with the fact that we'd never have children, because you were always be too absorbed in your work to be a devoted father—even that I could live with!"

He studied her as she closed her eyes and tried to maintain her composure. Bock knew something had been stirring in the pot for two years, and now, his wife needed to serve it hot.

"I vowed to love you through the good times as well as the bad times, August, but I'll be goddamned if I'm going to let your job make me a widow at age 37!"

Look at what I've done to this poor woman! How could I have not seen how much she was hurting?

She straightened herself in her chair, her eyes welling up with emotion.

"And what do you propose I do with the rest of my life? Rent out beach chairs in the Bahamas?"

Her chin quivered as she spoke. "Don't be ridiculous, August. You're a brilliant lawyer! You can hang up your own shingle. Start your own practice!"

The lights of the inner harbor twinkled like a Christmas celebration. August Bock had always wondered what it would be like to own one of those luxury boats he'd admired through his office window. Until this moment, something like that had always been just a pipe dream. How tough would it really be to start his own firm? Until a few weeks ago, he had built himself one helluva reputation.

In his mind, he weighed the options. Start anew, or drown in nameless files? Be your own boss, or kowtow to some self-serving bureaucrat until they were willing to take another chance on you? Work 9-to-5 and no weekends, or spend countless hours in the research library finding precedents for some ungrateful up and comer? *Yeah, the more he thought about it, this was a real toss-up!*

The waiter returned with the charge slip for Bock to sign, but before he could disappear again, Bock challenged him. "Do you know how much I love this woman?"

The waiter, a young man trying to look more sophisticated than his 19 years would allow, began to blush. "Excuse me, sir?"

Bock signed the slip, added a generous tip, and slid the leather folder across the table. "Did you know that this woman is the light of my life?!"

The waiter nodded at Gwen. "I don't doubt it, sir. She's very lovely."

Quite out of character, he grabbed the waiter's sleeve. "Hey, I'm not just saying it because it's her birthday either!"

Quickly, the waiter nodded, probably trying to remember how many drinks he had served to their table. "I'm sure you're not, sir."

August Bock reached across the table and gently stroked the side of his wife's face. "I don't ever say it enough!"

The waiter did a little half bow and wished Gwen many happy returns on her birthday before he vanished quickly into the kitchen.

Bock slipped the receipt into his wallet, stood up and walked around the table to pull out his wife's chair. "Who said chivalry was dead?"

His wife plucked her purse off one of the extra chairs at the table and gracefully stood up. She hadn't gained an ounce since she was in college and still managed to make quite a few of the heads in the restaurant turn. "Where are we going now?"

He turned her around until their eyes met. "Pick a state," he announced, catching her by surprise, "any state!"

* * * * * *

The drive home was normally a leisurely 20 minute ride taking them through the Harbor Tunnel and then over the Back Bay into the town of Essex. Downtown Baltimore, like any major city, is an ominous-looking place late at night. Somber gray buildings tower over the maze of one-way streets and avenues that only hours earlier channeled a steady stream of cars in and out of the city. Now, with the streets slick from a recent cloudburst, that bumper-to-bumper traffic was little more than a faint echo in the past.

"You can't believe the weight that's been lifted off my shoulders tonight," Bock admitted, as he reached over and turned down the volume on the baseball broadcast. Not only had he reached a new beginning in his life tonight, but the Orioles had won five in a row. Life was good!

His wife had her visor down, and was examining her face in the lighted vanity mirror. "Do you really mean that, August?"

He glanced up in the rear view mirror, but took no real notice of the single headlight beam that was bearing down on them. "I really do. I think this decision has been a long time in the making, Gwen. I'm just sorry that it took me so long to realize how big a jerk I've been over the last two years. I really want to make it all up to you."

His wife lifted the visor to its original position and looked out at the buildings whizzing by. There was a quizzical look on her face as though these surroundings were totally unfamiliar to her. "Where are we, August? This isn't the way home from the hotel. Did you blow a turn or something?"

The few halogen street lamps that were still functioning in this barren stretch of town cast an unearthly yellow pall on everything in sight. Along the seldom used sidewalk, a strong current of wind picked up the faded pages of a discarded newspaper, lifted them into the air and carried them across the street. Bock slowed the Lincoln down as he reached a deserted intersection. The names on the street signs were faded, but in the pale light, he thought he could make out Forest Street. He wasn't really sure. "Yeah, I think I must've screwed up. All this talk of picking up stakes, and I can't even find our way out of the damned city! We can't be too far from the freeway though. Maybe, I should just turn around and head back toward the hotel."

The intense glare from a headlight approaching from the rear turned night into day inside of the Lincoln. Gwendolyn Bock turned in her seat and shielded her eyes from the light's invading brilliance. "Does that lunatic behind us have his high-beams on?"

Bock squinted into his rear view mirror, but the reflection was blinding. "I'll open the window and wave him by."

Gwen grabbed her husband by the elbow to stop him. "Don't you dare open that window! Just drive!"

Bock wasn't nearly as paranoid as his wife seemed to be. He worked in this part of town and, although he wasn't familiar with the immediate area, he was sure that he would be able to find another entrance ramp for the freeway. "Just relax, Gwen. I won't open the window if it'll make you feel better."

Behind them, the rumbling ferocity of a massive motorcycle engine being revved to the red line rattled the Lincoln's windows.

"Obviously, our friend behind us has never been lost before," Bock said sarcastically.

Again, the engine raced, and the car windows chattered.

Gwen Bock turned back and instinctively slid lower in the seat. "Come on, August, drive!"

The Lincoln pulled away from the intersection, with the motorcycle hounding its every turn.

"I'm telling you, he's following us," Gwen said as she pulled down her visor and used the vanity mirror to maintain her fearful vigil.

Bock shook his head. "This is a public road, Gwen. Whoever it is has every right to be here."

She scowled, annoyed as usual by his authoritative tone. "But doesn't it scare you, when we're the only two vehicles on this desolate old street?"

The Lincoln passed a row of abandoned fish processing plants, which led Bock to believe they were heading in the right direction. "This is a rundown section of the city, sweetheart. There's not going to be much traffic around here this late at night."

Gwen held onto her shoulder harness with ashen knuckles, as the car splashed and bounced through a puddle of standing water. "Nice, smooth roads they've got down here!"

Bock clutched the steering wheel with both hands as the car jostled and rocked through the dingiest part of town. "Hang on. We should be able to see the freeway entrance soon."

The motorcycle pursuing them made a right turn and disappeared from view. "Now, you see there?" Bock said, nodding up at the rear view mirror. "That guy wasn't following us. You've got to learn to curb that rampant paranoia of yours, darlin'!"

The lights of the harbor were never a more welcome sight than they were for the Bocks that evening. Somehow they had driven in a complete circle and found themselves near the old wharf where the fishing fleet was moored. As they drove along the pier, the fishing trawlers bobbed gently in their berths. Even with the car windows closed, and the air conditioning blasting, the tolling of ship's bells was a comforting sound.

"I think I know where we're at now," Bock said optimistically. "The entrance to I-95 should only be half a mile or so up the road, and then we're home free!"

For the first time since they had found themselves lost, Gwen relaxed beside him. "Thank goodness! I guess I was acting a little bit irrational back there, wasn't I?"

Bock raised a sarcastic eyebrow. "Perhaps a bit."

"Hey, cut me a little slack, will ya'? It's so creepy around here at night!"

They passed a red and blue insignia that pointed the way to I-95. "There! You see?"

Gwen Bock leaned her head back against the headrest. "Thank God!"

The rider appeared again out of nowhere, cutting across their field of vision traveling from left to right, a blur of silver and black, a cloud of dust and gravel spitting out from behind the powerful machine.

August Bock jammed on the brakes and instinctively put out his right arm to hold his wife in her seat. "Did you see that idiot? Where did he come from? He drove right out in front of us! I almost nailed him!"

"Is that the same motorcycle that was following us?" his wife asked, fear filling her voice.

Bock blew out a nervous breath, trying to stop his hands from shaking on the steering wheel. "Don't be ridiculous."

They were still at a standstill when the big Harley circled back. Not more than 200 yards away, they could see the entrance ramp to the highway and the fog-shrouded spires of the city beyond that. The motorcycle did a slow semicircle until it was facing the Lincoln head on. With the motorcycle's headlight glaring in their faces, the ramp may as well have been 200 miles away.

Bock instinctively reached over and checked his wife's seat belt making sure it was secure. "What's he doing?"

The biker appeared to be deliberately lingering just beyond the range of the car's headlights.

"He's blocking the entrance ramp."

Gwen Bock never looked so scared. "August, I don't like this. Turn the car around ... please!"

Bock squinted into the rear view mirror trying to see what was behind him. The extremely narrow road ran directly between two fish packing plants. If a person were planning an ambush, they couldn't have picked a more perfect spot. "I think this service road is too narrow to make a U-turn, but I'll try!"

He spun the wheel to the left, and coaxed the car in that direction. Now to their right, the motorcycle engine revved like a hungry animal.

Gwen Bock turned toward the window and cupped her hands around her eyes, trying to see through the blinding glare. "Hurry, August! Hurry!"

The oversized Lincoln was now turned sideways on the narrow street, the passenger's side of the car facing their predator. The car's headlights fell upon a mangy-looking dog sitting atop a loading dock of one of the unoccupied fisheries. The disheveled canine stared down at the occupants of the Lincoln with bleary-eye indifference. "We're pinned in!"

"Back up!" Gwen screamed.

Bock yanked the Lincoln into reverse. "I'm trying, but we're wedged in here! I don't have any room to move!"

The motorcycle inched closer, its deafening engine causing the stray dog to turn and run for cover.

"He's getting closer!" Gwen screamed. "For God's sake, do something, August!"

Bock hit the accelerator and the Lincoln slammed into a storage area filled with empty 55 gallon drums. One of the containers fell onto the trunk and bounced into the rear window, shattering it.

It was at that moment that August Bock realized that his wife had lost it. She was screaming at the top of her lungs, struggling to undo the seat belt strapping her in. He threw the Lincoln into drive and turned the steering wheel as far to the left as it would go. The car lurched forward, hit the loading wall, and stalled. Frantically, he fumbled with the keys to get it restarted.

The Harley rolled ever closer, pulling up so near in fact that the tread of the front tire left a muddy impression on the passenger side door.

Gwen Bock tried to open the door, but it was blocked by the Harley and wouldn't budge. She began shoving her husband, wanting them to escape out his side, but he was too intent on getting the car started again.

"There's nowhere to run," Bock yelled, trying to calm his wife. "We're better off staying inside the safety of the car! In the glove box—use the cell phone—call 911!"

Through the windshield, Bock watched in horror as Earl Keely flipped down the kick stand using the worn heel of his boot, and lifted himself off the bike. Over the straining of the Lincoln's V-8 engine, Bock heard the biker's boots crackling on the gravel pavement as his worst nightmare headed up the stairs in front of the car to the raised loading platform. He was filthy-looking, wearing ragged blue jeans with holes torn in each knee. He wore no shirt, and the obscene tattoo that peered down on them from behind an unbuttoned black leather vest was more hideous than Bock could have ever described. The top of his head was covered by a blue and white bandana, and looking over at his wife, Bock realized she was staring at the man through the windshield, mesmerized by the way his ponytail swayed back and forth as he ascended the stairs.

Keely had probably been planning and anticipating this meeting since the beginning of the trial, and now that it was here, the moment was pure terror. The shotgun under his arm glinted in the pale light as he pointed it down at them. "Well, well. Looky who we got here! How ya' doin', Counselor?" He nodded down in mock courtesy at the female passenger. "*Mrs.* Counselor."

The voice came through muffled inside the car, but August Bock would have recognized it anywhere. "Don't do anything stupid, Keely!" he yelled as he went to open his door. If anything *were* to happen, he wanted to get as far away from Gwen as possible. "If you've got a problem with me, deal with me! You don't have to involve my wife!"

Bock never took his eyes off Keely as he continued to move the barrel of the shotgun back and forth like a prison guard. "Stay in the car, Counselor!"

Bock whispered to his wife. "Slide down in your seat, Gwen!"

Keely saw her starting to disappear behind the dashboard and shifted the gun at her. "Uh-uh, you stay right where I can see you, lady—and put down that telephone!"

"He's crazy, August!"

"I know that, sweetheart, but I think know how this guy's mind works, and I think I can talk our way out of this."

Something in the killer's malevolent grin told Bock they wouldn't be getting out of this alive.

"I love you, August!" Gwen Bock said proudly.

"I know you do, sweetheart. I love you, too!"

"More than anything, my love."

August Bock nodded softly. "Yes, more than anything."

"I really 'preciate you makin' that wrong turn back there, Counselor! Saved me the headache of havin' to kill you on some busy street on my way out of town!"

Bock held up both of his hands and tried not to sound as desperate as he truly felt. "Come on, Earl. Let's discuss this, okay, before any real harm is done?"

Keely leaned forward, his gold teeth sparkling in the darkness like diamonds on black velvet. "I got a news flash for you, Counselor! Too late! You ain't my first tonight!"

Bock looked over at his wife, and then back up at the maniac gawking at them from up on the loading bay. "What have you done, Earl?"

"That assistant of yours? The one that was in the courtroom with you? Ooh," he said, with a mock shiver, "she died real messy! Even tried to talk her way out of it by telling me she was pregnant!"

Gwen Bock covered her mouth. "Oh my God! He's killed Katie!"

August Bock slid his hand along the seat and grabbed hold of his wife's arm. "Now, let's just take a minute to talk about this, Earl. I'm sure we can come to some sort of understanding!"

But Bock knew then there would be no opportunity for negotiation. Earl Keely was not the understanding kind.

"My bags are all packed, Counselor, and Alaska is calling me! No one's ever gonna find me there!"

Bock could see it in the killer's eyes. He never had any intention of toying with his enemy, nor taking some perverted gratification at hearing Bock plead for his life. His blood ran as cold as the Yukon River.

"You're in my jurisdiction now, Counselor, and your sentence has already been decreed. I told you this tattoo would be the last sight you ever saw."

The Lincoln's windshield exploded in a shower of glass and buckshot. Three times Keely reloaded his shotgun, until he had no more ammunition, peppering the inside of the car in a hailstorm of lethal pellets. The thunderous report reverberated around the hollowed out buildings, while less than half a mile away traffic on the interstate cruised along as though nothing were happening.

Gwen Bock died instantly, the right side of her head blown clean off. August Bock was less fortunate. Broken glass pelted his face, with one of the larger shards piercing his right eyeball. A fountain of red-hot blood spewed through his fingers as he tried in vain to stop its flow. The force from one of the secondary blasts twisted his torso around in the seat, and the subsequent shots tore gaping holes in the muscle and tissue of his back and spine. He fell sideways against the inside of the door, his body shredded, his limbs tingling, staring one-eyed across the gore and blood-soaked seat at the lifeless body of his wife.

From this angle, Gwen's face appeared undamaged. In the encroaching haze that distorted his vision, she looked like a delicate angel who had simply decided to close her eyes and fall asleep. He wanted so desperately to reach out to her, to touch her, to hold her, one last time, but his arms would no longer heed his commands.

More than anything, my Love! Her words echoed through his mind.

As consciousness and Earl Keely both slipped away into the darkness, August Bock fell limply against the steering column. Now, the only sound remaining was the plaintive wailing of a car horn, shattering the tranquility of the night.

9

As Bock moved closer to the television screen, he couldn't help but see his reflection staring back at himself in the glass. It was like gazing into one of those three-dimensional pictures that had become all the rage lately. The harder he studied the screen, the more he could only see his own face. But the hideous distortion was not the glass's fault. It was a grotesque sight—one that he would never get used to, no matter how much he tried. Jagged scars disfigured most of his face, marring his skin like stitches on a patchwork quilt. Only one of his eyes had survived the ambush intact. The other was covered by a black patch that always reminded him of pirates and old Errol Flynn movies. Without the use of his legs though, swashbuckling was definitely out of the question. All he needed was a hook for a hand, a bandana to cover his bald pate, a parrot for his shoulder, and the image would be complete. Bock rolled his chair away from the monitor so that his reflection would become less apparent and allow him to concentrate on the events that had unfolded in the courtroom.

The dishonorable Nathan Waxman, mayor of the City of Miami Beach, was about to be acquitted of murdering his wife with a shotgun. There was no doubt in Bock's mind that the mayor was going to skate. After all, he was an expert at reading jurists' faces.

Waxman just sat there, squirming in his Italian suit, nervously primping himself as the verdict was about to be read. With a push of a button on his remote control, Bock backed up the tape again. Clever lawyering, allusions to a fictitious intruder, lost breathalyzer records, a detective's suddenly vague cognitive skills.... *What a farce! Smile while you can, you bastard ... judgment day is closer than you think.*

Bock stopped the tape. On each of the 15 screens, the mayor's larger-than-life frozen visage loomed down upon the crippled August Bock. It was only in his own twisted mind, but Bock imagined he saw Waxman turn and wink into the camera, taunting him, like an IRS agent at an audit. It never happened, but one didn't have to be a psychoanalyst to reason why the CEO of Worldwide Dispatch Incorporated was taking such a personal interest in this case: the innocent woman, the shotgun, the perpetrator still on the loose.

August Bock's entire face suddenly became glazed with nervous perspiration as he struggled not to let his mind spiral backward to that earlier time and place.

"Mr. Bock?" His secretary's interruption over the intercom on his desk thrust him back to reality. "You wanted to be reminded of your meeting this hour. Shall I send in Mr. Washington as well?"

Bock wiped away the stream of tears from his face and rolled himself over to the immense picture window that faced east toward the bay. The jade green water had a light chop to it, but it still shimmered under the midday sun like a precious gem. A handful of pleasure boats dotted the bay, while overhead the Goodyear blimp floated majestically northward, undoubtedly headed home to its airbase in Pompano Beach.

He wished more than anything that Gwen were here to share this picturesque view with him. He could still hear her voice, still see her face, just as if she were sitting across the table from him during their last dinner together. He could envision the way the candlelight glinted off her hair and smell the aroma of her perfume as they had spoken of leaving everything behind and starting a new life.

But fate stepped in, wearing a Nazi tattoo and mud-caked motorcycle boots, and rocked August Bock's world out of its orbit. In his wildest dreams, he never would have imagined he would be staring out over this tropical scenery without the love of his life by his side.

Still entranced, Bock never turned to look as his office door open behind him. "I'm sorry to bother you Mr. Bock, but when you didn't answer..."

Bock pointed the remote control and turned off all of the screens. "Are you alright, sir?"

Bock's good eye never wandered off the blimp gliding across his field of view; he just gestured over his shoulder with the remote control. "My mind was elsewhere."

The receptionist backed meekly out of the room. "No problem, Mr. Bock. As long as you're okay, I'll go ahead and send for Mr. Washington."

Beyond Biscayne Bay, attached to the mainland by a set of umbilical causeways, the skyline of Miami Beach stretched across the horizon. Where warm beige sand once greeted nothing but bare feet and colorful umbrellas, a fortress of high rise condominiums now blocked Bock's view of the Atlantic Ocean shoreline. These towers of decadence in turn were separated by a string of grandiose hotels that now stood as unoccupied reminders of a lost era in the city's history. It was no wonder the city was in such tragic financial straits, what with the immoral leadership it citizens had seen fit to elect.

The double doors to the office opened and Damon Washington stepped into the cavernous room. He was August Bock's right hand man, chosen from a list of technical geniuses fresh out of the University of Miami. Bock had taken an immediate liking to the young man but knew he needed more than just his technical expertise. Washington came from an Air Force family and learned to fly helicopters from his father. And while being computer savvy and knowing how to take off vertically were useful traits, Bock wanted more. He required someone who personally understood his ravenous hunger for vengeance. He hired Washington not only for his skills as a brilliant programmer and analyst, but because, deep within his file, his history revealed a sister who had been gunned down during a drive-by shooting. He would eventually prove to be the perfect collaborator.

After Washington served his internship and Bock finally trusted him enough to reveal the corporation's true intent, his sister's memory would make Washington eager to unite with WDI in its crusade against injustice.

Tall and lean, Washington liked to dress comfortably. No ties and jackets for him. He was as comfortable behind the rudders of the corporate helicopter as he was at his keyboard.

"Sit down. We need to talk," Bock said, pointing at one of the chairs before his desk.

Washington slipped into the cushy leather chair and crossed his legs figure four style.

"Where are we on this?" Bock asked, spinning the front page of the Miami Herald on his desk to face the young black man.

Washington leaned over and read the headline, then ran his hand over his goatee. "Everything is going as planned. One minor problem, but it was handled."

"Something I should know about?"

Washington ran his fingers along the crease in his trousers and shook his head. "Not at all. Now that the business in Arizona is done, we can focus on this."

Bock tapped his fingers on the arms of his wheelchair. "Why do I sense something about the Reverend's demise is bothering you?"

"It was messy, like Las Vegas. A lot of innocent people were killed."

"The loss of innocent lives will always be collateral damage in a war. And have no misgivings, Damon: this is a righteous war we are waging."

Bock rolled his chair in front of his panoramic window. Out on the bay, the wind had picked up and the water had a more noticeable chop. In the sky, a foreign jetliner was cutting through a pillow of wispy white clouds. He could tell it was of foreign origin because it trailed plumes of gray smoke from burning inferior fuel, something that domestic planes were banned from doing. "What's done is done, Damon. Tell me something that will put my mind at ease about our new objective."

Washington grabbed a notepad and pen out of his shirt pocket. "We agreed that, while it's not our usual formula, it won't matter. The outcome will still be successful. He is a very high profile target, and we needed a specific skill set." Washington leaned forward and tapped his finger on the newspaper. "Remember it was you who chose not to wait. And it was you who came up with this idea."

Bock watched the colorful sail of a windsurfer skim across surface of the bay. The jealous part of his heart had long since died off, along with plenty of other emotional nerve centers. "He will make a run for it if we don't act soon."

Washington nodded. "We both know that, but we can't be hasty. You make mistakes if you rush."

Bock pulled away from the window and spun his chair in behind his desk. "Then we concentrate on what we have control over."

Washington looked down at his notepad. "I'm listening."

Bock swiveled around and pointed the remote control toward the viewing wall. Nathan Waxman's jowly, duplicitous head suddenly filled each screen. Fifteen larger than life faces stared at him, frozen on video tape, grinning with disgraceful satisfaction. "I heard she ran interference last night."

Washington closed his notepad and slipped it back into the pocket of his shirt. "As far as I know, no one was the wiser."

Bock leaned forward and put his elbows on the desk. "Shayla tells me he's a real mess."

Washington agreed. "We knew he would be. We're doing what we have to. We just need to twist the screws a bit more," he said, spinning his fingers.

Bock reached into a pocket on the side of his wheelchair and pulled out a gold cigarette lighter, then opened a humidor sitting on his desk. Like a surgeon performing a delicate operation, he touched the flame to the end of a cigar as he rolled it between his lips. He lovingly blew a caravan of smoke rings into the still air and watched them float upward and then evaporate like ghosts. "I want to meet with him, but not here."

Washington looked surprised. "Why?"

"You have a problem with it?"

"Of course not," Washington said, thoughtfully stroking the short, dark whiskers around his mouth. "May I ask why?"

With his one good eye, Bock glared across the desk at Washington. "This isn't one of our ordinary recruits. He was chosen for his expertise and experience."

Washington was adamant. "Granted, he isn't like the rest, but why risk exposing yourself?"

Bock twirled the cigar between his lips. "We've never attempted this before. This problem is in our own backyard and I want to make sure for myself that he has the right incentive."

Washington drew in a deep breath. "I really wish you would reconsider."

As the sun slipped behind a cloud, a somber pall darkened the office. Bock set his cigar down in a Waterford ashtray. "What's the matter, Damon? Do you honestly think I'm somehow connecting my personal experiences to the death of the mayor's wife?"

Washington shifted uncomfortably in his chair. "Well, it's been like walking on eggshells around here since the trial began, August. It's doesn't exactly take a swami to know what must be going through your mind."

Bock waggled a disciplinary finger across his desk. "Don't you dare compare what happened to my wife to what happened to Anna Waxman. The man that murdered Anna Waxman is right there," he said, jabbing his cigar at the monitor, "while Earl Keely's still running around loose." He spun around until he was facing the panoramic scene outside his window once again. The bay was even choppier now, with whitecaps blowing from north to south foreshadowing an approaching cold front, but the vista still managed to obliterate Earl Keely's hideous face from his thoughts.

"And by the way," he said, turning to face Damon, "Shayla is not on a plane to Arizona yet. She asked to see me, so she should be here any minute. Why don't we wait and get her opinion?"

Washington sprang out of his chair like he had been sitting on an ejector seat. "She's coming here? Now?"

Bock spun his chair back to face the window and stared out wistfully at a powerboat cutting through the current. It was much like the one he and Gwen had dreamed about buying in Baltimore. "What is it about Shayla Rand that sets you off, Damon?"

Washington walked around the desk until he was confronting his employer face-to-face. "You're kidding me, right, August?" he inquired, banging his fist on the window for emphasis. "Why would you let a known terrorist set foot in these offices? What if someone recognizes her?"

Bock shook his head as he continued to stare out the window. "You're blowing her reputation way out of proportion. Besides, every time you've ever met her she's changed her appearance. She's a chameleon."

Washington wiped away the sweat that had suddenly appeared on his forehead. "That's not all she is. She doesn't kill because she has to, but because she enjoys it. We both know it. She didn't have to murder Strofsky."

There were two people on the deck of the powerboat and Bock imagined it was Gwen and himself out there. "She said he was a problem."

Washington put his hands to his head. "A problem," he screamed, spittle shooting out of his mouth in frustration. "He was an insignificant old man! We knew all about him! He was harmless."

Bock couldn't take his eye off the water. "She said she had her reasons. You worry too much."

Washington was incredulous. "Do you know how many strings I had to pull to cover up that little mess of hers? She's like the black plague, leaving a trail of corpses wherever she goes! Every time someone looks at her sideways, we have to clean up the collateral damage."

"No," Bock said, still daydreaming, "I haven't forgotten. She said the deli owner was trouble, and I believe her."

Washington tried to step between his employer and the window. "And what about the guy guarding the elevator in Vegas? What was her excuse for that one? Berger's credentials were flawless! He would have made it anyway."

The speedboat was slamming against the whitecaps in an effort to make headway. "Everyone has their own style, Damon. As far as I'm concerned, Shayla simply went above and beyond her responsibilities and ended those threats as she saw fit. You weren't there; she was. That's what we pay her for."

Washington was getting a queasy feeling in the pit of his stomach. It was the same feeling he always got whenever he thought about the psychotic Shayla Rand. "You know what, August? This time you've lost your compass. Shayla Rand has no conscience. You need to keep her as far away from this place as possible."

Bock glanced down at his wristwatch. It read 1:57. "If she terrifies you that much, perhaps you should go back to your office. I think I'd like you to run a status report of all our ongoing projects."

Washington put his hands on his hips. "Don't patronize me, August. Her coming here now is a huge mistake."

Bock glanced over at Washington and smiled contritely. "She's always on time. Maybe you shouldn't be here when she arrives."

Washington looked down at his own watch as the intercom on Bock's desk buzzed.

Bock saw all of the color drain out of Washington's face. "That would be her. Two P.M. and punctual as ever."

Washington backed away from the window. Fifteen floors was a long way down. "If you need me, I'll be in my office."

Bock rolled his chair away from the window. "You know you're more than welcome to stay if you want to."

"Mr. Bock, Ms. Rand is here," the voice over the intercom interjected.

"Last chance, Damon. Sure you don't want to hang around?"

That simple phrase had never sounded so ambiguous before. "I'll pass, but you can give her a big hug from me."

* * * * * *

Before Washington had the chance to make his cowardly departure, the door burst open and Shayla Rand strutted in, sucking all the air out of the room as she entered. "Hello, boys!"

Standing an imposing six feet tall in flat heeled sandals, she didn't only draw attention to herself, she demanded it. Today her hair was as red as a strong man's heart, but yesterday she could have been a brunette, and tomorrow a sultry blond or even a haggard, gray-haired waitress. "Greetings, Damon," she said as she walked by and toyed with one of the buttons on his shirt. "Always a pleasure to see you."

As she slithered into the room, Washington detected the hint of a foul odor trailing behind her. She was wearing a short, black sequined dress that she filled like concrete in a mold. Her legs and arms were muscular, but not so much as to be unfeminine. As she moved past him, Washington couldn't help notice that her rear swayed like it was dancing to a melody only she could hear.

In one hand she held the keys to the black Corvette she always drove; in the other, a roll of beige parchment—the type messengers might have transported in medieval times to relay an important communiqué from one kingdom to another. The scroll was tied with a simple red sash. It was like watching a train wreck. Washington didn't want to stare, but he couldn't turn away.

She walked around the desk and planted a generous kiss on August Bock's cheek and then wiped the lipstick off with her thumb. "How are you, Auggie?"

Bock smothered his cigar in the ashtray. "I've had better days."

Washington held his position near the exit as Shayla rounded the desk and took a seat.

"What an invigorating few days I've had!"

Bock watched her sit down. Her movement was as graceful as a flamingo. "We've been keeping you busy," he said.

She crossed her legs and both men held their collective breaths. "You don't know the half of it, love."

Washington instinctively reached behind his back and felt for the doorknob.

"To what do we owe this unexpected visit?" Bock asked, resting his elbows on his desk. "Don't you have a plane to catch?"

Shayla held up the back of her hand to examine her bright red nail polish. "I still have a few hours, but I thought this was important enough to stop by in person."

Behind her, Washington grimaced.

"On my way back from Vegas, I made a little side trip just for you, Auggie. I wanted to get here sooner, but yesterday's events were a bit more involved than we'd planned."

"I understand completely. So you stopped somewhere between Arizona and here? How did you find the time?"

Rand shrugged. "It wasn't really on the way, but well worth the extra trip. Ever heard of place called Chickaloo?"

"You flew from Sedona to Alaska?" Bock clearly knew the place.

She looked over her shoulder at Washington, like a mouse keeping an eye on the cheese. "Yes, my love. Alaska," she teased.

* * * * * *

Bock leaned as far forward as his immobilized lower torso would allow. He could feel the tension and excitement coil in the pit of his stomach like the spring on an old wind-up toy.

Shayla Rand set the scroll on her lap and clasped her hands together serenely. "Through my own discrete channels, I managed to track someone down there. Someone I've been meaning to pay a little visit to for quite a while now."

Shayla lifted the scroll off her lap, and tossed it nonchalantly onto the desk, where it wobbled into August Bock's waiting hand. "What is this?"

Damon moved closer so he could see.

Shayla looked at August Bock with merciless eyes that widened playfully at his excitement. "I brought you a gift, Auggie. It's just a little memento from my travels. I wanted you to know that I believe in what you're doing, and I wanted to get you something very special to show my admiration. You can consider this one a freebie."

Bock fumbled anxiously to undo the ribbon. When he pulled apart the scroll, both men gasped in horror. It wasn't parchment paper at all; it was a sheet of skin—human skin. It was heavily matted with gray and black hair, and at its center was the all too familiar tattoo of a skull wearing a Nazi helmet, the image that had been burned into August Bock's memory. The skull was as he remembered it, with that same venomous-looking serpent curling out of its dead eye sockets. Only now, the entire emblem was crusted with dried, black blood ... Earl Keely's blood.

It is much more important to know what sort of a patient has a disease than what sort of disease a patient has.
- noted physician Sir William Osler

10

Miami, Florida
Jackson Medical Center
Room 683

"Hey, sleeping beauty. You finally awake?"

Gabe Mitchell's eyes fluttered open, but he could barely discern the unfamiliar countenance of the old man looming over him. "Who... who are you?" the detective groaned, wiping the crust from the corners of his eyes.

The old man put his finger over his mouth. "Shhh ... the name's Chase ... Bennett Chase. Glad to finally make your acquaintance. Now don't try and talk if you don't think you can," he whispered softly. "You want me to ring the nurse for you?"

The room was pitch dark except for a ray of muted light coming from somewhere beyond the foot of his bed. "Where am I?"

"You're in good hands now, Mr. Mitchell. You're in the Jackson Medical Center," he said, his craggy face looking perplexed. "What do you prefer, Mr. Mitchell or Gabriel? I hope you don't mind, but I snuck a peek at your wristband, and that's how I know your first name. I figured since we're gonna be roomies and all, you wouldn't really mind. So is it Gabriel or Gabe? I don't want to seem too forward."

Something was tickling at Gabe's nose so he reached up only to discover a plastic tube protruding from his nostrils. "What...?"

The old man put his hand on Gabe's shoulder and pressed him back down on his pillow. "Conserve your strength, my friend. That's just an oxygen line to help you breathe easier."

Gabe's head felt like it weighed a ton, but more clarity returned to his mind with each waking minute. Talking was something else though. He could barely poke his tongue out between his pasty lips to speak. "Ohhh ... I feel like ... I was hit by a truck..."

Chase reached over to the stand beside the bed and grabbed a wet washcloth to blot Gabe's forehead. "You're still sweatin' like a pig. You must be running one helluva fever!"

The compress felt refreshing, sending a cool shiver down Gabe's body. "Why ... so dark in here?"

The old man shrugged. "Probably 'cause it's only three-thirty in the morning. I just got up to take my usual pre-dawn whiz..." He gestured with a nod back toward the bathroom. "I hope you're not gonna mind, but I gotta leave the light on to see my way at night. It's when I was coming out that I heard you moving around."

Gabe tried to focus but, no matter how hard he strained, his eyes wouldn't cooperate. In the faint light, he couldn't tell if Chase's hair was silver or white. He couldn't focus well enough to make out the color of the old man's eyes. He got the impression they might be gray ... or maybe even blue.

"So anyway ... I'm making my way back to bed," Chase continued, "and I hear you mumblin' something in the dark. Let me tell you, it scared me so much, I almost had to pee again!"

Gabe coughed hard and his whole body shuddered.

Chase cradled the detective's head in his hand and fluffed up the pillow beneath his head. "Take it easy, pal. Don't strain yourself."

The detective groaned as he shifted his weight in the bed. "Where's my son?"

The old man patted Gabe on the shoulder. "Ah, the little boy. An extremely large and affable Cuban woman brought him by here yesterday to visit, but the doctors thought it best for him not to see you like this. He seems like a strong young lad ... appears to be handling the situation fine!"

Gabe closed his eyes. *What would Casey do, if he wasn't around for him? He needs the influence of a real father, no matter what his grandparents said or did to poison the boy's mind against him.*

"Hey, I hope you don't mind me asking," Chase whispered, "but you're that cop from the television, am I right? I'd put money on it. This place has been a zoo ever since they rolled you in here!"

Gabe tried to wet his lips, but he couldn't seem to manufacture enough spit. "Television?"

There was a weird sense of excitement in the old man's voice that Gabe couldn't fathom. "Yeah ... you're the one that shot and killed that crazy bastard that was going around dicing up those poor women, right?"

Gabe tried to raise himself up onto his elbows, but he didn't have the strength to hold himself in that position. "Hold on a minute ... did you say, shot and killed?"

Chase nodded. "Hell yes! Don't you remember? They said you and your partner cornered the guy in an alley down on Flagler Street. You don't remember any of it?"

Gabe massaged his forehead. It was like staring into a deep, black hole. Nothing was there but darkness and missing time. "I ... can't..."

"The television said your partner held the guy at bay until you finally nailed him! You're a celebrity, pal!"

Gabe was getting frightened. No matter how hard he tried, he couldn't remember a damned thing about that night. He squeezed his eyes shut and concentrated, but it was no use—he was drawing a big goose egg. "What ... what about my partner? What did they say about her? Is she here too?"

The old man glanced around the room self-consciously.

"What? What's the matter? What aren't you telling me?"

Bennett Chase swallowed hard. "Uh, maybe we should put off the rest of this conversation until you're feeling up to it. You should get some rest now..."

With a lightning-like reflex that caught the old man by surprise, Gabe's right hand shot up and grabbed him by the wrist. Even in his debilitated state, he still could get his point across without saying a word.

"Okay," Chase gave in, prying off the detective's fingers. "I'm sorry to be the one to tell you this, but your partner," his voice trailed off, "that psycho killed her ... shot her in the head."

Gabe's head rolled back onto his pillow and he clamped his eyes shut to stem off the rush of heartache and the feeling of utter helplessness. Everything was so cloudy. *Shot her in the head? He didn't even remember the guy having a gun. Oh my God, Joanne. Was this somehow my fault? Why can't I remember?*

"I'm really sorry, Gabe. The guy on television made it sound like this Billy Ray Silva guy was a major nut-job. They said he's some kind of mute who had been abused by his mother. Do you know he was wearing all those women's tongues around his neck when..."

The detective turned his head away.

The old man caught himself. "You probably knew that already ... sorry..."

Gabe put his hand over his eyes. "Please ... don't say anything else."

Chase looked as though he could have swallowed his own tongue for being so insensitive. "Of course, Gabe, I understand."

It seemed like an eternity passed as Gabe tried to recollect those last few minutes of consciousness, like pieces of a jigsaw puzzle scattered to the unattainable corners of a table top. A piece too far away to reach, two more fragments way over there—his mental fingertips not long enough to grasp them—to fit them back together. A flash of blue light ... some red lights too. The macabre image of the giant's face emerging out of the shadows. Joanne Hansen ... arguing about his eating habits ... fearless as she headed into that rain-soaked alley. A steady drizzle and the booming thunder. The school building ... wind and splintering glass. *Was there a gun?* Snippets of blurred memories. A hazy recollection ... then a void. *He couldn't have shot his own partner by mistake, could he?* Gabe was balancing by the thinnest of threads over a bottomless pit of repressed guilt.

Chase paused with his hand over the light switch. "Do you want me to shut off the bathroom light so you can go back to sleep?"

The detective shook his head ruefully. "I may never be able to sleep peacefully again..."

After a long, looming silence, Chase attempted to change the subject. "You know it's about time you woke up anyway!" He said, trying his best to sound upbeat. "Do you realize that you've been lying around here like a sack of nails for nearly a week?"

The old man wiped the damp washcloth over Gabe's lips and then turned the rag inside-out. Now that his lips were moistened, the detective was able to exhibit the thinnest of smiles. "That feels good ... that's very kind of you. I ... I guess someone must have forgotten to set my alarm clock..."

The old man winked jovially. "Well, don't look at me! Besides, I was getting awful tired of staring across the room at your motionless carcass all day! A person can only play so much solitaire, you know what I mean?"

There was a steady beeping sound coming from somewhere off to Gabe's left.

"Don't panic," Chase assured him, "that's just the heart monitor they've got you hooked up to. Boy, oh boy, let me tell you ... it's probably a good thing you've been passed out for as long as you have been! Those doctors of yours have been poking and prodding at you as if you had grown a third testicle!"

Footsteps out in the hallway grew louder and then just as quickly padded away. Gabe turned his head toward the door to listen. "You ... you know anything about what they might have found out?"

Chase rubbed the washcloth around Gabe's neck. "Honestly? I'm the last person you should probably ask. I wouldn't understand that medical double-talk if they gave me a dictionary! I'm a retired pilot, not a doctor. Ask me the ascent rate of a 767 and I can tell you in a heartbeat, but when it comes to anything medical ... they may as well have been talking Portuguese!"

Gabe rubbed his hand over the week's worth of coarse growth that was sprouting from his cheeks. Missing days was one thing, but it was the frighteningly rapid growth of his beard that was always a more definitive and tangible means of marking the passage of time for him. Now his cheeks felt like the top of his head. "Oh, Jeez, I think *I've* gotta pee now..."

Chase scowled sardonically. "You've barely spoken fifty words to me, and '*I think I've got to pee*' has to be six of them? What is it about me that brings out the urine in people?"

It hurt to laugh, but Gabe appreciated the old man's effort at humor therapy. "Please ... it's too early..."

Chase squeezed his shoulder. "Jeez, I'm so sorry! I can be such an idiot sometimes. I didn't mean to make you uncomfortable. By the way, if you really need to go ... I know for a fact that when they brought you in, they inserted one of those tubes down there for you..."

If it was true, Gabe couldn't feel anything.

"...'cause they keep checking to see if you've been filling up that bag hanging over the side of your bed, so be my guest—whiz away to your heart's content!"

And so Gabe did ... but it burned ... *it burned a lot.*

"You want any more of this?" Chase asked, holding out the damp washcloth.

Gabe lethargically shook his head. "No thanks. I appreciate your kindness though. Since you seem to know so much about me, may I ask what you're in here for?"

Gabe watched the old man slowly walk over to the window, pry open the blinds with two fingers, and peek out. Beyond the confines of the darkened hospital room, it appeared that the world was continuing to spin. Six floors below, the shrill back-up warning signal from a van delivering baked goods defiled the purity of the early morning calm. It was one of those sounds only a person who was awake at this ungodly hour would ever be able to hear.

As the pale light seeping in through the window blinds cast prison stripes across the old man's face, Gabe could see a subtle change overtake his expression. It was the same expression Gabe had seen a million times while interrogating some young punk who was trying to come off braver than he really was. Bennett Chase was trying unsuccessfully to conceal his fear as he balled up the washcloth in his hand.

"I'm dying," he said, matter of factly, as he walked back to the bed and set the washcloth on a plastic tray on the night table.

Gabe's eyes widened, suddenly managing to snap into sharp focus on the old man's bulbous nose. "Excuse me?"

Chase stifled a yawn as though the disclosure of his imminent death didn't really matter that much to him. "We've all gotta go sometime, right?"

Gabe raised his right hand to grope for the old man's hand on the bed's cold steel handrail. For a long moment they just clung to each other in the gloom. "I'm so sorry, Bennett. I ... don't know exactly what to say in this situation. Isn't there anything the doctors can do for you?"

Chase patted the back of Gabe's hand, careful not to mess with the I.V. tube protruding from it. "Nope ... it's too late for me, I'm afraid. The big, bad C's got me by the prostate. Not much anyone can do for me now, I suppose. Six months from now, they tell me, I'll be landing on heaven's runway!"

Again, the sound of footsteps grew and faded beyond the closed door. Gabe wanted to scream out to whoever it was passing by: *hey, can't one of you people do something for this poor man?* "What about your family? Do you have anyone here to help you?"

Chase snickered. "Never had much time for family, what with flying all over the place. Spent 15 years with the Air Force overseas, then flying commercial planes ever since. It was only after I took ill that Southern-Air handed me my walking papers."

Even in the dim light, Gabe could see that the old man's eyes were beginning to tear up. "What about your immediate family? Your parents? Brothers or sisters?"

Chase reached down to Gabe's forehead and brushed back a lock of sweaty hair. "Jesus, Gabe! I'm 64 years old! You think that if my parents would have lived to be 90 that I'd be standing here talking to you? Cancer runs in my blood like salt in the ocean. Cancer took both my parents by the time they were fifty."

"No brothers or sisters?"

Chase pulled a tissue from a box on the night stand and sniffled to clear his nose. "Had a younger brother ... Warren ... died flying a sortie over Vietnam ... what a fucking waste of good life that was!"

"I'm sorry."

The old man shrugged again. "Hey, what are ya' gonna do? But you know what really sucks about this whole dying thing?"

Gabe's soft voice conveyed his sincerity. "What's that?"

There was a faraway, dreamy look in Chase's eyes. "What really bothers me is, even though I know I'm never gonna be around to celebrate another new year, I don't get to choose the way I wanna to go out."

"Choose? What are you talking about?"

The old man pursed his lips. "I mean, since I know I'm going to die anyway, I think they should've let me die with some style ... some dignity. Doing something that I want."

Gabe was astounded by the old man's honesty and candor. He wondered if their situations had been reversed if could be as courageous. "So? What's stopping you?"

Chase smirked. "Nah ... can't be done. Be kinda messy, to say nothing of the expense."

"Why's that? How would you choose to die if you could?"

A smile brightened the old man's rugged face. "'I guess I would have liked to have dotted my final period up in the air. You know ... flying."

Gabe nodded. "Now I understand where the expense and mess comes into the picture."

"I can't explain it ... but it's always felt to me like the only place I could ever really find true peace and serenity was at 35,000 feet." The old man's eyes took on that fanciful look once again. "It's tough to explain unless you've spent as much time up there as I have. The endless blue horizon ... pillowy white clouds shearing past your windshield ... the way the sun glints off the wings as you bank gracefully toward the east ... chasing an orange sunset that you would swear God created especially for you, as you knife your way through calm air toward the west coast. I'm telling you, Gabe: there's nothing here on terra firma that can even hold a candle to it."

Gabe almost felt jealous of not knowing such passion. "You make it sound so appealing."

Chase patted him on the shoulder. "There's nothing to compete with it down here on earth, my friend. Nothing even comes close."

"It sounds really terrific. I'm sorry you've been grounded."

Chase tried to smile as he pulled Gabe's blanket up to his chest. "Well, that's the way it goes, I guess. What was it some very perceptive person once said? It's not the years in your life, but the life in your years that counts?" He winked. "You'd better get some more rest now. Nurse Ratched will be in here around seven A.M. to deliver our medication. Wait till you see this old warhorse! Man alive, I'm telling you, she's got a face that would make a train wanna take a dirt road!"

Gabe laughed under his breath. "I don't know how you do it."

The old man sat down on the edge of his own bed and let his slippers fall to the floor before sliding his feet under the covers. "You think I should spend my remaining days feeling sorry for myself? Been there, done that, my friend. I've already cried myself a river, Gabe ... and you know what's left when the well's all dried up?"

Gabe stared up at the blank ceiling searching for the missing hours of his life. "What's that?"

"Jeez ... a dry well. I thought you were a detective."

Gabe swiveled his head to the right and saw the old man struggling to get comfortable. "That's it?"

Chase flipped the pillow under his head. "You were expecting something a bit more profound perhaps?"

Gabe pressed down on the tape securing his I.V. line to the back of his hand. "Why don't you travel? See the world!"

The old man rolled over onto his side. "You forgetting that I was a pilot? I've already seen more of this world than most people would in three lifetimes. Home and hearth ... that's what I crave now."

"But you don't have any family."

Chase fell back onto his pillow. "I didn't say the plan was perfect. You're lucky to have such a handsome son."

Gabe put the hand that didn't have the tube in it behind his head. "Well, except for Casey, I'm pretty much in the same boat you are. My wife and daughter were killed in a car accident a few years back. If I hadn't been trying to pull some overtime, I would have been behind the wheel that night and things might have turned out differently, you know?" He pondered reflectively. "Then my in-laws sued for custody of Casey citing my job and I as bad influences for the boy. Can you believe it? A police detective is all of a sudden a bad influence. Sure, I work some lousy hours, but I could have worked something out."

Chase frowned. "Boy that really stinks."

The detective struggled with a deep breath. "The funny thing is I know what it's like to grow up without your real parents. I never knew mine. I was raised bouncing from foster home to foster home. So, until my wife and kids came along, I was all alone in the world like you. Isn't it ironic that we should both end up here together?"

The old man snickered. "This conversation is turning into a real bummer, you know that? I think it's time we both got some rest—especially you. When they find out you're awake, this place is gonna be a madhouse!"

Gabe pulled the light blue hospital blanket up to his chin. "Bennett?"

Chase was sitting on the edge of his own bed arranging his pillow. "Hmm?"

"You're one of the good guys. I'm glad we got the chance to meet."

The old man smiled softly. "Me too, kid. But you're aware, because of my prognosis, this might be the shortest friendship in the history of mankind, right?"

Gabe held up his right hand. "One lesson I've learned through the deaths of my wife and daughter is that it's the quality and not the quantity of a relationship that's most important."

Bennett Chase pulled himself out of his bed and shuffled barefoot across the cold tile floor, and shook the detective's hand. "Let's stay in touch, okay?"

Gabe smiled warmly. "I'd like that."

The old man clasped his newfound friend's hand in both of his palms. "I would be honored to call you my friend, Detective Gabe. Anytime ... anywhere ... whenever you need to talk ... I'll be there for you!"

Psychoanalysts would have had enough fodder to write a thousand treatises on the bond that emerged out of the gloom of this chance encounter. There were missing father figures, dysfunctional families, death, two men exorcizing their demons and finding much more than they expected in the course of fifteen minutes. Improbable? Gabe Mitchell would have always thought so, but there was an inner strength that came with the acceptance of one's mortality that intrigued the detective. He had a lot to learn from Bennett Chase and, sadly, very little time to learn it in. "No, Mr. Chase ... the honor would be all mine."

11

Right on schedule. At 7:03 A.M., Nurse Ethel Grogan came into the room much the same way that the Nazis stormed into Poland. Pushing a cart of prepared doses of medicine ahead of her, she had a wizened, puckered face that made her look like much older than her actual years. Even through her stark white surgical stockings you could see the road map of bulging varicose veins running up her legs to a place nobody wanted to visit. As she stepped on the medicine trolley's wheel locks, the corner of her mouth curled upward into a devilish leer. It was as if she took a sadistic enjoyment in the early morning ritual of waking her patients out of their sound slumber.

Soundlessly, she strolled right past Gabe Mitchell's reposing figure and headed for the snoring Bennett Chase. With all the sensitivity of a longshoreman, she reached over the bed rails and, with one of her boney hands, jostled Chase by the shoulder. "Hey, wake up, Rip Van Winkle, it's time for your meds!"

She was halfway back to her cart to retrieve the old man's medication when she suddenly realized he hadn't budged from her cruel disruption of his sleep. Surprisingly spry for a woman of her age, Grogan spun around and stared for what seemed like an eternity at his motionless body. Chase, scheduled for release that morning, was no longer hooked up to any monitors, so there were no machines to confirm her suspicion. He was still on his back, the blue hospital blanket pulled up to his chin.

Gabe watched as she moved forward, pausing anxiously between the two beds, her hands growing clammier with each passing second. There was no visible evidence that Chase was still breathing. His chest remained static, his face peaceful and serene. She put her hand under his nose ... nothing. Reaching under the covers, she took his wrist to feel for a pulse...

"How's about some sugar, sugar!" Bennett Chase's eyes popped open and he was grinning and puckering his lips like a precocious six-year old.

Grogan stumbled backward and put her hands up to her mouth. "You vile old man ... how dare you!"

Gabe thought he would choke to death he was laughing so hard. "Oh, my God! You should have seen your face!"

She took two more steps backward until the cold, steel railings of Gabe's bed prevented her from retreating any further. "Your sense of humor leaves a lot to be desired, Mr. Chase. Has anybody ever told you that? If you weren't leaving us today, I swear to all that's holy, I would..."

As quietly as possible, Gabe inched his right hand over to the spot where the nurse's corpulent derriere was bulging through his bed rails and pinched it. Grogan nearly came out of her shoes!

No matter how hard it hurt both men to laugh, if laughter was truly the best medicine, then Chase and Gabe were overdosing. Grogan turned so pale at the sight of Gabe having regained consciousness that the detective thought he might have to ring for help for her.

"Did he put you up to this?" The nurse grumbled, nodding over toward Chase with the color and antagonistic scowl returning to her face.

Gabe shook his head apologetically. "I'm sorry, ma'am. He's the culprit ... he set this whole thing up. He had you going so good ... I just couldn't resist..."

She looked warily back and forth at both men. "So you're gonna be a troublemaker too, eh?"

"Aw, you're loving every minute of it..." Chase chimed in. "I'm better than orange juice in the morning."

She walked over to the medicine cart and then cast a Machiavellian glance back at Chase. "So you think you're a real wiseacre, huh, flyboy?" She began flipping through the assortment of drug packets. "There's gotta be an extra large suppository in here for you somewhere..."

Chase held up his hands. "Truce ... truce!" He turned his head toward Gabe. "See what they give you for just trying to put a little excitement in their life?"

Grogan flipped on the overhead light and then walked over to the detective's bedside. "Can you remember what time it was when you first woke up?"

"It was about three in the morning," Chase called out from his side of the room.

"I was talking to Mr. Mitchell ... would you mind?" she barked over her shoulder.

Gabe stared up at the nurse's wrinkled face. No matter how gruff her exterior appeared to be, the compassion in her eyes betrayed her gritty disguise. "Like Bennett said, it's been about four or five hours I would have to guess. I was up, and then I dozed back off until just before you came in."

She did a quick check of all the monitors above his headboard. "I'll notify your doctor. I know he'll want to speak with you right away."

Gabe reached up and grabbed her left arm. "Do they know what's the matter with me?"

"I think your doctor should..."

"But Bennett told me they've been doing all kinds of tests..."

She looked across the room at the old man lying sheepishly in his bed, her eyes turning hard as marble. "Mr. Chase should learn to mind his own business! All we've done is run some tests and draw a little blood from your arm. Doctor Sanborn will be able to tell you more when he arrives."

Bennett Chase stuck out his tongue at her. "You're gonna miss me when I'm gone ... go ahead and admit it!"

Her tongue popped out in rebuttal. "Yeah, like a bad case of hemorrhoids!"

Chase yawned and set his head back down softly onto his pillow. "Yeah, she loves me—you can tell!"

12

Doctor Kenneth Sanborn stood at the foot of Gabe Mitchell's bed less than half an hour later. Tall, clean cut, and sporting wire-rimmed glasses, Sanborn gave the impression of an accountant rather than a practitioner of internal medicine. With his white coat buttoned professionally to the collar, and holding a clipboard protectively against his chest, Sanborn studied the information the monitors above the bed were relaying. "Everything looks pretty steady," he said, matter-of-factly.

Gabe didn't say a word. No use in interrupting the man while he seemed to be in heavy thought.

Gabe watched the doctor open his metal clipboard and flip through his chart. "So, when was the first time you began to experience these blackouts, Gabe? Do you mind if I call you Gabe?"

The detective shrugged. "Sure, you can call me Gabe. They started about a month ago."

Sanborn walked around to the side of the bed and took his right wrist. He smiled sympathetically at Gabe. "Not that I don't trust what the monitors tell me, but taking your pulse manually always reassures me."

Gabe traded stares with the doctor.

"Your pulse is a bit high, but that isn't uncommon for a person who might be experiencing a bit of normal anxiety. Are you feeling alright now?"

Gabe shrugged as he looked down at the doctor's gloved hand. "Uh, yeah ... I guess so."

"You aren't feeling any discomfort anywhere? No physical pain?"

The detective shook his head.

Sanborn reached over the railing and lifted each of Gabe's eyelids, shining a brilliant penlight into each of his eyes. "Good. That's always a good sign. Think you're still running a fever?"

"I'm sweating."

Sanborn tapped at his chart. "All the sweating indicates is that your fever's probably breaking. That's another very good sign. We've got some fever reducers pumping through your I.V. You should be back to a normal temperature by tomorrow and the sweating should stop."

Gabe glanced over at Bennett Chase who was eavesdropping intently. "So all this is good news, right Doc? When do you plan on dropping the other shoe?"

Sanborn reached for the curtain that would surround the bed, but Gabe stopped him from pulling it shut. "Leave it, Doc. There's nothing that you can't say in front of my friend."

Bennett Chase waved his hands as if to say, *Don't worry about it, let him do his job.*

"Are you sure?" the doctor asked.

Gabe looked over at his roommate and received a reassuring smile in return. "So, how long do I have?" he kidded.

Sanborn didn't return his attempt at dark humor. "I'm really sorry, Gabe."

Gabe's eyes widened. "Wh-what are you telling me? I'm dying? You can't be serious."

Bennett Chase squirmed in his bed.

The doctor fretted nervously with his chin as he studied Gabe's chart. "Is your son your only surviving relative?"

Gabe took a double-take. "Surviving?"

Sanborn looked down at his shoes and then his head rose. "This part of my job is never easy."

Gabe turned to Bennett Chase in the adjacent bed whose eyebrows shot up, punctuating his craggy face like a pair of exclamation points.

"This can't be ... I just get a little dizzy sometimes," Gabe protested.

The doctor patted Gabe's shoulder. "We've run the tests twice, Gabe."

The detective tried to lift his head off the pillow. "What tests? What the hell is going on here?"

Sanborn shrugged. "I'm afraid your prognosis isn't good. In layman's terms, we've found an inoperable brain tumor. It's this cancerous mass that's been causing you to pass out and lose your motor functions. What's worse, the cancer is metastasizing."

Gabe winced. "What does that mean? Come on, speak English."

The doctor looked over at Bennett Chase. "Are you sure you want to discuss this in front of a stranger?"

The detective pulled himself up on his elbows. "He's not a stranger! Tell me!"

"Well, Gabe, without getting too technical, I'm afraid we've caught the mass too late. There's nothing we can do but try to make you comfortable in what time you have left."

What will Casey do? Gabe whispered under his breath.

Gabe looked over at Chase, whose eyes were moist with empathy and anger. Reaching up, Gabe grabbed the doctor by his one of his lapels. "Something's gotta be wrong here, Doc. You've gotta take more blood ... run more tests!"

"We already have, Gabe," he said, prying loose the detective's fist from his coat. "Your tests were confirmed and certified by one of the most reliable testing facilities in the state. These laboratories are run by very conscientious people. It is common procedure to run these kinds of tests twice. I'm truly sorry." Sanborn eased Gabe's head back onto the pillow.

"So, that's it?" Gabe asked. "How do I come down with something like this ... this cancer, or tumor, or whatever you say it is? What makes this happen?"

The doctor reached over to the nightstand for a washcloth that still felt damp. "I really can't tell you something I don't know, Gabe.

Sometimes it's genetic," he said, blotting Gabe's forehead, "but your chart said you didn't know your biological parents, right?"

Gabe closed his eyes with resignation. "No. I have no idea where or who my parents are."

"At this late stage, I don't think it would matter anyway," the doctor said, gently squeezing Gabe's arm and slipping his eyeglasses into the pocket of his lab coat. "It could've been brought on by anything, over-exertion, stress, even a blow to the head; who can say? The symptoms are not always cut and dry. Cancer can manifest itself in different people many different ways. We could treat you with chemicals and radiation, but with a mass as large as yours, the inevitable outcome is always the same. I see no need to put you through that ordeal when your prognosis is so ... terminal. Again, I'm very, very sorry."

The scene played out behind Gabe's closed eyelids like some horrible B movie. In the darkness of his own fear, he visualized this nebulous monster squeezing the life out of his brain. *How will Casey survive?* They were best buddies! He was working on getting him back from his grandparents. Casey deserved a real home ... with his real father! He would have turned things around ... he would have managed to pull it all together ... somehow.

The detective turned his disheartened gaze at the doctor, and then over to his newfound friend in the next bed. Bennett Chase's crestfallen expression said it all. There had simply been no words that could have conveyed the sheer hopelessness of the moment for Gabe Mitchell.

13

Normal visiting hours in the hospital didn't begin until 9 A.M., but at 8:50 when the elevator doors opened and Captain Leon Williams stepped out, he found the entire sixth floor congested beyond its approved capacity. Despite the best efforts of the overwhelmed nursing staff, the floor had been transformed into a carnival sideshow. The media contingent had set up camps lining the corridor outside of room 683 on the slightest chance that Gabe Mitchell would find the strength to grant them an interview. Television reporters primped over themselves in any reflective surfaces they could find, while inquisitive patients, who didn't know quite what to make of the hoopla, peered out of their rooms in fascinated curiosity.

Williams frowned at the fawning press and muscled his way through the crowd. A black man of immense proportions, a tackle for the North Carolina Tar Heels back in his college days, it would take all of his football acumen to clear a path through the snapping cameras, bright lights, and microphones being shoved in his face.

"Captain Williams," a disembodied voice yelled out, "what sanctions, if any, will your department be imposing on Detective Gabe?"

Williams snarled at the question like a pit bull backed into a corner.

Everyone was shouting at him, but a few voices carried louder than the rest...

"Captain Williams," a male voice shouted, "Is there any truth to the rumor that the department is investigating the shooting, and that Detective Gabe might be found responsible for his partner's death?"

Just keep moving ... no use even trying to dignify that question with a response.

"Captain Williams," *why did it always have to be the last room at the end of the hallway, the last gate at the airport, nothing but red lights, when you needed to get somewhere in a hurry?* "...is it his illness, or their animosity over Detective Hansen's death, that's kept Detective Gabe's fellow officers from visiting him?"

Now this was really starting to get out of hand. If I don't make some kind of statement, the press will just continue to crucify Gabe with their half-truths and innuendos. Bad press won't be good for anyone.

Halfway down the hallway, Williams abruptly stopped and turned. The slow, dynamic movement of his massive form was enough to silence the throng. Shutters clicked like locusts in a corn field, but one deliberate glance in their direction brought the camera bugs to a standstill. A flood of high intensity lights flashed to life, bathing the remaining half of the corridor in a surreal, stark white glow. Williams had to shield his eyes with the back of his hand. "You people aren't going away until you get some kind of statement, are you?"

The shouting started all over again, the questions coming faster than he could respond to them. "Captain Williams, how long has Detective Gabe known that he has an inoperable brain tumor?"

How were these people getting this information? Someone on the hospital staff had to be talking. Sound sympathetic, but stay neutral. "No one knew until a few hours ago."

"What was his reaction when he found out?"

"I wasn't there. You'll have to ask his doctor," he said, pointing to his left to field a question from that direction.

"What is the official position of the Police Department, Captain? Is it true that the detective is facing an internal investigation, or worse, the loss of his job and pension?"

Williams rubbed at his nose, annoyed. *Damn, how he hated the antiseptic smell of this place!* "I'm not at liberty to discuss the Department's official position in this matter, and, obviously, I haven't spoken to the detective yet, but I can tell you that knowing Gabe Mitchell as well as I do, the loss of his job right now is the least of his worries."

"So you're saying that the detective will be relieved of duty?"

They're like fleas, burrowing relentlessly until they've tapped blood. What good am I doing? They're going to write whatever they want anyway. "I don't know how, but you all obviously know the extent of the detective's medical condition. So, do you really think the future of his career is foremost on his mind? Come on, people!"

"Have you spoken with Detective Hansen's husband?"

Williams nodded solemnly. "Of course I have—it's been nearly a week! I called him right after I received the news."

"Did he say if he harbored any malice against Detective Gabe for his wife's death?"

The captain's eyes glazed over with anger. "Let me make this as clear as glass for you people; I'll tell you the same thing that I told Detective Hansen's husband: Gabe Mitchell did not kill Joanne Hansen! She gave her life in the line of duty apprehending a dangerous serial murderer. Her killer, Billy Ray Silva, is dead on a slab in the morgue because of Detective Gabe and her own selfless service to the people of this city! Why are you making Detective Gabe out to be the bad guy here? Why aren't you focusing your attention on the real criminal in this case?"

"But isn't it true that the majority of Detective Gabe's fellow officers feel betrayed by him, and believe he should never have been on active duty the night of his partner's death?"

Aren't these vultures listening to anything I say? They're not letting up! "As I stated before, Detective Gabe did not know how seriously ill he was until a few hours ago!"

There was a voice from the back of the crowd, barely discernable. "But this wasn't the first time he had passed out in the past few weeks, was it, Captain?"

Williams shook his head. "From what I've been told, no, it wasn't."

"But the detective never had himself checked out, even though he knew this could affect his performance on the job?"

The captain adjusted the knot on his tie. Suddenly, the lights were making him feel much too warm. "With the exception of random drug testing, and a thorough yearly physical, the Department is not responsible for the health of each individual on the force. It was left up to Detective Gabe's discretion to see a doctor about his condition."

"Are you saying that the Department was aware of the detective's blackouts, but chose to overlook them?"

Don't let them know you were aware of the problem ... they'll drag you into this for sure! "You're putting words in my mouth. That's not what I said!"

"Well, what exactly is the position..."

The hallway fell under stunned silence as though some omnipotent watcher had suddenly hit the mute button on a remote control. There was no sound but for the familiar clicking of shutters and whirring of auto-winders. Leon Williams looked over the crowd with a perplexed expression on his face as though he had suddenly gone deaf. He quickly realized that he was no longer the center of attention. All eyes were looking past him. He turned to see a frail, solitary figure poised outside of a doorway, dressed in only a pale blue hospital gown, a mobile I.V. stand flanking his side. "Maybe I should take it from here, Captain..."

The reporters rushed past Williams like they were commuters trying to catch an express train and he was a turnstile, trampling each other with no regard for their own well-being.

"Detective Gabe," they screamed in unison. "Please Detective, one question..."

Gabe held up his hands in an effort to keep them at a distance. There were more flashbulbs popping than at a Hollywood movie premiere, as Williams shouldered his way through the crowd to stand next to his man. "We have to talk, Gabe," Williams whispered with his back to the crowd.

"I know Captain, but they're not gonna leave us alone until I say something."

Williams' enormous frame eclipsed most of the light, casting an ominous shadow on the far wall of the corridor. "Okay, just keep it short and sweet," he grumbled. "And for God's sake, don't go into any details!"

Gabe nodded. "I understand, Captain."

"Detective Gabe," a perpetually perky female reporter from Channel 6 blurted out, "what is your prognosis?"

Williams leaned over and whispered in Gabe's ear. "Don't answer this one, Gabe. You're not a doctor."

"Maybe you should speak with my doctor."

"We already have. He told us to speak to you!"

Gabe looked at his boss for help, but there was none forthcoming. "Uh, I'm feeling alright for now, I guess. Isn't that what's really important?"

"Why didn't you ever visit a doctor before this most recent blackout?"

Gabe rubbed the back of his hand where the feeding tube extended from. "To be honest, this whole thing just kinda snuck up on me..."

Someone from the *Herald* blurted out. "Didn't you realize you could be putting your fellow officers and public at risk from these fainting spells?"

"I think that's enough ... we should end this now," Williams announced.

Gabe Mitchell looked contrite as the cameras continued to snap away. These were the photos that would grace tomorrow's front page and the evening newscasts. "If I ever thought that I was putting anyone at risk..."

"A little too late for that, isn't it, Detective?" someone yelled from the middle of the crowd.

"Are you surprised that none of your colleagues appear to sympathize with your plight, Detective?" a reporter from one of the Latin stations asked. "The ones that we've interviewed think you acted irresponsibly for your lack of honesty with them. What do you have to say to these fellow officers?"

Williams shook his head for Gabe not to answer.

Gabe entire body seemed to sag. "They're probably right..."

A rumble of stunned disbelief rolled through the audience. Williams, granite-eyed, tried to get Gabe to stop, while not wanting to appear like he was trying to hush up some kind of secret complicity.

"So you agree that you knowingly put your partner at risk?"

Gabe held on to the I.V. stand for support. "I should have had myself checked. It never crossed my mind..."

Williams stepped in front of his detective and waved his arms. "That's all for now. Detective Gabe was considerate enough to come out here and answer your questions to the best of his ability. He needs his rest."

As they turned to leave, the questions came at them like automatic gunfire.

"Are you planning on contacting Joanne Hansen's husband? If so, what will you say to him?"

"What about your family, Detective?"

"Have you told your son yet? How is he handling all of this?"

"Does Detective Gabe know you're relieving him of duty, Captain Williams?"

"What's your opinion on Mayor Waxman's acquittal, Captain?"

Williams guided Gabe back into room 683 and let the door slowly close behind them. "You shouldn't have gone out there, Gabe."

Bennett Chase pointed up at the television that was broadcasting a live picture from out in the hallway. "Well, I think that went just peachy," he said, sarcastically.

Gabe sat down on the edge of his bed and let his slippers fall to the floor. "Yeah, I'm very charismatic, aren't I?"

The old man lowered the volume from his bedside control. "Especially in the nifty gown with the slit up the ass! Rumor has it they want you for the cover of next month's *G.Q.!*"

Standing at the foot of Gabe's bed, Williams gestured over at the old man. "Who is this?"

Gabe obliged with a quick introduction. "Captain Williams—Bennett Chase. Bennett—my boss, Captain Leon Williams."

Chase held up his hand, but Williams didn't reciprocate. "We need to talk, Gabe ... alone!"

Gabe arduously lifted his legs up onto the bed and propped himself up against the headboard. "There's nothing that you can't say in front of Bennett."

Chase flipped off the television. "Nope. This is important stuff. I'll just make myself scarce for a little while. Maybe those reporters will want to talk to the first person who spoke to you when you woke up!"

Gabe watched as the old man struggled to rise to his feet.

"Don't say anything bad about me!"

Williams blocked Chase's path to the door. "I would appreciate it if you didn't speak to anyone out there, Mr. Chase."

The old man shuffled forward in obvious discomfort. "Now, don't get your knickers in a knot, Captain. I was only trying to lighten the mood. Gabe knows I wouldn't say anything. You want all those reporters out of here? Just leave it to me!"

Gabe winked at his newfound friend. "You can trust him, Captain."

Chase opened the door and stepped boldly out into the corridor. This was his shot at fifteen minutes of fame and he wasn't going to let it pass him by. Through the doorway, Williams looked on as the old man was engulfed by the frenzied mob. Amazingly, though, as the door crept closed on all the tumult, the only voice he could differentiate was that of Bennett Chase yelling at the crowd...

"Hey, any of you people know where the supply room is? We're out of T.P. in there, and I've got one helluva case of the trots..."

14

"Well, that was fun!" Williams sniped, pulling up a chair alongside Gabe's bed and straddling it backward.

"I'm afraid this is only the beginning, Captain," Gabe apologized, sighing as his shoulders sank in resignation. "I really screwed this up, didn't I?"

Williams inched his chair closer to the edge of the bed. "I'm not here to pull any punches with you, Gabe. You know that's not how I operate."

Gabe adjusted the pillow under his head as he studied the somber expression on his captain's face.

"The timing on all of this couldn't be worse. First, every police department in South Florida is feeling the fallout from Waxman's not guilty verdict over on Miami Beach."

Gabe was genuinely surprised. He heard the reporter mention something about the story, but he wasn't really paying attention. "What did you say about Waxman?"

Williams squirmed in his chair. "Can you believe it? That son-of-a-bitch was acquitted a few days ago and, even though our department had nothing to do with the investigation, suddenly every law enforcement official in Dade County is under the microscope from every federal alphabet agency you can think of!"

Gabe wondered just how much more of the world had whizzed past him in the last six days. "But how is that possible? I thought the D.A.'s case against him was airtight?"

"Well, you know what happens to a jar when it's supposed to be airtight and it springs a leak? You don't notice anything until you go to use it, and then find everything inside has turned rancid and stinks to high heaven!"

"So what stunk inside?"

"Ah," Williams said, waving his hand carelessly, "the D.A.'s making some noise about jury tampering, but he's coming off sounding like sour grapes. If they can't find enough evidence to prove that the Mayor of Miami Beach shot gunned his wife in cold blood, how the hell do they plan on ferreting out a bribed juror?" He shook his head. "Ain't never gonna happen. The prosecution screwed the pooch."

Gabe frowned. "And now, my mess."

Williams rubbed his enormous hand over his bloodshot eyes. "Yeah, and now your mess."

There was a pregnant pause while both men sat quietly and contemplated their futures. Finally, Williams stood up and put his foot on the chair. "This situation is no good, Gabe. You've put the department in a very tenuous position here."

Out in the hall, a series of chimes rang out, followed by a female voice calling for a "Code Blue in room 622." Someone's life was on the line, but Gabe's Captain never flinched.

"So is it true?" Gabe asked.

Williams crossed his arms over his expansive chest. "Is what true?"

"What the reporters were saying out there? That no one in the department trusts me anymore?"

Williams walked over to the window and peered through the curtains. The parking lot was jammed with television vans, and the lawn was blanketed by a flock of news anchors all setting up for their midday broadcasts. The captain let the drapes fall shut. "Well, I wouldn't say anyone's exactly taking numbers to be your partner!"

Gabe tried to sit up. "I don't need a partner, Captain!"

Williams looked down at his spit-shined Florsheims and shook his head. "You can't be serious, Gabe! You can't come back. I already spoke with Doctor Sanborn. He told me how far along you are."

"Did he tell you that I can have radiation therapy and there are other things that can prolong..."

Williams stopped him mid-sentence, his voice as determined as his expression. "Prolong what, Gabe? The inevitable? Forget the fact that none of your fellow officers want anything to do with you. If it were only that simple, I would have gladly issued a transfer, or written a letter of recommendation for another division in a heartbeat. But dammit, Gabe, you've got terminal cancer ... in your *brain*! I don't mean to sound heartless, but good God man, you're dying! Spend whatever quality time you have left with Casey. Take in a ballgame with him. Smell the roses."

Gabe looked down at his hands. They were trembling. "So you want my badge?"

Williams kicked his toe harmlessly at the floor. "I've already got your badge, Gabe. I had it before I ever stepped foot in this hospital."

"Oh..."

"This visit was nothing more than a formality to bring you up to speed ... I'm really sorry."

Gabe took in a deep breath and let it out slowly. There was no way in hell he was going to fall apart in front of his boss. "So what now?"

The captain stood at the foot of Gabe's bed and toyed with the buttons that adjusted the bed's elevation. "I can't tell you what to do. You could probably hire a lawyer and come after the department for some kind of settlement, but you know what the courts are like. Casey would probably be your age before he saw any reparation." Williams walked around the bed and leaned on the back of the chair. "If I were in your shoes, I think I'd forget about the past, focus on making the most of the time you have left. In two weeks, the newspapers will have played out this story, and those hyenas out there will be chasing after their next meal. As far as the department is concerned, you've been cleared of any wrongdoing or accountability. There are no charges you'll have to face in regard to Joanne's death. You'll be given the usual severance package..."

Gabe raised a skeptical eyebrow. "But no pension."

Williams frowned. "Uh, no. No pension. Considering the circumstances, I think the chief is being more than fair with you. Of course, the medical expenses for this visit will be taken care of."

Gabe winked wryly. "But not for future ones."

Williams shook his head.

"Tell the chief that's very magnanimous of him."

Williams rubbed his forehead. His hands were tied. He wasn't going to come out and say it, but he had already been warned by his commander that if he had any aspirations for higher office, he had to cut his association with Gabe as quickly as possible. The climb to City Hall was a steep one for blacks in law enforcement—especially in the South—and this whole Gabe Mitchell fiasco could prove to be a very slippery rung on the ladder for him. He didn't want to sound uncaring, but the sooner the public forgot about Detective Gabe Mitchell, the better it would be for everybody involved. "Look, Gabe," he said with a straight face, "I'm just the messenger here. I went to bat for you when no one else in the department would!"

"I appreciate that, sir."

Williams reached out and squeezed Gabe's foot. "I'm telling you, use whatever time you've got to give your boy a lifetime of memories. Take him away somewhere where you two can be together without all those buzzards out there stalking you. If you can manage to impart one-tenth of your courage and tenacity into the boy, he'll be set for the rest of his life."

Gabe nodded. "Thanks for those kind words, Captain. I'll think about it. Right now, I just think I've got to start getting all my ducks in a row. I may not have a future, but I sure as hell have to ensure that my son has one."

Williams walked over toward the door. "Well, you know, if there's anything that you need..."

The captain's departure was interrupted by the door swinging open. Bennett Chase was back, this time escorting Gabe's son Casey and his overweight, silver-haired housekeeper, Marta Diegas, into the room. "They're like a pack of rabid wolves out there!" Chase declared. "Absolute insanity!"

Williams mussed the boy's thick brown hair. "How 'ya doin', butch? All those reporters didn't frighten you, did they?"

Casey pulled himself close to the housekeeper and buried his head against her rotund thigh. "He's just a-scared," she apologized in her best fractured English.

Williams rubbed the young boy's back tenderly before he stepped out into the corridor. He could only imagine the hardships that lay ahead for the kid. *Yeah, this world really sucked sometimes!*

15

Gabe lowered the railing alongside his bed and patted an empty space on the mattress where he'd made room. "Hey, lil' bud, jump on up here!"

Casey Mitchell was every bit a seven-year-old boy. Wearing a blue checkerboard flannel shirt, faded jeans, high top Chuck Taylor sneakers that he refused to lace, and carrying a teal and black Marlin's cap, the youngster looked up skeptically at his housekeeper and nanny, Marta Diegas. "It's okay, child. Don't be afraid of the machines!"

Gabe patted the bed again. "Come on, slugger. Here, I made some room for you! How's grandma and grandpa treating you?"

The child looked over at Bennett Chase who was leaning against the railings of his own bed. "Go on, kid. He's your old man, for gosh sake! He ain't gonna bite ya'!"

Gabe watched his son inch closer toward the bed, reminding him of the time the boy had climbed into the dentist's chair for the first time. Gabe wondered what was going through his son's mind. He sure looked like his father, but there were all of these electronic gizmos around him—it was enough to traumatize an adult, much less an impressionable seven-year-old.

"What the matter, Casey?" Gabe asked. "Don't you have a hug for your old man?" He patted at the sheets beside him for a third time.

Casey reached out an arm and Gabe grabbed it. No matter how weak he felt, that small palm in his hand gave him the strength of an entire army. In one fluid motion, he swept his son up onto the bed.

His mother's face ... it was a gift that was more precious than gold. Even tearing up, Casey's eyes seemed to sparkle like amber stones in a pool of clear water. Gabe reached up and brushed a few errant curls off the boy's forehead. "Why the sour puss, kiddo?"

Casey didn't respond; instead, his face began to knot up as the small boy's anxiety bubbled to the surface. Marta reached into her oversized purse and pulled out a handkerchief and blotted his face. "Everything ees fine now, Casey. No need to be sad. You see? Your father he loves you."

"Those ... people ... out ... there," the boy whimpered, "they ... they wouldn't leave us alone!"

Gabe glanced over at Bennett Chase. "Those sons of bitches," the old man growled, "pardon my French, kid ... they were all over them. It was a good thing I was out there to run interference."

Gabe shot the old man a "thumbs up." "Thanks Bennett, I owe you one."

"Maybe next time, they should call first ... or maybe come up some back way."

Marta Diegas nodded emphatically. "Sí, I will."

Gabe didn't want to lose his cool in front of his son, but all this hounding was absurd. "They shouldn't have to call first or sneak around to see me!"

Chase agreed. "Yeah ... maybe in a perfect world."

All of this intrigue and suspicion was clearly too much for Casey. All his son wanted was to be held, so Gabe pulled him close and kissed the top of his head. "Everything will be alright, kid ... I promise."

Gabe nodded to the housekeeper, who understood what lay ahead for the boy.

"When are you getting out of here, Dad?" Casey asked, pressing his face into his father's chest.

Gabe ran his hand up and down his son's back. "Pretty soon, I'm told," he whispered, kissing his son's head again.

No matter how naive the boy appeared to be, whether it was intuition or some inner-vibe he picked up on from his father, Casey reached around and embraced Gabe tighter than he had ever done before. It was a moment to be cherished ... a breathless, spectacular epiphany for both father and son ... a bonding few children would ever hope to share with a parent ... an unspoken, heartfelt, declaration of their unbounded love for one another.

"Can I stay here with you, until you're better?"

Gabe cradled his son's head against his chest. "I wish you could son, but the doctors are pretty strict around here."

"Like Marta strict?"

The housekeeper's eyes opened wide.

"Marta isn't strict, is she?"

Casey looked up at his father. "She wouldn't let me stay up for Law and Order last night."

Gabe pushed the boy away until they were facing each other eye to eye. "And did I ever let you stay up to watch it on a school night?"

Casey shook his head. "No, but you know how to work the VCR ... she doesn't! All she can do is make it flash 12:00!"

"Well, I should be home way before next Sunday, so what do ya' say I come over to Grandma and Grandpa's and we can watch it together?"

"I can stay up?"

Gabe buttoned one of his son's buttons that had come undone. "Sure. We got a date?"

Casey stuck out his tongue at his nanny, and then shook his father's hand one time with emphasis. "It's a date!"

Gabe took Casey's baseball cap and slipped it onto his own head. The petite hat sat atop his hair like a beanie. His son looked at him like he was crazy. "What's the matter? Too small?"

"You look silly, Dad!"

Gabe looked over at his roommate. "What d'ya think?"

Bennett Chase shrugged. "Looks like a swell fit to me."

Casey snatched the cap off his father's head and put it on proudly, displaying it for everyone in the room to admire. "See? This is how it's supposed to go!"

Bennett waved it off. "Nah, I liked it better on your old man."

"Really?"

The old man shambled over and stood next to the housekeeper. "Yeah, I think so. It makes his head look like it's got more in it than it really does."

Casey narrowed his eyes suspiciously and put the cap back on his father's head. "You sure?"

"Hey," Gabe interrupted, "don't I get a say in any of this?"

Casey had crawled onto his knees and Gabe found himself scooting to the far edge of the bed to make enough room. It felt just like Sunday mornings used to be at their house. Forget about watching the Cartoon Network. If he knew his father was home, at six-thirty on the button, come hell or high water, Casey would storm into his bedroom like a Tasmanian Devil, leaving total havoc in his wake. Not always a welcome sight if Gabe had been pulling overtime by working the Saturday night 9 P.M. to 2 A.M. shift—how he had fantasized about throwing his kid through a wall on more than a few of those mornings—but now, how lucky he felt recalling those bittersweet times.

Casey ... seven years old, and so easily distracted. It was scary the way this kid could go from despondency to hyper-activity in less than a nanosecond. Today was the first time Gabe thanked heaven for his child's naiveté.

"Maybe we should find one that fits me better," Gabe said, handing the cap back to his son as he made the decision. "As soon as they let me out of here, we'll go shopping for one, and then we can walk around town looking like twins! Maybe we'll even go to a Marlin's game! How's that sound?"

Again his son looked at him incorrigibly. "It's only February, Dad! Baseball season doesn't start for another two months!"

Gabe held up his hand. "Go ahead and hit me. I forgot."

Casey playfully slapped his father's wrist, careful not to touch the feeding tube. "But maybe we can go to one in April? Box seats?"

How far off April seemed, even though he knew the seconds, minutes, hours and days, would zoom by before he knew it. What kind of physical shape would he be in by then? He had seen it all before on the streets, on television, in the movies—skeletons with skin, frail walking corpses, oxygen bottles and open lesions. He'd kill himself before he ever let himself deteriorate to that point. "Sure, kiddo, pick a game and we're there ... box seats!"

Casey stretched out his legs and took up a position lying next to his father. Side by side, their forms seemed to fit together perfectly. Someone might take Gabe Mitchell's place in his son's life, but no one would ever be able to replace him.

With a nod of his head toward the hallway, Gabe signaled to his roommate that the moment he had been dreading had arrived. Without further urging, the old man took Marta Diegas by the arm and escorted her toward the door. "Why don't you and I take a walk down to the cafeteria and see if we can't get ourselves some of that cafe con leche that's been known to grow hair on a person's teeth ... whatd'ya say?"

Now it was family time. There were grownup realities and harsh truths that Gabe needed to simplify for his son, and he had to do it in private. Gabe watched Marta look lovingly at the boy and then reach down into the collar of her blouse and pull out the gold cross that her mother had given her as a child. Gabe knew it was a sacrosanct charm which she wore around her neck everyday of her life. The housekeeper kissed the cross, closed her eyes, and recited a silent benediction. When she returned to the room, none of their lives would ever be the same again.

Innocence would be lost—but inspiration and courage would be found. He hoped.

16

For reasons they both chose not to verbalize, the hospital room felt colder and lonelier than usual this morning.

If his years of flying commercially had taught Bennett Chase anything, it was to pack his belongings economically. First, he laid out the few pairs of underwear he had brought with him, and then neatly rolled them into tight little logs. He followed those with his t-shirts, three pairs of white socks, two pair of velour sweat pants, and a royal blue and orange University of Florida sweatshirt. Once his cord of clothing logs was complete, everything fit easily into his garnet and gold Florida State Seminole duffle bag.

Chase could feel Gabe's eyes on him, watching in reverence as the old man packed his things. "So where'd you learn to pack like that?"

Chase stuffed the underwear in first, filling the nylon bag layer by layer like an Egyptian slave building a pyramid. "Years of practice."

Small talk. A way to fill the uncomfortable minutes. Chase wasn't very good at it. It was going to be tough to leave his newfound friend behind. They had grown close over the past few days, sharing a lifetime of thoughts, dreams and experiences. Chase had begun to think of Gabe as the son he had always regretted not having. Everything he tried to say sounded so forced and stilted.

"Being able to pack a bag like that is a skill that must come in handy," Gabe said.

Chase began to fill up his black leather toiletry kit with shaving items off the nearby sink. The melancholy in his voice betrayed his normally jovial manner. "Not anymore. I learned to pack like this when I flew for the airlines. It's just another one of those trivial talents people seem to acquire over their lifetime."

Gabe sat up in his bed, his elbow accidentally pushing the switch that turned on the overhead television. The local morning news was on, but both men ignored it. "You can still travel, Bennett. The doctors didn't say you couldn't."

The old man leaned both hands on the sink. From behind, Gabe could see his shoulders sag with resignation. "But they advised against it."

"Hey, we're not gonna let those pill jockeys tell us how we can spend the rest of our lives, are we?" Gabe interrupted. "If you want to pack up and see the world, then why the hell don't you?"

Chase carried his sundry kit over to his bed. The small bag only weighed a few ounces, but he walked like it weighed a ton. "You're forgetting that I've already seen most of the world. Besides," he said, running his fingers through his soft thicket of silver hair, "starting next week, they want me to check in for a weekly treatment, so I guess it's time to say *adios* to the silver mane!"

Not only were they stealing the old man's freedom, they were also depriving him of his dignity. The worst part was Chase knew Gabe was a younger version of himself. He would be going through the same treatments and loss of pride a few months from now.

On the television, the newscast was interrupted by a special bulletin, providing a much needed distraction for both men. A young reporter stood on the steps of the Miami Beach City Hall, trying to keep her long blonde hair from blowing out of control in the cool, blustery wind. "The press liaison for Mayor Nathan Waxman has just announced that the mayor will be granting his first press conference since being exonerated on the charge of homicide in the shotgun death of his wife, Dorothy. This will be the first interview the mayor has given since retreating into seclusion with family and friends to celebrate his acquittal. As you undoubtedly know, the jury of seven men and five women returned the controversial verdict earlier in the week, after less than twelve hours of deliberation. Waxman stood accused of the August 19th, 1996 brutal slaying of his wife at the family's townhouse on Washington Avenue." The harried reporter kept looking down at her quickly written notes. "Throughout the trial, the mayor steadfastly adhered to his claim that an intruder killed his wife, even though he admitted to a violent argument with her earlier that tragic evening—an argument that was overheard and testified to by the couple's resident housekeeper. Also, despite the fact that the murder weapon was registered to the mayor, and only his fingerprints were found on the weapon, the defense team shed enough reasonable doubt in the juror's minds for them to return a verdict of not guilty. Mayor Waxman, not surprisingly, has resigned his office under the cloud of negative publicity following the trial. Once again, the press conference scheduled for later this afternoon will be the mayor's first public appearance since his acquittal on homicide charges. Of course, this station will bring it to you when it happens. This is Michelle Schaefer reporting live from the steps of Miami Beach City Hall. Now, back to the studio..."

Bennett Chase walked over to the window and opened the blinds. For some reason, the room suddenly needed the cheering effect of warm morning sunlight. "What a farce! Can you friggin' believe it? That bastard's gonna get off scot-free after committing an act of cold-blooded murder, and we're both condemned to death!"

Gabe nodded. "It sure is a tough pill to swallow."

"It seems like it's happening more and more these days," Chase sadly admitted, as he pushed his bag aside and sat on the edge of his bed. "It's like the justice system in this country has lost its rudder. Is it just me, or does it feel like the inmates are running the asylum?"

Gabe scratched his head. Even though this case was in the Beach's jurisdiction, you still heard things through the grapevine. *The buzz was that a conviction for this guy was supposed to be a slam dunk.* "I can't figure what those jurors were listening to." He shifted his weight uncomfortably in the bed. "I'd have staked my reputation on the D.A.'s case."

The old man glanced up at the television. Like a microcosm of the real world, the attention of the news anchors had already shifted to the weather. "So what are you saying? You think there was monkey business going on?"

Gabe waved his hand as if he had already said far too much. "I'm not exactly the one to be casting aspersions anymore."

Chase zipped the duffel bag closed. "I guess at least one good thing is coming out of all of that Waxman nonsense."

"What the hell would that be?"

Chase pointed up at the television. "At least it's taken you out of the headlines! You're now yesterday's news, my boy!"

Gabe nodded. "I guess you've got to be thankful for what they give you. You always manage to find the silver lining, don't you, Bennett?"

The old man lifted his duffle bag set it down on the edge of Gabe's bed. "Hey, since this jerk took over the headlines, I've actually been able to take a stroll in the hallway without being bombarded by reporters!"

Gabe took a sip of water from a paper cup. "Damn! And to think, I ended up spending my fifteen minutes of fame flat on my back!"

Chase patted the back of Gabe's hand. "If there's one thing life teaches you, son, it's to always look at the bright side. If life deals you a deuce, you've got to turn it into a wild card!"

Gabe reached out and took the old man's hand. "Life sure has dealt us both a bunch of deuces, hasn't it?"

Chase reached into the pocket of his sweat pants and pulled out a note card and a ball point pen. "Okay now. That's the last time I want to hear any of that pessimistic shit coming out of your mouth, young man!" He scribbled his address and phone number onto the card. "Here's my number. If you need *anything*," he said, emphasizing what he felt was the most important word, "you call me, and we'll talk."

Gabe sat up and snapped his fingers towards himself. "Got another one of those cards?"

The old man reached into his pocket and handed another one over, along with the pen.

"And this is *my* number. If *you're* ever not feeling well, or you just need to get something off your chest, you do the same, you hear me?"

"Deal."

"Promise?"

Chase raised an eyebrow. "What are you, my mama? I said I promise."

After five emotionally draining days of sharing the same claustrophobic hospital room, Bennett Chase had discovered a fellowship that few people could ever dream of sharing. They were two completely different men who'd come upon each other at a defining moment of their lives. Though years apart in age, and after arriving at this place by two quite distinct paths, fate had thrown them together into a very special kinship. Without ever saying it aloud, they agreed to fulfill their separate destinies together, sharing the final leg of their journeys down the same short road.

17

Gabe hadn't heard the door open.

In the doorway, backlit by the stark white light flooding in from the hall, stood a fantasy in a navy blue business suit. She was incredibly tall, and both men's eyes were drawn to her shapely stems like lemmings to a cliff. Her green eyes were soft but piercing, hidden behind a pair of large fashion lenses. Her hair was midnight black, pulled tightly behind her head and held there with a blue fashion clip. While her coat sleeves were long, her skirt was much the opposite. Bennett Chase was the first to break the awkward silence. "Please tell me you're here to wheel me out of this place and I'll die a happy man!"

"No, that would be my job," grunted Nurse Ethel Grogan as she lumbered into the room pushing a wheelchair. "Let's go, Casanova! I've been looking forward to this day for two weeks now. It's time to boot your wrinkled old ass outta here!"

Chase flipped his middle finger at the old crone before turning his salacious consideration back to their alluring visitor. "Pay no attention to her, doll-face. She's never been the same since Dorothy's house fell on her sister!"

Grogan's face always seemed twisted, like she was in the midst of having stomach cramps. "In the chair, wiseass!"

The old man grabbed his bag off Gabe's bed and proceeded to beam his most beguiling smile at their visitor. "I'm sorry, miss, but I never caught your name."

The young woman's demeanor remained extraordinarily business-like. "That's probably because I never threw it." Her Irish accent was subtle, but there was a definite lilt to it.

Chase took a seat in the wheelchair, placing the duffle bag on his lap, and feigned a shiver. "Aye-chi-mama! Did the temperature just drop fifty degrees in here, or is it me?"

The tall stranger shook her head. "My name is Sheila Randall, and I'm here to see Mr. Mitchell."

The old man looked over at Gabe and mouthed the words "you lucky bastard."

Gabe laughed, then held up the card with Chase's phone number on it. "You remember what I told you, right?"

Bennett Chase flashed a "thumbs up" at his friend, and let himself be spun around toward the open door. "Onward husky," he shouted, pointing into the hallway.

Nurse Grogan billowed in a deep breath and gave the chair a hearty push, letting it roll unchecked into the corridor. "That old fool sure better pray that the elevators are working!"

Gabe rolled his eyes and offered his visitor a seat. "I'm sorry, Ms. Randall. You said you were here to see me?"

She crossed her legs in a long, fluid motion that made Gabe lean up on his elbows. "Yes, I am."

Gabe suddenly felt awkward and vulnerable lying prone in the bed. Something about this situation made him feel less a man than he really was. "Have we met before? I get the feeling that we might have. You're not another reporter, are you?"

"You must be mistaken. We've never met and I'm not a reporter."

Gabe nodded. "Work for the hospital then?"

She picked a piece of lint off the hem of her skirt. "No, Mr. Mitchell..."

"Call me Gabe."

"Okay ... Gabe. I don't work for the hospital."

Gabe scratched at the nearly week's worth of thick stubble that had sprouted on his face. "Well, Sheila, I could keep guessing if you really want me to. I used to be a detective."

"I'm here to talk to you about your situation."

Gabe closed one eye warily. "My situation?"

"The police department has turned its back on you."

Gabe should have known it. The business suit should have been the tip off. "You're a lawyer?"

She clasped her hands around her exposed knee. "Oh God no, I despise lawyers."

"See? Now, if we had continued playing twenty questions," Gabe said, pushing himself back on the bed until he was propped up against the headboard, "you would have won, 'cause I don't have the slightest idea what you want from me then."

"The insurance policy you have through the police department will probably take care of this hospital stay, but not the rest of your treatments."

Gabe had no idea how this stranger knew so much, and it made his radar flip on. "First of all, getting back to the force, and having them turning their backs on me ... you should know that my case is still under internal investigation and I have been assured that there are no charges pending."

Sheila Randall's matter-of-fact tenor never wavered. "Those investigations move so slow you'll probably be dead a year before any determination is actually ever reached."

"Okay, well I can definitely rule out you being a doctor, what with this uplifting bedside manner of yours!"

"What about your son?"

Gabe gnashed his teeth. "What about my son?"

She crossed her legs in the other direction, only this time Gabe was too incensed to take notice.

"Have you thought about his future? What will happen to him after you're dead? How will he get by?"

Why did she keep using the word "*dead,*" instead of saying "*gone,*" *as in "after you're gone?"* That was so strange to use harsh language like that to the dying person's face.

"Look, Ms. Randall. I just found out a few days ago that I'm not gonna be around to put milk and cookies out for Saint Nick this year, okay? So cut me some slack, will 'ya? My son Casey is the most important thing in my life and, as soon as I get out of here, I intend to see that he is taken care of." He ran his fingers thoughtfully along the cold silver bed rail. "I don't know how yet, but I will."

Randall slid her chair closer to the bed until she was talking in just over a whisper. "That's what I'm here for, Gabe—to see that Casey's taken care of for the rest of his life."

Gabe nodded as though he finally understood. "Ah, so you're from an insurance company! That might have been my next guess."

She reached up and put her hand over his. "You haven't had a personal visitor except your son and his nanny since you were admitted. Your fellow officers hold you responsible for your partner's death. You have $683 in your savings account. Two years ago, you took out a second mortgage on your house."

Gabe lashed out and grabbed her by the wrist. "How the hell do you know so much about me? You're no insurance agent!"

Randall never flinched. Even as he increased the pressure on her wrist, she seemed to be enjoying it. "Think of me as your guardian angel, Gabe. I've come here to solve your predicament."

Gabe eased his grip and looked at her skeptically. "So, you know someone that can cure cancer? I know about a billion people who would be real happy to hear that!"

Randall pulled her hand away and flexed her wrist. "Mr. Mitchell, this is just a preliminary interview, but if you'd care to be serious for a moment, I'm here to make you a very generous offer."

Why not? Gabe thought. *I've got nothing better to do at the moment. Sure, I'll play along with her.* "How generous?"

"Four million dollars."

Gabe's mouth went dry.

"...untraceable ... in a secret numbered account ... payable to your son ... however you stipulate the funds should be disbursed to him ... upon your death."

This had to be some kind of elaborate gag, but Gabe didn't know anyone, besides himself, who had the ingenuity to think up such a sadistic scam! His mouth tried to form words, but he couldn't even make spit. When he finally managed to shake out the marbles, he spoke the prophetic words half-jokingly that would change the rest of his life: *"So, exactly who do I have to kill for that kind of cash?"*

18

Traffic was light on I-75 as the black stretch limousine crossed the imaginary boundary line into Broward County. Gabe stared out at the scenery as it flew by at 70 miles per hour. Like so many residents who had relocated to Broward County since the devastation caused by Hurricane Andrew in 1992, both Gabe Mitchell and his in-laws now made their homes further north in the town of Davie, a suburb west of Fort Lauderdale. Once a sleepy little community that prided itself on its country charm and leisurely, rustic lifestyle, the town now found itself in a showdown with developers to maintain its identity in the midst of the ever-encroaching urban sprawl. Where once all he could hear on a cool winter morning was the plaintive trumpeting of a herd of milk cows grazing in a windswept farm field, now that tranquil scene had been replaced by the coughing of backhoes, and the thunder of dynamite blasting through sheetrock to clear the land for more homes and commercial centers. Things change.

Office buildings and homes under construction weren't necessarily a cheerful sight, but perhaps it was because Gabe was suddenly more attentive to the everyday things others might take for granted. Most upsetting to him was his muddied perspective of the bright blue sky that was being soiled a mossy shade of green by the dark window tinting. Indeed, the inside of this limo wasn't a very cheerful environment for someone who had very few things to be optimistic about.

Behind Sheila Randall's head, a pane of thick black glass separated the nameless chauffeur from where they were sitting. "Are you feeling alright, Gabe?"

Gabe glanced impassively across the car's whorish red velour interior at Randall, but chose not to respond. There was an awkwardness in the way she had posed the question, as though her interest in his welfare was unnatural and well-rehearsed. She was one of the few things Gabe thought he understood about this whole deal. Randall was only the messenger ... albeit a long-legged, utterly breathtaking one, but still, nothing more than a chunk of bait fish used to lure him into ... what? He didn't know that yet.

Maybe the average prospect would let Sheila Randall's knockout good looks lead him around by his short hairs, but from the minute she had walked into the hospital room, Gabe's internal warning system started to flash. No matter how hard she tried to mask it, there was something cold and lethal behind her eyes. His late partner had that same dangerous edge to her personality, but he didn't want to think about that now. Feigning a toothless smile, he returned his attention to the passing landscape.

Gabe watched with envy as a flock of colorless birds fluttered across the skyline in a perfect arrowhead formation to whereabouts unknown. *Why did they do that ... and why couldn't he?* Just another strange mystery of life he would never have the time to unravel. Something about watching that convoy of birds fade away on the horizon made him think back to one of the many reflective late-night discussions he held with Bennett Chase. He remembered sitting in their darkened hospital room, the only light bleeding in from beneath the door, ruminating over paper cups filled with warm apple juice. Chase warned Gabe that no good would come out of him dwelling on his limited mortality. Thoughts of what the future held would only serve to drive him mad. Concentrate on the present, he urged, and only on the things *he* could directly effect. They were simple but profound words and a difficult maxim to master.

Concentrate on the present...

So then, what was this woman up to? For the hefty sum of $4 million, he knew they weren't just going to ask him to donate his organs to science. He had accepted her cryptic proposition on a fluke ... at least that's what he tried to convince himself. But it was what she had said about Casey that really got him thinking. His son deserved a shot at a full life ... a good life ... whatever the price. Hell, what did he have to lose? His own life? Yeah, right! They couldn't take it away from him twice! The more he thought about the cash, the more tempting that busload of zeros trailing after that number four were becoming! Call it curiosity, or a cop's intuition, Gabe had elected to purchase a ticket on this mystery train.

"You seem depressed, Gabe. That's only natural."

Gabe drummed his fingers on the plush crimson armrest as the car lurched over a pothole in the road.

"Do you want to talk about it?"

Gabe rubbed a hand over the growth of beard he had decided to leave on his face. He remembered staring at himself in the hospital room mirror, and warning himself not to put a razor blade anywhere near his throat. He hadn't been feeling suicidal at the moment, but again ... things change. "You think I'm depressed? Then tell me something that will cheer me up," he muttered, still looking out at the passing scenery.

"Like what?"

"Why don't you fill me in on what you really need me for and what all this cloak and dagger shit is about? And where are you taking me?"

"Such a curious man, my goodness! We're just taking you by your in-law's house," she said, shifting her weight in the seat. "You're going to see your son! Isn't that where you want to go?"

Gabe fumbled for the window switch and finally managed to crack the window a bit. He needed the cleansing effect of some fresh air. Suddenly the inside of the car was making him feel penned in. "I mean after that. You've got to want something from me. You're not running a limo service here, right?"

Randall inched her way across her bench seat until she was sitting directly across from Gabe, next to the partially opened window. "So much mistrust in the world ... you're doing the right thing."

Gabe raised an eyebrow that insinuated he understood more than he really did. "Where are you taking me after I say goodbye to my son? I mean, that is what this little side trip is all about, isn't it?"

There wasn't even the slightest hint of a smile to crease the woman's exquisite features. "Don't be so melodramatic, Gabe. It doesn't become you. You're going to see your son again, and I promise, all of your questions will be answered very soon. In the meantime, why don't you just enjoy the trip," she said, stretching out her arms, her voice shifting coquettishly into the drawl of a southern belle. "I swear, don't you love riding in the back of a limousine? It's just so luxurious! Personally," she added, fanning her hand in front of her face, "I think it's the greatest thing since ... since ... well heck, I don't know, it's the best way to travel ... don't you agree?"

A faint trace of horse manure wafted into the car, a welcome home signal that only Gabe seemed to pick up on. "And you people are still interested in me, knowing full well that I'm a police detective?"

Randall intertwined her fingers and cupped them over her knee. "Correction ... you *were* a police detective."

Gabe never took his eyes off the enchantment that the afternoon sky seemed to hold for him. "That's where your dossier on me is dead wrong, Ms. Randall," he disagreed. "They can take away my badge, and they can take away my gun, but I'll always be a cop."

For the first time since they had met, Sheila Randall's stoic countenance splintered into a telling smile. "*That*, my dear Mr. Mitchell ... is exactly what we're counting on!"

* * * * * *

Westbrooke Trail was an unpaved thoroughfare until two years ago. Still too narrow for two-way traffic, the thin ribbon of asphalt was lined on both sides by a pair of drainage canals that eventually wove their way into the Everglades five miles to the west. Cut into a dense grove of eucalyptus and oak trees, Westbrooke Trail meandered past very few homes and had only been modernized upon the insistence of the U.S. Postal Service who had lost more than their share of vehicles to either the potholes, rough terrain, or, even once, a wayward alligator.

Owning a home on Westbrooke Trail was like living within the walls of a fortress constructed by Mother Nature herself. At night, with its blacktop illuminated only by the occasional patch of moonlight filtering through the dense thicket of tree branches, the street always proved to be a worthy antagonist to anyone unfamiliar with its disconcerting twists and turns.

"Your in-laws must really like their privacy to live way out here," Randall said, as she squinted to see anything that might lie beyond the impenetrable wall of overgrowth whizzing by the window.

Gabe rolled down the window halfway to get a better view. The cool wind felt refreshing against his face. "Yeah," he agreed somberly, "the more secluded, the better."

Randall spoke matter-of-factly. "No love lost between you, is there?"

Gabe held onto the armrest as the limo slowed to take a large winding curve in the road. "So I suppose you know everything about the custody fight too?"

Like Gabe's question had never been asked, Randall changed the subject. "Your son enjoys living out here?"

"Very much."

"Seems isolated. Not many neighbors."

The limo slowed again to pass a garbage truck that was making its bi-weekly pickup. Gabe had never been aware of it before now, but the truck's awful odor and its unrelenting backup signal were defiling the pristine atmosphere of the forest like a mugger. *Don't dwell on the things you have no control over...* "He's made a friend or two at school ... and he really loves playing in these woods!"

"He sounds like a bright young boy."

Gabe nodded dreamily. "You wouldn't believe how fearless the kid is, when he's exploring out there. I used to worry about him, but I swear he's got more guts and creativity than I ever had at his age."

The limousine turned into the driveway of his in-law's residence. "You're very proud of him."

Gabe's face saddened. "Casey's practically grown up on his own. I haven't exactly been around for him..."

Randall was as dispassionate as a foreclosure banker. "Don't worry. Just the fact that you're here shows how much you care."

Leaning forward in his seat, Gabe stared into her unyielding eyes. "You keep assuring me of that, but I don't even know what the hell I'm doing!"

Randall tapped her wristwatch. "We're on a tight schedule. You've got 15 minutes."

Gabe reached for the door handle. "You know that the only reason that I'm seeing this game of yours through to the end is because you've got my curiosity meter flying off the register."

Randall leaned back comfortably. "So the financial benefit for your son has nothing to do with it?"

Gabe opened the door and stepped out into the bright winter sun. The smell of the trees came like a fine wine to his nostrils. "That was $5 million, right?"

Never sticking her face out of the shadows, Randall shook her finger back and forth naughtily. "Please don't push me, Mr. Mitchell."

Gabe slammed the door and shaded his eyes to see in through the half opened window. "Lady, when I push you, you'll know it."

A well-muscled wrist jutted out of the darkness displaying a Cartier timepiece. "Now you've only got 14. You've wasted one."

19

1171 Westbrooke Trail ... what a glorious sight! As Gabe stepped off the paved driveway and onto the flat stone path that led up to the screened-in front porch, he took a moment to drink in the entire 3,200 square feet of split-level housing, sitting on one and a half acres of prime South Florida bottomland. The pale blue house was fully air-conditioned, but even in the most blistering summer heat, the surrounding woodlands kept the thermostat from ever climbing above 72 degrees. There was a towering oak tree in the front yard with an old tire hanging from one of its lower branches. Gabe remembered back to better times, during family get-togethers, when he would spin Casey in that tire until he thought the boy would throw up. Casey was too big to be spun anymore, and now the tire hung there as a memorial to more carefree times, and perhaps as an occasional target for football practice.

Continuing up the path, for the first time Gabe noticed that the wooden shutters outside of Casey's bedroom on the second floor were in sore need of a fresh coat of cherry varnish, and that some of the gutter flashing was in disrepair as well. Just a simple few hours work for a handyman, but as he trudged up the stone steps and opened the door to the porch, he wondered if he should say anything—they hated him enough.

As was the usual case, the screen door was unlocked and the front door wide open. This was yet another infraction on a long laundry list of things his in-laws did that drove Gabe crazy. Stepping inside the house, he was surprised to find the living room empty, so he called out for his son and the housekeeper. "Casey? Marta? Anyone around?" He let the screen door slam shut behind him.

It sounded more like a stampede across the wooden floorboards as Marta Diegas came storming into the living room from the kitchen, drying off her hands vigorously on her food-stained apron. "Señor Gabe," she shouted joyously. "What you doing here? I'm surprised to see you! When did they let you out? Why didn't you call me to give you ride?"

Gabe raised his hands over his head as the rotund Cuban woman wrapped her arms around him with a crushing passion that would have made a python envious. He could hear the air blow out of his lungs as she continued the pressure; she was so caught up in the moment, totally oblivious to the fact that the veins in Gabe's neck looked ready to burst. Sure that he would pass out if he stayed in her clutches another second, Gabe pushed down on the housekeepers' shoulders to extricate himself. "Enough, Marta!" he blurted out, gulping for some much needed air at the same time. "I'm very glad to see you too. It's good to be out! Where are the Gibsons?"

She clasped her hands in front of her and shook them. "Señor Gibson went to play the golf club, and the Señora is went to play cards at Señora Coldwell's house. Ah, Señor Gabe, you don't know how much the boy and me miss you!"

Gabe's respiration had about returned to normal as he looked around the room. "Where is Casey? He should be home from school already, right?"

"Oh sí, he is playing out in the backyard woods with his friend..." she quickly covered her mouth as if she had already said too much.

Gabe stepped back, his arched eyebrow conveying his displeasure. "Not with that Dylan James kid?"

Marta stared down at her white nursing shoes. "Sí..."

"Marta, how many times have I told you..."

"But Señor Gabe..."

Gabe stormed through the dining room toward the door that led out to the backyard. "I'm telling you, Marta, that James kid is gonna grow up to be a career criminal! Thirteen years old, and he's already been arrested for arson and shoplifting—twice! If I hadn't owed his old man a few favors, and hadn't called in some of my own markers down at the D.A.'s office, that kid would be rotting away in a juvenile facility somewhere in the middle of the state!"

Marta waddled after him. "But he seems like such a nice boy and Casey really..."

Gabe stepped out onto the porch and shielded his eyes from the sun. "That's not the kind of influence I want around him, Marta! Believe me, if that James kid ever makes it to high school, which I seriously doubt, they're gonna vote him Most Likely to Take a Life. Take my word on it!"

Marta stepped out onto the wooden landing. "Do not be upset with me, Señor Gabe. Casey has been very lonely since he's been living here. He spends most of his time in his bedroom sitting in front of the computer. I see him typing on the screen back and forth to Dylan. You may not like him, Señor, but Dylan is the only one that will come all this way to visit. They are both two lonely boys. I really think they need each other."

Gabe leaned against one of the oak beams that supported the patio roof. Why was he getting himself so worked up? Maybe because in less than a year he wouldn't be around to play guardian angel for his son any longer, and the boy would be doing whatever he wanted, hanging out with whomever he wanted, and learning life lessons all on his own. *Perhaps dying is the easiest thing you do in life...*

He turned to the housekeeper who looked genuinely frightened. "I'm sorry, Marta. This isn't your fault. I just want..." his words trailed off. He was so confused. "...I don't know what I want..."

Marta put her hand on his shoulder to comfort him. Together they stood silently on the porch for a long moment, the cool afternoon breeze stirring the dead leaves on the dry, brown grass. They were like two spies speaking in a cryptic code, both afraid to actually broach the delicate subject that was really weighing so heavily on both of their minds. "I know, Señor. It's no fair for a seven-year-old boy to think about such things. He's too young to understand. He just wants to play in the woods and have fun with the only friend who ever comes to see him."

Gabe understood and nodded. "But it's people like that James kid that are exactly what I want to talk to him about. There's so much stuff I need to teach him."

The housekeeper pointed her finger toward a rustling in the undergrowth. "When the time is right," she said softly, "he will listen ... and he will carry your advise with him here," she added, putting her clasped fists over her heart, "...for his entire life!"

"Dad!" Casey came bursting through the bushes, brushing a spider web away from his face.

Dylan James, nearly two heads taller than Casey, followed the seven-year-old out of the trees. A cigarette dangled between the teen's lips, his t-shirt torn off at the sleeves—he paused at the edge of the property, seemingly impervious to the cool afternoon's drop in temperature. Gabe watched him stop there, the teen suspiciously watching as Casey tore across the backyard toward the porch. Gabe wore his hostility towards the youthful offender like cheap cologne. Gabe never let his gaze drift off the teenager. They stood silently like opposing knights across a chessboard, the teenager holding his ground defiantly, letting Gabe see the smoke curling past his face.

Casey bolted up the steps and grabbed his father around the waist. "I can't believe you're here! Why didn't anyone tell me you were coming? How did you get here?"

Gabe stooped down and let Casey grab him around his shoulders. Ordinarily, he might have picked the boy up, but today he just didn't have the strength. "You're sure the curious owl today, aren't you? They let your old man out for good behavior, so I thought I would surprise you. Actually, I thought about going to the beach first and catching some rays, but then I thought, 'Hey, why not stop here first and see my rotten little kid?'"

The youngster pulled away from his father and glared at him with one of those incredulous smiles that only seven-year-olds can seem to muster. "You're lyin', right?"

Gabe went down to his knees and held the boy close. "You really think I'd ever choose going to the beach over being with you?"

Casey rested his head on Gabe's shoulder. "Me neither, Dad."

Gabe winked up at Marta, whose eyes were tearing and lips were quivering. He kissed his son on the forehead and whispered into his ear. "...Besides, I figured it was way too cold for the beach!"

"Dad!"

Together they held each other and laughed heartily for a long time. Forget the drugs—this was the kind of therapy that Gabe really needed.

Casey let his father stand up and began waving toward his friend still loitering at the edge of the woods. "Can Dylan come in? He knows you've been sick. I've told him all about it."

Gabe looked out at the boy who was busily crushing the butt of his cigarette under the heel of his sneaker. "Actually, Casey, I'm only home for a few minutes, so I really wanted to talk to you alone..."

"But you just got here! Aren't you staying here with me? Where you going?" the boy interrupted, disappointment evident in his voice.

Gabe hated lying to his son, but he didn't have the time or the inclination to make up some elaborate story right now. He said the first thing that popped into his head. "I've ... I've got a few more tests to take."

Casey stuck his hands in his pockets. Gabe could see that the boy was withdrawing into himself. "Why didn't they do these tests at the hospital?" he pouted.

Gabe reached down and took his son's hands out of his pockets and held them both. "I guess they didn't have the right machinery at the hospital, son. But don't worry. I should be back again real soon."

Casey wouldn't look at his father in the face. "When?"

Gabe couldn't answer what he didn't know. A car horn shattered the tension of the moment.

"Who's that?"

Gabe squeezed his son's seemingly tiny hands. "Those are the people that are taking me for the tests. But I made them drop me off here first, so that I could see you."

Heartbroken, Casey backed away. It was only a short measure in actual distance, but to Gabe it felt like the breadth of eternity.

"I think I wanna go goof around with Dylan now."

When Gabe looked across the backyard, Dylan James had already lit another cigarette and was scraping away dirt from under his nails with a Swiss Army knife. Suddenly, the $4 million was looking mighty appealing. Private schools, book knowledge instead of crook knowledge ... he had to see this thing through. Life was so full of wrong turns, he had to give Casey a fighting chance.

The car horn sounded again.

"You'd better go, Dad."

Gabe went to ruffle Casey's hair, but the boy stayed out of his reach. "You gonna be okay?"

"We're going to be fine, Sénor Gabe," Marta said, trying to ease the anxiety of the moment.

Casey nodded. "Can I go play now?"

Even the emotional trauma of learning he was terminally ill didn't hold a candle to how depressed Gabe was feeling at this very second. Giving up his own life was one thing, but to be responsible for the sorrow and letdown written all over his only child's face was enough to make him want to slit his wrists right then and there. "Are you mad at me, Casey?"

The horn blared from around the front of the house for a third time.

The youngster inched his way back down the steps. "Just go, Dad. I wanna play."

Gabe held out his arm, reaching for something intangible and came away with just that ... the cool afternoon breeze on his palm. "I love you, Casey!"

But the youngster didn't answer, and in seconds had disappeared with his friend into the underbrush, through a flurry of rustling branches, like the ballplayers vanishing into the cornfields in the movie *Field of Dreams*.

Gabe brought his arm down and stared at his empty hand. "What just happened here, Marta? What have I done?"

"Everytheen will work out alright for him, Sénor Gabe. I make that swear promise to you!"

The car horn trumpeted impatiently.

"Well, Marta," Gabe said resolutely, as he walked back into the house, "it looks like I'm about to sell my soul to make sure it does."

20

5:15 P.M.
Heading Southeast
Somewhere over the Caribbean

Approximately 35 miles south of San Salvador lies the pockmarked shore of a sparsely populated islet that is ravaged by a ceaseless onslaught of crashing turquoise waves. Twenty miles square, this fleck of land is barely worth mentioning on most nautical charts. It was first known as Mamana by the Lucayan Indians, and later renamed Santa Maria de la Concepción by Christopher Columbus. More recently in its history, Spanish explorers once found a lone rum keg washed up on a shore and changed the name to Rum Cay, the name it still maintains to this day.

Shayla Rand smiled to herself as the island loomed larger on the horizon; Gabe Mitchell was about to learn firsthand that the island's infamous legacy of harboring ruthless cutthroats was still going strong.

The Bell Jet Ranger III rocketed 1,250 feet over the dark blue waters of the Gulf Stream at a hair-raising speed of 125 miles per hour. Strapped into one of the rear-facing seats, Gabe found himself clinging onto his shoulder harness with both hands. Occasionally, he would summon up the nerve to glance out the window, but fear of flying and heights had never been two of his admirable traits. Reaching above his head, he adjusted one of the air vents to redirect its cooling breeze onto his profusely sweating brow. If he had known a helicopter ride was involved in this arrangement, he might have seriously reconsidered.

Shayla Rand was sitting across from him, her face the epitome of dispassionate composure. She hadn't even strapped herself in, choosing instead the freedom of movement to flip casually through the leisure section of the most recent *Miami Herald.*

A school of bottle-nosed dolphins failed miserably to keep up with their airborne rival as it rocketed southeastward. It was the high-pitched whine of the jet engine that had first attracted them, but even with their incredible speed, the graceful mammals were no match for the curious black airship leaving them at a near standstill in its stormy turbulence.

Damon Washington, who was up front at the controls, was the first to notice the dolphin's fluid performance across the wave tops. "Wow! Look down there! Those fish are really hauling ass!"

Rand glanced away from her paper momentarily to see what he was referring to. Sure enough, there was a school of porpoises leaping from crest to crest below the belly of the helicopter. She adjusted her headphones and the attached microphone in front of her mouth.

"They're mammals."

"Whatever," came Washington's reply. "They're really hauling ass!"

Rand turned her attention back to Gabe, whose fingernails were firmly embedded into the straps of his harness. "Porpoises do nothing for you, Gabe? You seem distracted."

"How much longer 'till we're back on solid ground?"

She smiled sadistically, finding it hard to mask her amusement in the pale shade of green his face had taken on. "You're not enjoying the ride? That's a shame. I love everything about helicopters."

"When do we land?"

Rand glanced at her wristwatch. "Five, ten minutes perhaps. Are you going to make it?"

The helicopter righted itself, and Gabe blew out a strong sigh of relief. "I'll have to admit that I've never been much of a flyer."

Rand adjusted the earphones on her head again. "You could've fooled me," she joked, rolling her eyes. "Do you think it's the medication that's rotting your stomach?"

Gabe let go of the harness just long enough to wipe the sweat off his forehead. "No, that stuff tends to put me to sleep if anything. This phobia with flying goes way back. I've just never been able to buy into the concepts of lift and thrust. I don't understand them, and I don't trust them."

Rand reached across the cabin and lowered Gabe's microphone until it was directly in front of his lips. "That's very strange. I don't remember reading anything about this in your dossier. Is it a fear of all heights, or just flying?"

Gabe covered his mouth to hold back his queasiness. "Look, do we really have to discuss this now?"

Shayla Rand wasn't pleased that her information packet was incomplete, but she didn't let it show. "No, of course we don't have to discuss it now. Close your eyes and think pleasant thoughts ... like the fine future your son has in store for him now. That should make you feel better. Just try to relax, and in a few more minutes we'll be back on terra firma."

* * * * * *

Gabe had been trying awfully hard *not* to think about Casey. Seeing him in his new surroundings, hanging out with that hoodlum friend of his, no parental supervision to speak of, what could $4 million dollars possibly add to that situation? Nightmarish visions of his son as a teenager crept in from the dark edges of his subconscious mind. As if the nausea wasn't bad enough, now he had to deal with images of Casey perched on the back of a gold-plated motorcycle, tattoos plastered all over his arms with long, scraggly hair held back with a studded headband. In the distance, he could picture his in-laws sitting on the veranda of some expensive country club, dressed in multi-colored golf togs from head to toe, cardigan sweaters draped around their suntanned necks, holding up their gin and tonics in a toast to their dearly departed, but philanthropic son-in-law. *Oh God, he had to stop thinking like that, or he was going to throw up for sure!*

Rand reached over and grabbed him by the knee, snapping him out of his horrible daydream. Her voice came into Gabe's headphones amidst a filtered chorus of static pops and hisses. "You sure you're alright? We can't afford to have you spacing out on us."

Gabe nodded as the sleek black helicopter glided into a low dive over the Caribbean and began its final approach into Rum Cay. "Don't worry, I'll make it."

Rand cupped her hand over her microphone to be heard better. "We need you as sharp as your reputation leads us to believe you are."

Gabe leaned back and combed his fingers through his week-old beard. "Just get this thing onto Mother Earth, and I'll be fine."

Rand held up one finger. "Another minute."

21

As the Jet Ranger drew closer to the island, the water transformed from an inky shade of indigo to a glistening shade of aquamarine as the ocean floor began its subtle climb toward the surface. The Jet Ranger's elongated shadow trailed behind the helicopter, the dark mirage climbing and tumbling over each whitecap and rolling wave.

With the exception of the palm trees and the miscellaneous undergrowth indigenous to the island, the northwestern shore of Rum Cay was as remote and barren as the surface of the moon. Gabe first caught glimpse of the rocky shoreline as the helicopter banked steeply to the right, tilting nearly on its side, as the pilot followed the jagged coastline southward toward their ultimate destination. Thick brown clumps of washed-up seaweed edged the beaches, outlining the island like an ocean demarcation line. Amid a whirlwind of dry sand, the helpless palms that were caught in the flight path were nearly bent sideways from the percussion of the Jet Ranger's blades.

Seeing the shoreline race by so quickly, and realizing they were barely one hundred feet off the ground, gave Gabe no consolation. If anything, the sight of land only increased the impression of blistering speed and his sickening sensation of motion-sickness.

The blue and white striped canopy stood out like a carnival tent in the desert of rock and seaweed. The 40 by 40 square foot awning had been erected on one of the few barren areas on the windswept western shore of the island. Four half inch cables had been driven into the coral rock to brace the canopy from the blustery gusts blowing in off the ocean. Less than one hundred yards from the tent, a round landing pad had been designated by a ring of bright orange traffic cones.

A wide path assembled from sheets of plywood led from the landing area to the tent. Beneath the tent, the natural sand surface had been overlaid by more hardwood, creating a more stable surface. Under the canopy, a veritable grotto of potted plants along with three high-backed wicker chairs and a matching rattan bar had been set up for the special summit.

The Jet Ranger settled back to earth like a feather falling from the sky. The skids settled into the soft sand just as the sun was painting the horizon using a pallet of indescribable shades of pink, orange, gold and pale blue. As the rotors slowed to idle speed, a bank of floodlights came on, bathing the entire temporary compound in soft white light.

When the soles of Gabe Mitchell's shoes finally touched the plywood boards, his legs almost buckled beneath him. Damon Washington climbed out of the hatch behind him and literally had to hold him steady. "Whoo, cowboy, you gonna be okay?"

Gabe put a hand against the side of the helicopter to brace himself. "I don't suppose there are any trains back to the mainland from here?"

Washington put his arm around Gabe until he got his footing. "We could've rented a boat, but if you think you were queasy up there," he said, pointing a thumb at the radiant sky, "I'll guarantee you'd have been hocking up a lung out there on the water!"

Washington then turned back toward the open hatch and held out a hand to guide Shayla Rand down the stairway, but she rudely brushed it away. "Isn't that sea breeze just remarkable?" she said, stepping onto the plywood walkway and inflating her ample chest with the salty air. "I really don't get enough of this stuff. Don't you just love the tranquility of the beach, Gabe?"

Gabe leaned his shoulder against the fuselage until he could feel his circulation getting back to normal. With the swipe of his hand, he blotted still more perspiration off his forehead. "I do now!"

Washington climbed back into the helicopter and within a few seconds, the rotors once again began spinning at top speed. "Unless you want to get your skin sandblasted," Rand yelled, over the whining of the engine, "you'd better get under cover!"

"Where's he going?" Gabe screamed back.

She took Gabe by the arm and chaperoned him toward the well-lit canopy. "Don't worry, he'll be back," she assured him, "the Bahamian authorities might not approve of our little impromptu rendezvous, so he's heading up to Nassau to smooth everything out. When we need him, he can be back here in less than 10 minutes."

Straining to move forward against the wash from the blades was taking every ounce of strength that Gabe had left. "By smoothing everything out, you mean..."

Rand lowered her head against the blowing sand. "Money makes the world go 'round. You should understand that as well as anybody, right, Gabe?"

As the last trace of the sun sank beyond the horizon, the Jet Ranger gracefully lifted off, and quickly disappeared—a speck against the darkening sky. Within seconds, the high-pitched drone of the engine was replaced by the incessant hum of gasoline powered generators, and the gentle lapping of the waves along the beach.

A wheelchair bound older man held out his hand as Gabe stepped beneath the canopy. The wheelchair-bound lawyer was dressed in a mustard-colored jacket and a black open-collared shirt with matching slacks. "Mr. Mitchell, or may I call you Gabe? It is a pleasure to finally meet you in person."

Gabe took his hand and shook it, but his eyes were instinctively scanning the area, taking it all in, including the host's distressing countenance. "And you would be?"

"The name's August Bock. Sit down, relax," he said, pointing to one of three folding chairs grouped around a large bamboo table.

"Three chairs. Are you expecting someone else?"

Bock smiled approvingly at Shayla Rand. "No, we're not expecting anyone else. That third chair is for my pilot, Mr. Washington, if he should finish his errand quicker than anticipated. Can I offer you a drink? I know you're on medication, so all I've stocked is soft drinks."

Gabe walked over to the ocean side of the pavilion and looked out toward the water. The sound of breaking waves like the harmony of the rustling palm trees was one of life's hypnotic melodies. "I'll just take a bottle of water, and calling me Gabe is fine."

Bock pointed toward the bar for Shayla who willingly obliged. "Welcome to Rum Cay, Gabe. I know it's a bit cloak and dagger to fly you all the way to a remote island like this, but I've got my reasons. Besides, who wants to sit in some stuffy old office when you can have all of this wonderful scenery around as you transact business?"

Gabe took the bottle of ice water from Shayla. "Lime or lemon?"

"Neither," Gabe said, downing the cold water in one long pull.

"Fetch our guest another one, Shayla."

Gabe rubbed the cool green bottle across his forehead. "No thanks. I'm okay for now."

Bock rolled over to one of the chairs and pulled it away from the table. "Then please, sit down and let's talk. I'm sure you have a million questions for me, and I get very weary at having to look up at people all the time." He rubbed the back of his neck. "To say nothing of the crick it gives me right here."

Gabe hated to leave where he was standing. The ocean seemed so alive, so full of motion. The salt air that stung his nostrils never smelled sweeter than it did at that moment. The orange and purple hues of dusk seemed so somber, yet so vibrant to him now. He despised himself for taking so long to appreciate these simple pleasures.

Shayla reached into the cooler and pulled out a plate of giant prawns and cocktail sauce that had been prepared ahead of time. Each of the pink and white shrimps were as big as her fist. She unwrapped the plate and set it in the center of the table along with a few cloth napkins.

Gabe took a seat facing opposite of August Bock. "Well, Mr. Bock, you said I'd have a million questions to ask, and I'm sure that number is pretty low, but, for the life of me, I don't know where to start."

Bock took one of the prawns by the tail and dipped it in the spicy condiment, savoring each mouthful. "These are really tasty. You really ought to try one."

Gabe set the empty bottle down on the table. "I'll pass for now. I think my stomach's still up in your helicopter."

"Ah," Bock acknowledged as Shayla stepped behind him and began massaging his neck. "I fully understand. A few more minutes breathing this wonderful sea air and you'll be right as rain."

Gabe nudged the green bottle a few inches across the table's surface, as though moving a chess piece. "You didn't bring me out to the middle of nowhere to eat shellfish, did you, Mr. Bock?"

Bock reached up and patted Shayla on the hand. "Pour me a ginger ale, won't you sweetheart?"

Gabe watched as she walked over to the ice chest and unscrewed the lid off the small bottle of pale soda. Under different circumstances, the sight of her shapely figure bent over like that might have deserved a second glance, but not now. "You called her Shayla. At the hospital, she introduced herself as Sheila. So, which one is it?"

Shayla handed the glass to her employer. "My given name is Shayla Rand," she said, finally liberating her thick Irish brogue. "I'm sure you can forgive my deception, Mr. Mitchell, but your roommate and that nurse were both with you at the time."

Gabe raised an eyebrow, wondering what else about her was bogus. "And you *still* insist that we haven't met before today? I could've sworn..."

August Bock held up his glass derailing Gabe's train of thought. "Cheers, Gabe. Here's to your son's bright future."

The wind suddenly changed directions, causing a nearby palm to shed one of its fronds. The branch came crashing to the ground, startling Gabe. "Okay, that's as good a place to start as any ... let's talk about my son's future."

Bock wiped the corner of his mouth with his napkin. "Okay, what do you want to know first?"

Gabe sat up rigidly. "Why not start from the beginning? Who are you, and what is this all about?"

"You see," Bock chuckled. "I told you it would only take a few minutes and you'd be your old inquisitive self again. Have another bottle of water, and I'll try to fill you in."

Shayla replaced the empty bottle, but Gabe was no longer thirsty. "Exactly what do you people want from me?"

August Bock rolled his chair to the end of the makeshift deck. The sky had turned to night, and a long white ribbon of light shimmered across the surface of the water leading to a half moon that hung just above the horizon. He locked his wheels in place and folded his hands across his lap. "Simply put, Gabe ... because of a horrific twist of fate, I find myself in the most enviable, dare I say, divine position to do what's right ... to do what's needed ... for my fellow man."

Gabe's eyes narrowed.

Bock smiled. "Now, before you think I'm some crackpot millionaire whose wheelchair has rolled round the bend of sanity, I can assure you that I am quite sound of mind. Even without the use of my legs, I can march where no one else would dare—I can reach out with the mighty hand of vengeance and balance the scales of justice. I do what needs to be done to fix the system when it breaks."

Gabe wiped some blowing sand off his cheek. "And exactly which part of that philosophy is supposed to convince me that you're not bat-shit crazy?"

Bock unlocked the chair's brake and spun around to face Gabe. "I fully understand your skepticism, but let me tell you how this campaign came to be. The idea came to me while I was in rehabilitation for my accident and I met the most amazing young girl. Like you, she was dying, but much too young. We would talk whenever our sessions coincided, discussing what she wanted to do with the time she had remaining." Gabe saw Bock's uncovered eye begin to well up. "She told me that her father had been shot and killed a year earlier while waiting in line to cash his paycheck during a robbery. The thief was apprehended quickly, but escaped during his transfer to the county stockade. The authorities blamed it on a procedural mix up, and he was still at large—but not for long." Bock borrowed the devil's grin. "I came to know her well over the last weeks before she succumbed to the disease, and what I'll always remember about her was her desire for revenge. She knew it was wrong, and she thought herself a better person, but she couldn't get the thought of retribution out of her head. Neither could I."

Thoughts of Gabe's wife and daughter swirled through his own mind as he listened.

Bock blew out a deep breath. "So that's the history; now let me reveal the reality. I seek out terminal patients such as yourself, Gabe, who for one reason or another not only find themselves down on their luck physically, but monetarily as well. Maybe they've used up their nest egg battling their illnesses, or perhaps their insurance companies have canceled their policies," he said, waving his hand disgustedly. "You wouldn't believe how often *that* happens. Whatever the reason, if the patient fits the profile of what we feel is a potential candidate, we step in and offer them a solution to their fiscal crisis."

Gabe leaned forward, resting his elbows on the bamboo table. "In exchange for..."

Bock unlocked his wheels and spun around to face Gabe. His face was laced tight as a boot. "In exchange for...performing one last heroic service for humanity."

Gabe never let his eyes waver from Bock's face. He was analyzing the man in front of him, trying to figure out whether he was staring into the eyes of a genius or a madman.

"And this service would be..."

"In your case," Bock said, looking over at Shayla, who was seated on the edge of the table, "we want you to rectify another heinous miscarriage of justice."

Gabe sat back in his chair. It had all become so crystal clear. "You talk in circles like a lawyer, but what you really want, is for me to kill someone ... plain and simple."

A horsefly landed on the table, curious about a lemon pit. With cobra-like agility, Shayla's hand whipped out, and flattened the bug beneath her palm. She grinned with contentment and wiped the guts onto her napkin. "Someone very special, love."

Gabe rose out of his chair and held up his hands. "I thought you were only kidding at the hospital. You're really serious about murdering someone? Is that what you do? You find dying people and send them off on suicide missions?" He rubbed his forehead.

"You're all insane! You can't take justice into your own hands. That's what we have courts and lawyers for."

August Bock's calm facade showed its first hint of structure failure. "Courts and lawyers? You think we should respect the decisions that come out of a court of law in this country as if those decisions are sacrosanct? You know, I believed that one time too— until the woman I loved was slaughtered by a man that 12 jurors said was 'innocent.' He wasn't innocent when he killed my wife and left me in this chair. No, no, I know the average person walking around out there might say they want to honor the decisions of our courts. Not me. Not anymore."

Gabe could feel the sweat dripping down the back of his neck as he shook his head with incredulity.

"There is a fine line between insanity and brilliance, Mr. Mitchell," Bock said as he slowly regained his composure. "I need not remind you of all the brilliant people in history who were initially regarded by their peers as crazy."

Gabe looked around for the nearest escape route, but it was pitch dark and the helicopter had left. There was nowhere to run. "Well, I'll be sure to add both your names to that list because you're both lunatics."

"Hear me out," Bock said, pointing for Gabe to return to his seat. "Just listen to what I have to say, and being an ex-law enforcement officer, I'm sure you'll come around to our way of thinking."

Gabe shook his head incredulously and sat back down. This whole thing was like some kind of farce. At any moment he expected someone to pop out of the underbrush and tell him he was being pranked. "I don't think so."

"You don't? Then let me ask you a hypothetical question. That mass murderer that killed all of those poor defenseless women and then killed your partner? What if he had survived that shootout in the alley?"

That thought grabbed Gabe's attention and stirred his ire.

Bock continued. "Now suppose he had gone on trial, and through some procedural technicality or legal loophole, had been set free? How would you feel about that?"

Gabe could feel his teeth grinding, and now August Bock was smiling. "Wouldn't be too happy, would you? We handle *just* those types of situations, Gabe. Consider us the alternative. We specialize in correcting mistakes made by an overwhelmed and very corrupt justice system."

Gabe rubbed his hand over his heart. "By using people like me."

"Exactly! Can you think of a better way? Everybody wins! Now, are you beginning to understand how important our job is?"

"Are you funded by the government?"

Bock frowned. "Oh Lord no, although they are one of my best clients. They give us blanket immunity and, in return, we're occasionally called upon, how should I put this? To clean up their dirty laundry? So again, it's a win-win situation for everyone."

"And what you want me for? To clean up a government mess?"

"I told you, the government isn't my only client. Through very discreet channels, we're approached by people from all over the world who feel someone has escaped justice. Of course, I'm very particular about the cases I take on. I will only deal with the wrongfully acquitted. I don't do divorces," he laughed. "This independent work is the backbone of my operation. These wealthy clients pay for our service, and, in turn, that enables us to pay you. All of this gives me the resources to fulfill my main objective and that is to see that our brand of terminal retribution is carried out wherever and whenever it's called for."

"So this operation of yours has been going on for quite a while?"

Bock reached across the table for his ginger ale and took a sip. "I don't believe that anything we've done in the past is of your concern, Gabe. Let's just deal with the here and now, shall we?"

Gabe crossed his arms over his chest. "That being?"

"A very high-profile case has come to our attention. Yet another jury has seen fit to allow another criminal to go unpunished. It's the one great flaw of our system of jurisprudence: relying on average people with no legal background to pass judgment on these defendants who are obviously guilty."

"You talk like a lawyer, and you seem to know a lot about the law."

Bock ignored the comment. "For this particular assignment, we require someone with a very specific skill set when it comes to police procedures. We need someone who would be familiar to his fellow officers. Someone who could slip through a tight security net unnoticed, provided he had the right credentials."

Fellow officers? Gabe didn't have to be hit over the head with a Louisville Slugger. Now he knew exactly who the intended target was. "This is all about Nathan Waxman, am I right?"

Bock smiled over at Shayla. "I told you, didn't I?"

Shayla nodded. "He's good."

Gabe rubbed his lips; suddenly they were bone-dry. "And if I kill him, my son will get $4 million."

"That is absolutely correct," Bock confirmed.

"But you're assuming that I'll be killed in the process. What if I were to get away somehow?"

Shayla smiled. "You can rest assured that there's no chance of that happening, love."

"Why's that?"

Bock clasped his hands on his lap. "Let's just say, we plan on giving the ex-mayor of Miami Beach an explosive send off."

Gabe remembered the news reports about Waxman taking his private yacht on a week-long getaway. "So when's this all supposed to happen?"

Shayla walked around behind the bar and pulled out a hand-held radio and whispered something into it.

"Tomorrow night," Bock said matter-of-factly. "Everything has been planned down to the minute."

Gabe looked incredulous. "Tomorrow night? You're telling me I've got less than 24 hours to live?"

Shayla set the radio down on top of the bar and smiled. "Twenty-three, actually. He's planning on leaving at sunset."

Gabe felt like his world was spinning out of control. "But that's impossible! There's too many things I still have to take care of! Tomorrow night's too soon!"

"That's why we let you visit with your son this afternoon," Bock said. "That's a very unorthodox policy for us, but we thought seeing him one last time would help put your mind at ease."

Off in the distance, the sound of thumping rotor blades grew louder.

"And what if I don't want to go along with this plan of yours? You know, I'm a cop and you've just confessed to a massive terrorist conspiracy."

Shayla Rand stepped forward until her face was close enough that Gabe could feel her hot breath. "You *used* to be a cop ... and I don't think you'll be telling your story to anyone."

"Gabe ... Shayla ... please," Bock pleaded, trying to avert the standoff. They stood eye to eye with neither of them flinching. "Gabe, the plan's already in motion. There's nothing you can do to stop us."

Unblinking, Gabe inched his face closer to Shayla. "What are you going to do, lady?" he growled like a predatory cat. "Kill me here?"

Bock shook his head. "Please, Gabe, don't be foolish. If I let Shayla kill you now," he said, never considering that the outcome would be otherwise, "Nathan Waxman will go sailing off into the sunset exonerated from justice for a second time. That would be a tragedy I would find reprehensible. I have no intention of letting you die here."

A whirlwind of sand was whipped into the air as the landing lights from Bock's helicopter illuminated the tent.

Gabe shrugged defiantly. "Well, you can't *make* me do it."

Back nodded to Rand and from behind the bar; in response, she retrieved a small brown paper sack. It was the same size bag that a child would store his peanut butter and jelly sandwich in for school. Slowly, deliberately, she unrolled the top of the bag. Sensing Gabe's anxiety and savoring every moment of it, she never took her eyes off of him as she methodically reached inside...

The blades of the idling helicopter continued to spin and the drone from the engines made speaking at a normal volume virtually impossible.

"That's Casey's baseball cap!" Gabe screamed.

Shayla held up the teal and black Florida Marlins hat as though she were displaying it at an auction. "It would be a real shame if something were to happen to your boy, love. He's a real charmer!"

Gabe was feeling weaker than ever, but he still couldn't control his outrage. With no thought of his own regard, he leapt for Rand with both his hands balled into fists. "If you so much as look at my son!"

It took very little effort for her to sidestep his feeble attack and spin around, catching him in a choke hold from behind. "I would love to kill you now," she taunted in his ear, "but I'd take even more pleasure in torturing and then killing your boy instead." She shoved him toward the table where he slumped over, clutching at his throat.

"I was sincerely hoping it wouldn't come down to this," Bock said, regretfully shaking his head. "I promise no harm will come to your son, and he will be amply rewarded—if you do what we tell you."

Gabe was having a difficult time catching his breath. "So, this is what it comes down to? Petty blackmail?"

Bock shook his head. "Blackmail? Maybe. Petty? We do what we must. If you think about it, Gabe, we're actually saving you a great deal of suffering and hardship by giving you a quick and painless way out. Dying from a brain tumor is such a horrible way to go. You'd be sacrificing yourself for the benefit of mankind, and at the same time, your son will be set for life! Now, what's so hard to swallow about that deal?"

Gabe tried to stand upright, his hands still rubbing his tender neck. "I guess you've left me no choice."

Bock looked over at Shayla and raised his glass. "You see what can be worked out through a little negotiation? A toast to Gabe Mitchell and the successful completion of his mission!"

Damon Washington stepped out of the darkness and into the brightly lit tent. "Everything went well, I assume."

"Splendid," Bock announced. "Now please fly Gabe back to the mainland. I want to speak with Shayla privately, and, since it's such a glorious night, I thought we might stay on a bit longer. You can return for us after you've seen to his accommodations."

Gabe poured the water from the bottle onto a napkin and blotted the cold compress against his face. Combined with the cool breeze blowing in from the ocean, it quickly revived his spirit and energy. "I suppose there's no chance I'd be allowed to go home first?"

"I'm afraid not," Bock said. "It would be better if you were to stay where we can keep an eye on you. It's not that I think you'd try anything foolish—it's just a precaution for your own welfare. Believe me: you'll be very comfortable in the room we have set up for you, and you'll be fully briefed there as well. But if there's anything else you want, just let one of my associates know."

"You mean, like a last meal?"

Bock held open his hands. "If that's what you wish. The sky's the limit. Money is no object. Food, companionship—whatever you'd like, it's yours ... just name it. I want to make your next 22 hours the most pleasant you've ever spent on earth."

Gabe started walking with Damon Washington toward the helicopter, but paused at the edge of the walkway and turned around. "Don't you mean my *last* 22 hours?"

* * * * * *

The moon had risen halfway up the night sky, and a band of fluffy white clouds drifted aimlessly across it. Out to sea, the lights from a smattering of Bahamian fishing boats blinked along the horizon, like stars that didn't have the ambition to reach any higher into the sky. The whine of the retreating helicopter had long since been replaced by the slapping of the surf on the shoreline and the continuous hum of the electrical generator. August Bock noticed none of it. His wheelchair sat perched at the edge of the wooden floor facing the ocean, but his mind was elsewhere as Shayla Rand handed him another drink.

"So, what do you think of my choice?" he asked, with his focus somewhere far beyond the starlit horizon.

"Do you want my honest opinion?" she asked, leaning against one of the thick metal cables that supported the canopy, "or do you want me to tell you what you want to hear?"

Bock frowned. "I take it you're not enthused about Mr. Mitchell. I value your opinion. Why not?"

Rand stepped down onto the sand and walked around to face Bock. With the difference in height of the sand and platform floor, they were now at eye level. "He's not like the old Jew, or the crippled girl, August. I've seen this man in action twice. He's dangerous. I don't trust him as far as I can throw him."

"In the entire time I've known you, I've never seen you scared of anyone."

She bent down and picked up a shell and tossed it into the incoming tide. "No man frightens me, August, but I'm warning you. You might be getting more than you bargained for with this man."

"What makes you say that?"

"Because you've backed him into a corner and this is the type of man who won't be intimidated like that. I've seen him with a gun in his face. He's as dangerous as a ricocheting bullet. I don't like him, and I wouldn't turn my back on him if he'd already been dead a week."

Bock took a sip from his drink. "I think you worry too much. By tomorrow night at this time, it will all be over."

Shayla leaned forward in the sand, her hands resting on the arms of Bock's wheelchair. "You're not listening to me August. You asked my opinion, and I am telling you right now that the only good Gabe Mitchell is a dead Gabe Mitchell."

"You're worrying yourself over nothing, my dear. He will perform exactly as we've planned. We've strung him along like a marionette to this point. And now, he honestly believes we have him over the proverbial barrel."

But Shayla Rand was not so self-assured. "A lot can happen in a single day, August," she said, digging her heels into the sand. "As far as I'm concerned, tomorrow night cannot come soon enough!"

22

Tropic Garden Motel
20 hours to live

Damon Washington untied the knot on Gabe's blindfold and slipped the black scarf into his pocket.

"Was that really necessary?" Gabe asked, rubbing his eyes.

"Just a precaution, Mr. Mitchell."

"Do you treat all of your recruits this way?"

Washington folded the black scarf into a neat little square. "No, just the ones who used to be police detectives."

After Gabe's eyes had sufficiently adjusted to the dreary lighting, he couldn't decide if the foul shade of yellow on the walls was caused by decaying paint, or the dismal gloom cast off by the stained lampshade. One thing was for certain: the room smelled musty and needed to be aired out. Everything about this place said *don't touch me without rubber gloves.* "Not exactly the lap of luxury, is it?"

Damon Washington closed the door behind Gabe. "Be it ever so humble, Mr. Mitchell. Eric here will see to anything you might need."

Gabe sat down on the edge of the bed. It felt too firm to sleep on, but he had a feeling that, in a dump like this, sleep was not the main purpose of the beds. He smiled across the room at Eric, the bodybuilder henchman, who was leaning heavily against the door. Not even at full strength could Gabe have taken on this block of chiseled granite that masqueraded as a human being. The way the man's pectoral muscles strained at the silk fabric of his shirt made Gabe think of the *Incredible Hulk*. "Wazzup?"

The guard's sullen expression never wavered. His single eyebrow wrinkled a bit, but he never offered a verbal response. Gabe figured if he *had* answered, it wouldn't have been more than a grunt anyway.

"Not a big talker?" Gabe asked.

"We hire Eric occasionally," Washington said, walking toward the bathroom, flipping on the light inside, looking around, and then shutting the light off again. "He does his job well and that's all we care about. We don't ask him to be congenial."

"Ah," Gabe nodded, "and he's just going to stand there staring at me all night?"

"We just want you to get some rest, Mr. Mitchell. In the morning we'll be back to brief you about tomorrow night's plans. Until then, relax, watch some television, have a nice meal ... whatever. Just tell Eric what you want and he'll contact us."

Gabe looked over at the empty night stand next to the bed.

"We've had the phone removed. I'm sure you understand ... precautionary."

Gabe reached over for a copy of the latest *TV Guide* that was on the dresser and flipped through it. "You don't have to explain."

"Perhaps if you had been a bit more cooperative with Mr. Bock."

Gabe tossed the *TV Guide* onto the night stand. "Bock must really have it in for Nathan Waxman."

"My *boss*," Washington said, "has it in for *anyone* who commits a crime and gets away with it."

Gabe reclined backward on his elbows. "So do I, but you've gotta work within the system's limits. Otherwise, you've got nothing but..."

"Justice?"

"I was going to say anarchy."

"I'd like to stay and debate you all night, Mr. Mitchell, but I have more preparations to make. Can I at least get you something to eat before I leave?" Washington asked.

"No, I can't eat anything after that flight," Gabe said, putting his hand on his stomach. "My belly's still doing flip-flops. All I want is to take my medicine, lie down, and let it knock me unconscious until morning."

"If that's all you want, Eric can get you something cold to drink from the machine outside so you can take your pills. Have a good night's sleep, Mr. Mitchell," Washington said, his hand on the doorknob, "and we'll see you bright and early in the morning."

The door slammed, and the room went deathly silent. Gabe thought he heard scratching coming from inside one of the walls. *Rats.* But he tried to block it out of his mind. "So," he said to the bodyguard, "how long have you been working for these people?"

The bruiser flipped open his cellular phone to check on its battery, and slipped it into his breast pocket. "You want something to drink so you can take your pills?"

Gabe looked surprised. "A sentence? Jeez, for a minute there, I thought I was going to have to use sign language!"

The corner of the bodyguard's mouth sagged downward. "Whad'ya want?"

"I don't care. If there's something caffeine-free, that'll be perfect. I don't need caffeine fighting off the effect of my pills when I'm trying to sleep."

"I'll get you whatever's in the machine."

"You need some change?"

Eric shook his thick neck. "I got it."

Gabe saw the latch click after the bodyguard shut the door. The lock was brand new—he could tell that from the polished brass. It stood out like a third thumb. He had to work fast...

Gabe sprinted for the bathroom and quickly unwrapped two plastic glasses. Through the flimsy walls, he could hear the can of soda dropping out of the machine. There was a small window above the old porcelain toilet, but it was painted shut. Besides, it was three floors down to the street. He figured he could burst through the window and jump if he had to, but he hoped it wouldn't come to that. Above the peeling sink, the vanity mirror was cracked, a wide strip of silver duct tape holding the broken glass in the frame. No doubt that was cheaper for the landlord than putting in an entire new mirror in this dump.

"All they had was regular Diet Pepsi."

Gabe walked out of the bathroom with the two opaque plastic glasses. "It'll have to do, I guess."

"Why two glasses?" Eric asked.

"I hate to drink alone. I just thought you'd want a drink too."

The bodyguard took a seat in one of the room's cheap wooden chairs. The rickety material creaked under the tremendous load. "You take as much as you want. I can finish the rest out of the can."

This wasn't going the way he planned. "Hey, at least let me wipe the top off for you. Look how gross it is." He didn't have to exaggerate. The can was disgustingly dirty.

Eric inspected the top of the filthy can. "Yeah, okay."

Gabe casually walked into the bathroom, keeping the bodyguard engaged entire way. "That's why I never drink out of the can or the bottle if I can help it." He flipped on the light in the bathroom, but kept his back to the outer room. "Whoo! You should see all of the crap that's coming off on this towel!" He came back out with one glass filled and the rest of the can, which he handed to Eric. "Cheers!"

The bodyguard finished the remainder of the soda in one slug, his Adams apple bouncing in his throat like a rubber ball. Letting out a belch, he crushed the aluminum container in his fist, without the slightest effort. "I'll be outside if you need anything."

"Hey," Gabe said, "why don't you stick around a few more minutes? We can talk or play some cards. It'll take a few minutes for my pills to work."

The bodyguard held up his hand. "I don't get paid to babysit, mister. Washington told you to get some sleep ... so sleep."

Gabe reached for the television's remote control, but it didn't work.

"So how much does babysitting go for nowadays?" Gabe asked.

Eric yawned. "More than *you* can afford from the looks of you."

Gabe took another sip from his soda. "I guess I *have* kinda let myself go lately. Exactly how did you get into the kind of great shape you're in?"

Eric yawned again and rubbed his eyes. He stopped halfway to the door. Gabe figured it was a better than fifty-fifty chance that Eric would love talking about his own physique. *First principle of hostage negotiation: there's only one thing that can flourish without nourishment ... it's the human ego.*

Gabe yawned so Eric could see him, and the bodyguard copied him. "I guess it don't really matter if I'm inside or out, so long as you stay put."

"I'm not going anywhere," Gabe assured his captor as he fluffed up the two droopy pillows on the bed and braced them against the rattan headboard. "I'm gonna get nice and cozy, and if I should nod off, then do me a favor and shut off the lights, will you?"

The bodyguard sat back down in the same rickety chair as before, this time leaning with his elbows on the table. "Is it warm in here, or is it me?"

The only thing that *was* comfortable about the room was the temperature. "Seems fine to me," Gabe said. "So tell me about your fitness regimen. How'd you beef up like that?"

Eric tugged at the collar of his shirt which he suddenly found very constricting.

"I ... uh ... I work out a minimum of two hours a day with free weights..."

"How about those machines?" Gabe asked, genuinely showing interest. "You use the Stairmaster and stuff like that?"

Eric shook his head heavily. "Uh ... no cardio. Don't ... like the machines."

Gabe stretched his arms above his head and took in a long, protracted breath, stretching lazily as his pills continued their work. "How about food supplements? You take any steroids or stuff like that?"

Eric's left eyelid wilted slowly and then blinked open again. "No ... drugs ... never take any drugs."

Gabe nodded. "That's a good philosophy to live by, you know? If you ask me, drugs are the scourge of our modern society, don't you think so? For all the good they do for some people, when used indiscriminately, they can do terrible damage."

Eric's enormous head hit the table with a leaden "*thud.*"

Gabe sprang off of the bed. *Wow, those things work fast!* Eight capsules. It was all the medicine he had left. He knew it was going take a lot to bring down this elephant, and he hadn't wanted to take any chances.

He figured he had four to five hours leeway while Eric was in dreamland, but, to play it safe, he would be back in under three. His first priority was Casey's safety. Moving on the balls of his feet, he inched closer to the sleeping bodyguard who was now sawing wood like a lumberjack. The phone was in his shirt pocket and the keys were undoubtedly in his trousers. One thing at a time...

Sweat rolled off of Gabe's forehead as he inched his hand closer to the pocket with the phone in it. Who knew how powerful those pills were, or how strong Eric's constitution was?

The bodyguard was sleeping on his crossed arms, his face pressed flat against the table. Gabe had to get onto his knees and work upward from below, using the tip of one finger to nudge the phone ever-so-slowly out of Eric's pocket. The weightlifter stirred ... and Gabe held his breath. His hands were surprisingly steady considering the awkward position he was in.

Once the phone was in his possession, the keys were next. He wanted them as insurance, just in case something went wrong, and he needed to return before Eric awoke. After a few seconds of careful consideration, he realized this might take a bit of surgery. He remembered the broken vanity mirror...

The jagged sliver of glass Gabe returned with from the bathroom would do nicely. A fraction of an inch at a time, he cut open Eric's pants pocket. Once again, the bodyguard rustled, this time shifting his face on the table away from Gabe. The material tore with a ripping sound until the tip of the glass hit the metal key ring. With one swift tug, Gabe freed the keys from the slumbering bodyguard's pocket and stifled their jingling between his palms.

Gabe tiptoed toward the drapes and pulled them back just enough to see outside. His view was partially obscured, but, even in the eerie amber tinge from the streetlights, he could see most of the parking lot. Only three spaces appeared to be filled, but, from this third floor height, he couldn't tell if any of the vehicles were occupied. It would be a chance he would have to take.

As Gabe left, he decided to leave the light on, fearing that if someone else was watching the room, they might find it strange that Eric would stay inside once the lights went out. Carefully, he opened the door just wide enough to hold out the sliver of broken mirror. He tilted it in both directions to see if the landing was clear. Thankfully, it was.

The stairwell was closer to his left. Only one room to cross and then the stairs. The cool night air rushed into the room, drying up the perspiration on Gabe's face and making him want to sneeze, but he pressed his fist hard against his nose to suppress the urge. He couldn't keep the door open; the cold air would wake Eric like a slap from an Eskimo. Staying low, he crept on his belly through the door, closing it slowly behind him so the lock would make as little noise as possible.

Now that he was out on the landing, two more cars came into view. These were parked right up against the building below. Lying prone on the floor, Gabe crept forward until his head was flush against the ledge and the metal railing. The car on the right, an expensive import, looked empty. Gabe rifled through the keys he took off Eric. The import had to be his—the key matched. Next to the import, there was a light blue *(or what appeared to be blue under the amber lights)* sedan. At first Gabe thought it might be unoccupied as well, until he saw a faint orange dot glowing through the windshield ... the telltale tip of a lit cigarette. It could have been another one of Bock's hired goons keeping an extra eye on the outside of the place, or just some innocent passerby who was in the wrong place at the wrong time. Either way, it ruined any chance Gabe had of misappropriating Eric's car.

Making his way down the stairs, he paused behind a garbage dumpster to catch his bearings. He knew Miami like the back of his hand, but nothing around here seemed familiar. Maybe he was just too tired, or perhaps it was the all the confusion of the moment, but, for the life of him, he couldn't spot a recognizable landmark. Behind the motel, a tall fence ran the perimeter of the parking lot, another clue that this wasn't the best of neighborhoods. Gabe stayed with his back pressed against the fence for a long moment and listened to the sounds of the night. He stayed in the shadows, creeping ever-so-slowly toward the entrance to the parking lot, stopping whenever the sound of a passing car would grow too loud. *Look at me! I'm slinking around a parking lot in the middle of nowhere! Go back upstairs. Let the chips fall wherever they fall. Three weeks or three months—it would still never be enough time to fill all the holes in Casey's life. He'll be better off with all that money.*

In the midst of the stillness, he could feel his heart beating. It felt weak and feeble, like termites burrowing inside of his chest.

But who says they'll hold up their end of the deal? Who knows what they'll do to Casey after I'm gone? He's just another loose end for them. I've gotta make sure Casey's alright. I've gotta keep going. Gotta put an end to this insanity.

Gabe was wheezing as he walked as fast as he could for the opening in the fence. When he finally reached the street, he looked to his left ... more motels. To his right ... even more motels. Across the busy street in front of him ... yet another row of motels. *Where was he?*

Thunder boomed on a cloudless evening. It came from his left, exploding from out of the darkness. It grew louder with each passing second. It came from across the street, behind the row of motels. *Wait ... not thunder. Too nice out for thunder.*

A boat. A racing boat to be exact. They called them "cigarettes"— sleek hulled firecrackers that raced across the surface of the water trailing a rooster tail of spray in their turbulent wake. He was near the water. He turned to what he figured was the east and drew in a deep breath. *Salt air.* Now things were starting to fall into place.

23

He was on Hollywood Beach—a narrow strip of real estate north of Miami Beach and southeast of Fort Lauderdale. Motels by the hundreds flanked the Atlantic Ocean here for the convenience of all the tourists that called this place home during these winter months.

This was no out-of-the-way place. He remembered from the television report that Nathan Waxman's yacht was docked at a marina on the Intracoastal Waterway not very far from here. That had to be where the roar of the boats was coming from.

Gabe's mind was clearing. Being in Hollywood wasn't good though. He was half an hour ride from Miami with no transportation. Gabe reached into his back pocket and checked his bankroll. Fifty-three dollars ... more than enough for cab fare.

Waiting for his ride to show up, Gabe phoned his in-laws number, but there was no answer. He knew tonight was Marta's night off, so he could only hope and pray that Casey was with one of them and that his son was safe.

The yellow cab came screeching to the curb ten minutes later. Once inside, Gabe couldn't decide which smelled worse: the motel room he had just left, or the interior of the car.

"Where to, mister?" the cabbie asked, in a heavy Haitian accent.

"Drive south," Gabe ordered from the back seat.

"South?"

"I'll tell you exactly where in a minute. Head down toward Miami."

The Haitian driver stared at Gabe quizzically in the rear-view mirror, and then nodded. "Okay, south. Boulevard or expressway?"

Gabe messed up the number he was punching into Eric's portable phone. "I don't care! The quickest way!"

The driver nodded again. "Boulevard is quicker this time of night."

"Then take the damned boulevard!"

Gabe re-dialed the police station and was told Captain Leon Williams had left for a quick dinner. Now Gabe knew *exactly* where to tell the cabbie to drive.

The lights along Biscayne Boulevard, a.k.a. U.S. 1, streaked by like a meteor shower. This four lane blacktop had been the main thoroughfare in South Florida years before the interstate brought new meaning to the word "congestion." Now a secondary road, one could still get a taste of the evolution of South Florida by studying the neighborhoods the boulevard passed through. It was like looking at a cross-section of a sedimentary rock, the newer layers of stone forming atop the older and crushing them beneath their weight.

Restaurants that had once served celebrities as well as scoundrels now stood as boarded-up monuments to a bygone era. The signs on most of the stores were written in Spanish as well as English, a by-product of the new ethnicity of the area. Hookers still patrolled the sidewalks of North Miami, leaning into the cars of anyone who would slow down and show an interest in their wares. Gabe smiled to himself as the taxi pulled away from a red light. As he watched those ladies of the evening move from car to car, he couldn't help but remember back to those early years of busting johns and running down pimps. Although most of those years working under Leon Williams' command were memorable, he sure wouldn't miss a single minute of those exhausting footraces.

Gabe tried his in-law's number one more time, but still no luck. There would be no leaving his voice on their message machine. He didn't want to risk it. "Make the next right, driver."

Once in Miami, the taxi turned off Biscayne Boulevard and onto Flagler Street. "Two more blocks on the left," Gabe instructed.

The car slowed down to a crawl in front of Strofsky's Late-Nite Delicatessen. "This the place?" the driver asked.

Gabe stared at the restaurant's red neon sign through the taxi's window, his hand paralyzed on the door handle unable to turn it. The last time he'd been here, Joanne Hansen was still alive. He'd known nothing of August Bock or Shayla Rand, and the only threat his son ever had was from kids that were bigger than him at school.

"Are you alright, mister?"

Gabe tried desperately to shake off the sudden anxiety attack. "Yeah, but do you mind if I sit here for a second?"

The driver shrugged. "The meter's still running. Sit as long as you want."

The door to the deli opened, and a young black couple holding hands strolled out. The husband or boyfriend offered his wife or girlfriend his coat and she accepted it, throwing it over her shoulders for warmth. Yes, life did go on.

"Can you wait here for me?" Gabe asked. "I'll need a ride back."

"All the way back to Hollywood?" the driver asked over his shoulder.

"Is that a problem?"

The cabbie pointed to the meter and shrugged. "You already owe me $21."

Gabe reached into his pocket and pulled out a twenty and a five. "Please, this is very important. Shut off the meter and wait for me."

The driver scratched his head and shut off the engine. "Well, it was a slow night anyway. Make it quick; I don't like this neighborhood."

Gabe got out of the car and patted the driver's door. "Hopefully this shouldn't take long. I'll be as fast as I can."

Gabe hurried across the sidewalk and into the diner.

"Detective Gabe!" Morris Strofsky shouted as he stepped from behind the counter, drying his hands on his apron. "I'm so sorry about Detective Hansen. She was such a nice young woman," he said apologetically as he shook Gabe's hand. "I sent a platter of food to her house. So how are you feeling? All I heard was what they said on the television and then some gossip from the other policemen that eat here. So how are you doing ... really?"

"Nothing I can't handle, Morris. So, what are they saying about me back at the precinct?"

Old man Strofsky waved his hand. "Fuck what they say. You've always been tops on my list. I told them all about the way you talked that guy out of robbing me last week. They said that was wrong of you too. I don't agree with them."

Gabe surveyed the clientele of the deli as he spoke. "They might be right, Morris. Look, I'd like to kibitz some more, but have you seen my captain tonight?"

Strofsky pointed to a booth in the rear of the restaurant. The back of the seats were built purposely high to offer privacy. "You're in luck; I just served him tonight's special ... meatloaf and mashed potatoes. Can I get you something? It's on the house, no matter what anyone else thinks."

"How about a creme soda just for old times? Send Gladys over with one, okay?"

The old man's face turned dour. "Gladys doesn't work here anymore. She hasn't shown up in more than a week. Always rude to the customers. Good riddance to bad rubbish, as far as I'm concerned."

Gabe looked honestly surprised. "Really? She was always nice to me."

Strofsky was having a difficult time dissolving the angered look from his wrinkled old mug. "Then you must have been the exception to the rule. But don't worry: the Doctor Brown's Soda is still on me. I'll bring it right over."

Captain Leon Williams was studying the financial section of the *Miami Herald* when Gabe walked up to his booth startling him. "Hello, Captain."

Williams looked impeccable as usual in his custom tailored suit and matching silk neckwear. "Gabe? What are you doing here? Is everything alright? Shouldn't you be resting or something?"

"You mind if I sit down, Captain?"

Williams folded the newspaper and set it down on the space beside him. He pointed to the open side of the booth. "Of course you can sit down. Is everything okay?"

Gabe slid into the booth and began to fidget nervously with the utensils in front of him. "It's all so unreal. I don't know where to start..."

"Well, call the tabloids. I've never seen Gabe Mitchell at a loss for words before," Williams joked, as he pushed his half-eaten dinner off to one side. "You look troubled and tired, Gabe. Lord knows what you're going through. You wanna talk about it?"

"This has nothing to do with my illness..." Gabe said. "Well, I guess it has *something* to do with the illness. I mean, if it wasn't for my illness..."

Williams reached across the table and took Gabe's hand. "Slow down. You're talking in riddles."

Gabe pressed his hands against the sides of his head and squeezed his eyes shut. "It's just so hard to believe ... too much to comprehend."

"Start at the beginning then," Williams said, as he peeked around the edge of the booth to see if anyone was within earshot. Luckily the restaurant was almost empty.

Gabe let his head loll against the back of the booth. His eyes looked dreamily at nothing in particular on the ceiling. "You're going to think I'm making this whole thing up..."

Williams sat upright. "What thing? What is this all about?"

Gabe took a deep breath. There was no time for small talk. He just had to tell his story and hope that his ex-captain didn't call for the guys in the white jackets to haul him away. "There's this guy ... well no, wait a minute ... let me start from the beginning..."

Williams crossed his arms and listened intently to Gabe Mitchell's tale of red-haired hit-women, wheel-chair bound megalomaniacs, kamikaze assassinations, post-mortem payoffs, blackmail, mysterious tropical islands, and an escape attempt that would rival any Harrison Ford movie.

"Are you still taking your medication like you're supposed to?" Williams asked, sincerely.

"This isn't some drug-induced hallucination. I'm not making this up," Gabe growled, slamming his hand on the table and nearly knocking over the creme soda he never even noticed old man Strofsky had brought. "You've got to believe me! Do some research!

If you connect all the dots, you're going to find a bunch of suspicious deaths ... all people that have been acquitted of major crimes!"

Williams put his finger over his mouth. "Calm down, Gabe. You've been under a helluva lot of stress lately. I'm sure there's gotta be someone who can give you the help you..."

Gabe reached across the table and grabbed his captain by his $800 lapels. He pulled him so close that, when Gabe spoke, little beads of spittle splattered on Williams' face. "Don't patronize me, Captain. I'm trying to tell you that by tomorrow night at this time, Nathan Waxman is going to be dead!"

Williams leaned back and Gabe released his grip. "The Mayor of Miami Beach?"

Gabe nodded. "Tomorrow night on his yacht. Bock recruited me to kill him!"

Williams pulled out a small note pad out of his pocket and jotted down the mayor's name and the name of August Bock. "Getting rid of that son-of-a-bitch wouldn't be the worst idea I've ever heard."

Gabe leaned forward, his face ashen and sour. "I know you believe Waxman killed his wife, Captain. Everyone does. But he had his day in court and justice was served."

Williams dabbed at the corner of his mouth with his napkin. "What about this option: we forget about this conversation and you go ahead and kill him," he said with a conniving grin.

"Captain?"

Williams shrugged. "I'm only kidding. And you're supposed to murder him ... how?"

"I don't know yet. They're filling me in the tomorrow."

"And this is going to happen where?"

"I think they said on his yacht, but I'm not sure. I got the impression it was supposed to happen when he's leaving town."

Williams closed the notepad and shook his head skeptically. "I don't believe I'm going to do this. I swear Gabe, if I come out of this looking like an idiot..."

Now it was Gabe's turn to reach out for his captain's hand. "Thanks for having my back, Leon. I feel better now that someone I can trust knows."

Williams looked at his wristwatch. "So where are you off to now? What are you going to do?"

"I think I need to warn Waxman's people."

Williams put out a hand to stop Gabe from leaving the booth. "Let me handle that. I'll make a few phone calls and if anything in your story checks out, I promise I'll contact the Mayor personally."

Gabe nodded. "Of course, you're right. Now that I've got you working on this, I can breathe a bit easier. I need to go back then and find out what the plan is. When I learn more, I'll figure out a way to contact you again."

Gabe slid out of the booth and shook his captain's hand. "Thanks Captain. I knew I could count on you."

Old man Strofsky waved to Gabe as he hurried out the front door, then he walked over to the booth. The first thing he noticed was the full glass of creme soda. "He didn't even touch his drink."

* * * * * *

Captain Leon Williams flipped open his notepad and tore out the page he had just scribbled on. Shaking his head, he tore the slip of paper into tiny pieces and threw the confetti onto his scoop of uneaten mashed potatoes. "Poor bastard is crazy as they come. That tumor must really be eating away at his brain. We can only hope the end comes quickly and peacefully for him."

Morris Strofsky nodded sadly in agreement. "It's so sad. He looks so normal."

Williams pulled out his cellular phone and smiled at the old man. "Looks can be deceiving, Morris."

"Sure, Captain. You want some privacy?"

Williams nodded and waited while the old man cleared away the dirty plates. Williams then reached into his billfold and withdrew a beige business card bearing only three capital letters and a telephone number printed in raised brown lettering. He dialed the number and waited. The voice that finally answered was direct and to the point. "*What?*"

"Let me talk to him."

"He's unavailable."

Williams' voice countered hard as concrete. "Tell him we've got a problem."

"What kind of problem?"

Williams tipped his head downward and whispered. "Gabe Mitchell just showed up and sat down across from me."

Silence filled the line like a third presence.

"Yeah, I had a feeling that would get your attention."

"Where are you?"

"I'm at Strofsky's Deli. I was eating dinner and he just waltzed in here like nothing was wrong!"

"That's impossible."

Williams leaned forward and rolled his eyes. "You wanna lay some money on that? How about I give you a million to one odds?"

"You did right to call."

Williams was seething. "You'd better listen to me buster, and you can relay this to your boss." His finger jabbed at the air like he was trying to burst invisible balloons. "What kind of Tinker Toy organization is he running over there? You wanted this guy and I handed him to you on a silver platter. You said nothing about killing his partner. You said nothing about threatening the life of a seven-year-old boy. Now I'm an accomplice to murder and kidnapping! I got you all the credentials you needed for tomorrow night. And now you people can't even hold onto him?" Williams was squeezing the phone so hard he thought it might snap in half. "You need me to do that too?"

Again, there was an awkward pause.

"Where is he now?"

"Heading back."

"We'll handle it."

"I warned you about him. I've known Gabe Mitchell for 15 years. Before his wife and daughter died, he was the best man I ever had under my command. Even after his breakdown, I'd still take another ten cops just like him. Now that he's got the scent, he's not going to let up."

"I said, we'd handle it."

Williams fussed with the knot on his tie. "Well you'd better, because it's my keister on the line too, and everything you promised me ain't gonna be worth shit if I'm spending the rest of my life behind bars. You got it?"

"We'll deal with this."

Williams slapped the phone shut. "You'd better deal with it," he snarled, storming out of the deli, "or we'll all be eating slop off tin plates!"

24

"You can drop me off here."

"Are you sure?" the cabbie asked. "This is more than a block from where I picked up you up."

Gabe reached over the back seat and tossed the remainder of what money he had onto the front seat. "That should cover it and then some."

The taxi pulled over to the curb outside a store that rented and sold scuba equipment. A red neon dive flag sizzled in the front window of the darkened shop.

"You want me to wait again for you?"

Gabe leaned into the passenger side window and smiled. "No thanks, I'm good."

The driver counted his fare and folded the bills in half before slipping them into his shirt pocket. "Anytime you need another ride to Miami, you just call my company and ask for Nelson. I'll give you a special discount."

Gabe stepped back onto the sidewalk and pulled his collar up to ward off the cold breeze blowing in off the water. "Have a good night, Nelson."

"Same to you, sir," the driver replied. Then the taxi pulled away from the curb and sped off into the night.

The smells of the beach overwhelmed Gabe's nostrils as he hustled across the empty street. Gasoline fumes from outboard engines, salt sea air, Chinese food ... no, something fried but not Chinese ... the aromas all mingled together and wafted around him like angel dust on the bracing wind.

He paused a few hundred yards from the entrance to the Tropic Garden Motel, standing in a darkened doorway of a store that sold inflatable rafts, beach towels, sea shells, and anything else someone visiting the area could buy. He leaned his head out of the shadows as a car pulled out onto the street from the motel's driveway. It turned right onto A1A and drove right past him. Gabe recognized it as the sedan whose driver liked to smoke in the dark. He made out two figures in the car—male and female. Seeing a couple inside the car put his mind at ease a bit. Gabe realized that a lot of these motels would lodge prostitutes attracted to this section of the beach. The smoker was probably just some john who didn't want to fork out the additional fifty bucks for a room he'd only be spending a few hours in.

Ah, don't you just love a free market economy.

Gabe moved toward the motel like a cautious ninja, staying in the shadows with his back pressed up to the fronts of the buildings. When he was finally close enough to get a glimpse of the parking lot, he could see that there were only two spaces occupied. Quite strange, he thought, for a motel during the height of the winter season. Long past midnight, the parking lot should have been flooded with the cars of tired vacationers. Only two cars ... Eric the goon's expensive import, to which Gabe still held the keys, and now a slick-looking black Corvette parked right next to it.

Past the ice and soda machines and up the stairs, Gabe stopped to catch his breath. He never remembered working this hard when he was healthy, much less now. Pausing on the landing, he once again took out the piece of broken mirror and held it out around the corner. The hallway appeared clear, and there was no sign of trouble. Home free.

Ever so deftly, he slipped the room key into the lock and twisted the doorknob. Everything inside the room seemed as he had left it. Eric was still in the same chair sleeping off the medication. His head was still flat on the table. Gabe checked his watch. It had been three hours. His pills had performed well above their prescribed purpose. Now all he had to do was to set Eric's keys on the floor below his torn pocket, and slip into bed making it look like he had been sleeping the entire time.

The bodyguard looked like he was sleeping so peacefully. Gabe knelt down to place the key ring on the carpet when he noticed a large dark spot on the rug. He touched his fingertips to the stain ... they came away dark and sticky ... blood!

Gabe moved around to examine the bodyguard's face. There was a black hole above the bridge of Eric's nose. A muzzle burn circled the wound which told Gabe the barrel of the assailant's gun had been placed flush up against his skin. No mercy. A stream of syrupy brown liquid flowed from the wound and spilled onto the table. The excess drained over the edge and onto the floor, one life-depreciating drop at a time.

"Someone's been a bad boy. Out gallivanting when they shouldn't have been."

The unmistakable Irish voice came from the bathroom doorway.

Gabe spun around, startled, but not surprised. "Why did you have to kill him?"

Shayla stepped into the room, her silencer-equipped pistol pointing at Gabe. "Anyone that stupid doesn't deserve to live."

Gabe's body trembled. "It was my fault. I drugged him. You didn't need to kill him."

Shayla motioned with her gun for Gabe to take a seat on the foot of the bed. "Then take comfort in the fact that he was sleeping and probably never felt a thing."

So many things were running through Gabe's mind. How many times had he found himself staring down the barrel of a gun? There were too many to recall, but never one belonging to such a stone-cold killer. There was no telltale twitching in her arms. Most guns weighed less than a pound but seemed to weigh a ton when it was pointed at another human being. There was no sweat on her brow— no agitated darting of her eyes. Those two lifeless green orbs never moved off Gabe's face.

"How did you know?"

Shayla stepped into room, backlit in the yellow haze coming from the bathroom. She had changed clothes into a black leather miniskirt with a matching top and jacket. Her blazing red hair was held back with two small black barrettes above each ear. "Did you really think you could move a muscle without us knowing about it? We're not running some dog and pony show here, love."

Gabe never looked up at her, choosing instead to focus on the bloodstain beneath the table. "So you know where I went."

Shayla moved slowly around the room, never losing focus from her target. "To get help from someone you trust—a very predictable move on your part."

Gabe cocked his head. "I was striving for predictability."

"Joke all you want, Gabriel, but your police contact doesn't concern us."

"And why not?" Gabe asked, raising his eyebrows.

Shayla knelt down, still facing Gabe, and picked up the set of keys he had placed on the floor. "Because your superior thinks you're insane."

Williams? Gabe's heart beat a little faster. Had they killed him too?

"I told you we were thorough," she said, launching into her rehearsed response. "After you interrupted his dinner, we had someone call him claiming to be your doctor. Our man told him you had refused to take your medication, and that you might become delusional without it. Needless to say, whatever you might have revealed to him about such a bizarre story, made a pretty strong case for your insanity. So you see? Your trip to Miami was nothing more than three hours out on the town. And now," she said, with a malicious grin, "you've come back to me."

Gabe was incensed. They had anticipated his every move. "If you knew I was going to run, why did you let me go in the first place?"

Shayla held out an opened palm. "Give me the phone."

Gabe handed her the bodyguard's cellular phone.

"You were never a threat to us."

"What? You put some kind of tracking device in the phone?"

Shayla shook her head. "Nothing so James Bondish, Gabriel. We blocked your son's number from this phone. You could never get through to him, could you?"

Gabe remained silent, stewing inside at his own stupidity. He could have kicked himself for not having tried to call from the landline in Strofsky's Deli.

"So now the question is," Shayla said, raising the gun a few feet from Gabe's right temple, "what should we do with you?"

Gabe's body stiffened, only his eyes shifted to the right. "Can't live with me, can't kill without me."

"Crack wise, Gabriel, but I'd be crazy to let you live another five minutes. You've proven to us what I've thought about you all along: you can't be trusted."

"So what are you gonna do, shoot me like you did Eric over there? What happens to your plan to kill Nathan Waxman if I die before I'm supposed to? I'll bet your boss won't be too happy about that."

Shayla shrugged. "August Bock trusts me implicitly. He'll come up with another plan. He always does."

Gabe shot up from his vulnerable position on the bed. "Wrong, lady," he growled, slapping her weapon away from his face. "I'm the best chance you've got. Hell, with less than a day to go, I'm the only chance you've got. I've got the face everybody knows. No one can get closer to Waxman than I can! Isn't that why you chose me in the first place? I'm your golden opportunity."

He moved closer until he could feel the tip of the silencer pressed up against his chest. The two of them faced off in the center of the dingy motel room like a pair of prize fighters sizing each other up. Gabe could hear his own breathing, and he could swear she wasn't breathing at all.

"Your son lost his $4 million inheritance the minute you stepped foot out of this room."

Round and round they went ... never letting their stares waver ... neither one daring to blink. Gabe waited patiently for an opening.

"Your boss needs me. No matter what you'd *really* like to do, you can't lay a finger on me."

They continued to orbit each other in a macabre dance of killer and terminal victim.

"After I kill you, I plan on paying your son another visit."

She was taunting him, daring him to make the first move so she could justify pulling the trigger. They both knew it.

"I told you before: you go near my son and I'll kill you."

The malevolent grin was back on her face. She was beginning to enjoy toying with her quarry. A simple pleasure she had never taken the time to indulge in before. "You'll kill me?" she cackled. "And just how do you propose to do that? Come back from the grave?"

"You so much as drive into my son's neighborhood, and I promise ... that's exactly what I'll do."

Shayla showed her forearm. "Look, no goose bumps."

"Well, maybe this'll make your skin change texture..."

Gabe let loose with a right hand that Shayla dodged as easily as if the punch had been thrown underwater.

"That's it? That's the best you've got?"

Every muscle in Gabe's upper body pleaded for him to lie down and take a nap, but his will was stronger. He lashed out with his left, which Shayla casually blocked with her right arm. Her satanic smile took on a yellowish hue from the tainted bathroom light. "I'll tell you what I'm going to do. Since I'm in a sporting mood, and I need the exercise," she said mockingly as she threw her pistol onto the middle of the bed. "Here's your chance. All you've got to do is go get it."

Before Gabe could even wince, the heel of her left boot was in his mid-section. In his weakened condition, it felt like he had been hit with a jackhammer. He doubled over, coughing up blood and spitting bile. She stepped to her left, looking for her next point of attack. "Come on, sport. You're not just going to stand there blowing air, are you? If I wanted to waste my time working out on a heavy bag, I could have gone to the gym."

Gabe tried to stand erect, but his insides felt like they had been roasted with an acetylene torch. "Can't ... breathe..."

Shayla danced around on her tip-toes, every muscle in her fabulous body working together in perfect symmetry. "Come on, Gabe," she taunted, bouncing from side to side gracefully. "It's gut check time. You're going to die regardless, but at least I'm giving you a fighting chance. Come on. Think about what I'm going to do to your boy."

Gabe hugged his stomach. "How can I fight you? I can't even catch my breath."

"Itty-bitty pieces," Shayla teased as she shadowboxed a circle around him. "I'll cut him up while he's still alive and screaming for mercy. One prepubescent limb at a time."

Gabe grimaced, understanding fully these were not empty threats. "I think I'm going to pass out..."

Shayla's eyes narrowed. "Don't you dare pass out on me!"

Gabe turned his back on her and surreptitiously slipped his hand into his trouser pocket. The shard of mirror was still there. He palmed it easily.

Shayla reached out and grabbed him by the right shoulder, preparing to spin him around to finish him off, but she was not as agile as she thought...

The murky light glinted off the jagged piece of glass as it slashed upward toward her face. The skin running from her chin all the way up to her right cheekbone cleaved open, like a razor tearing through tissue paper. Blood gushed out of the gaping wound as Shayla stumbled backward, holding her hands to her face to stem the crimson torrent. "You bastard ... I'll kill you!"

Gabe dove for the bed with Shayla in crazed pursuit. Blood was spraying and splattering everywhere. The bedspread and walls were quickly turned into abstract works of ghoulish art. Gabe got hold of the pistol by the muzzle and Shayla elbowed him on the side of his face, causing the gun to flip out of his hand and skid across the carpet. He was trying to claw his way off the bed, but Shayla was straddling him, the skin on her face splayed open like a freshly cleaned trout, pummeling his kidneys relentlessly. "A bullet is too easy for you! I'm going to rip your heart out with my bare hands!"

She might not have had the strength of a man, but what she lacked in muscle Shayla Rand more than made up for in precision and technique. Every punch felt like it ruptured his kidneys. Gabe's fingers tore at the bed sheets as he gasped for every breath. The pain was excruciating, traveling all the way down the back of his legs, making them nearly ineffectual. Ten more seconds and he knew he was a goner.

Just as Gabe thought he was about to meet his maker, the door to the room burst open on its hinges...

The weight was suddenly peeled off Gabe's back.

"Let go of me!" Shayla screamed. "Look what he did to me! I'm going to kill him!"

Damon Washington was grabbing her around the waist, trying to hang on for dear life. "You're not going to kill anyone..."

Her face was half cloaked behind a hideous mask of dripping blood and flapping flesh. "Let go of me, or I swear I'll kill you too!"

Washington dragged her backward, lifting her off the floor and pulling her toward the bathroom. "Stop fighting me!"

Her screams were blood-curdling. "The bastard cut me!"

Gabe was hanging off the side of the bed, his upper torso bent toward the floor, arms dangling limply by his side. All he could make out was a muffled argument; his eyes weren't seeing, his ears not hearing.

"What are you trying to do," Washington grunted, "ruin everything?"

"I don't give a damn about anything else!" Rand seethed, a firestorm in her eyes. "That asshole cut my face!"

Washington didn't know how he was managing to control her. His fists were locked together around her waist, but it was like trying to harness a wild animal. "You've got to calm down! We've got to get you some medical attention."

Blood was running down her neck and onto her leather top. There was no sign of pain on her face, only anger and total revulsion. Just as quickly, her body suddenly relaxed in Washington's grasp. "You're right," she coughed. "I need a doctor right away."

"I'm going to let you go then," Washington huffed. "Are you going to stay calm?"

She nodded. "Yes, I'm okay."

"Are you positive?"

"Yes."

Washington released his grip, and she sprang for the gun lying in the middle of the room. Shayla dove to the floor and, in one swift acrobatic move, had the pistol and rolled to her feet, pointing the silencer at Gabe's prone and inert body.

"Shayla don't!" Washington screamed.

She put her free hand up to her face, feeling the horrible damage the blade of glass had caused. "I warned August from the beginning that he was going to be trouble."

Washington held up his hands and like a referee, moved between her and Gabe. "We all knew this wouldn't be an easy target, Shayla, but he is our best bet. Please! We need him alive."

"But he cut me. How am I supposed to do my job now? Shayla Rand, the woman of a thousand faces, and oh, by the way, she's got a fifteen centimeter scar running from her eye to her mouth?"

Washington motioned for her to calm down. "We'll get you the finest plastic surgeon in the entire world, Shayla. You will be as beautiful as ever ... I promise."

She put both hands up to the gun. "I still want him dead."

Washington checked once more to make sure he was still standing between Shayla and her target. "He will be dead ... tomorrow night. Don't do anything crazy here and *everyone* will get what they deserve."

The flow of blood from the repulsive gash on her face was showing no sign of letting up. The rest of the skin on her face was turning a sickly ashen shade. "But it won't be the same."

Washington held open his hands trying to look diplomatic. "Sure it will ... and we'll both be right there on the water to see all the fireworks."

Gabe made a groggy grumbling sound and the shard of bloody mirror plopped out of his open hand.

"We're so close to wrapping this whole thing up," Washington said, "don't let your temper screw this up for everyone."

Shayla touched her torn skin again. "I want this mended tonight."

Washington let out a sigh of relief. "Sure. I can arrange that."

Shayla lowered her gun. "What are you going to do about this mess?"

"Don't worry about it. I'll take care of everything here."

"Where should I go?" Shayla asked, walking into the bathroom and coming out with a wet washcloth pressed against her mutilated face.

"Go to the emergency room at Jackson Medical Center. I'll give our doctor a call and tell him to meet you there."

Shayla looked skeptical. "He's not a plastic surgeon. I *need* a plastic surgeon!"

"Calm down. When I tell him what we want, I'm sure he'll pull some strings and get you the best plastic surgeon they've got on staff to stitch you up. I promise you'll be ready to go by tomorrow night."

Shayla moved slowly toward the door leading outside and paused in the doorway. "I want you to know something, Damon."

Washington turned to face her. "What's that?"

She never looked back, but the icy calmness was back in her voice. "I want you to know that if something should go wrong tomorrow night, not only will I hunt Gabe and his child down to the ends of the earth," she said, most assuredly. "I'll kill you too for stopping me tonight."

Let justice be done, though the heavens fall!
           -Earl of Mansfield

25

Gold Coast Marina
6:45 P.M. One hour to live

For the first time in his life, Nathan Waxman hated being the center of attention. All he wanted to do was leave. To the west, beyond the heavy stand of pine and oak trees that lined the far side of the Intracoastal Waterway, the day's colors were draining out of the sky. It couldn't have been a more artistic sunset; an orange fireball settling below the horizon, the stars twinkling to life to take its place—as serene a moment in time as Waxman could imagine ... a stark contrast to the all of the bustling activity taking place at the marina.

Gold Coast Marina housed some of the most opulent sailing and motorized vessels in the southern United States. Everything from majestic three-mast windjammers to economical 16-foot runabouts all moored here. Twenty-four long wooden docks stretched out from the shore, some berthing only one enormous yacht, others harboring five or six smaller vessels that took up that same amount of dock space. Security was never very tight here, and, on a clear Saturday evening such as this, curious people often strolled the docks after a hearty dinner at one of the nearby restaurants.

But not tonight...

Gold Coast Marina had been turned into a madhouse of glaring lights and screaming people. The police had cordoned off the entire property, but it did no good. Protesters who believed that Nathan Waxman had gotten away with murder picketed around the barricades, screaming their disapproval, waving their signs, on some of which were scrawled "Visit Miami Beach and get away with murder!" and "I voted for a murderer!"

The press was having a field day with these people. Every local television station as well as a few of the national news networks were carrying the event live. Even tourists who had no idea who Nathan Waxman was were drawn into the media feeding frenzy.

This was Nathan Waxman's first public appearance since his acquittal of his wife's murder and, whether he liked it or not, the entire world was tuned in. He needed this vacation more than wanted it, and the stress of the trial was evident on his face. He no longer bore the boyish good looks that voted him into office six years earlier; now his face was pale and lined, and his hair was peppered with premature gray.

He stood on the starboard deck of his yacht, *Mystique*, one sneaker propped up on the railing, smiling and waving out at the crowd. Like any accomplished politician, he acknowledged his well-wishers while ignoring the rest of the angry hecklers.

Behind him, the window to the bridge slid open. "We'll be ready to shove off in about another half hour," Tyler Kennedy said, his weathered face peeking through the opening. "The last of the provisions are being loaded onboard. You think you can keep that shit-kickin' smile on your puss 'till then?"

Waxman never glanced back at the only traveling companion he'd have on this trip. "The smile is rented. It's my arm that I'm worried about. It feels like it's about to snap off."

Kennedy chuckled under his breath. "Love to stay and keep you company, but I gotta make sure the beer's iced up. The devils in the details, ya' know?"

"None of your imported suds I hope."

"Hey, if we're gonna share the same vessel for two weeks, you had better stay on my good side. You can drink that piss you call beer, and I'll drink the good stuff. Just keep your paws off my stash."

Waxman switched hands. "Good thing this is my boat or I'd probably die of dehydration."

"No chance of that," Kennedy said, sliding the window shut. "I promised my goddaughter I'd bring you back in one piece."

* * * * * *

At a private fuel dock just over a mile away, dressed completely in dark colors, Shayla Rand waited. With a five inch strip of white gauze taped to half her face, she stood at the helm while Damon Washington continued to pump marine-grade fuel into the sleek black cigarette's twin tanks. The powerboat bobbed gently in the oily water, drinking up the fuel like a thirsty camel. Overhead, a helicopter swept low over the water heading north, the same direction Shayla was facing.

She pulled out her night-vision binoculars and followed the helicopter's flight up river. "More police," she said calmly.

Washington continued his pressure on the pump handle. "Fast too. I got to fly one of those beauties once. You think Bock's Ranger is fast? Whoa, you ain't seen nothing! That puppy right there can spin on a dime, and climbs like a space shuttle. You blink and it's adios muchacho."

The helicopter was little more than a dot on the horizon now. Shayla set down the binoculars and checked her wristwatch. "How many do you think will be out there?"

Washington shrugged nonchalantly as he watched the numbers click away on the pump. "Don't worry your pretty little ... uh..."

Shayla turned her disfigured face toward him. Even though the remark was clearly unintentional, she was still livid.

Washington's eyes grew as big as ping-pong balls. "Sorry."

Shayla wordlessly turned her gaze back to the choppy water.

"That's probably just a routine beach patrol," Washington said. "The only extra security is going to be onshore. We're covered. No one suspects a thing."

"And when should Gabe arrive?"

Washington checked his watch. "He should be there already."

"You're positive he understands what he's supposed to do?"

"I went over it a dozen times with him. He's ready."

Shayla took another look at the surrounding landscape through the binoculars. Even in the waning sunlight, the panorama was still well lit, except for the slight green tinge to everything. "You're sure he'll follow through?"

"Well, he's still weak from the junk pumping through his veins, and that beat down you gave him last night didn't help."

She put her hand up to the bandage on her face and gently caressed it. "It helped me."

Washington pulled the handle from the gas tank and screwed on the cap. "That should do it," he said, climbing up the ladder onto the dock and setting the handle back into the pump. "Let me just take care of the bill, and we're good to go."

Shayla slipped the leather strap around her neck and let the binoculars hang down over her ample chest. "Get a move on. I don't want to miss the fireworks."

26

Mystique was lit up like a Christmas tree. From stem to stern, the 94-foot yacht screamed opulence. Most people on the dock that night would have been in seventh heaven just owning the 16-foot runabout that hung from two large davits on her stern. She was stark white, floating like a grand dame, contrasted with the pitch night sky. Her epithet was artfully gilded across the transom in large cursive, gold-leaf letters. Three decks high, she was truly a sight to behold.

Moored at the longest berth in the marina, the one usually afforded to the occasional small cargo ship when dock space at nearby Port Everglades was at a premium, a steel ramp extended from her starboard side, where delivery men carted up dollies full of edibles and drinks. It looked to Gabe as though there were enough provisions for a small army, but there were only two passengers on this voyage.

Gabe remained in the shadows for now. Huge wooden crates and 55-gallon steel drums were scattered all over the place, making it very easy for him to stay out of sight. The last thing he wanted was to have some unsuspecting spectator accidentally bump into his belt buckle and blow everyone in a quarter-mile radius to Kingdom

Come. Washington had told him the belt was completely tamper-proof, but Gabe didn't see any reason to tempt the odds. He had to admit that the explosive device was ingenious. Holding up his pants was probably enough high explosives to take the down a large building. That image wasn't exactly putting his mind at ease. They told Gabe it would be painless, but how could they know? He just prayed they were right.

Another cold front was cutting though South Florida, bringing the evening's temperature into the low 40s. Gabe asked Washington if he could get him something warm to wear, and was given a dark nylon windbreaker. It wasn't keeping him toasty the way a down-filled jacket would have, but what was it going to matter in an hour anyway? The chilly wind blowing in off the water tore into each and every one of Gabe's aching muscles. Shayla had really done a number on him. When he'd awoken this afternoon, he could barely swing his legs off the bed. His back was covered with lumpy purple bruises that felt like raw meat to his touch. He moved so slowly, it took him nearly two hours to shower and get ready. He had asked Washington for something for the pain and was grateful for the nondescript pill he was given. Whatever the medication was, it eased the soreness and gave him a bit more mobility.

The plan, as Washington had explained it, was very straightforward. Proximity to the mayor wasn't really an issue. He only had to sneak onboard, wait until the boat was at least a quarter mile from the marina and ... *painless.*

Sitting on the dock, with his back pressed up against one of the wooden crates, he pulled his knees up against his chest, careful not to jostle the belt too much. It didn't fit too snug, but after the dinner they served him back at the motel, he was thankful it was a bit on the loose side. He had been pleasantly surprised by the food's preparation. Everything had been exactly how he ordered it. The steak was cool red inside and charred on the outside, while the lobster tail was sweet and succulent. He was astonished that he had any appetite at all, but then this all seemed like some sort of surreal dream anyway.

He was going to be dead in less than an hour. Was that possible?

Gabe had never worked on a case where the criminal had been sentenced to death ... many had been sentenced to life in prison, but no candidates for the chair they called "Old Sparky." Surely, the maniac he had chased into the alley would have been convicted and eventually executed, but that sentence had already been carried out without a jury's recommendation. Gabe found himself wondering many of the same thoughts that a criminal awaiting his execution might have. What will the weather be like tomorrow? For that matter, what will the *world* be like tomorrow? A chill ran down Gabe's back as he crawled toward a larger stack of crates to block the escalating breeze. The regrets in his life had been so many ... his wife and daughter, his partner, and now his son.

What will Casey do when he finds out I'm dead? I'll miss him so much. Will the feeling be mutual? What sports will he grow up to play? Now that he'll be able to afford it, where will he go to college? What line of work will he choose? Who will he marry? How many children will he have? Where will they live? Will he even remember me then? He had to clear his mind or his heart would shatter. He had to stay focused, if not for himself, then for his son's sake.

Gabe was 200 yards from the stern of the yacht with nothing between him and Nathan Waxman, except half a dozen news crews, a handful of delivery men, and about 300 screaming onlookers and protestors. *Sneaking on board? Nothing to it!* He reached into his pocket and pulled out his wallet. Flipping it open, he had to tip it into the moonlight to read the credentials. Even in the chalky glow, if it was a forgery, it was a darn good one. It looked exactly like his old police badge and identification card, right down to his signature.

Gabe peeked around the corner of the crate. Waxman was still waving out at the crowd and trying to answer any questions he could discern over the rabble. Lights from the television cameras danced back and forth across the hull of the yacht like floodlights on a prison wall. Uniformed patrolmen as well as plain-clothed officers mingled in the crowd. To Gabe, some of the cops who were trying to look inconspicuous stood out more than the uniformed sentries. They were the ones not looking at the yacht. They circulated through the mob like people searching for a lost friend. Gabe spotted them easily. He counted more than a dozen. *Maybe they were expecting trouble.*

Footsteps...

Gabe quietly slid himself back into the shadows behind the shipping container. Two patrolmen from the sound of it. They took their time, pausing every few seconds and then moving on. Hard heels clicking on the wooden dock ... getting closer.

"Hey," one said. "Time for a cigarette break."

They were right on the other side of the crate. Gabe pulled himself into a tight little ball.

"Sure," came the response in a huskier voice. "Why the hell not?"

Of all the places to stop! Don't you know not to smoke around all of this combustible stuff?

Gabe could hear the crinkling of the cigarette pack and the repeated attempts to ignite a lighter.

"Too damn windy," the first one said. "Stand over here."

The husky one must be turning to block the wind. More tries at lighting the smoke.

"Damn! I think my lighter must be out of juice. You got any matches?"

"Yeah, here."

Of course he'd have to have matches with him! Don't either of these two palookas know that smoking can kill you?

The lit match came sailing over the top of the box and landed directly on the top of Gabe's right thigh. The burning pain was instantaneous. With his eyes pinched tight, and a grimace that belied his true anguish, Gabe flicked the match into the water where it sizzled to death. *Son-of-a-bitch!*

"Can you believe all of this bullshit?" the first one said, between drags.

Gabe wasn't really trying to eavesdrop on the conversation. He was more intent on rubbing his thigh through the hole in his pants and biting his lower lip.

"Hey, after what that guy's been through, don't you think he deserves some R & R?"

One of the guards leaned against the crate. It didn't budge, but Gabe could tell there was someone pushing against the other side.

"So the guy got off," the first one said. "I always thought he should have."

That remark perked up Gabe's ears.

"What are you talking about?" asked the second one.

Gabe tilted his head. *Yeah, what are you talking about?*

"You know who his wife was, right?"

"Just what I read in the papers," the second one admitted, as he took a long drag from his smoke. "I knew she was a congresswoman or a senator or something like that."

"A state senator," corrected the first one, "up in Tally."

"So?"

"She was a real powerful woman, had a lot of clout, but then she had her daughter and gave up her political career to raise the kid."

A daughter? I didn't know Waxman had a daughter.

"And your point being?"

Aw, say more! Please, say more!

The first one let out a long, throaty cough and then spit something into the water. "Well, I could never leave my little girl motherless."

"So you think somebody else killed his wife?"

"Change the subject," the first one said. "You almost done with that thing? We gotta go."

The voices started to fade as the two patrolman moved off in the opposite direction.

Gabe collapsed back into the shadows. His heart was pounding and his hands were trembling. What had just happened here?

Have I even taken the time to think this whole thing through? What if Waxman really didn't kill his wife? Who else would have benefitted from her death? These are the basic questions that any rookie cop would've asked, so why haven't I? The jury found him innocent, yet Bock insists he's not. Why am I taking that psychotic's word for it?

The engines of *Mystique* roared to life, interrupting Gabe's thoughts. White water churned and smoke fumed from beneath the transom as the throttles were gunned and then set back to idle speed. *It's almost time. What am I supposed to do? I can't do this if there's a chance Nathan Waxman's really innocent. But if I don't do it, they'll kill Casey for sure!*

The delivery ramp on the side of the ship was almost secured, and with only a few more cases of food-stuffs to be rolled onboard, a forklift was preparing to pull the steel loading ramp back onto the pier.

Gabe stepped out from behind the crate and, as planned, hung his badge around his neck. *It's simple. I don't have any choice. I've got to see this thing through or my son is dead!*

27

The sleek black cigarette boat glided effortlessly through the water. This was manatee season and the protection of those gentle mammals gave them the perfect excuse for moving so slowly up the river. Shayla Rand stood next to the wheel with her red hair tucked tightly beneath a dark-colored baseball cap. With one hand holding onto the frame of the windshield, she pressed the zoom on the side of her night-vision binoculars and brought the distant marina into sharp focus. "This is close enough."

Damon Washington eased back on the throttles although the boat's mighty engines continued to protest like a caged animal. With a predator's eye, Shayla surveyed the waterway. A flotilla of pleasure boats were moving both up and down river, while a few ships she spotted in the distance were circling near the marina. Curious boaters would soon be in for the surprise of their lives. "We can't just sit here bobbing in the middle of the channel," Washington warned. "We've got to keep moving or someone's going to hit us."

Shayla never lowered the binoculars. "I don't want to get any closer. As soon as it's done, we'll get the hell out of here."

Washington spun the wheel to the right. "Then let me circle at least. Otherwise, someone might think we're having engine problems and call the marine patrol."

As the cigarette boat began its slow loop, Shayla turned her body to face the opposite direction, never losing sight of *Mystique*.

"Why are you so worried about him? He'll do it," Washington asked over the low drone of the engines.

"If you want to know the truth," Shayla said, wrinkling her nose and feeling the fresh stitches tug on her facial skin. "I'm really hoping the bastard will chicken out. I've got some unfinished business to settle with him."

28

Gabe's hair was hanging down on his forehead in sweaty ringlets. He wasn't sure if it was nervous perspiration or the lack of medicine over the past eight hours but, either way, the waterworks were flowing. He made his way toward *Mystique*, keeping a low profile by skirting along the edge of the pier, moving from crate to barrel and blending in with the crowd whenever it was necessary. His breath was coming in short gasps, puffing out of his mouth in little clouds of warm vapor. He wasn't aware of anything or anyone but his intended destination, and he lumbered single-mindedly on the most surreptitious route to reach it. The crowd noise and all the lights had turned the entire scene into a blurry dreamscape that he found himself stumbling his way through.

The mob grew more boisterous and chaotic the closer Gabe got to the yacht. Overhead, a police helicopter did a low sweep over the marina, causing most of the gallery to cover their ears and hold their collars tight around their necks.

If they thought that was loud...

Gabe had no specific plan as to how to get onboard. Bock's guidelines left much to be desired in that department. All he had were his very authentic-looking credentials and his own instincts.

Two boxes of paper goods, one case of assorted vegetables, and one box of Idaho potatoes. These looked like the last provisions being loaded onto the ship. Gabe decided to make his move as they were being readied by a dockworker to dolly up the ramp. "Whoa, hold on a minute there, partner. I've got to look inside those boxes," he said, displaying his badge hanging from his neck chain.

The dock worker, who wore a credential badge of his own pinned to his coveralls, wiped his forehead on his sleeve and shot Gabe an irritated glare. A ponytail dangled out of his baseball cap, and the name Rick was embroidered on his pocket. "Excuse me?" Rick asked, peering around the side of the stack of cumbersome boxes.

"I said, I need to see inspect inside those boxes."

The longshoreman was obviously having a hard time juggling the cartons on the inclined ramp. "Why are you hassling me man? This is like my 15th load already. Why are you starting to check this stuff now? Don't you got something better to do with your time?"

Gabe sized Rick up quickly. He was little thinner than Gabe was, but Gabe had been losing so much weight lately that the clothes would probably be a good fit. "This is just routine. We don't want anything getting onboard that shouldn't be here."

Rick propped his elbow onto his dolly. "But we've probably loaded over 100 boxes already! Why are you waiting until now?"

Mystique's engines revved and her twin propellers boiled the dark water behind her stern.

"I want you to come with me," Gabe ordered over the noise.

"Say what?"

"You heard me," Gabe shouted, matter-of-factly. "Follow me."

Rick hung his head in disgust. "Why are you giving me such a hard time, man? I just want to load these last few boxes and get the hell out of here!"

It sounded like *Mystique* was almost ready to depart.

"The boxes can wait. This boat isn't leaving here until I say it is," Gabe said, trying to sound as official as possible. "I have some questions to ask you, and I'm not going stand here screaming at the top of my lungs!"

Rick stabbed his hands into his overall pockets and grudgingly let Gabe lead him off the pier. "Where are we going?"

"Away from all of the commotion," Gabe said over his shoulder. "Just follow me."

There was a storage shed at the far edge of the marina's property. A single light pole dimly illuminated the old wooden cabin that housed a variety of electrical tools, hoses, and various other items used for maintenance of the docks. A rusty padlock and hasp was the only security preventing anyone from stealing any of the shed's contents. Gabe lifted the lock in his hand and tugged on it. Despite its decrepit appearance, the lock held firm.

"Can't you just ask me whatever you want to know out here?" Rick asked anxiously.

Gabe shrugged with his back to him. "I guess I've got no choice."

Rick was too busy stomping his boots on the pine needle-covered ground trying to keep his warmth circulating to even see the blow. Gabe's trained fist moved like a piece of the darkness; it was nearly invisible—a spinning roundhouse that focused all of his weight and energy upon five small and otherwise insignificant knuckles.

Rick's head snapped to the side, his ponytail whipping around face in protest. He had no time to react anyway, as the opposite set of knuckles caught him squarely beneath the jaw and nearly lifted him out of his Timberland work boots. His head lolled backward, his eyes gazing blankly skyward at a panorama of night that now held twice as many stars as it did only a few seconds before. He stumbled backward, but Gabe caught him before he hit the cold hard ground.

"Sorry about that," Gabe said, trying to rub out the painful stinging sensation in his fist. "It was all I could think of at the moment." He pulled Rick's limp body behind the storage shed, quickly stripped off the worker's overalls and threw them on over his own clothes, but not before removing his windbreaker and draping it over the motionless longshoreman. The coveralls buttoned up the front, so Gabe left two or three buttons unfastened so he could easily access the belt buckle detonator. He removed Rick's baseball cap and adjusted the plastic strap in the back to loosen it. Pulling the brim low over his face, he headed back toward *Mystique* knowing full well he had only minutes before the dock worker would regain consciousness and all hell would probably break loose.

Shuffling through the crowd, Gabe never looked up. Every time he would hear someone say *"hey,"* or some similar acknowledgment that he felt was directed toward him, he would brusquely flash Rick's security tag and continue along toward the ramp and the waiting dolly of provisions.

Another helicopter buzzed low over the waterway. In the distance, Gabe could see that the night sky was now filled with blinking red and white lights. Every network station had probably sent their own crew to cover the story.

Gabe had been advised there would be only two people on the yacht: Nathan Waxman and his one man crew, Tyler Kennedy. He had no reason to doubt Bock's information since he had been right on the money so far. This was a good thing, since maintaining stealth in his anemic condition would be no easy task.

Out of the corner of his eye, Gabe spotted Waxman winding down his impromptu press conference. Onboard *Mystique*, standing at the top of the loading ramp, was a middle-aged, silver-haired man with his fists planted firmly on his hips. It had to be Kennedy. The description fit. From his overt body language, it was obvious that he was miffed at something. "What the hell is taking you so long? You should have finished loading this stuff 15 minutes ago!"

Gabe pushed the load up the incline, keeping his face to the far side of the boxes. "Nature called," he answered, trying to disguise his voice in case the man possibly knew who Rick was.

Kennedy held up his wristwatch and pushed on the tiny stem that illuminated the dial in a soft shade of green. "We're running behind schedule because of your weak bladder, mister. I know you guys get paid by the hour, but I've got a schedule to keep."

Gabe gave him a cursory flip of his hand as he moved past him. "My apologies, skipper. Just give me two minutes to stow these last four boxes, and you can have them pull the ramp."

Gabe thought Kennedy was going to say something else to him when a floodlight swept across the length of the ship, illuminating his silver-hair in its brilliance. The man turned back to the railing, waving like an excited tourist on his first cruise, forgetting the worker and his supplies. Luckily for Gabe, the distraction was good enough to prevent the skipper from noticing the dock worker's sudden lack of a ponytail, or his switch from work boots to tennis sneakers. Gabe never realized this was a mistake in judgment that the man would end up paying dearly for.

29

"What do you see?" Damon Washington asked, as he cut back on the throttle.

Shayla steadied herself against the windshield as the boat rocked gently in its own wake. "They're pulling the ramp away."

"Any sign of Gabe?"

She shook her head without lowering the night-vision binoculars. "It's too crowded to see much of anything in particular." She glanced down at her watch. "We'll know in a few minutes though."

Washington surveyed the sky. "Look at all of those news helicopters. They came out of nowhere!"

"It must be a slow news night," Shayla said sarcastically. "Don't worry. Once the boat leaves the dock, they'll be gone."

"Until..."

"Yes, until."

"I hope Gabe has the guts to go through with this," Washington added.

Shayla stared through the green tinted glasses as the water began to smoke and churn like a boiling cauldron behind the luxury yacht. "Guts have nothing to do with this. Gabe will press that button because he *believes*. Just keep your eyes in that direction and, in a few more minutes," she said, once again feeling the bandage on her face, "and you..."

Out of the darkness, a voice bellowed through a bullhorn. *"This is the Marine Patrol. You, in the black cigarette: turn off your engine and make ready a tow rope."*

Both Washington and Rand turned to see a green and yellow outboard approaching across the channel. "What did we do?" Washington asked under his breath. "We're just sitting here minding our own business."

"Good evening," the lone marine patrolman called out, taking the end of the rope Washington handed him and tying it to his vessel's portside cleat. "Can I see your boat's registration and some form of personal identification for each of you please?"

"What's the matter, Officer ... Martinez?" Washington asked, eyeing the officer's name tag. "Were we breaking some kind of law I don't know about?"

"Is this your boat, sir?" the officer asked.

"Of course it is, Officer," Shayla said.

The patrolman waved his left hand while keeping his right firmly on the butt of his pistol in its holster. "I was talking to your friend..."

It whistled through the air with a heated *"thwip,"* like a dart from a blowgun, narrowly missing Washington's left armpit. The hollow point bullet struck the deputy just below his chin. The shell went into his throat the size of a dime, flattened out against his spinal cord, and exited through a hole in the back of his neck the size of a silver dollar. The marine patrol officer clutched wildly at his throat as blood spewed between his fingers. He stumbled backward, falling against his seat and cracking his head on the throttle handle. He lay draped over the driver's seat, his head arched backward, blood spraying the fiberglass decking, his arms flailing like a downed power line.

"Have you lost your mind?" Washington screamed incredulously, unable to take his eyes off of the twitching body. "You didn't need to kill him. All our papers were in order."

Shayla had already slipped her gun back into the waistband of her pants and was staring through her binoculars as though the dead law officer only a few feet from where she was standing didn't even exist. "Forget him. It looks like the yacht is getting underway."

Washington paced back and forth, running his hands through his hair. "What are we supposed to do now?" he yelled. "We can't leave him bobbing here like a cork."

"Sure we can," Shayla said, never lowering the glasses from her eyes. "By the time anyone finds him, we'll be long gone."

Everything Damon Washington had ever thought about Shayla Rand had just been confirmed in less than a second. He was in shock, he was aghast, but mostly he was very afraid. She was a soulless killing machine that had been programmed to be devoid of mercy. "What if he called it in?"

"Just untie the boat. He's the Marine Patrol, not the Coast Guard. He hands out tickets for expired tags, or at least he used to," she chuckled out of the corner of her mouth.

Instinctively, Washington grabbed a rag and wiped down the hull where he might have left fingerprints before untying the rope and setting the green and white marine patrol boat adrift. "I can't believe you just turned around and shot him!"

Shayla momentarily glanced to see which direction the current was taking the wafting boat. Pleased that it would soon be carried into the far bank and swallowed up by the mangrove overgrowth, she continued with her surveillance. "He would have been pestering us for half an hour or more."

Washington didn't realize his hands were shaking until he saw the nylon rope vibrating in his hand. "We can't stay here. Someone might have spotted him questioning us," he said, more to himself than to Shayla.

"You worry too much, Damon," she said, calmly adjusting the focusing ring of her binoculars. "I spotted him across the channel nearly an hour ago. I'm sure we were nothing more than just another routine stop to him."

Washington wrapped the rope around his arm and let it fall to the deck in a coiled heap. "I still say we should get out of here."

"I agree with you one hundred percent," Shayla said, stepping aside to make room for Washington next to the boat's throttles. "It's time to crank her up. *Mystique* just pulled out."

30

Inside the provision hold, the temperature was a bone-numbing 45 degrees, and Gabe felt every icy degree of it. Fumbling with the snaps on his coveralls, he could see the tips of his fingers turning a sickly shade of blue. He removed Rick's coveralls, rolled them into a clumsy wad and stashed it between two boxes of assorted vegetables. His breath billowed from his mouth like smoke from a Vermont chimney as he rubbed his arms trying to get some sensation back in his extremities.

Becoming a stowaway had been easier than Gabe thought. All he had to do was hide beneath the metal stairwell leading to the upper decks and drag over a few boxes of canned goods to complete the camouflage. Five minutes later, the outer cargo hatch was sealed, and he emerged from his burrow ... cold, tired, shaking, and with less than ten minutes to live.

The fiberglass decking beneath his feet rumbled to life with the drone of the engines. Even in this windowless compartment, the feeling of movement was evident. It was a gentle rocking motion that one felt in their inner ear rather than beneath their feet. The instability was affecting Gabe's equilibrium so badly that he had to steady himself by holding onto the metal banister at the base of the stairs. He stared up at the twenty or so steps that led to the upper decks. The gleaming metal steps were as daunting as the Himalayan Mountains with the way he was feeling now.

Step by excruciating step, Gabe pulled himself toward the hatch that looked down upon him like the entrance to the promised land. He struggled upward, hand over hand, with every muscle in his arms straining beyond their limits to lift him to the next landing. If there was a correct time to die, Gabe thought, when one's body had been completely depleted of energy, then this was it.

He finally reached the hatch. He could no longer feel the boat swaying as it had settled into a steady pace, its sharp bow gently slicing through the dark water like a scalpel. With the utmost caution, he released the latch that opened the heavy steel door. A rubber gasket around the door frame had created a vacuum inside the refrigerated compartment, demanding Gabe to use what little power he had left in his shoulder to help force the hatch open. When it finally hissed open, the cold salt air rushed over Gabe like a damp smog.

To his left, he could see the west bank of the Intracoastal Waterway sliding past. Pine trees reaching up into the darkness, their brown needles and dried cones resisting Winter's attempt to shake them loose. Gabe figured the yacht was running at minimum pace, what was called "no wake" speed, so any waves kicked up by the massive engines didn't damage the seawall behind some of the more elegant homes that lined the eastern bank of the channel.

Closing and sealing the hatch behind him, Gabe moved to his left along the port side of the ship. This was the side of the yacht away from where the crowds had been on the dock. All that faced him now was the tree-covered west bank, a smattering of pleasure boats headed in the opposite direction, and the occasional channel markers poking their wooden supports out of the water, guiding boats through the deepest section of the waterway. The helicopters had all disappeared, undoubtedly summoned to cover some news event that *really* mattered.

As he moved steadily toward the bow, Gabe remained crouched as he passed beneath the portholes to the main cabin, galley, and staterooms. He would pause beneath each one only long enough to glimpse inside for any sign of movement. As he found each one empty, he would continue toward the front of the ship. The sound of the waves slapping against the surging hull was soothing, but Gabe would have no chance to revel in its tranquilizing effects.

Gabe glanced back toward the stern of the ship. All he could see were the bright lights of the shore to the east, and the pitch blackness of the horizon to the west, but he could feel she was out there somewhere ... watching ... waiting. He could feel her eyes on him like an invisible hand on his shoulder, urging him onward. A voice on the wind...

He was a few yards from the open hatch to the bridge, still crouching with the tendons in his knees burning like wildfire. Black strands of his hair were matted against his forehead even though it was too cold to sweat. The time was fast approaching and he knew it. His mouth was dry and pasty, and he couldn't have conjured up spit if he wanted to.

With his back to the smooth fiberglass bulkhead, Gabe inched his way toward the bow of the ship. The voices he heard rang familiar. It was the same voice that had given him a hard time on the loading ramp only a few minutes earlier and that of Nathan Waxman.

Tyler Kennedy stood alongside Nathan Waxman. "Everything looks good, Nate," he said. "We'll be out of the channel in 20 minutes."

Waxman looked disdainfully at the sidearm Kennedy was sporting on his hip. "Do you really need to be wearing that thing?"

The friend and bodyguard patted the Colt .45 his father had given him long ago; he patted the butt of the weapon. "This baby is staying on my belt until we're out to sea, and then it might still take some convincing to make me take it off."

Waxman raised an eyebrow. "What's the matter? You afraid of pirates?"

Kennedy shook his head. "Nothing scares me so long as Mr. Colt is by my side!"

"Well, keep it holstered. You know how I feel about guns."

Kennedy looked skeptically at his longtime friend. "What's really bothering you, Nate? You're a free man. This should be a victorious moment for you."

Waxman slipped his hands into his pockets and stared off into the distance. "Not as long as whoever killed her is still out there. I feel like I'm running away, when I should be mustering a search to find her real killer."

Kennedy patted his longtime friend on the shoulder. "They'll be time enough for that when we get back. Right now, you've got to regroup. That's what this trip is really all about."

Waxman frowned. "I'm really starting to have second thoughts about leaving Haley behind too. Maybe I should call the house and have her throw some stuff in a duffle bag. I can fly her to Exuma."

Kennedy resisted. "Hasn't she been through enough losing her mother and with you standing trial? You said yourself, she needs to work it out too. It's only for a few weeks, and you can still call her anytime you'd like."

Waxman thought about his daughter, who was the spitting image of her mother, and nodded. "Get me my phone."

Kennedy nodded and worked his way toward the bridge on the opposite side of the ship from where Gabe had heard the entire conversation while hiding in the shadows.

A few seconds later, Kennedy returned with a cell phone. The ex-mayor worked his way toward the very tip of the bow where he felt more alone. When Waxman finally reached the bow of *Mystique*, the only light shining on him was lunar. Haley answered the phone on the first ring.

"Hi, dad."

He could almost see her cradling the phone against her ear with her large brown eyes making her look like one of those doe-eyed Mexican children in a velvet painting. He'd even be willing to bet she'd asked Isabel, the housekeeper, to braid her ponytails the way her mother always did it for her. It was her way of keeping the love alive. "Hey princess. How's my little baby-girl tonight?"

"I'm okay. I wish you were here though."

"Yes, I know baby-girl. I really wish I was there too. But you remember what I promised you, right?"

"Yes."

"And what was that?"

"That as soon as Easter comes, we'll take a trip together."

"Are you looking forward to that?"

"Uh-huh."

Waxman stared up at the cloudless night sky and the brilliant full moon. "So am I."

"Dad?"

"Yes, princess?"

There was a long pause on the line. Waxman first looked at the phone thinking it had been disconnected.

"When you come back, can we go see mom's grave?"

The dark water surrounding the yacht suddenly looked endlessly deep and ominous, but not nearly as empty as the void in their lives. What would one more drop mean in such an infinite amount of salty water? He wondered about that as the tear trickled off his cheek and joined its brethren in the channel. "You know you can visit her anytime you want, princess. If you want, you can tell Isabel I said it was okay, and she'll take you to mom's resting place."

"But it's not the same. I don't like going there without you."

Waxman drew in a deep breath of the pungent air, and wiped his face with the back of his hand. "Okay. I promise we'll go together to see mommy as soon as I get back."

"You really promise?"

"Cross my heart and..." He stopped himself mid-sentence. "You know. Pinky promise."

"Dad!" she reprimanded him. *"You can't pinky promise over the phone!"*

"Sure you can! Where are you?"

"Up in my room, doing my stupid math homework."

"Does the phone cord stretch all the way to the window?"

"I think so."

"Then walk over to the window and look for the moon." He could see her in his mind's eye, struggling with the phone as she hauled it over to the window.

"I see it."

"Me too. Now, point your pinky up at the moon. We'll do a long-distance, bounce-it-off-the-moon, pinky promise."

"Okay, I'm pointing."

"So am I." He must have looked crazy to the reporters, but he didn't give a damn. "I promise to take you to see mommy, and to take a trip wherever you want over Easter break."

There was another long pause on the line.

"And I promise to miss you until you come home."

The ex-mayor couldn't talk anymore. Not without his voice betraying his heartache. "I've got to go now, baby-girl."

"Will you call me again?"

"Of course I will, baby. I'll call you back later to wish you sweet dreams."

"Aren't those people ever going to leave us alone? They scare me sometimes."

"I know this has been really difficult for you, princess. It will all go away very soon though, I promise. Just remember: no matter how scared you get, you know I love you, right?"

"I love you too, Dad."

Nathan Waxman pushed the button to shut off the phone and then, holding onto the chrome railing so tightly his knuckles turned white, began crying uncontrollably.

31

Since he was manning the bridge, Gabe assumed this had to be Kennedy. He was speaking into the radio, asking for weather and ocean conditions for the northern Bahamas and surrounding area. Gabe peeked through the opening and confirmed his suspicion. Kennedy was tapping his foot, impatiently waiting for the weather report, shrouded in an eerie red glow from the bank of electronic instruments before him. With all of the expensive technology at Kennedy's disposal, Gabe's focus was still drawn to the most utilitarian piece of equipment he saw inside the control room: the pistol strapped to Kennedy's waist.

The weather report came back forecasting moderate seas with a light breeze blowing out of the northeast. This would be wind and water that would never get the opportunity to weather *Mystique's* hand-polished teak veneer.

Gabe waited for Kennedy to set the microphone back in its cradle. He wanted to leave no chance for him to radio for help. On the control panel, a carnival of lights blinked and oscillated in a myriad of functions as Gabe closed in. Kennedy was leaning forward, shifting his eyes from the sweeping green beam on the radar screen to the front and back windows. *Mystique* was closing in on the last overpass before the Port Everglades inlet, the tributary that would take her out into the Atlantic Ocean. As a matter of courtesy and safe boating, it is customary for a ship's captain to signal the bridge tender when their vessel requires the drawbridge to be raised. This was a practice Gabe should have accounted for before deciding to make his move.

The horn blasted three long blasts, causing Nathan Waxman, who was still standing out on the bow, to cover his ears and shake his fist up at the wheelhouse window.

The unexpected noise caused Gabe to stumble backward and trip over the large captain's chair that was bolted to the floor behind him. Tyler Kennedy spun around without drawing his weapon, as startled by the intruder as Gabe was by the blaring claxon.

"Who the hell..."

Since Gabe was already low, he dove for Kennedy's legs. Kennedy fell backward with a bone-jarring *"thud,"* hitting the inflexible deck with tremendous force. Gabe clawed his way up the prone captain's body, twice slapping away his hand when he reached for his gun. "Stop struggling with me," Gabe snarled, "I'm trying to save..."

A left cross came out of nowhere and caught Gabe on the side of his face; Gabe thought he heard his brain rattle the punch nailed him so flush. Kennedy seized the opportunity to shift his weight and roll to his right. Now he was on top, trying to keep the intruder's flailing arms from inflicting any damage.

"How'd you get on my ship?" Kennedy growled, spittle dripping down from his lips.

He straddled Gabe, with all of his weight on Gabe's waist, all of his bulk upon the belt and buckle.

Squirming flat on his back, Gabe was able to look up through the window and see that they were passing beneath the opened span of bridge. A few more minutes and they would be inside Port Everglades, a deep harbor filled with commercial vessels, cruise ships, restaurants with water-view windows, the Broward Convention Center, and other buildings built out of glass to afford the most scenic view of the ocean. The concussion from the blast would turn all of those windows into glass grenades, and hundreds of innocent people would surely be killed or maimed by the shrapnel.

Kennedy was surprisingly strong for a man nearly twice Gabe's age. His arms were sinewy but powerful from years of yacht racing and deep sea fishing. He struggled to keep Gabe's arms pinned to the floor, but as long as he did, there was no chance he could reach his weapon.

Gabe shifted his weight, juking to his left the way a prizefighter would feign a punch and counter with his opposite hand. Kennedy let go of Gabe's right wrist for a split second, but that was all it took for Gabe to grab the pistol.

"Off of me," Gabe said between exhausted gasps. He had the barrel of the gun pressed against Kennedy's throat. "Stand up slowly."

Kennedy raised his opened palms in compliance and rose warily to his feet. "What do you want?"

"How much longer until we reach Port Everglades?"

Kennedy looked over Gabe's shoulder through the window. "I'd say about 10 minutes, why?"

Gabe was standing now, leaning against the control console, the gun never wavering from its target. "Does this thing have an autopilot?"

Kennedy looked puzzled. "You mean like an airplane?"

"Yeah," Gabe said, glancing back and forth between the high-tech equipment and Kennedy. "Like an airplane."

"I can lock the steering in place, that's about it," Kennedy admitted.

Gabe saw that it was clear sailing ahead, and motioned at Kennedy with the barrel of the gun. "Do it."

"Tell me what you want and maybe I can help you," Kennedy said, as he tightened a small wheel screw beneath the steering yolk.

"No one can help me anymore," Gabe said, waving the gun between Kennedy and the hatch leading outside on deck. "After you."

Kennedy moved sideways, never turning his back on the intruder. "If it's money you're after..."

Gabe smirked. "It's not money, pal. If it was money, you'd never have seen me coming."

Kennedy was standing against the railing, the muzzle of his own gun pressed into his spine. His silver hair was blowing wildly in the wind and the cold salt air was making his eyes tear. "Is this about blackmail? A kidnapping? You'll never get away with this!"

This guy talked way too much. Gabe was fighting the urge to club him on the back of his skull and dump him overboard, but he knew he'd probably drown in the process. "Shut up, I'm trying to save your life."

Kennedy turned to face Gabe, incredulity in his eyes. "Yeah, right."

"Jump."

"Excuse me?" Kennedy said, glancing down at the dark water racing past the hull of the yacht.

"You heard me ... jump, or I swear to God I'll shoot first and toss your corpse in afterward."

"You've got to be kidding me! That water must be freezing!"

Gabe held the gun up to Kennedy's temple. "The water's gonna be warming up real soon, I promise. Now jump!"

"What are you going to do with Nathan?" Kennedy demanded to know as he hoisted one leg over the railing.

Gabe couldn't take it anymore. With one swift push, Kennedy flew overboard, did a head over heels pinwheel, and splashed into the water legs first. "Son-of-a-bitch wouldn't shut up," Gabe grumbled to himself as he began to make his way toward the nose of the ship.

Nathan Waxman was standing at the pinnacle of *Mystique's* bow, the state flag of Florida flapping rigidly on a chrome mast above his head. He was facing away from Gabe, engaged in a conversation on his cellular phone, oblivious to his unexpected guest.

Gabe's first impression was that Waxman appeared smaller in person. It might have been an optical illusion, with the ex-mayor silhouetted against the shimmering lights of the Port on the horizon, but Gabe didn't think so. Waxman seemed to be standing a full head shorter and was much leaner than Gabe had always thought. Gabe had always found himself a bit star-struck by the famous and the infamous, but none of that mattered anymore.

Careful not to let the squeaking from his tennis sneakers give him away, Gabe crept up behind Waxman and placed the muzzle of Kennedy's gun against the base of his head. The ex-mayor stopped his phone conversation in mid-sentence and froze in place. With his free hand, Gabe reached around and took the cellular phone.

"It's my daughter."

"*Hello?*" Gabe listened to the innocent voice.

"*Dad?*"

Gabe put his hand over the mouthpiece and motioned for Waxman to turn around. "How old is she?"

Waxman wasn't sure what to say. "Seven ... going on 20."

The corner of Gabe's mouth curled up. "I understand that age. Look, I'm going let you finish talking to her, but say anything out of line, say anything to warn her, and the last sound she'll hear is a sound she'll spend the rest of her life in therapy trying to forget."

Waxman nodded and took back the phone. "I ... I'm sorry, baby. Are you all tucked in?"

The lights in the distance were growing brighter and clearer as Gabe gestured for Waxman to wrap up the call.

"You're my everything, princess. Always remember that."

Gabe zipped up his windbreaker as the cold wind pelted his body.

"I love you, too. Sleep tight ... I'll talk to you..." He looked questioningly at Gabe. "Soon?"

Gabe grabbed the phone and threw it overboard.

"Who the hell are you, and how'd you get on my yacht?"

Gabe took a step forward. "Who I am isn't important, neither is how I got here."

"What do you want? Is it money?" Waxman asked, pulling his wallet out of his back pocket. "If it's money, we can work something out."

"I was sent here to kill you," Gabe said, tiredly.

Instinctively, Waxman took a step back, but he was already standing against the railing. His wallet was trembling in his hand. "Who sent you?"

Gabe lifted up the waistband of his windbreaker to expose the belt. "I don't have time for all your questions, but I do have time for you to answer one of mine."

Gabe stepped closer, until he was close enough to see Waxman's facial muscles twitching from fear.

Waxman stared at his assailant, examining his weary face. "You don't look like someone who could kill another human being in cold blood. What is it you really want from me?"

"Look at me."

The ex-mayor was too afraid to stare into Gabe's face directly.

"I said, look at me," Gabe growled, sticking the barrel of Kennedy's pistol directly beneath Waxman's chin.

The ex-mayor had no choice but to lock eyes with Gabe.

"Did you kill your wife?"

The question took Waxman by surprise. "What?"

Gabe cocked the hammer on the pistol. "I don't have time to repeat the question."

Waxman's eyes opened wide like picture windows that Gabe stared right into. "No, I didn't kill my wife. I don't know who did. I loved her ... and now, all I've got left is our daughter. I'm begging you ... please don't take me from her!"

It had all come down to this one moment. This wicked trade-off. His son's future for the life of this man. "I never intended to shoot you," Gabe said, as he took a deep breath, stepped back, and confidently placed his finger on the buckle of his belt...

32

Through her binoculars, Shayla Rand watched the impact of the explosion; it was so thunderous—so violent—that fish as far as 500 yards in both directions were boiled alive. One moment *Mystique* was the envy of the waterway, cruising majestically into the Port, and then, instantaneously, she completely disintegrated. A glowing plume of orange and red fire and billowing black smoke shot thousands of feet into the night sky, igniting it like daylight. The plastic explosive and the additional 200 gallons of highly combustible marine fuel left little trace of the once sleek ship. The hull splintered into infinitesimal fragments, raining harmlessly down on the churning water like an early December rain.

A crater 20 feet deep and 500 feet long was blasted into the limestone and coral riverbed beneath ground zero. The shockwave created a tsunami of water 30 feet tall that roared out in every direction. On the west bank, shallow-rooted pine trees fell in on each other like toothpicks when caught in the destructive path of the massive wave. As the wave moved down the walled-in waterway, it seemed to gain momentum and height. Smaller boats that were moored to wooden or concrete docks behind some of the more opulent homes were thrown from the river like a bar of soap out of a bathtub. One 16-foot runabout was launched so high, it tumbled end over end before busting through a massive screened-in patio, crashing bow-first in the shallow end of the homeowner's pool.

The tidal wave stormed out of the Port without mercy. Sea walls that had withstood more than 50 years of hurricanes and blistering weather crumbled like stale cheese from the violent impact. Fuel docks pummeled by the wave sprang leaks and exploded, sending pillars of fire and caustic fumes rising like torches into the darkness.

Most of the larger cruise ships had already set sail in the afternoon, but a handful of remaining ships that had been converted into floating casinos transporting gamblers just beyond the legal distance from shore to try their luck for a few hours weren't as fortunate. Most of these fortune hunters were standing out on deck enjoying their complimentary bon voyage cocktails when the thunderous blast hit. Any passengers who weren't blown off their feet from the force of the explosion were pelted with flying glass from their shattered drink tumblers. Two men who were caught in the middle when one of the gangways tore loose were dumped into the water between the ship and the concrete berth. When the wave struck the opposite side of the ship, they were mashed against the sea wall—two gory blotches that were quickly washed away with the surging tide.

This was also the first aftermath of the belt that Damon Washington had witnessed firsthand. He stood at the controls of the cigarette, his mouth hanging open in dumbfounded awe. Beside him, Shayla screamed and dropped the binoculars, blinded by the flash from the explosion. They were over half a mile away, and they could still feel the warmth from the blast. The invisible heat wave rippled through the air at an alarming speed, warping the horizon like an airport's tarmac on a hot summer day. "You've got to be shitting me," he marveled under his breath.

Shayla clawed at her eyes, praying her sight would quickly return. She could still make out the tower of flames, but it was blurry and her field of vision spotted. "Video doesn't do it justice, does it?" she said, putting her hand on Washington's shoulder. "I'll be damned. I had Gabe figured out all wrong. I never thought he would go through with it."

Suddenly, Washington's demeanor turned from one of devout reverence to one of sheer panic. "Good God almighty! What the hell is that? It sounds like a freight train!"

Shayla continued trying to clear her eyes, but still couldn't make out what had Washington on the verge of hysterics.

"Hang on," Washington screamed as he gunned the throttles and sent the cigarette boat spinning in a 180-degree donut turn. Rand was flung to the deck as the twin engines thundered to life. The bow of the boat lifted itself out of the water, defying gravity in a pirouette of spewing foam and screaming exhaust. Shayla slid on her back across the deck, groping wildly for anything to give her a hand-hold. Washington had the throttles pushed as far forward as they would allow, but kept fisting them, as though the pressure from his hand would somehow increase the engine's capabilities.

Pulling herself to her knees by grabbing onto one of the aft line cleats, Shayla looked behind them to see what had Washington so terrified. At first, she thought her eyes were still playing tricks on her. It was massive! A liquid phantom of monolithic proportions was bearing down on them ... dark as a blackout, but full of unnatural life. The monstrosity was swallowing small boats whole and spitting them out onto dry land. It seemed to moan in a low bass rumble as it approached, like it was trying to communicate in some terrifying language. The terrifying sound was punctuated by the splintering of wooden piers and the exploding of outboard engines.

The cigarette boat rocketed past another boat that was also running for its life. This smaller cruiser had less horsepower and quickly fell behind in the high speed retreat. There was an entire family aboard, who had undoubtedly been enjoying a pleasant night on the water until all hell broke loose. Shayla saw the horror on the parents' faces and the confusion on their children's.

The wave caught up with them seconds later, seizing them like a caged animal grabbing a piece of fresh meat. It pulled them straight up out of the water, flinging their helpless bodies to different points on the compass. The boat flipped over, its whining propeller chewing at the empty air. When it hit the surface, the gas tank erupted, but the flames were instantly doused by the wave engulfing it.

"Jesus, Mary and Joseph," Washington screamed in shock. "Did you see that?"

Shayla had pulled herself to the front of the boat and was hanging with white knuckles onto the windshield next to Washington. She didn't want to look back, but the sound was growing louder, like a locomotive on steroids. "It's gaining on us!"

Washington leaned forward, his face stinging from the salt spray, as if leaning forward would somehow help the boat become more aerodynamic. The cigarette skipped across the surface, its keel barely skimming the water. One slip of the wheel, or if they hit an oncoming wave the wrong way, and they'd be dead long before the wall of water ever reached them.

"We're not going to make it," Shayla screamed. "It's almost on top of us!"

Washington didn't have to be told. The stern of the cigarette slowly began to rise out of the water.

"Hold on, this is going to be tight!"

The Intracoastal Waterway is fed by hundreds of smaller canals, creeks, rivers and rivulets. The Dania Cutoff Canal was just one such tributary. Washington threw the wheel hard to starboard, and the cigarette boat cut a 90-degree swath through the channel. Shayla had to wrap her leg around the seat behind her to prevent from being catapulted out of the boat. The engines wailed in opposition as the portside of the cigarette lifted itself out of the water. For a second that seemed like an eternity, the speedboat skidded on its side, slicing a thin bubbling wake that was barely a foot wide. Washington shifted his weight to the left and commanded that Shayla do the same. With the center of gravity sufficiently compensated, the hull once again slapped the surface and the cigarette's engines dug into the water.

"Wahoo! What a ride!" Washington howled as he wiped the water from his face.

Shayla wasn't nearly as enthusiastic. "Stop this boat right now!"

Washington throttled back and the cigarette fell still in the water, its twin engines smoking from the burden. "Oh my God! Did you see that? Did you see the way this baby hooked around that turn?"

As the raging wave roared on past the mouth of the canal, Shayla bent over the side of the boat and proceeded to retch up her dinner of poached salmon and wild rice. After a full five minutes of repeating this ordeal and green to the gills, she wiped her mouth with the back of her sleeve. "Are we still alive?" she asked between throaty coughs.

Washington was hopping around with frenetic energy. "Yeah, mama. We're still here. Alive and kickin'. I ain't seen nothing like that shit before! Whoo-hoo!"

Shayla sat herself down and leaned forward, letting her head hang down between her legs. "That was very quick thinking on your part, Damon," she groaned. "I owe you one."

Washington set the throttles onto idle speed and turned the bow back toward the Intracoastal. "It'll be okay now. I think we can head back."

Shayla put her hand on his arm. "I don't think we should go back. They'll be too many reporters asking questions of anyone who was on the water tonight. Let's just find somewhere to torch the boat, and we'll hoof it to the nearest road."

Washington grinned. "I guess you're pretty tired of being on the water anyway."

"Are you kidding?" she said, rising shakily to her feet. "It may be months before I even step into a bath."

Washington snickered as he pointed to a decrepit pier coming along the port side. "That looks like good a place as any to tie up."

Shayla felt the bandage on her face. It was moist from sweat and smelled of bile. She tore off the soiled gauze and tape, wadded it up, and threw it into the water. She watched it float away on the current, and, like the bastard who had given it to her, it sank to a watery grave.

Washington drew in a deep breath. "Now what's bothering you? You should be dancing on cloud nine now that this one is over."

Shayla pulled off her baseball cap and shook her head, letting the cool breeze dry her hair. "The son-of-a bitch took the easy way out."

"I wouldn't exactly say getting blown to smithereens is taking the easy way out, Shayla," Washington said with a grimace. "The important thing is: everything was a success, and now we can move on."

As the cigarette boat bumped into the rickety wooden dock, she ran her finger along the stitches on her face. The jagged scar was still tender to her touch. "I would have given my eye teeth for the chance..."

Washington shut off the engines and moved toward the stern storage compartment where he pulled out the spare five-gallon container of fuel and began pouring it over the deck. When he was through, he hoisted himself up onto the pier and held out a hand for Shayla. "Forget about him, Shayla. It's all over. He's nothing but fish food."

Shayla took a step back as Washington lit a match and tossed it into the boat. "Yeah," she repeated with a dissatisfied scowl, "nothing but fish food."

33

Fifteenth Floor
Tower of the Americas

The office was oppressively dark, illuminated only by the flickering glow from the wall of television monitors. "I'm watching it as we speak," August Bock said into the speaker phone, as news reports of the same evening's volatile events filled the 15 screens in front of him. He was dressed in casual attire—a bright crimson blazer accompanied by an open collared black silk shirt. At the far end of his desk, a silver serving tray waited with the leftovers of a steak dinner that had been delivered as a special favor by the owner of one of the finest restaurants in the city.

"You should have seen it, August. I can't begin to describe it," Washington's amplified voice said, excitedly.

Almost every local and national news channel had helicopters circling over the devastated section of waterway, pointing their floodlights and cameras down on the oily patch of water where *Mystique* had simply vaporized. Police boats and Coast Guard cruisers glided back and forth between the spots of light that illuminated the river. Marine officers skimmed the water with handheld nets, trying to sift for any evidence of debris that might lead them to a reason for this cataclysmic tragedy.

"It looks like there's nothing left of her," Bock said as he lifted a glass of cognac to his lips. "Very clean. Very well done."

"Did they say anything about that damned wave?" Washington asked. "It nearly killed us both."

Bock swiveled in his wheelchair so he could see out into Biscayne Bay. The body of water that separated Miami from Miami Beach was also the southernmost outlet for the Intracoastal Waterway. The water looked perfectly peaceful. The red and green lights from the channel markers sparkled off the water like strings of Christmas lights, and, in the distance, the colorful pastel lights of South Beach cast the foundation of the night sky in a soft rosy glow. It was hard for Bock to imagine from Damon's incredible description that one of those harmlessly rolling waves might have been such a savage marauder not so long ago. "They never caught anything on tape," Bock said as he took a long puff from his Cohiba cigar, self-satisfied at another completed mission of his righteous campaign, "but it looks like it did quite a number out there."

"It was crazy!"

"Collateral damage. It happens all the time when you're fighting a war."

"I've never been so scared."

"Are you trying to hit me up for extra combat pay?" Bock joked.

"If anyone ever deserved it..."

Bock rolled his chair closer to the television screens as the cameras panned closer to the water. "How's Shayla doing?"

"You know her ... she's a stone-cold bitch, although I don't think she'll be going near the water again anytime soon. We decided to catch separate cabs."

"Did she behave herself?"

There was a nervous pause. "Uh ... we'll have to discuss that later on."

Bock drummed his fingers intolerantly on his desk. "Tell me now, before I hear about it on the television."

Washington's lowered his voice to a whisper so the cabbie couldn't hear, even though he doubted that the Pakistani driver understood more than a dozen words of English anyway. "Scratch one Marine Patrol..."

Bock knew what was coming next. "Why?"

"It all happened so fast."

"Was he trouble?"

"Hell, August, I don't know; we barely got past the introductions. It was all a blur. One minute he's standing there talking to me, the next second not. That was the first time I ever saw someone ... up close and personal..."

Bock gnawed on his lower lip. "Well, that's what we pay her for. Kill first and ask questions later."

"I'm telling you, he just looked at her the wrong way, and *bang*, the dude never knew what hit him."

"If she didn't think he was a threat, he'd still be ticketing boating violations."

"Anyway, I think we lucked out this time."

Bock took another swig from his drink. "How so?"

"I can't be certain, but I'd be willing to bet that wave took care of any incriminating evidence there might have been. It was flinging boats left and right like they were kids' toys. It destroyed anything that got in its way. Nothing to worry about."

Bock watched the smoke curl away from the end of his cigar. "I'll keep an ear to the media just in case. As long as The Department of Homeland Security continues playing the blame game with international terror cells, they'll be chasing their tails for years. God bless America."

"Just wanted to give you a heads up. I'm sure you'll eventually hear something when all the bodies start floating to the surface. Meanwhile, I'm going home and taking a nice warm shower. I need to wash the stench of death and seawater off of me, and then I'll come in. Shayla's doing the same. We said we'd meet up around 11 o'clock. Is that okay with you?"

"That's fine. I'll be glad to finally close the file on this one so we can start discussing California."

There was another long pause on the line. "Damn, August."

"What's the matter now?"

"Don't you ever take a night off? It's Saturday night, man, and I've just been to hell and back. Can't California wait a few hours?"

"We'll see," Bock said, as he tapped the ashes from his cigar into an ivory ashtray on his desk.

Bock pressed the lit button on the phone and disconnected the line. Reaching across his desk, he pointed his remote control unit at one of the screens. A familiar female reporter's skittish face filled the monitor. She had the collar of her tweed coat turned up to battle the cold wind blowing off the water. Unlike any of the rehearsed reports she was accustomed to doing, she looked confused, looking around nervously to make sure she wasn't in any danger herself. Behind her, fire crews were working feverishly to quench a demonic blaze still burning out of control in the Port.

"This is Carmen Ochoa, coming to you live from Port Everglades, where less than an hour ago, Ex-Miami Beach Mayor Nathan Waxman's luxury yacht, the Mystique, inexplicably exploded less than half a mile from where I'm now standing. There is no doubt that Mayor Waxman was killed in the blast." She was holding her earpiece firmly against her ear. Through it, Bock imagined her producer was filling her in on the latest developments. *"It has been speculated that there might have been a fuel leak in the engine compartment, but none of that can be confirmed until divers are able to salvage what remains of the boat from the bottom of the Intracoastal."*

Bock pressed a button on the remote control and the audio portion of the broadcast went silent. He took another swig of his drink, and maneuvered his wheelchair to face the sparkling lights of the city. Staring out into the void, his mind couldn't shake loose a single line of haunting prose—a powerful string of words that had been the driving force in his life for the past six years. Repeating it to himself always seemed to relieve any pangs of guilt or remorse he might have been feeling at a time like this. It was a quote he had memorized from Edmund Burke, an Irish-born writer from the eighteenth century.

It went simply like this:

"The only thing necessary for the triumph of evil, is for good men to do nothing."

34

The sky was an ethereal blue—so pure in its splendor, that it would make one gasp just to gaze upon it. Birds, too far away to distinguish their species, flecked the sky like a shake of pepper. There was a wooden fence in the distance that stretched in both directions to the limits of the horizon. It was clearly not a fence to keep people out, but perhaps the boundary of a country road or two lane highway.

The field in which the antique quilt had been placed was filled with wild flowers, yellow, blue, white, green and purple—all swaying to the gentle harmony of the breeze. There was giggling and happy noises rising from the colorful meadow. Casey and Kimmie Mitchell were in hot pursuit of a butterfly that seemed to be toying with them, flitting just beyond their outstretched hands. They were romping joyously together, not a care in the world, their entire lives a mystery yet to be unraveled in their own time.

"What a glorious day," Renee announced as she sat up on the blanket. "Not too warm, nor too windy."

Gabe was lying prone on one elbow, unable to take his eyes off his wife. Her dress was as white as daisy petals, and her soft blond hair glistened like spun gold under the bright afternoon sun. "It's absolutely perfect. This is what life is all about, isn't it?"

Renee didn't answer him, as she began to pull food out of a straw picnic basket by her feet. "All of your favorites," she said. "You name it, we've got it."

Gabe knew his wife better than she knew herself. He could tell when something was troubling her. She had this way of keeping it to herself that was more revealing than if she had told him outright. "What is it?" he asked, sitting up and putting his hand softly on her back. "You can talk to me. Didn't I always say that I'd be here for you?"

A plastic plate clattered back into the wicker basket as she hung her head and began to sob. "You always promised me you would be, but you weren't."

Gabe put his hand on her shoulder and turned her towards him. "When? When wasn't I ever there for you?" He took his fingers and blotted the tears from her face. When he pulled them away, the clear, salty fluid had somehow changed its consistency. It was thick and sticky ... and red. The more he tried to wipe his hands, the more saturated they became. It was blood, and it was on his hands, and he couldn't get rid of it. He tried wiping his hands clean on the leg of his pants, but it did little to absolve the stain. "What is this?" he screamed, holding up his opened palms for her to see.

His wife once again turned her back to face the wooden fence on the horizon. "You promised me, but you lied."

His head was thumping ... thumping...

Thump ... Thump ... Thump ... Thump...

Gabe's eyes fluttered open. The deafening sound echoed inside the decrepit framework of the old school bus like thunder in a tin can. Light poured in through the buses' shattered windows, illuminating the tattered benches that had long since torn free of their rusted bolts. Gabe was lying on the cold metal floor, his back propped up against the rear door and soaked to the skin. He tried to move, but his legs were paralyzed. An anemic-looking gray rat, who scampered out of a hole in the floor, stared curiously at the intruder, his beady red eyes glowing like dying embers in the meager light.

Thump ... Thump ... Thump ... Thump ... Thump...

The rat stood up on his hind legs, gazing up at the roof of the bus, his nose and whiskers twitching nervously. Frightened by the noise, it took one last look at Gabe and darted back into his hole in the floor.

Outside, a police helicopter hovered over the junkyard, shining its floodlight over the jumble of old clunkers and disassembled engine parts strewn all over the two-acre junk lot. Damage here was impossible to assess since the place always seemed to look like it had been hit by a tidal wave. The two Doberman guard dogs were reported missing by the proprietor, but there was a good chance they had been swept out into the river by the receding water. Only a makeshift wooden fence protected the junkyard from the river, and an entire section of it had been washed away. Quite a few homeowners' family pets left to roam in their backyards had drowned the same way that night.

The light crossed over Gabe's face again and he had to protect his eyes from the glare. Slowly, the noise faded out, replaced by the echoes of his own heavy breathing. He tried to shift his position, but his legs wouldn't answer the call. He pressed his hands against the corrugated metal flooring for support, but his lower body still wouldn't budge. With no strength left for a second attempt, he leaned back and let his body rest. His memory was an impenetrable maze, filled with winding passageways and congested intersections. No two thoughts could be linked together to make a single cohesive image. What couldn't he remember? How did he come to be in this place?

Behind closed eyes, the recollections rushed by like an out of focus movie. He watched them whiz by, unable to differentiate between reality and those impressions concocted by his energy starved brain. Yachts and fences. Handguns and picnic baskets. Belts and flowers. Truth and fiction.

The air inside the decaying bus smelled of grease and mildew, but there was another scent stinging Gabe's nostrils. He tilted his head back and drew in a deep breath ... salt air. The bus creaked beneath him, settling into the well-saturated earth.

Salt air ... just concentrate on that.

He let his mind lock onto that aroma and it homed in on it like a trained pigeon. *Think...*

Okay, there were lights, lots of colored lights, looming in the distance. His eyes narrowed, as his face showed the strain of his focus. *You were on the water. Your footing was unsteady, as it swayed beneath your feet. As what swayed? A boat? No, bigger ... there was a lot of deck space.* Gabe closed his fist and rapped it against his forehead in frustration. His hand came away drenched in red; he was bleeding from a large gash above his right eye. He wiped his hand on the leg of his pants, but the stain was persistent. *Don't worry about that now, the thoughts are starting to clear...*

There was a figure standing there ... no, well yes, standing, but talking on the phone. Sirens pierced the stagnant air inside the bus. Gabe put his fingers up against the side of his head to block out the distraction.

You're talking to him, and then you reach for your ... belt!

Gabe reached down to his waist. His belt was gone.

Okay, it's all coming back to me now...

He was detached, watching it all happen in the third person as though he were omnipotent, floating above it all. He saw himself removing his belt and scampering up the ladder to the yacht's flying bridge. Once up there, he watched as he took the belt and wrapped it around one of the flexible radio antennas. Carefully, he had let go of the antenna, letting it spring back to its original 20-foot height.

Innocence. I remember thinking he didn't do it...

The yacht was on automatic control and approaching the entrance to Port Everglades. It was plain to see from all the activity on the docks that the port was in the midst of another bustling Saturday night. To the east, a few small cruise ships were docked at one of the terminals preparing to set sail. He had no time for a second opinion.

This was insane; what was I thinking?

Nathan Waxman remained cornered in the bow, afraid to go anywhere near the lunatic on the bridge.

Nathan Waxman? Yes, of course ... I remember him now.

"There's no time to explain. You've got to trust me on this."

Waxman had his back pressed against the chrome railing; to either side, the dark water of the Intracoastal hissed by below. "What have you done with Tyler Kennedy?"

Gabe grabbed the ex-mayor by the shoulders and spun him around. "Your friend's safe. Now, I'm gonna need you to climb over the railing."

"Are you crazy?" Waxman cried, looking down at the 25-foot drop and turbulent water. "I'll be crushed."

"You're going die for sure if you stay here," Gabe warned. "We've only got one chance and that way," he said, pointing down at the waves crashing against the hull, "is it."

The cold wind was cutting right through both men as they argued the logic of abandoning *Mystique* by such a perilous method.

"Please tell me why you're doing this," Waxman pleaded as he lifted his leg over the starboard railing. "I told you, if it's money you're after..."

Gabe glanced back at the belt dangling from the wobbling antenna. He wasn't sure he was that good a marksman, especially in his weakened condition. "I'm not going to say it again. I don't have time to explain. You've got to do this. I'm going to give you to the count of three."

"I can't do it," Waxman stammered. "I've got a young daughter to think about."

Gabe put the barrel of Kennedy's pistol against the side of the ex-mayor's neck. "And I've got a boy of my own, *now jump!*"

Waxman's hands were gripping the railing like they were welded to it. "I can't do it, I'm telling you."

"Do you want me to shoot you right here? I swear to Christ I will, unless you jump on three."

The sounds of the port were becoming more discernable. Baritone horns sounded from a fleet of tugboats heading out to sea. A train whistled its arrival at a concrete plant, as it prepared to load another boxcar full of gravel.

"Then go ahead and shoot me. I'd rather die that way than drown."

Gabe cursed under his breath and climbed over the railing. He took hold of Waxman's forearm and twisted it halfway around. Even for a great shot standing on steady ground and facing flush to the target this would have been a tough target, but then why should anything in his life be that easy?

The concussion hit them like a sledgehammer.

The blast warped the air around them, sending a sonic shockwave slamming into their defenseless bodies. There was no oxygen to breath. Their lungs had compressed and were temporarily incapable of inhalation. The heat was unbridled, but they were propelled so fast they couldn't feel a degree of it. They somersaulted through the night sky, riding an invisible wave of air, their eyeballs bulging out of their skulls from the momentum. Both men were catapulted toward the shore like they'd been shot out of a circus cannon. Their ears only rang once. It was a high-pitched, deafening screech, followed by muffled silence. Behind them, *Mystique*, once breathtakingly majestic, simply vaporized in a towering gold, black and orange hell storm.

Gabe hit the water with all the grace of a hippopotamus doing a swan dive. He missed the hard, rocky shore by less than a few yards, but colliding with the water at the speed he was falling was still like landing on a sheet of plywood.

I pulled us onto the shore ... the ground was unsteady and full of rocks ... he was unconscious ... my arms ... my entire body was spent ... fell flat on my face and couldn't move ... wasn't there long ... two new sounds ... dogs yelping and then a deafening rumble ... never heard anything like that before ... like a buffalo stampede ... closing in from behind...

The gargantuan wave rose out of the depths, snuffing out and devouring what little was left of the smoldering hull of Mystique. In slow motion, it crawled toward the shoreline, dredging up 1,000-pound boulders from the riverbed and relocating them effortlessly, the way a person might toss a gum wrapper.

What about Waxman? Is he still alive? Too spent ... can't think anymore...

Gabe was too exhausted to run. Every cell in his body had just about given up. The shore was muddy and felt so cool and refreshing against his skin.

Nothing could make him move now...

The wall of water tore them from their earthen cradles. Unsympathetic to their fatigue, the wave flipped them onto their backs, sending them crashing through the dilapidated wooden fence. It carried them 50 feet inland as it swallowed up old cars and howling Dobermans whole. White foam and seaweed boiled into the junkyard, tearing free anything that wasn't nailed down.

Miraculously, Gabe found himself tumbling head over heels atop the crest of the wave, like a surfer thrown from his board while riding the Banzai Pipeline. Twice he hit something with a jolting impact, but his body was too battered and bruised to register the pain. The wave lifted him over the tree line, enveloping both the tallest pines and tearing loose the shallower-rooted queen palms. With a thunderous roar, the wave reached its apex and then broke, leaving scores of fish and crustaceans gasping for air or scrambling back toward the river.

As the torrent of water began to recede, Gabe was lowered, almost lovingly, back to the mucky ground. He laid there for what seemed like an eternity as a catfish squirmed in the mud mere inches from his face, contorting in an excruciating dance of death. It sounded like a gentle rain as gravity drained the water back, slicing rivulets into the soft ground to facilitate the river's reclamation. Gabe lifted his head out of the silt and coughed out a mixture of mud and seawater. His eyes were swollen and felt like they were on fire as he tried to focus in on his surroundings.

I'd trade my right arm for a fistful of aspirins right about now...

As Gabe pulled himself to his knees, everything was shrouded in a gauzy haze. Junkyards might be considered pretty spooky places even during the day, but cloaked only in moonlight, the odd contours and jagged shapes created an even more ominous impression. The whiskered catfish lying by his side had slowed its wriggling, its gills panting for its last few breaths. Gabe closed his eyes and rolled his head from side to side as the vertebrae in his neck crackled in protest. A breeze hit him from behind. It was a caustic smell filled with fire and gasoline fumes. It made Gabe lightheaded and he fell forward, his brain suddenly taking a nausea-inducing rollercoaster ride. He put his hand over his mouth and tried to hold his breath, but cutting off his oxygen only made the situation worse.

Can't stay here...

Like a man who had just been shot in both legs, Gabe began to drag himself away from the river—away from the toxic smoke. His hands groped at the soggy earth, pulling away chunks of top soil peppered with rusted bolts and discarded screws. With every muscle in his body screaming for him to stop—to just roll over and let the inevitable finally happen—Gabe strained on. Incredible willpower or sheer stupidity, he refused to be found like this, face down in the mud, surrounded by dead fish, crabs nipping the flesh off his bones.

Sirens...

They came from some distant place, growing louder with each passing second. He pulled himself along on his elbows, like a soldier at boot camp shimmying beneath a stretch of barbed wire. He had no clue where he was headed, but instinctively knew he didn't want to be found. Another 20 feet may as well have been a mile. Elbow ... knee ... elbow ... knee. The ground smelled disgusting too.

Onward another 10 feet, and his hand hit something soft ... he jumped back.

A groan...

Gabe reached out into the darkness and felt a face. A silhouette stretched out before him. "Mr. Mayor?"

Gabe scurried forward. Nathan Waxman was lying on his back, his face blackened with mud like the master of ceremonies at a minstrel show. Gabe crawled up beside him and tried to clear the dirt from his airways to ease his breathing. He was unconscious, but alive ... barely.

As if hauling himself through the muck wasn't enough of a superhuman endeavor, now Gabe found himself towing an extra 200 pounds of dead weight.

Dear God, why don't I just roll over and die?

Call it self-preservation, or a cop's intuition, but as clouded as his mind was, some fervent voice in the back of his mind urged him to seek cover.

The veins in Gabe's neck protruded like drinking straws as he struggled onward. He had Waxman by the lapel of his waterlogged jacket, his fingers feeling as though they would snap off at any second. He had to find some shelter.

Like a mirage appearing in the middle of the Gobi, a large shape loomed out of the darkness.

Is that yellow?

One of the most recognizable things in the world: a public school bus. The tires were missing, and it was pitched to one side, its hinged front door torn loose.

Oh momma! What a beautiful sight!

Out on the street that fronted the junkyard, a fire engine raced by with its shrill horn warning traffic out of its path. It was quickly followed by another siren, probably a police car or an ambulance in hot pursuit.

Gabe hoisted himself up the three metal steps that led into the bus while still holding onto the back of Waxman's collar. Bracing his feet against the bottom step, he groaned in agony as he lugged the motionless ex-mayor up the stairs and inside the bus.

Got to rest ... just want to close my eyes for a minute or two, that's all...

Thankful his memory had returned, Gabe tried to move his feet again. This time they budged, and he realized his paralysis wasn't internal. Nathan Waxman's torso was draped across his legs. Gabe leaned back against the rear door and laughed to himself.

If this situation wasn't so tragic, it would almost be funny.

Where would he go now? He had to get some medical attention for the ex-mayor, but...

Wait a damned minute now ... everyone is going to assume we've both been killed in the blast. Hold on now ... this could work to my advantage ... if Bock believes I've gone through with the assassination, there should be no more threat to Casey's life.

Gabe thought long and hard about this new twist of events. Any military leader worth his salt knows that the element of surprise is a formidable ally.

So why not stay dead?

Who knew how much time he had left? But now that his son was no longer in danger, why not find a way to throw a monkey wrench into August Bock's plans? It would be tough not contacting his son—he wanted to see him, to hold him, more than anything—but he couldn't take that risk.

So, who can I trust?

Gabe bent forward and checked the pulse on Waxman's throat. It was weak, but discernable. If he didn't get him out of this drafty rust bucket soon, he would be responsible for his death. Another helicopter hovered overhead, temporarily turning night into day.

If I just had some loose change, there's got to be a pay phone around here ... I can call a taxi ... but where can we go that's safe?

Gabe patted down his pockets and came up empty, except for a slip of paper that was drenched and barely legible, which he tossed haphazardly onto the floor. Thinking that perhaps Waxman might have something of use, he carefully rolled the ex-mayor onto his back and began scouring his pockets. Like a blessing from above, he found Waxman's eel-skin wallet intact, although his family pictures were beyond salvation. Rifling through the billfold, Gabe found nearly $200 and enough plastic money to clog an ATM.

There's got to be a pay phone nearby. But who to call? There's no one I can trust...

The blazing beacon from the police search helicopter once again flooded the bus with its intrusive white light. Out of the corner of his eye, the discarded slip of paper glistened on the wet floor like a well-polished jewel. Gabe tilted his head to read the name and phone number that had been scribbled in bleeding red marker, and, like lightning striking from above, he suddenly knew exactly who to call.

35

He soared like an eagle, a billow of woolly white and silver clouds passing beneath him. He gazed down on the earth, his arms spread out in joyous flight. The ground was green and brown beneath his makeshift wings, and the water passing below shimmered like a sheet of aluminum foil in the bright afternoon sun. No one was here to bother him, and the only sounds he heard were the envious rustling of the earthbound trees, and the wind's serenade singing in his ears.

He banked to the left and then back to the right. Floating aimlessly on the thermal currents, dodging the fluffy clouds like they were pylons in an air race. Just ahead, he spotted a v-shaped formation of migrating birds and accelerated to join up with them. Performing an effortless barrel roll, he slid into the center of the wedge and flew along with them for a while, smiling politely whenever one would turn its head and squawk at the outsider in their midst.

This was where he truly belonged—not down below with the dead and the dying. Up here he was free! Up here, he could go wherever he pleased, whenever he pleased. Up here, there were no enlarged prostates, no throwing up from chemotherapy, no one telling him what he could or couldn't eat or what his body was capable of. Up here, there were no restrictions.

With a courteous wave of his hand, he let the birds continue on their journey and soared upward, bending over backwards, letting the warmth of the sun caress his face. He flew that way for a while, over on his back, staring up at nothing but the pale blue canopy drifting peacefully overhead. He flew that way until he heard the *banging*...

Five times, then five times more. Impatient ... unrelenting in its urgency.

Bang ... bang ... bang ... bang ... bang...

He began to tumble, falling out of the sky as though the invisible strings supporting his body had suddenly been snipped. He fell through the gauzy clouds end over end, the hard brown earth rushing up at him. His arms and legs instinctively flapped as he tried desperately to regain lift. A rugged cluster of trees waited like a bed of jagged spines to impale him. The cool blue water beside the forest began to swirl in a fierce vortex waiting to swallow him up at his point of impact.

He screamed, but the sound choked off in his throat. It looked like a water landing was inevitable, and so the whirlpool began to froth and widen, nothing but pure darkness at its core. He put his arms over his eyes to brace for the collision, but none ever came. He plummeted past sea level, continuing to fall headlong into the center of the cataract, his entire body getting soaking wet, but yet, miraculously, not drowning.

Bang ... bang ... bang ... bang ... bang...

Something had his legs. He started kicking, his feet becoming entangled in whatever it was. His heart was pounding like the pistons in a World War II spitfire, as the faceless creature wrapped its tentacles around his lower torso. He reached down and grabbed it, tearing at it, pulling it off himself.

Bang ... bang ... bang ... bang ... bang...

Bennett Chase sat bolt upright in his bed. His body coated with nervous perspiration, his bed sheets twisted around his legs. His mouth hung open gasping for breath as his eyes slowly orientated themselves to the darkness. He reached over to the nightstand and turned the alarm clock so he could read the time. In big, bright, LED numbers, the clock read 4:18.

Bang ... bang ... bang ... bang ... bang...

Someone was at the front porch, but who the hell, would be pounding on his door in the middle of the night? He threw off his blanket and ran his fingers through his thick silver hair like a makeshift comb. He sat for a long moment on the edge of his bed collecting his thoughts. He wasn't as sharp as he used to be, and nowadays it always took him a few quarts of coffee to reach his potential first thing when he woke up. He slipped his feet into a pair of fur-lined leather slippers and grabbed his terrycloth bathrobe that was hanging off a hook on the back of the bedroom door.

Bang ... bang ... bang ... bang ... bang...

"Hang on," he muttered, as he felt for the light switch at the top of the stairs. "Keep your shirt on."

He trudged down the stairs, wiping the crust out of his eyes as he descended. He had lived in this old two-story wooden house his entire adult life, having bought it some forty years earlier when he first flew for the Air Force. Now the stairs and floorboards, like him, creaked under his weight.

Reaching the first floor, he avoided the front door and opted to make a left, heading instead into the living room where he always kept a loaded shotgun behind the curio cabinet that was filled with old aviation memorabilia. An ounce of prevention ... his daddy always said.

Bennett Chase looked very peculiar toting the double-barreled shotgun toward the front door, kind of like Santa Claus gone bad.

Bang ... bang ... bang ... bang ... bang...

He peered through the fisheye peephole, but it was too dark to make anything out. Resting the barrel of the gun on his shoulder, but with his finger still on the trigger, he flipped on the outside light and looked out again. A distorted face stared back at him. It belonged to someone he never thought he'd see again...

The front door flew open and Gabe Mitchell practically collapsed into his arms.

"Gabe! What the hell happened to you?" he asked, leading Gabe over to his couch.

Gabe pointed with his thumb back over his shoulder. "One more."

Chase put a throw pillow behind Gabe's head. "One more what?"

"Someone ... outside ... bring him in."

"There's someone else with you?"

Gabe managed to nod.

Chase set the shotgun down on the floor behind the couch and waddled back to the porch. There *was* someone else there, a crumpled heap of a man. Chase tried to lift him to his feet, but it was dead weight. After many failed efforts to stand the man upright, Chase ended up having to grab the limp man by the collar of his scorched windbreaker and haul him into the house like a sack of potatoes. He dragged him through the living room, huffing and puffing like an old steam engine. When he finally made it into the guest bedroom, he boosted him up onto the queen sized bed, never realizing he was now boarding a local celebrity. The room was dark, and Chase couldn't have cared less who the stranger was. He was more worried about Gabe.

Out of breath, but too energized to notice, Chase shuffled back into the living room and knelt beside the couch. "Jeez, Gabe," he said, feeling Gabe's forehead for signs of a fever. "What the hell happened to you? You look like a zombie!"

Gabe tried to smile, but every muscle, including his lips, hurt. "Well, hell was full," he groaned, "so I decided to come back."

"You're burning up! I'm gonna get you a cold washcloth."

Gabe grabbed him by the arm. "You can't tell anyone we're here."

Chase found just enough space on the edge of the couch to settle his rather rotund posterior, albeit uncomfortably. "Anything you say, son. I know there's got to be a logical explanation for the shape you two are in. Now, let me get you that damp washcloth."

In the few minutes it took for Bennett to return with the wet rag, Gabe had already drifted off to sleep. Ever so delicately, Chase folded the washcloth into quarters and began to mop Gabe's brow. "That feels great," Gabe moaned.

"I didn't mean to wake you."

"I wasn't sleeping; I was resting my eyes."

Chase smirked. "Sure you were, kid. Now, why don't you ... rest your eyes some more, and we can talk in the morning."

Again Gabe grabbed him by the sleeve of his bathrobe. "I tried calling you."

"Sorry about that. I don't sleep very well these days, so I've been turning my phone off at night."

"Please, you can't tell anyone we're here."

Chase gave the back of Gabe's hand a reassuring pat. "You already told me that, son, and I promised you, I wouldn't."

"It's very important, Bennett."

"Don't worry. You have my word."

"You can't let him out of your sight either."

Chase looked toward the hallway leading to the guest bedroom. "Believe me: if he's in half the shape you're in, he's not going anywhere."

"You can't let him try to contact anyone either."

Chase wiped the washcloth around Gabe's throat. "I'm sure the need for all of this secrecy will become clear in the light of morning, son. Till then, I promise not to let him talk to anyone. I'll even remove the phone in his room, how's that?"

Looking up at the old man, Chase's head was backlit by a small table lamp, making it look like he was sporting a halo. Gabe reached out his charred and muddied hand to touch the angelic mirage. "I'll never be able to repay you for this."

"Hey, the fact that you trusted me enough to come here is all the thanks I need. All this secrecy and excitement is putting a spark back into this old jet jockey's engine. Whatever kind of trouble you've gotten yourself into, we can figure it out together."

Gabe sighed. "I don't know..."

Chase continued to pat down Gabe's forehead. "What can they do to us? Put us in jail for the rest of our lives? Neither one of us is supposed to make it past New Year's Eve anyway. Those would be the shortest life sentences ever handed down, right?"

Gabe tried valiantly to hold his eyes open but they felt as heavy as garage doors. "I'm just so ... tired."

Chase cupped Gabe's smudged face in his hand. "You get some sleep now, son. I'm going to take the phone out of the other room."

Tiptoeing to a hall closet, Chase found an old brown and beige afghan and returned with it to the couch. Like he was wrapping a breakable Christmas ornament, the old man tucked the blanket all around Gabe's peaceful form. "Sleep tight, my boy," he whispered.

Chase clicked off the table lamp and headed for the guest room. A small nightlight plugged into one of the wall sockets cast the hallway in a pale sapphire glow. Holding the door so that the squeaking hinge wouldn't wake Gabe's buddy, Chase found him just as he had left him: curled up in the fetal position. There was an awful smell coming from both men, but the close quarters of this windowless bedroom seemed to magnify the putrid odor. Chase couldn't quite put his finger on it. Smoke was a primary ingredient judging from all their singed clothing, possibly stale sea water too, but the rest of the smelly compound was a mystery. This stench would never do. He would have to undress this one now and then find them both some fresh clothes in the morning.

There was a small lamp on the desk in the corner where Chase had the personal computer he used to surf the Internet and pay his bills. Holding down the lamp's "on" button, the weak yellow bulb hummed to life. The old man hiked up the bulky sleeves of his bathrobe and with grimace of repulsion, and he gingerly turned his second unexpected houseguest onto his back. In the dim light, Chase got his first good look at the unidentified guest's face.

"Dear Lord, forget about New Year's..." he gasped, as his hand automatically covered his mouth, "...we might not even make it to Easter!"

36

The smoky aroma of freshly cooked bacon teased Gabe out of his dreamless slumber. As he struggled to open his eyes, an achy groan was all he could muster out of a mouth so dry, his tongue had stuck to his lips. He stifled a yawn and tried to get his eyes to focus, but, in these unfamiliar surroundings, that was easier said than done.

A ceiling fan modeled after the nose cone of a vintage RAF Spitfire airplane stirred the air, complete with a growling red mouth and shark-like white teeth. The four wooden blades painted silver to resemble the WWII fighter's propellers held Gabe spellbound. It took a few seconds for his clouded mind to register that he wasn't being strafed by an outdated warplane. To his relief, he quickly took note of the wooden ceiling beams and the afghan he clutched in his trembling hands.

"You finally awake?" a voice called out from some not too distant place.

Gabe shifted on the couch and grunted.

"I'll take that as a 'yes.' You must have smelled my home cooking."

Coughing to clear his throat, Gabe clawed his way out of the knitted blanket that had him covered.

"I hope you haven't gone vegetarian on me," the familiar voice announced. "I'm eating everything they say I can't, until my arteries clog like a bathtub drain. I don't give a rat's ass whether it's good for me or not. Screw those doctors!"

Gabe threw his feet off the couch and sat up, cupping his head in his hands. He could feel the rough stubble of his beard against his palms and it made him feel dirtier. Another more pungent aroma quickly expunged the mouth-watering smell of the cooking bacon. It was coming from him, and it was nauseating. Now, if he only had the strength to strip and take a shower.

"Hey, sleepyhead," Chase said, carrying a skillet into the living room. "Nice to see you finally up and at 'em."

More bizarre than the sight of a jet fighter dive bombing you from above would have to be seeing this roly-poly of a man carrying a frying pan and wearing an apron stretched to the limitation of its fabric, which read *"I'm the cook, and what I say goes."* "So, how do you like your eggs?"

Gabe cracked one eye to glance up at the jocular chef standing before him. "Nice apron," he moaned.

"Never, ever antagonize the cook," Chase snickered, "especially when he has ample opportunity to spit in your food."

"Maybe just something to drink," Gabe muttered, as he rolled his neck from side to side.

"Uh-uh," Chase shook his head. "You're going to take a nice hot shower, and then you'll get some food into your system, even if I have to shove it down your throat. When was the last time you ate anyway?"

Gabe scratched his head. "Uh, what day is it?"

Chase flipped the pot holder onto his dining room table, and then set the hot frying pan on top of it. "Yeah, I thought as much. We've got to get some nourishment into you, son. Come on ... let me give you a hand."

Chase lifted Gabe by his elbow and assisted him through the house that resembled more of a shrine to aviation than a place to call home. There were photos of old warplanes adorning every inch of wall space, and scale models of jet fighters everywhere Gabe looked.

"Just toss your clothes out into the hallway," Chase instructed as they reached the bathroom, "and I'll get rid of them like I did the mayor's."

Gabe put his hand to his forehead. "Oh God ... the mayor. Where is he?"

"Don't worry about a thing," Chase said, prodding Gabe to keep moving. "He's sleeping like a baby, and he's not going anywhere in his birthday suit. I stuffed his clothes into a garbage bag, and that's the same place yours belong, as soon as you strip out of them." Chase reached around Gabe and switched on the bathroom light. "Just throw those smelly old rags out to me, and I'll go up to the Wal-Mart after breakfast and get you both some fresh jeans and a couple of shirts. There's an extra bathrobe hanging behind the door for you to wear in the meantime. It probably won't fit, but I wasn't exactly expecting company, you know?"

Gabe leaned against the sink and began to unbutton his shirt. Suddenly, his hands became so inept. "I'm sorry to put you through all this trouble, Bennett."

The old man stepped in front of Gabe and, swatting his hand away, began unbuttoning his shirt for him. "Nonsense. You're obviously in over your head, and I want to help you. Christ's sake, boy! This is the most excitement I've had in years! My blood's pumping and my heart's doing the rumba! This is great!"

"Not great," said Gabe between raspy coughs.

Chase kicked the pile of offensive garments into the hall. He would later use a broom to scoot them into a garbage bag. "You going be able to shower by yourself?"

"I can do it."

"I'll be in earshot if you need me."

Gabe turned and stared at himself in the mirror. The haggard mug that frowned back at him was barely recognizable. It looked as though his face had been shoved through a meat grinder. His eyes were dark and hollow. Soot formed a dirty "V" around his neck where his collar had been open. His hair hung down in drooping ringlets like a Rastafarian's dreadlocks. Not a bad look, if he had ever considered himself fashionable enough to try it. Maybe a shower *would* help. *Yeah*, he said to himself, as he tenderly touched one of his swollen cheeks, *and if a frog had wings, it wouldn't bump its ass every time it hopped.* "What about the mayor? Is he doing alright?"

Gabe gazed into the mirror at the old man's reflection leaning against the door jamb behind him. Gabe didn't realize he'd repeated the question. Chase smiled back at him patiently. "He seems okay to me ... still sleeping. I keep checking on him every half hour or so."

"Yes, you need to do that for me."

"Of course I will. I *did* notice, though, that he had some dried blood around his ears ... probably from the blast."

Gabe looked up, suddenly feeling more naked than he actually was. "How did..."

"All over the morning news, my boy! You can't switch on the television without hearing about the explosion."

Gabe reached for Chase's shoulder. "I want to explain..."

"Relax," the old man comforted him. "No one's more interested in finding out how you're involved in this mess than I am, but you can tell me your story all in good time. Right now, though, the first order of business is getting you back on your feet."

"But..."

Chase stepped past Gabe and twisted the knobs inside the shower stall. "But nothing. Get in there and wash the worries off your back. You'll be surprised how much better you'll feel once you get yourself cleaned up."

Gabe hobbled into the shower and closed the glass door behind him. "Then, will you stay and talk to me?"

"Well, this is a situation I don't find myself in too often, but I don't think this day can get much more bizarre," Chase said, setting his prodigious girth atop the closed toilet seat. "Yeah, I'll stay if you want."

Gabe twisted off the hot water tap, and let the icy chill overrun his bare skin. Staring down at the drain, he watched a swirl of dark water stain the tiled floor. "So tell me what they're saying."

The old man slapped his hands down on his knees, clearly uncomfortable talking to another man while in a position in which he was more accustomed to doing light reading and contemplating universal truths. "The details are still sketchy, but all they're saying is the boat had some kind of engine malfunction and blew up. Nothing's positive, but they're supposed to be sending divers into the area this morning to search for clues."

Gabe rubbed a bar of soap onto a fresh washrag. "They won't find anything."

"Yeah, it didn't look like it."

"I still don't know how I'm standing here talking to you," Gabe admitted as he scrubbed at his chest. "But for the grace of God..."

"They interviewed one guy who worked on the docks..."

Gabe flashed back to the delivery man he had switched clothes with.

"The guy said someone identifying himself as a policeman had assaulted him just before the boat got underway."

"Yeah, that was yours truly. I'm not proud of it, but I had to get onboard. Is the guy okay?"

"He'll live. I don't think you have to worry about it too much though. They're not putting much credence in his story. They said he's got a reputation for distorting the truth to cover the fact that he drinks on the job."

"Like The Boy Who Cried Wolf."

Chase arched his back and stretched his stubby arms toward the ceiling. "I guess so."

"There was another guy on the boat with Waxman..." Gabe said as he began to shampoo his hair.

"That would be Tyler Kennedy, the friend of Waxman who was supposed to be at the controls."

Gabe cleared his throat. "I threw him overboard."

"Excuse me?"

"I knew what was coming; we struggled, and I tossed him over the side," Gabe said, letting the water pressure rinse the minty-smelling lather out of his hair. "I didn't want him to get hurt. Did they find him?"

Chase slid around on the toilet seat until he was facing the shower. "You have no idea what happened out there on the river last night, do you?"

The knobs squeaked as Gabe shut off the water and reached for a towel. "Can I borrow a razor?"

Chase stood up and retrieved a disposable razor and can of shaving cream from the medicine cabinet over the sink. "Here."

Gabe smiled graciously and began to carefully apply the foam to his face. "You're right, that shower really helped."

"Gabe?"

"What?"

"We were just in the middle of a conversation."

Gabe dragged the razor down the side of his face. "What were we talking about again?"

Chase's eyes narrowed. "Are you sure you're alright?"

"Of course, I'm fine. Why do you keep asking me that?" Gabe asked as he cleaned out the razor under the running tap.

"You seem a bit discombobulated, that's all."

"Nah, I'm fine, Bennett. My ears are still ringing a little, but I'm sure that'll go away in time."

Chase handed Gabe a washcloth to wipe the remaining streaks of foam off his face. "I'm gonna go check on Waxman again, and then finish making you some breakfast. Why don't you dry off and meet me in the kitchen? We can talk some more while you eat."

"Sounds like a plan," Gabe agreed.

37

Four pieces of toast, three eggs sunny side up, and six rashers of bacon. Gabe was scarfing down the hot food like a condemned man. "This is very good," he complimented Chase.

The old man scrubbed down the frying pan in the sink. "I've learned to cook pretty well over the years. It was either that, or live on fast food." He patted his enormous stomach. "Maybe too much of both come to think of it."

Gabe leaned back in his chair and blew out a satiated puff of air. "I'm stuffed."

"I don't doubt it."

"Waxman still asleep?"

Chase flipped a dishtowel over his shoulder. "He's hardly shifted position since I laid him down last night. He's so out of it, I had to check his chest for signs of life. I'm wondering if that much rest is good for him. Maybe we should wake him?"

"Let him sleep," Gabe said, shaking his head. "It's nature's way of repairing his body."

Gabe picked up his plate, utensils and juice glass from the table and walked them over to the sink.

"Gimme, I'll take care of them," Chase said.

"I can do it."

"Come on, I'm elbow deep in soap suds already. Hand them over."

Gabe passed Chase the dirty dishes and took his seat once again at the kitchen table. "You really miss flying, don't you?"

The old man's shoulders noticeably sagged. "Like an amputee misses a limb."

"This place is quite a museum," Gabe said, looking out into the living room.

"God gave us memories, so that we might have roses in December."

Gabe sat silently for a long moment, suddenly feeling very melancholy for his friend. "You should be very proud of this wonderful collection you've put together."

The plates clattered in the sink. "It keeps my mind off the serious stuff."

Gabe drummed his fingers on the table self-consciously. "I'll never forget what you told me in the hospital about your passion for flying and wanting nothing more than to die in the air. I'm envious."

Chase set a plate onto the drying rack. "Of what?"

"Of that kind of passion."

"Can we change the subject?" the old man asked brusquely as he hung up the dishtowel and took a seat across the table from Gabe. "There's more important things we've got to deal with than my propensity for collecting memorabilia."

Gabe brushed the damp hair away from his eyes. "Okay, let's talk."

Chase turned serious, and his seemingly indelible grin was nowhere to be found. "I don't know what this is all about, but it's obvious you're neck-deep in something big ... and I want to help."

"I appreciate that; you already have."

The old man held up his hand. "Just listen now. It's my turn to talk."

Gabe wasn't used to being hushed. It caught him by surprise and it showed.

"Before you tell me what this is all about," Chase continued, "there's a lot of other stuff you need to know."

Gabe was almost afraid to hear the rest.

"A lot of innocent people died last night on the river, Gabe."

Gabe was taken aback. "What the hell are you talking about?"

"I could let you hear it on the news, but I think it would be better if I told you myself."

Chase went on to explain as much as he knew about the aftermath of the explosion and the carnage and loss of life left in its wake. Gabe was shaken by the news, his face crumbling to pieces from the weight of his grief. "How many died?" Gabe asked, wiping his eyes on the sleeve of his borrowed bathrobe.

"They're not sure yet."

"What about Waxman's friend?"

"Kennedy?"

"Yeah, Kennedy. He ended up alright, didn't he?"

Chase looked up toward the ceiling and grimaced with regret. "I'm sorry, son. He was one of the first ones they found."

Gabe stood up and began pacing around the kitchen like a caged leopard. "All of their planning ... all of their attention to detail..."

The old man turned his chair so he could follow Gabe around the kitchen. "Who are you talking about? All of whose planning?"

"Those sons-of- bitches. It would have happened anyway..."

"What would have happened anyway?"

"All of those innocent people would have been killed anyway," Gabe said, waving his hands in the air. "They didn't give a damn about that ... all those innocent lives probably never even entered into their equation. Even if I had gone through with it, all those other people would have died anyway..."

Chase grabbed at Gabe's sleeve as he walked by. "Come on, son. You're rambling. Sit back down and talk to me calmly."

Gabe pulled out the chair next to Chase and sat down. His eyes were filled with an animalistic rage that could easily have been mistaken for insanity. "Don't you see," Gabe lamented as he leaned forward and took hold of the old man by his shoulders, "they're nothing more than common terrorists who're using terminal patients like us for their ammunition. I don't know how long this has been going on, but someone's got to stop them before any more innocent people die!"

Chase pulled loose of Gabe's grip and stared at him like he had been speaking in a foreign language. "What do you mean, they're using terminal patients like us? Who is? What are you talking about?"

Gabe ran his hands through his hair. "I know this all sounds crazy..."

The old man huffed in agreement. "You think?"

"You can't tell anyone what I'm about to tell you," Gabe warned as he reached out and put his hand on Chase's knee, "promise me."

The old man gnawed on his lower lip faintheartedly. "In for a penny, in for a pound, I guess..."

Gabe leaned back in his chair and folded his arms across his chest. "I was recruited to kill Nathan Waxman."

The old man shot out of his seat like a teenager, and backed himself against the kitchen counter. "Recruited? By whom? Why?"

Gabe stood up and walked over to Chase. He spoke in a whisper. "They strapped a bomb to my waist and gave me the credentials to slip through the crowd at the marina unnoticed."

Chase ran his fingers through his hair. "They knew I was dying and my face would be familiar to most of the security staff on the dock, and that's why they chose me."

"Who chose you for Christ's sake? You're not making sense."

"I know it," Gabe said, putting his hand on Chase's neck. "I know how insane this all sounds. I barely believe it myself."

"So who put you up to this?" the old man asked. "And more importantly, why would you go along with it? You're a police officer, for crying out loud!"

Gabe rubbed his forehead trying to get the logical sequence of events in order. "First, this woman showed up at the hospital..."

The old man's eyes lit up. "You mean, the one with the stems that wouldn't quit? The one that looked like an attorney?"

Gabe realized Chase had actually met her too and pointed. "Exactly! That's the one ... her real name is Shayla Rand, and trust me: she was no lawyer."

"Great looking though."

"Not anymore," Gabe snickered. "First she arranges to have me discharged, and, the next thing I know, I'm being whisked away by helicopter to some isolated slab of rock somewhere in the Caribbean."

"The Bahamas?" Chase asked skeptically.

Gabe scratched his head. "I guess it was the Bahamas ... whatever ... that doesn't matter."

The old man's eyebrows arched like a pair of window awnings. "And what did you do on this island in the Bahamas?"

"I know how insane this must sound."

Chase walked over to refrigerator and took out a plastic jug of ice water. "I don't think you do," he said as he opened a cabinet and reached for a drinking glass.

"There was this guy there waiting to meet me. He said his name was Bock, August Bock. Have you ever heard of him?"

"Never," Chase said sincerely.

"Yeah, I wouldn't doubt that. He spends most of his life in the shadows. Even as I think about him now, it's a very unsettling image."

"How so?"

Gabe instinctively rubbed his own legs. "He's confined to a wheelchair, his face is hideously disfigured and he wears a patch over one eye..."

"Sounds like he's had a difficult life himself."

"Yes," Gabe said, speculatively, "I'd be curious about that."

"So you meet up with this Bock character on the island and..."

"And ... he offers me $4 million."

The glass fell out of the old man's hand and shattered in the sink. "Four million dollars?"

Gabe nodded. "That was my reaction too."

Chase reached over the sink and closed the window blinds, as though shutting them would somehow keep the conversation more private. "And where exactly did he expect a dead man to spend $4 million?"

Gabe began to pick the broken pieces of glass out of the sink. "He told me Casey would inherit the money after I was gone."

Chase opened the cabinet under the sink and pulled out a wastebasket for the glass. "And you believed him?"

"Yes."

"Why?"

"Well, I wanted to believe him for Casey's sake ... but it didn't matter anyway."

Chase dropped the last shard of busted glass into the plastic lined can. "And why was that?"

"Because I turned him down."

Chase put his hand over his heart. "I would hope so."

Gabe took a deep breath. "But then the woman pulls Casey's baseball cap out of a brown paper bag."

Chase's face balled up into a snarl. "Those evil, scum-sucking..."

Gabe coughed into his fist. "They said if I didn't go through with it, they'd kill him." The familiar pangs of nausea were returning to his stomach. "I didn't know what to do."

Chase took a long swig directly from the mouth of the plastic water jug. "I've never heard of anything so villainous."

"I got the impression these people were old hat at this type of thing," Gabe said, stuffing his hands into the pockets of his robe. "It was a well-oiled operation."

Chase walked back to the refrigerator and put the water away. "Did they say why they wanted to target Waxman?"

"I can't remember."

"Well, *somebody* wanted him dead."

Gabe winced at the pain in his stomach and turned toward the sink just in case. "Before this all happened, half the city would have liked to have seen him behind bars ... or worse."

Chase closed the door to the refrigerator. "Because he got away with killing his wife."

Gabe shook his head. "But he didn't do it."

The old man rolled his eyes in amazement. "You've got to be kidding."

Gabe coughed again and spit into the drain. "Let me finish..."

Chase shrugged. "I can't wait."

"I felt like my back was against the wall. I didn't know where to go, so I managed to sneak away from where they were holding me and I contacted my old boss..."

"The captain that came to visit you in the hospital..."

"Exactly. I told him my story, and, in not so many words, he told me I was deranged and that I needed to spend whatever time I had left with my son."

Chase shrugged. "Well, I can understand that … it's pretty unbelievable."

Gabe tore off a paper towel and wiped his mouth. "So, with nowhere else to turn, less than six months to live, and the promise of $4 million to secure my son's future, I decided to go through with it."

Chase looked astonished. "You actually decided to kill the mayor? And then what?" he asked excitedly.

"And then," Gabe said, balling up the paper towel, "I was on the docks and I overheard these two patrolman saying they had proof of Waxman's innocence and that it was all a set-up."

The old man's mouth hung open. "Whoa, sensory overload! This story gets more incredible by the minute! You're like James Bond, for Christ's sake! So, who did they say set him up?"

Gabe shook his head. "They didn't. I'm guessing it has to be whoever paid Bock to have Waxman killed after he was acquitted."

"But isn't that what they would call 'hearsay' in a court of law? You can't believe the word of two cops that you overheard talking."

Gabe agreed. "I know that, but when I confronted Waxman face to face, I just knew it. Call it my gut instinct. Call it whatever you want. I could see it in his eyes. He was really torn apart by his wife's death. I know that look. I've worn it myself."

"So now Bock has to assume you're both dead. That's why you didn't want me to let the mayor get in touch with anyone."

"An advantage I'd really like to keep."

"So, what's your next move?"

Gabe took a labored breath. "The first thing I've got to do is get some more of my medicine. I don't know how long I'll make it if I don't. I think I should wait until dark though; I want to stay as inconspicuous as possible. If you'll let me borrow your car, I'll go see Dr. Sanborn at the hospital. He'll write me a prescription."

Chase undid his robe and threw it over one of the kitchen chairs. He was a sight to behold in just a t-shirt and an enormous pair of boxer shorts. "You're not going anywhere unless I go out and get you some clothes first."

Gabe followed his friend out into the living room. "I can't tell you how much I appreciate this, Bennett."

The old man turned and held out his hand. "You're sending me away with a bang, son. I'm the one that will never be able to repay you."

Uncharacteristically for both men, they stood in the center of the living room and hugged ... friend to friend ... father to son. When they pulled apart, Chase looked up at Gabe's swollen face and smiled. "You know, I still can't believe he didn't kill his wife. Everything pointed at him. I was so positive..."

"Then I'm glad you weren't on my jury," Nathan Waxman announced, as he stood stark naked in the doorway of the guest bedroom.

38

All three men sat around the kitchen table while Nathan Waxman devoured the tuna fish hoagie that Chase had brought back for him. Both men were wearing their new clothes—Gabe, a pair of tan jeans and a long sleeve navy blue pullover, and Waxman, denim blues and a red and blue plaid, long sleeved cotton shirt. Their shoes were identical—blue and white running sneakers—Chase having opted for economy over style.

Waxman took another swig from his diet cola, his eyes darting back and forth dubiously at both men over the raised lip of his glass. His mind was still mired in quicksand and an incessant buzzing plagued his hearing. He hadn't said much since emerging from his slumber, choosing instead to remain reticent until he had completely sized up his situation. Like any experienced politician, he learned much from just observing the mannerisms of his opposition. Whether it was during an election debate or arguing for legislation, Waxman could smell doubt or sense apprehension a mile away. His wife had been the same way. In this modern era of ascending to higher office by slinging mud and climbing over the disgraced reputations of your revered adversaries, a candidate who was worth his salt couldn't aspire to any major political position without that intuitive skill.

Taking the last few bites of his sandwich, Waxman's analysis of the two men sitting across from him was ambiguous at best.

Gabe Mitchell...

On the apparent physical side, he's battered to a pulp, so he's obviously not afraid to mix it up, if the situation demands it. But there is a sorrow on his face. His brooding eyes reveal a tormented soul—a tragic manifestation Waxman himself was acutely familiar with.

The old man, Bennett Chase...

He was the wild card in this scenario. Not quite sure of how he fits in here. This was obviously his house, but he doesn't seem like the conspiratorial type. Apply four pounds of pancake makeup and he'd look to be more at home under the big top. Where was the connection between these two men?

Judgment is reserved on him for now.

They were both eyeing him like he was some kind of a science experiment, which would have made anyone feel very self-conscious. Whether it was out of their concern for his well-being, or the fear that he was going to do something drastic, neither man ever appeared to blink.

He decided to try something and held out his drinking glass.

"He wants more soda," Chase said, as the chrome legs of his chair screeched on the floor when he pushed his hefty frame away from the table.

Waxman pulled the glass back, and Chase mistrustfully lowered himself back onto his chair. "What? Now he doesn't want more?"

Gabe raised a swollen eyebrow. "We were staring at you, weren't we?"

Waxman wiped the corner of his mouth clean with a paper towel and pushed his plate away with his thumb. Thankfully, he was able to decipher Gabe's question even through the filter of white noise that droned in his ears. "Yes," he answered simply.

Gabe reached out and put his hand on Chase's shoulder. "We apologize," he said. "We're just glad you're getting your strength back. Is there anything we can get for you, Your Honor?"

Waxman grimaced, massaging his temple. "Aspirin?"

Chase retrieved the drug from a cabinet over the sink filled with pills and medicinal syrups. "Here," he said, taking Waxman's glass, "let me get you something to wash that down with."

Waxman swallowed the pills and, tilting his head back, closed his eyes while he waited for the tablets to take effect. "Please don't call me that," he said, groaning toward the ceiling. "I'm not the mayor anymore."

Gabe leaned forward to begin his interrogation. "Are you up to answering some questions, sir?"

Waxman brought both palms down on the table with a thunderous *slap*. "Am I up to answering questions? Where do I start? In the last 24 hours, I've been shanghaied, had my beloved ship blown to bits, woke hard of hearing with a swarm of bees zipping around inside my head, and found myself dressed like a country bumpkin, and sitting in an air force museum across from one guy who looks like they just dug him out of the ground, and another one who should already know if I'd been naughty or nice." Bits of tuna flew from his lips as his anger reached a fevered pitch. "And you've got the *chutzpah* to want to ask *me* questions? What stops me from walking out that door right now," he said, jabbing a finger toward the living room foyer, "and having you two lunatics turned over to the proper authorities?"

Gabe's countenance turned solid as sheet rock and he said, "I guess I do."

Almost in unison, Chase confirmed that matter-of-factly with a wave of his thumb in Gabe's direction. "I guess he does."

Waxman fell silent for a moment as he considered his odds. He was never much of a fighter, having been taught early in life to use brains over brawn. There really wasn't much of a decision to be made here. This wasn't his home court; this wasn't a political arena. Words had no clout compared to a good left hook, and he quickly came to the conclusion that it probably wouldn't be in his best interest to provoke the man who looked like he had just gone 15 rounds with Evander Holyfield. "Well..." he declared, "I'm not answering any of your questions until I first get some answers of my own."

"Fair enough," Gabe said, easing back in his chair. "Fire away."

The questions came fast and furious and Gabe tried to answer as many as he could, as concisely as he could.

"So you're telling me that both of you have been diagnosed..."

"It's a fact we've both come to terms with, right Bennett?"

The old man nodded in confirmation when Waxman looked over at him. "Spin of the wheel, luck of the deal."

"And that's how you met?"

"In the terminal ward," Gabe said. "It'll create friends in a hurry."

Waxman empathized with both men's situation, but it still didn't excuse what they had done to him. He had to know more, and the questioning went on for almost another hour.

"And you know nothing about this August Bock character?" Waxman asked.

Gabe shrugged. "I was hoping you might be able to shed some light on who he is."

"I've never heard of him either. Despite what the press and half the city might think, I'm just an average guy and I really don't associate with any shady people."

Outside the kitchen window, a garbage truck rumbled to a stop as the regular bi-weekly trash pickup was made. Chase walked over to the window, pushed the blinds to one side, and gave a familiar wave to the garbage collector who waved back.

Waxman rubbed his forehead. Never in his wildest dreams could he have imagined such a thing. "You know, I still can't believe what you're telling me. This is something straight out of a paperback thriller."

"Believe it," Gabe nodded. "Thankfully, we're both living proof that it exists."

"But why would they target me?"

"Because you were acquitted," Chase interrupted from across the room.

Gabe waggled his finger in the air. "You know? That's what I thought at first, Bennett, but the more I think about it..."

Waxman stiffened up defiantly. "Well, I can tell you one thing ... if this Bock joker had bothered to do his research, he would have discovered that I never killed my wife."

"That's exactly what I mean," Gabe said, tapping his finger on the table. "I got the impression that August Bock *was* a very meticulous person. I mean, every detail of his plan to kill you had been precisely worked out. No," he said, a concerned look on his face, "I've got a feeling that there's something else going on here, and for some reason, everything keeps coming back to your wife."

"My wife?" Waxman said, suspiciously.

Gabe's face was twisted in thought as he stood up from the table. "Just hear me out..."

Chase stepped out of Gabe's way as he began to weave around the small kitchen.

"Your wife was a seasoned politician too, right?"

Waxman took another sip of his soda. "She was a state senator ... but she wasn't even running for another term," Waxman added.

Gabe toyed with his inflamed lips as he paced. "This is the part that bothers me: if Bock wanted *you* dead, why was your wife killed first? That's not the way he works. He's not in the business of framing people."

"I don't understand the point you're trying to make."

Gabe tugged on his lips again. "Follow me on this ... if Bock wanted you dead, he could have just sent me, or someone like me, to kill you right from the beginning. That's the way he works. Why did your wife have to die?"

No matter how much Nathan Waxman tried to erase the vision of finding his wife's body nearly torn in half from a shotgun blast, he still shivered at the thought of it. "So you're saying you believe someone else killed my wife?"

Gabe nodded his head. "That's what I'm beginning to think. I think someone needed *both* of you out of the way."

Chase stepped forward. "I think I see where you're going with this, Gabe. Someone wanted the senator dead, and the mayor out of the way too, so they framed him for her murder. And when the jury didn't come through for them..."

Gabe looked across the room at Waxman. "August Bock was brought in."

"This is all too incomprehensible for me," Waxman moaned. "Why would anyone want to kill my Anna?"

"It's a sad fact of life, but politicians are gunned down all the time," Gabe frowned.

Waxman lowered his head and began to rack his brain. "This makes absolutely no sense. Anna didn't have an enemy in the world. If anything, people thought more of *her* than they did me. She was the rock. I was *her* husband. She could have held any office she aspired to, but she had decided to chuck it all and become a full-time mother to our daughter at the end of this term." There was a whimper in his voice. "Why?"

"That's what I intend to find out," Gabe said confidently. "But I need you to promise me that you'll stay put here until I can dig up some answers."

"My daughter," Waxman suddenly realized. "What about my daughter? My God, I've got to speak with her ... got to see her ... she thinks I'm dead!"

Gabe walked over and put his hands firmly on Waxman's shoulders, holding him down in his chair. "I know what you're going through. I've got a son that's her age too. You've just got to give me just a little time. I've got to stop Bock before he kills anyone else."

Waxman swatted away Gabe's hand. "Not seeing your son might be fine for you, Mr. Mitchell, but I'm not going to let your investigation run roughshod over *my* little girl's well-being. She has to know that her daddy's still alive."

Gabe shook his head, never trying to disguise his incredulity with Waxman's callousness. "Don't you understand the situation we're in here? If August Bock finds out you're alive, he'll assume I am too," Gabe said, swatting a dishtowel on the counter. "He's already threatened my son's life to get me to participate in his scheme, so what makes you think he wouldn't go after your daughter to keep *you* quiet? Let me make you a simple guarantee: if you come out of hiding, your daughter and my son are as good as dead."

Waxman frowned. "Your scare tactics don't frighten me, Mr. Mitchell. Throwing my daughter's life in my face is no way to ensure my cooperation."

Gabe looked over at Chase who just shrugged. "Then think about this, sir: I saved your life. Don't you think you owe me something for that?"

Waxman stared down at his hands and then up to the man whose face looked like 40 miles of bad road. His daughter's life was well worth the gamble. "Well, never let it be said that Nathan Waxman wasn't a fair man. You've got 24 hours."

"Forty-eight," Gabe begged. "I still have to go to the hospital later tonight to get more medicine, or I won't be able to function. These next few hours until night falls are a waste for me."

"Thirty-six hours," Waxman comprised, "and then I call my daughter."

Gabe reached out his hand, and the two men shook on their pact.

"Maybe *I* can see that these next few hours aren't wasted," Chase interjected.

"How's that?" Gabe asked.

Chase spread his hands in front of him. "Greetings from the Internet genie. Your wish is my command. Perhaps I can interest you both in some information..."

"You mean over the computer?" Gabe asked.

"Well, despite what you probably think of me, my computer isn't just for downloading porn, my boy. Maybe we can scrounge something up on Mr. August Bock," Chase said disgustedly as he pronounced the name.

"Well, it's better than just sitting around and watching the grass grow," Waxman conceded.

39

All three of them huddled around the computer in the guest room like witches around a cauldron. Chase sat in the squeaking swivel chair with Gabe looking over his shoulder and Waxman a step behind him.

"'Flyboy029?" Gabe asked, pointing to the screen.

"You got a problem with it?" Chase snapped sarcastically.

Gabe pursed his lips. "None whatsoever."

"Where to first?" the old man asked.

"Just look up August Bock by name," Waxman suggested.

Chase typed in the name into the browser. Almost instantaneously, the search engine reported no listings for an August Bock. It came back with an August Brothers, a bread bakery, and an August Max, a restaurant in Broward County, plus even more obscure partial matches.

"Well, that's a big goose egg," Chase said. "What now?"

Gabe turned to Waxman for advice. "You seem to know your way around cyberspace; what do you think?"

"Try the news groups," Waxman said, pointing at the screen. "If there's been something in the newspapers about him, or an article written anywhere, you might track it down there."

Chase shrugged. "Okay, it's worth a shot."

They all stared at the screen like it was an oracle.

Three hits.

"There's three old articles from the *Baltimore Sun* listing an August Bock. They're consecutively listed by date."

"Baltimore?" Gabe said, sounding surprised.

"You want me to pull up the first one?"

"Sure," Gabe said, "how many August Bocks can there possibly be?"

Chase highlighted the first listing and double clicked on his mouse.

"This might take a second; she's old, but she's reliable."

Now all three men were gathered around the screen, holding their collective breaths in anticipation.

"Uh, here we go," Gabe announced as the first newspaper article from the *Baltimore Sun* scrolled onto the screen. It was dated some years earlier. Gabe and Chase begin to read it silently to themselves until Waxman wedged himself between them and began reading aloud the tragic headline. "Baltimore Prosecutor and Wife Gunned Down."

"It seems," Gabe began paraphrasing as he scanned down the article, "that Bock was a successful Federal Prosecutor at one time. On this night he's eating dinner with his wife at some swank harbor side restaurant and, next time he's seen again, his car has been riddled with holes in a deserted warehouse district of the city. When the paramedics arrive, he's barely breathing and his wife is dead."

"How the heck does that happen?" Chase asked.

Gabe shook his head. "Pull up the next one. Maybe it'll tell us more."

The next clipping appeared to be a follow-up. "Here we go," Gabe continued. "According to Bock himself, when he first regained consciousness in the hospital, he pinned the ambush on a repeat felon he failed to convict named Earl Keely."

Waxman shook his head in disgust. "And I thought our local problems were bad. I'm telling you, all of our cities are going to hell on the express train."

Gabe gave a quick biting glance over at Waxman. "You can quit your campaigning, Mr. Mayor. No one here voted for you."

Waxman cleared his throat as Gabe continued to summarize the article aloud. "It says here that Earl Keely was one of those renegade biker types. He was known for his tattoos and disregard for anyone but his fellow gang members and his motorcycle. According to the court records, he'd been tied to over ten rapes and robberies in less a than two year period."

"Sounds like the kind of guy only a mother could love," Chase said under his breath.

"Yeah, a real prince," Waxman added.

Gabe put his finger on the screen and traced it back and forth as he spoke. "Bock tried repeatedly to convict the guy, but Keely kept getting off on technicalities."

"Damned lawyers," Chase grumbled.

"Hey," Waxman said, defensively. "Come on now. We're not all shysters."

"The jury's still out," Chase said, with a wink at Gabe.

"It seems that Bock and Keely had quite a little ground war going on," Gabe said as he read the last paragraph.

"But Keely fired the last shot," Chase sadly surmised.

"This just doesn't sound like the same guy I met on the island," Gabe said as he motioned for Chase to pull up the next article. "I almost feel bad for this guy."

"Keely Still At Large," Waxman read the new headline.

"They never found him," Gabe remarked. "This article is dated a few weeks later and he's still on the loose. One sources speculated that he was heading for Alaska."

"Why Alaska?" Waxman asked.

"Who knows?" Gabe said, jotting the exact spelling of Earl Keely's name on a nearby note pad. "So, at the time of this article, Bock is recovering in the hospital, but he's taken a bullet in the spine, which accounts for the wheelchair, and glass from his car's windshield has irreparably damaged one of his eyes. I can tell you firsthand: his face is still a mangled mess, so he's probably not too keen on plastic surgery."

"Or," Waxman speculated, "perhaps he chose to keep those scars so he wouldn't forget."

Gabe nodded. "That's a possibility too, but do you really think the loss of his wife is enough to send him off on this crazed campaign of his?"

Waxman chuckles.

"What's so funny?"

"Don't you see?" Waxman said, motioning his hand in a circle. "We're three peas in a pod. Bock, you, and me. All three of us have lost our wives, and we're all tortured souls."

Gabe stood up rigidly. "Don't you dare compare me to August Bock."

"No, no, no," Waxman said apologetically, "while I certainly don't condone his methods, believe it or not, I think I almost admire the man for his passion and dedication. Don't you? If you could avenge *your* wife's death, wouldn't you go to the ends of the earth to do it? We all *would*, but in his own twisted way, August Bock is actually doing something about it. Plain and simple: he's killing everyone he believes has gotten away with murder!"

Gabe thought he understood what the ex-mayor was feeling, but could only think of how many people had died, justly or not, because of Bock's perverse passion and dedication.

Gabe asked Chase to clear the screen again, and this time asked him to log onto the actual *Baltimore Sun* newspaper website and had him search their archives under the heading Keely, Earl. One small article appeared, dated two years later than the previous ones. "Assailant's Mutilated Body Found," Gabe read aloud. "Point Barrow, Alaska. The mutilated body of Earl Keely, the biker thought to be responsible for the shotgun ambush of Federal Prosecutor August Bock and his wife, was found in an abandoned fishery by a state trooper. His throat was slit, but this wasn't the most disturbing aspect of his death. There was a 12-inch patch of Keely's chest missing, where police said he sported a large tattoo of a Nazi skull." Gabe read the next line twice to make sure he was correct, as the two other men cringed at the graphic description, "It appeared to have been carved or torn from his chest and was never recovered."

"Revenge is mine saith the Lord," Chase said, humbly.

But Gabe knew better. "Not unless the Lord is sporting red hair nowadays and speaking with an Irish accent," he said sarcastically. "Well, at least that answers one question for us."

"What's that?" Chase asked, as he powered down the computer.

"It means August Bock was *never* hired by anyone to have you assassinated. If what we're postulating is the truth, and Bock is staying true to form, he, like so many others who watched the reports of your trial, thought you had really gotten away with murdering your wife. It must have hit a nerve."

The ex-mayor looked deep in thought. "So you're saying he just came after me on his own?"

Gabe nodded. "Exactly! That's what he does. Bottom line is: I don't think your wife's death and August Bock are even related. And I'm sure whoever killed her, and tried to frame you for the murder, is eternally grateful for his help!"

Bennett Chase swiveled around in his chair and rested his arms on his stomach. "So, we're still minus one mystery guest in this whole mess. Got any, pardon the pun, *candidates*?"

"No," Gabe said with a renewed sense of determination, "but I intend to find out."

"So, what's the plan?" Waxman asked.

"Well, Your Honor," Gabe said, as he lead both men out of the darkened bedroom, "I think it's time for us dead guys to kick some ass."

40

The hours that followed were filled with solemn introspection, sound bites from the local news channels, Quarter Pounders from McDonalds, and, for Gabe, shivers and night sweats. His system was beginning to shut down, and the cover of darkness couldn't have come too soon. His eyes were sunken and surrounded with pale red rings, and his skin had taken on a bluish-ashen shade that foreshadowed future circulation problems.

"Are you sure you don't want me to drive you?" Chase asked, dangling his key ring on the end of his finger. "You don't look so hot."

"Multiply that times a hundred, and that's how I feel," Gabe said, snatching the keys. "I think you should stay here with the mayor and wait for me."

Chase took a sip from his soda and covered his mouth to stifle a burp. "You're just going to get the medication and then come right back, right?"

"That's the plan," Gabe insisted. "I called Sanborn's office at the hospital and he's working late tonight. He just has to write me a prescription, and then I'm heading back. Believe me: I don't want to be there any longer than I have to. I've had my fill of hospitals."

"Amen to that," the old man concurred.

In front of the television set, Nathan Waxman took the last bite of his hamburger. "I wish you two would stop addressing me as 'Mayor.' I don't hold that office anymore, and hearing you call me that makes me feel very pretentious. Call me Nathan or even Nate, but please, no more Mayor, or Mr. Mayor, or even Your Honor. Suddenly it feels dirty."

"I don't have a problem with that," Chase admitted. "I always thought it was kind of pompous, myself."

Gabe didn't say anything as he examined the keys on the ring until he found the ignition key. He would have a tough time referring to Nathan Waxman by anything other than his official title. It was something to be proud of—a sign of respect. "Time for me to go."

The old man ushered Gabe back through the kitchen to a door which led into the garage. Opening the door and reaching around the wall, he tugged on a chain that illuminated a single yellow light bulb. Immediately, the odor accosted Gabe's nose. The garage smelled from old oil and musty blankets. "She's been around the block a few times," Chase said like a loving parent as he pointed to the rust-pitted body of the 1984 Chrysler, "but it's what's in her heart that counts."

Gabe shuddered. "Do I need to get shots before I climb in there?"

"Make all the jokes you want, but she'll get you there and back in one piece. And, take my word as an old fighter pilot: that's all that ever matters."

Gabe walked around to the far side of the car and unlocked the door. He pulled on the handle, but the door wouldn't budge.

"Sometimes she sticks," Chase called from the opened doorway. "Just give her a little elbow grease and she'll pop right open."

Gabe propped his right foot up against the car's molding and yanked. The door squealed open.

"There you go."

Gabe shot his friend a skeptical glance before climbing inside.

"The garage door opener is on the visor," Chase called out.

"You've been through too much to die in this bucket of bolts," Gabe mumbled to himself as he crossed his fingers and slipped the key into the ignition.

The old Chrysler coughed to life, with the radio blasting out "Flight of the Valkyries" from the cassette deck, an inspirational tape Chase always listened to while either behind the wheel or in the cockpit. Gabe fumbled with the radio to squelch the music and then reached up and pressed the button that raised the garage door. As the old Chrysler pulled out into the brisk South Florida night, Bennett Chase flashed Gabe a 'thumbs up'—his way of wishing good fortune.

41

The old man had been right. After the old Chrysler warmed up, she drove as smooth as a brand new car. It was only a 15 minute ride to Jackson Medical Center from Chase's home, along a circuitous route Gabe knew would avoid the major traffic thoroughfares. As he drove past landmarks he had seen countless times before, they all seemed different to him. Perhaps because, for the first time, he was *really* noticing them. He felt like a stranger in a familiar land, appreciating everything around him, soaking it all in, committing it all to memory so he wouldn't forget what it was like to have been *alive* here. The Cuban cafeterias with their Latin music blaring so loud, you could tap your feet to the frantic rhythms nearly a block away. Street vendors selling everything from bags of limes and lemons to charred mystery meat on wooden skewers ... it all smelled so wonderful. Overhead, the city's Metrorail train system glided by, transporting its faceless passengers to the concrete and glass spires of downtown Miami. In the distance, the bright lights of the city, glittering like a million chandeliers with their colors only limited to one's imagination, gave this routine night its carnival-like atmosphere. Gabe didn't realize it, but he was grinning uncontrollably, awestruck by its majestic beauty, like a newborn child.

One of the largest publicly funded hospitals and teaching facilities in the entire United States, Jackson Medical Center's reputation for quality care and its elite staff are unparalleled in every field of medicine. With campuses and satellite centers spread out over the whole city, its primary facility is a complex of towers and buildings that house both hospital patients as well as medical offices, situated on the western side of downtown Miami. It was an office on the fourth floor of the main 10-story building that Gabe was interested in.

As he guided the old Chrysler into one of the hospital's covered garages, Gabe tore a stub from the automated ticket dispenser and began hunting for a parking spot. On the third level, he finally found a vacancy. Pulling into the space, he made a mental note of the color and level number he was parked on. When he shut down the engine, the car back-fired twice and sizzled for a full 30 seconds before falling silent.

Gabe climbed out of the car and the brisk wind seemed to intensify, chilling Gabe to his very core. The swirling breeze howled through the structure, making a sad, lamentable sound that made Gabe want to pick up his pace. Walking as quickly as he could, he continually clenched and unclenched his fists to keep the circulation and feeling in his fingers going. Even under the harsh glare of the florescent lights, Gabe could see that the skin under his fingernails was turning blue. He needed his medication ... and soon.

There was no entrance into the hospital from this level, so Gabe had to take the elevator up one floor. The warmth of the enclosed lift was a welcome respite, giving Gabe brief chance to thaw his bones. The doors opened and he stepped past two women, probably a mother and her daughter, who had obviously been crying. Gabe remained silent, but tried to look understanding as he used his arm to block the door from closing before the mourners had made it inside. *God, how he hated hospitals.*

The acridly antiseptic smell of the hospital accosted Gabe's nostrils the instant he pushed through the glass doors. A staccato chime was tolling over the speaker system, and like the ultra-high pitched frequency of a dog whistle, it appeared that only the hospital's staff cocked their heads to heed it. Gabe never remembered being aware of it during his stay; he was sure it was always there, calling *someone* to go *somewhere*, but he'd never really paid attention to it ... until now.

A large digital clock hanging over the nurses' station read 8:35. Gabe tried to avoid eye contact with the two nurses manning the desk as he pressed the "down button" on the elevator. He could feel one of them staring at him, and he instinctively kept his back turned to her and jabbed at the button, hoping, but knowing, it would do nothing to increase the speed of the lift's descent.

"Are you alright, sir?" came a gentle voice from behind.

Gabe did his best to ignore her.

"Sir ... are you feeling alright?"

"Hmmm?" muttered Gabe naively. "Were you talking to me?"

The nurse, a young blond with that "extra perky" smile and deep blue eyes came around from behind the desk. "Yes, sir. You look peaked. Are you okay?"

Gabe gouged at the lit elevator button hard enough to almost splinter his fingernail. "Just a bit under the weather tonight. That's why I'm here. Came to see my doctor."

The nurse moved around to Gabe's left, but he turned away not wanting her to get a good look at him. "May I ask your doctor's name?" she asked suspiciously.

Why the hell is taking this elevator so long?

"Sanborn," Gabe said, his nose nearly pressed against the cold silver doors.

This answer seemed to appease the nurse. "Ah, Dr. Sanborn. His office is on the fourth floor ... one floor down."

Gabe growled between clenched teeth. "Yes, I know."

A bell chimed and the doors hissed open, but not soon enough for Gabe. Thankfully the lift was empty, or he would have trampled any passengers as he rushed inside.

"Have a good evening," the nurse called out as the doors slid closed. "And feel better."

It wasn't like Gabe to snap like that. His nerves were frayed, and his entire body was trembling like he was a junkie going through the symptoms of withdrawal. As the lift came to a stop, Gabe touched his palms to his face and realized they were like two slabs of ice.

Stepping out of the elevator, he cupped his hands around his mouth and blew into his fists to warm them. *It's like the Arctic Circle in this place.*

There was no nurses' station on this floor, just offices and what appeared to be storage and examination rooms. Hanging on the wall across the hallway was a directory. Gabe quickly scanned the listing and found Sanborn, Kenneth ... 422. There would be no need for skulking around here; with the exception of a two man janitorial crew shampooing the carpeting, Gabe couldn't see anyone else. When he had anonymously phoned the hospital earlier in the evening, he had been told that Sanborn would be in his office until 9:00 P.M. Gabe just prayed a medical emergency hadn't changed all that.

This floor was so disorienting. Like spokes on a wheel, darkened corridors spread out from a central hub. With the drone of the shampooing machine rumbling through his head, Gabe identified the correct hallway.

A few landscaping plants would do a lot for this place, Gabe thought as he padded down the sterile passageway. "416 ... 418 ... 420," he counted under his breath.

A sliver of light illuminated the pale green carpet beneath the door to room 422. Gabe put his ear up to the door and listened, but heard nothing. He took hold of the door knob and twisted ... it was unlocked. Knocking as he entered, Gabe found himself in an empty outer office. A single desk lamp illuminated a small work station. Three walls were adorned with the same nondescript artwork found in most receptionists' cubicles, while the fourth wall, which separated this room from Sanborn's office, was manufactured out of frosted glass. All Gabe could make out behind it were a few vague shapes and some distorted shadows. He thought it was a very unsettling effect for a doctor's office. As he stepped further into the receptionist's quarters, there was a picture on the desk, a family portrait, none of which was of Kenneth Sanborn.

From the main office came a shuffling of papers and the creak of a chair.

"Dr. Sanborn?" Gabe called out.

A voice responded from behind the glass wall. "Yes, who's there? It's after office hours."

Gabe poked his head around the doorway and found Sanborn sitting at his desk, opening his mail with a fancy pewter letter opener. This office was dark as well, except for a lamp on the doctor's desk which illuminated a small framed photograph of Sanborn and his wife. "Someone forget to pay the electric bill in this place?" Gabe asked.

Sanborn still hadn't looked up from his mail as he exhaled a weary sigh. He assumed he was just talking to one of the cleaning crew. "This is the only chance for peace and quiet I get after a day full of surgeries and I cherish the solitude and subdued lighting. If you'll come back in about 15 minutes, my garbage will be ready. I'm just going through the last of my mail."

"I think you've mistaken me for someone else, Doc."

Sanborn looked up and squinted into the darkness. Gabe's face was shrouded in shadow. The doctor reached across his desk and bent the neck of the desk lamp to shine its focus on the visitor.

Gabe covered his eyes from the glare of the beam. "Remember me, Doc?"

The letter opener dropped out of the doctor's hand. Pale astonishment fell upon Sanborn's face, and his entire body began to tremble uncontrollably. "This ... this is impossible," he stammered. "You ... you're supposed to be dead!"

"Dead?" Gabe countered. "Hey, I'm sorry to disappoint you, Doc, but wasn't it *you* that told me I still had six months to live?"

Sanborn seemed confused and began looking around the room like he was searching for another exit. His finger waggled at Gabe nervously as his breathing began to come in gasps. "The yacht blew up! I saw it on the television! I saw it with my own two eyes! You were supposed to have been killed in the blast!"

Gabe entire body went rigid. What was going on here? How did Sanborn know about his involvement with *Mystique*? It was impossible ... he couldn't have known. There was nothing on the news tying him to the explosion. Gabe's mind was calculating and shifting events and ideas around like slats on a Chinese puzzle box. Somewhere, all of this fit. *Of course! Bock would need a connection in the medical profession to help him procure terminal recruits. Who better than someone who deals with them on a daily basis?*

Gabe's only purpose here tonight had been to acquire more medication, and suddenly he found himself staring into the frightened eyes of someone who knew way too much. The pills could wait. Gabe needed to play out this hand. He stepped further into the office. "I think we need to talk, Doc."

Out of the corner of his eye, the doctor found where the pewter letter opener had landed on his desk, and subtly covered the blade with his right hand. Sweat beaded up on his forehead and his fingers raised to fiddle with his collar as if it were five sizes too small. "I have nothing to say to you," he said as he eased his high-backed chair away from the desk. "Now you'd better leave before I call hospital security."

Gabe held up his hands innocently. "Sure Doc. Don't get your stethoscope in a knot. I'll leave..." He turned to the door, but, instead of retreating, Gabe closed the door and clicked the lock shut. "...when hell freezes over."

"What ... are you doing?" Sanborn quavered.

"Take a good look at me, Doc," Gabe said as he walked closer into the spotlight from the desk lamp. "Do I look like a guy who's in the mood to screw around? I want some answers, and I want them now!"

Sanborn reached for the phone, but Gabe was surprisingly quick as he yanked the receiver out of the doctor's hand and ripped the cord out of the wall. "Sorry, Doc. Security's not coming."

Sanborn pulled his hand back ever so slowly, keeping the letter opener secreted beneath it. "I don't know what you want from me. I just did whatever they told me to do."

Gabe put both hands on Sanborn's desk and leaned across it menacingly. He was at the end of his physical strength, but this new disclosure seemed to pump a little gas into his tank. How deep did this conspiracy run? *How is it that August Bock could have manipulated every event, every nuance of his life?* Gabe would have to start thinking on a different plane ... believing that everyone was now under Bock's influence. Who could he trust? August Bock was a more than just a madman—he was a deadly virus that infected everything and left no one unsusceptible. "You know I've got nothing to lose, Doc, so don't play games with me. How long have you been working with August Bock?"

Sanborn tried to put up on an intrepid facade, but his voice couldn't mask his desperation. "I don't know who that is, or what you're talking about."

Gabe leaned back and took a long dramatic pause. Years of breaking alibis across an interrogation table had made him a master in the subtle techniques of intimidation. Slowly, he began to walk around the desk, tapping his fingers across its surface as he closed in on his cowering prey. "Ehhh," he said, imitating the sound of a buzzer. "Wrong answer, Doc. Strike one." Gabe grabbed a stapler off Sanborn's desk and sent it flying across the room into one of those amorphous pieces of artwork. The glass in the frame shattered into a thousand fragments. "Two more strikes and you're out," he snarled. "You want to try again? Tell me about your association with August Bock."

Sanborn had pressed himself so far back into his chair, there surely had to be two rows of button impressions on his spine. "I have no idea what you're talking about," he faltered.

"Ehhh," Gabe buzzed again. "Strike two." He picked up a trash can by his feet and heaved it through the opaque glass wall separating Sanborn's office from the receptionist's. The subsequent crash was loud ... too loud. Unless the cleaning crew was deaf, they must have heard it. Gabe would have to pick up the tempo. He grabbed Sanborn by his red paisley tie and jerked him out of his chair. They stood eye to eye, doctor to patient, conspirator to victim. "I'm through dancing with you, Doc," Gabe hissed. "Now it's time to fess up. Was August Bock using you to recruit terminal patients like me? Tell me the truth, or I swear I'll knock your nose so far down your throat, you'll have to breathe through your ears."

"Not like you," Sanborn stuttered.

Gabe didn't understand. "What does that mean, *not like me*?"

With the speed of a striking snake, the letter opener came out ... arching upward at Gabe's abdomen. Gabe pivoted to his right as the blade ran up the front of his shirt and glanced off the bottom of his chin. Blood oozed from the inch-long gash along his jaw line, but his adrenaline was pumping far too fast for him to feel the sting of the exposed wound. With lightning reflexes of his own, Gabe caught Sanborn's wrist before the blade could make another pass.

The doctor was out of his chair, forcing Gabe back onto his desk, the tip of the letter opener pointing directly between Gabe's eyes.

Gabe was on the defensive. Bent awkwardly backward and losing more precious energy-giving blood every second, his options were few.

Sanborn was grinning like a jackal, his face flushed beet-red, his eyes filled with frenzied fanaticism. "Maybe this time," he grunted, "you'll stay dead!"

Gabe had both arms locked straight out above him, the blade poised at their apex like the sword of Damocles. He had no leverage—only the waning strength of depleted muscles ... but his head was hitting something. He tilted his head back and caught a glimpse of the desk lamp ... he had to go for it ... it was now or never.

Gabe's right hand came off Sanborn's wrist, and, in what seemed like slow motion, the blade started its downward sweep. Gabe had the lamp by its neck and swung it outward, catching Sanborn square on the side of his head with the heavy chrome base. The letter opener never hit its mark as the doctor screamed in pain and stumbled backward, tripping over his chair in the process. The cord from the lamp snapped out of the wall and the office was filled only with what meager light managed to filter in through the broken window to the outer office.

Gabe could hear Sanborn crawling to get away, but until his pupils fully adjusted to the darkness, the doctor may as well have been invisible. Gabe held his breath and listened. Sanborn was prone on his stomach, wriggling toward the office door like a miner crawling through a tunnel. Light glinted off the letter opener Sanborn was still clutching in his hand, and it caught Gabe's attention. Throwing all thoughts of self-preservation to the wind, Gabe dove for the fleeing doctor and grabbed him around the waist. Together the pair continued their struggle with the blade. Rolling back and forth across the floor, the two men fought. Just a few short weeks ago, Gabe would have had no problem drubbing a weaker adversary, but with all of his vitality robbed by his illness, even fending off someone as uncoordinated as Sanborn was proving to be more than a handful for him.

Gabe could feel the letter opener between them, pressing against his stomach. Sanborn was on top of him, forcing the blade downward with all of his strength. Gabe was gasping for every breath, his fists locked around Sanborn's, the veins on his forearms protruding like drinking straws, not letting the makeshift weapon get any closer.

"You have to die," Sanborn strained. "You can't even begin to understand what you're up against." He was straddling Gabe on the floor, but the standoff was taking its toll on a set of arms that was more used to performing delicate surgeries than hand-to-hand combat. He needed more leverage. Flexing his knees, he rose up, enabling him to apply more of his bodyweight behind the blade. This was also his fatal mistake.

Gabe felt the weight lift off his body, and, with crushing power, brought his right knee up into Sanborn's now vulnerable groin area. No one, with the possible exception of a pregnant woman in her 30th hour of labor, could commiserate with the sheer torture a man feels when he's had his crackers crumbled. Sanborn's eyes rolled back into their sockets as he face contorted in pain. In a decisive, swift movement, Gabe pulled down on the doctor's hands, guiding the letter opener into Sanborn's own stomach. The rounded blade tore through the fabric of his lab coat and clothing, and buried itself to the hilt in the soft tissue above his abdomen. Blood gushed from the puncture as Gabe yanked his hands free.

Kenneth Sanborn reared back and howled like a dying sea serpent. The horrifying expression on his face was a mixture of disbelief and agony. His fingers clutched for the handle of the letter opener, but barely half an inch of it was left protruding from his stomach. His entire body began to shudder as his life drained out in an ever spreading crimson stain on the front of his white coat. "Maybe ... maybe it's better this way," he sputtered as he began to cough up blood. "I deserve this ... for what I've put you through."

Gabe was panting like a pack mule. "I'm not letting you off that easy," he said, gently lifting the doctor's head off the floor. "You're telling me what I want to know, or I'm calling for help, and you'll spend the rest of your life in jail receiving rectal exams from an inmate named Butch."

Sanborn's head flopped to one side, and Gabe knew all of his harsh threats were futile. The doctor would never live to see the inside of a prison cell.

"Come on, Doc. Talk to me," Gabe urged as he cradled Sanborn's head in his hands. "What did you mean when you said *not like me*?"

The doctor gurgled; his teeth were coated with blood. "My wife ... killed by a drunk driver. The bastard who did it ... set free. I had to do something..." He clutched in vain at Gabe's arm. "Had ... to do something."

Gabe wiped away a stream of blood that was dripping down the side of the doctor's face. "And that's how you met up with August Bock?"

One of Sanborn's eyes flickered open. It was so filled with blood, Gabe could no longer tell what color it was. "A woman."

"Shayla Rand."

Sanborn nodded ever so slightly. "Made a deal. I'd do anything..."

Gabe leaned down and placed his mouth right next to Sanborn's ear. "And in exchange for murdering the man who killed your wife, you gave them..."

Doctor Kenneth Sanborn looked up bleary eyed at Gabe and said one last blood-curdling word before he died: "You."

42

In moments, the cleaning crew would discover Sanborn's body. Gabe had to think quick. There was no time to ponder over the doctor's cryptic confession, or to wonder how he would get his hands on more medication. Gabe's mind was such a jumble, he wasn't even sure what kind or dosage of medication he was taking.

Lining the far wall of the office was a row of filing cabinets. If there was a folder in there with his name on it, perhaps it held some answers. If he could just get the name of his pills, maybe he could find another way to get a prescription filled.

The cabinets were all alphabetized, making it a snap to locate his folder. But, in his haste, Gabe was getting careless and didn't realize he was leaving a trail of blood every time he touched a fresh surface. Gingerly, his fingers danced over the file tabs in the cabinet marked "Mc – Mo." Mickens ... Miller ... Mintzer ... Miranda ... Gabe, Gabe. But, to his surprise, there were two folders with his name on them. He pulled them both out.

Gabe walked over to the doorway and held open the files in the light. Giving the contents of each folder a quick going over, nothing appeared peculiar. Not that he would have been able to spot anything out of the ordinary—it all looked like medical mumbo-jumbo to him.

Except ... one word that was repeated highlighted in yellow marker in the second folder: *Digitoxin*. Gabe might not have been able to remember the name of the medicine he was taking, but he was sure that Digitoxin wasn't it. And something else he found puzzling—in the same folder, there was a business card stapled inside the back cover. It was a simple beige card containing the rendering of an 18-wheeler, the name of what appeared to be a freight company, and its toll-free phone number embossed in gold filigree. It read:

Worldwide Dispatch Incorporated
(800) 555-7700

Why would his doctor have the business card from some cargo hauler attached to his medical records? Gabe looked down at the Sanborn's lifeless body and shook his head regretfully. Another victim who'd fallen prey to Bock's heinous plot. So many answers had died with him. He was probably a good husband who was blinded by the love for his wife, and one of the most powerful aphrodisiacs known to man: revenge.

Gabe studied the card again for a long moment, but, in his mind's disoriented state, he never deciphered the play on words. He wouldn't have the time to make the connection either, because more trouble was on the way—the faint chatter of voices coming down the corridor. Once they found the body, all hell would surely break loose.

Tucking the two manila folders into his waistband behind his back, Gabe hustled into the outer office and hid behind the opened door to the hallway. His heart was thumping a mile a minute as he heard them standing just outside the office. There were two of them, and they spoke to each other in broken English with thick Spanish accents.

"Ay Dios," Gabe overheard one say. "Did you hear about that football player, J.R. Jackson?"

Seconds later, a vacuum cleaner was turned on and their conversation turned into a shouting match as the men tried to be heard over the droning machine. "He got what was coming to him," the one pushing the vacuum yelled. "The Lord ... he works in mysterious ways!"

"Ay Dios," the first one shuddered, "no one deserves to die like that."

There was two ways Gabe could handle this: wait here for something to happen, or take matters into his own hands. The decision was an easy one; time was no longer a commodity to be wasted.

Gabe pulled the files out of his trousers and took a deep breath. There was blood all over his clothes, but if he moved fast enough and looked official enough, he might just get away with it. He tucked the folders under his arm, grabbed hold of the doorknob and stepped out into the corridor, closing the office door behind him. "Good evening, gentlemen," Gabe said to them, as he brusquely shoved his way between them.

* * * * * *

The worker pushing the vacuum paid no attention to the stranger—he just gave a wave of his hand and continued humming a song to himself. But the janitor doing the dusting was another matter. He only glimpsed the stranger from behind, and probably wouldn't have thought twice about him, until he wiped down the doorknob and his dust rag came away smeared with blood.

"Orlando. *ORLANDO*," he shouted. "Apaga la maquina (shut off the machine)! Mira esto (look at this)," he said franticly in his native tongue, and waving the discolored rag in his co-worker's face.

Both men looked at each other unsure of how to handle the situation. "Look inside the office," Manny said.

Manny shook his head. "You look, Orlando."

Orlando held out his hand. "Give me the rag. I do not want to touch anything. I learned that on the television."

"Sí, es muy astuto (Yes, that's very smart)."

Like he was wrapping the cloth around an eggshell, Orlando slipped the rag around the doorknob and turned it. Apprehensively, he peeked inside the outer office with his co-worker bobbing and weaving behind him, trying to get his own glimpse through the doorway.

43

Gabe was rounding the landing between the fifth and fourth floors when the chimes began to toll like a slot machine paying off a jackpot. There was no doubt in his mind—the cleaning crew had found the corpse. Far below, down the coil of concrete stairs, he could hear the echoes of metal doors opening and slamming shut, and the rapid clattering of running feet. He wasn't going to make it.

Upon reaching the fourth floor exit, Gabe pushed ever so slightly on the bar that released the door. He could only see down the corridor in one direction, but at least there was no sign of security ... yet. Unfortunately, the direction Gabe was looking was the opposite way of the parking garage. All he could see were numbered patient rooms and one door marked "linen storage." At the far end of the hallway, he spotted the same young blond nurse who had hassled him at the elevator, but she appeared to be preoccupied with helping an elderly patient back into her room. Gabe let the door close again.

The footsteps in the stairwell were growing louder, and now they were accompanied by heavy, commanding voices barking out instructions. He couldn't just stand here and let himself be captured. It was at this critical moment of decision that Gabe noticed the blood on the outside of the file folders. Then, for the first time, he glanced down at his soiled clothes and scowled forlornly. He may as well have been wearing a neon sign that flashed *"Here I am, boys. Come and get me."*

There was nowhere to run. Going back up to the fifth floor was crazy, and it would only be a matter of minutes before the police arrived and sealed off every exit ... time to improvise.

Gabe cracked the door again and got his bearing on the door labeled "linen storage." He prayed it housed more than just neatly folded bed sheets and dinner napkins. Shoving open the heavy metal door, he made a beeline across the hallway for the storage room. Head down and hunched over, it was the quickest 50 feet Gabe had ever traversed.

Gabe burst inside the room, which was more like a closet, and felt around for the light switch. When he finally found it and flipped it on, he realized he had struck the mother lode. First aid kits, lab coats, operating greenies—everything he would need. He spun around and locked the door behind him. He had to work quick.

His clothes were the first to go. He removed the few dollars he had brought with him for parking from his pocket, and then balled up the clothes and shoved them into a red garbage bag labeled *"Medical Waste."* He quickly found a set of teal green operating scrubs and put them on. No sooner had he tightened the pants' drawstring than he moved on to the first aid kits. He popped open several of them before he found one with a mirror attached to the inside lid. The face that stared back at him in the glass was too pathetic for words, but there was still a glimmer flickering in those eyes ... maybe it was from the excitement of one last chase, but that flicker of fire was definitely still in there.

Gabe leaned his head back and swabbed clean the gash below his chin. The combination of denatured alcohol meeting raw flesh was enough to make a tear come to the eyes of even the most rugged of men. Gabe had to bite down hard on his lower lip to quell the urge to scream. He used five more alcohol drenched swabs to remove the blood from his neck and hands. By the time Gabe was done, the red garbage bag was nearly filled to bursting. Rummaging one last time through the shelves of clothing, he came across boxes of paper bonnets, face masks and booties. They would be perfect to complete his disguise. He tucked his hair under the paper cap and slipped the booties over his sneakers. Actually wearing the face mask might draw too much attention, so he just tied it loosely around his neck and let it dangle there, in case he needed it. Before he switched off the light, Gabe jammed the loaded garbage bag behind one of the metal shelves and covered it up with a stack of bed sheets. There was no doubt that someone would eventually find it, but he made sure it would take them quite a while.

Gabe emerged from the storage room looking like a surgeon who had just stepped out of the operating theater. He switched the order of the medical folders so that the bloody covers were a little less obvious. Now all he had to do was make it less than 100 yards to the doors the led out to the parking garage.

He walked quickly, but not so much as to look like he was rushing. Walking in paper boots was obviously an acquired skill, one that Gabe had yet to refine. He nearly slipped twice as his feet fumbled for traction. What Gabe didn't know was, the paper boots were usually the first thing a surgeon removed after his gloves and mask when he left the operating room. They were designed for hygienic purposes only, not for quick getaways.

Gabe was just passing the nurses' station when two uniformed patrolmen stepped out of the elevator. They stood in the corridor directly blocking Gabe's exit. Gabe came to a grinding halt and, turning his back to them, began studiously flipping through his folders as though he was searching for something important. Out of the corner of his eye, he watched the two patrolmen talking amongst themselves. One pointed in one direction, the other pointed toward Gabe. *This wasn't good.*

"Excuse me, doctor," the one walking toward Gabe called out. "Can I talk to you a minute?"

Gabe tried not to panic. Holding up the clean side of the folders to block his face, Gabe stepped toward the closest room he could find. "Not now officer," he said, trying to sound as harried as most doctors usually were. "I'm busy with a patient."

Out of the frying pan and into the fire. Gabe found himself in the midst of a quorum of young interns huddled around the bed of an old woman. Everyone turned to look at Gabe as he burst through the door—even the old woman.

"Good evening, doctor," they all said in unison.

Gabe nodded seriously as the door opened behind him and the patrolman popped his head in. "I said I was with a patient!" Gabe snarled, kicking the door closed, almost decapitating the meddlesome officer. "There's some big emergency up on five," Gabe said, with an indifferent shrug.

One of the interns, a young Asian girl, handed Gabe a metal clipboard containing the patient's medical chart. "Here is Mrs. Applebaum's chart, Doctor..."

"Uh ... Bennett," Gabe came up with. "But I'm not here to assist you on your rounds." He said, looking down at his own files. He had a brainstorm. "Your attending physician will be here momentarily I'm sure." Gabe hoped to God it wouldn't be too momentarily. "I'm just here to see which of you bright young doctors has the sharpest diagnostic skills."

They all looked at each other curiously. An overweight young man standing at the head of the bed was the first to break the skeptical silence. "But we're with a patient, Doctor. Don't you think we should address Mrs. Applebaum's prognosis first?"

Cop, doctor—it didn't matter. The skill of intimidation was all the same. "What's your name, doctor?" Gabe growled.

The chubby intern swallowed hard. "Caputo, sir. Ellis Caputo."

Gabe tore a ball point pen from the pocket of the young Asian doctor and pretended to write down the name. "Anyone else agree with *Doctor* Caputo?"

It was like he was staring at the statues on Easter Island. No one budged, no one inhaled. "I didn't think so," Gabe said, walking up to the foot of the bed and patting the old woman on the ankle. "You don't mind if I borrow these young doctors for a minute, do you Mrs. Applebaum?" Gabe didn't wait for an answer. He turned and walked toward the door, pushed it open and ushered the small group of interns out into the hall. "We can talk and walk at the same time, okay?"

Stepping into the corridor, they all looked at each other and then back at the door to Mrs. Applebaum's room. The hallway was jammed with hospital security and patrolmen. Gabe huddled the young doctors around him and began making his way toward the exit leading to the garage. "How's your knowledge of medicines, Caputo?" Gabe asked.

The overweight intern was anxious to have his name erased from wherever Gabe had written it. "Give me your best shot, Doctor Bennett."

"Digitoxin. What is it? What does it do?"

Caputo never hesitated. "Digitoxin. Used for congestive heart failure to regulate the heart rhythm."

Congestive heart failure? That made no sense. "Anybody else?" Gabe asked.

The Asian girl spoke up. "An overdose can cause nausea, vomiting, diarrhea, blurred vision and cardiac disturbances, such as tachycardia and premature contractions."

Gabe didn't realize it, but he had stopped moving. Sanborn's words came racing back to him in a flood of thoughts. When he asked the doctor about the recruitment of terminal patients like himself, Sanborn had said "*not like you.*"

"Let me ask you another question," he said, glancing from one young attentive face to the next. "I'm going to throw a hypothetical at you, and tell me what you think..."

They hung on each of his words.

"If you wanted to make someone *think* they were dying, would Digitoxin do the trick?"

"But why would anyone want to do that?" Caputo asked.

"Hypothetically, Ellis," Gabe snarled. "Would Digitoxin be your drug of choice?"

The Asian woman interrupted. "There are others that might work better, but yes, I guess Digitoxin would do the job ... as long as you regulated the absorption rate. I mean, you give the person too much at one time," she said, snapping her fingers, "and it's all over."

"What's your name?" Gabe asked.

"Hayashi. Nancy Hayashi."

"Okay then Doctor Hayashi. How would you administer the drug?"

Hayashi looked over a Caputo and the others. "I'd grind a pill into their food, I guess."

"Or use the liquid form and mix it in a drink," Caputo chimed in.

"But it would have to be a sweet drink, like a sweet soda to mask the bitterness," Hayashi added.

Gabe's mind was working like a Rubik's Cube. Suddenly, all of the colors were clicking into perfect alignment...

Creme soda ... his favorite! How many of them had he downed over the last month? How many times had that waitress at Strofsky's plied him with sodas free of charge... Oh, dear God! Could it be? The Irish accent ... of course it was her! Shayla Rand was the old waitress working at Strofsky's! Didn't old man Strofsky say that she had quit right after he went into the hospital? It all made perfect sense now.

This whole thing had been a set up from the get-go. He was never dying of a brain tumor—they were systematically poisoning him so that he'd believe he was dying of a brain tumor! But wait ... I thought they only use terminal patients for their operations? Maybe they couldn't find someone that was actually dying that met all of their requirements. Of course, that had to be it! If you can't get someone who's actually dying, do the next best thing: find someone who's just lost most of his family and has no reason to live. They had done their research well ... in that respect, he was the perfect candidate!

Gabe didn't know whether to do a back flip or fall to his knees and thank the Almighty for this reprieve. All that mattered now was that he was going to see his son grow up after all. There were no words that could do justice to the delirium that enveloped his heart. It filled every fiber of his being with a newfound energy that seemed to reinvigorate him.

Gabe grabbed Nancy Hayashi by the shoulders and spun her to face him. "The treatment for Digitoxin poisoning ... what's the antidote?"

She looked over at Caputo. "Uh ... that would be tannic acid, right?"

Caputo nodded. "That's right. Flush the system with tannic acid."

Gabe turned his head toward the chubby doctor. "Tannic acid?"

"Tea," Caputo said, suspiciously.

"Tea?" Gabe asked, excitedly. "You mean like ... regular tea ... tea?"

"Yeah," the overweight intern concurred as his eyes narrowed and his hands went to his hips. "Regular tea ... tea."

"So just drink lots and lots of it?"

"Who the fuck are you?" Caputo asked gruffly.

"Excuse me?"

"You're no doctor. Who the hell are you?"

Gabe began to slowly back away from the group, trying to look and sound as unassuming as possible. "Well, you've been a very helpful group of young doctors. I wish you all the best in your medical careers." Spinning around in his paper shoes, Gabe slipped and nearly collided with the wall. Enough was enough; clumsily, he tore the fabric off his sneakers and bolted for the exit just ahead of him.

Gabe exploded through the doors and ran into the bracing night air. The cold no longer chilled him to the marrow, though, as a new warmth pumped through every tissue in his body. It was amazing how a single hour could change a person's life. Just knowing that his destiny was no longer predetermined put a spring in his step that had been missing for months.

As he raced across the catwalk that led to the parking structure, Gabe glanced over the railing at the squad of patrol cars that had already surrounded the main building. A battalion of officers were bathed in the red and blue flashing lights from the roofs of their vehicles. From his bird's-eye perch, they looked so small and insignificant as they scrambled from place to place ... but Gabe knew better. He wasn't out of the woods quite yet.

There would be no taking the elevator this time; Gabe felt too spry. It was only one flight down, and he vaulted the stairs two at a time. When he reached Chase's old Chrysler, he popped open the trunk and found a tool box. All he needed was a screwdriver, but he had to work quick. Less than a minute later, he had removed the license plate off the car in the next parking stall and affixed it to the rear bumper of the Chrysler. Then he tossed Chase's original plate and his medical folders into the trunk and put the screwdriver back in the tool box. Now the car was untraceable.

Climbing behind the wheel, Gabe turned the key in the ignition and the Chrysler backfired twice before chugging to life. A plume of foul gray smoke blossomed from the tailpipe of the old car. If he needed to make a run for it, Gabe thought, this would be the shortest hot pursuit in the annals of law enforcement. Down and around in a never-ending spiral, Gabe drove cautiously until he reached the toll booth. He found the parking ticket above his visor and handed it to the attendant.

"Why didn't you park in the employee lot?" the attendant asked, noticing Gabe's hospital garb.

"My other car's in the shop and it had my parking decal on it."

"You could have gotten a temporary at the security office, you know."

Gabe tried not to sound impatient. "It's no big deal; I'll have the other car back tomorrow."

"Well, that repair's gonna cost you an extra three dollars," the attendant said, holding out his hand for the toll.

Gabe handed him a five. "Say, what's all the excitement about?"

The words *"Thank You"* lit up on the side of the booth as the attendant put the money in his register. "I heard some doctor got murdered, but I don't put any stock in rumors."

Gabe drummed his fingers on the wheel as he waited for his change and for the wooden barricade to lift. "Well, something's up."

Gabe blew out a sigh of relief as the attendant waved him through. The jubilation was to be short-lived though. Right around the corner, a road block had been established. There were two cars in front of him, and now one pulled in behind him. He was stuck.

Gabe watched as the patrolman shined his flashlight inside the car ahead of him. This was all normal police procedure, and, if he maintained his composure, he might make it through.

The patrolman signaled Gabe to move up. "Good evening, doctor. Can I see some form of identification, please?"

Gabe rubbed his eyes and yawned as he read the patrolman's name tag. "What's this all about, Officer ... Kelsey?"

"May I see your I.D. please," the patrolman reiterated.

Gabe patted his pockets. "I know you may not believe this, officer, but I've just finished pulling a 48-hour rotation and I've left all my street clothes back in my locker. I'm promising you that if I don't get home and get some shut-eye in the next 20 minutes, you may find this old battlewagon wrapped around a telephone pole somewhere."

The patrolman glanced down the length of the old Chrysler. "This is a pretty nasty piece of transportation you're driving here, doctor. Malpractice insurance been taking its toll?"

Let him make fun of the car, Gabe warned himself. Don't say anything that will antagonize him. Just make your excuses and let the subject drop. "This car belongs to my neighbor, Mr. Bennett Chase. He was nice enough to lend it to me while my car's in the shop. Do you want to see the registration?"

Kelsey shined his light in Gabe's face and then pointed it toward the sidewalk. "That won't be necessary, doctor, but I *am* going to ask you to pull your car over to that curb."

Gabe feigned exasperation. "Oh, for Christ's sake! Can't you see that I'm exhausted? What if I give you my name and you verify it with hospital security? Won't that be good enough?"

The patrolman shook his head. "No sir. I can't let you take to our city streets without your driver's license now, can I?"

Grab a bigger shovel, Gabe. This hole you're digging just keeps getting deeper and deeper.

Gabe let his head fall against the steering wheel. "Please Officer," he moaned. "I live less than ten minutes away from here. If I promise to have Mr. Chase drive me back tomorrow morning to retrieve my wallet and identification, can't you find it in your heart to let me slide this *one* time? Be honest: do I look like I have the energy to lie to you?"

If anyone gave the appearance of having worked 48 hours straight, it was Gabe. The patrolman shined his light in Gabe's haggard face one more time before finally acquiescing. Besides, there were now four more cars cued up behind this one, and the line wasn't getting any shorter. "Okay, doctor. Just let me have your name."

Gabe never hesitated to give Patrolman Kelsey his most disarming smile.

"Thanks a lot, officer. Now, you see what a little honesty can do for you? The name's Caputo ... Ellis Caputo."

Excerpt from the Los Angeles Tribune:

Famed Running Back J.R. Jackson Killed in Bizarre Accident on Palm Springs Golf Course

Palm Desert California

American Football League Hall of Famer, and 1974 All Collegiate Trophy winner, Jordan Roosevelt Jackson was killed yesterday when the golf cart he and a fellow player were driving in mysteriously exploded shortly after they pulled away from the first tee at The Desert Palm Golf Links.

Jackson, the perennial all-star running back for the Buffalo Bulls, had been playing golf and staying out of the public spotlight since his notorious acquittal last December of the murder of his ex-wife, Janice Bowen Jackson, and her recent companion, Robert Feldman.

Jackson had just finished signing autographs for a group of his supporters when his golf cart "literally disintegrated," an injured eyewitness commented.

Everyone in Jackson's playing foursome were killed instantly and eight others waiting to tee off had to be airlifted to Palm Springs Memorial Hospital for treatment. The eight survivors suffered various injuries ranging from third- degree burns and concussions to one player with a shattered spine. The force of the blast left a crater in the ground measuring eight feet deep and 25 feet across.

The other members of the foursome that killed in the blast were John Watkins, 43, and Mark Petersen, 46, two friends of Jackson that he regularly played with. The fourth player was a guest of the club filling in for Simon Kaplan, a very fortunate record executive vacationing in the Bahamas with his family.

The guest, whose identity police are checking into at this time, was said to have been an older man whom employees in the pro shop said looked to be unusually frail to be playing a strenuous 18 holes of golf.

Police and arson investigators are not ruling out foul play, but, there is so little physical evidence left to sift through, investigators say that it will be nearly impossible to piece together any clues.

"I've never seen anything like this," the course superintendent, Roger Perkus, said. "It's physically impossible for a golf cart to just vaporize like that, even these gasoline-powered models. We're going to suggest that the cart manufacturer take a long, hard look into their design."

Over the past four months since his controversial acquittal, Jackson had received countless death threats, but none were ever substantiated.

A police spokesman now says each of those cases will have to be reopened to see if there is any connection between those threats and this tragedy.

44

Fifteenth Floor
Tower of the Americas

Less than ten minutes after the hospital workers discovered Kenneth Sanborn's bloody remains, the phone beside the bed in August Bock's private quarters rang. Unlike the adjacent business offices, this cluster of rooms was decorated in an elegant Oriental motif, with red, black and gold flocked wall trimmings, Asian designed furniture, and unique Mandarin sculptures that ornamented the black marble floors. This was August Bock's personal hideaway—a restricted retreat, where he could escape his physical limitations and let his imagination and libido run free.

When the phone interrupted him, Bock was lying on his back with his head lounging on two down pillows. Between his legs, his amply-endowed paid escort for the evening was practicing her masterful oral techniques beneath the rumpled silk sheets. Bock's head was turned toward the panoramic glass wall that looked out over the city's sparkling skyline, but his functioning eye was sightless. He was staring beyond the flickering lights at some invisible spot on the horizon; as the world became a blur, his body shuddered with its climactic release.

The phone continued to ring ... seven ... eight ... nine times, before Bock, totally annoyed, stretched over and snatched the receiver off its cradle. Captain Leon Williams was on the other end of the line. He sounded out of breath and very impatient. *"I wanted you to be the first to know."*

It took a few seconds for Bock's head to clear, and to distinguish the voice. Throwing off the bed sheets, he gestured impatiently for the prostitute to leave the room. She stood up—her long, dark hair all tussled—and stripped the red silk top sheet off the bed. Her high heels clicked on the marble floor as she wrapped her curvaceous form in the sheet and obediently headed for the bathroom. August Bock paid her well, so she was never offended and always did what was asked of her.

Bock waited until he was alone, and then used his elbows to pull the dead weight of his lower torso into a sitting position, up against the headboard. "Wanted me to be the first to know what?"

Williams lowered his voice until it was barely audible. "We've just found Ken Sanborn dead in his office."

Bock listened indifferently to the news and let a bored yawn escape. This information was of little consequence to him. Sanborn had already served his purpose. "The truth is, the doctor's probably done us a favor by taking his own life," Bock said, pitilessly. "He was a gutless bungler who would have eventually had to been silenced. One loose end Shayla won't have to deal with."

"You didn't let me finish," Williams chided. "I never said, Sanborn took his own life."

There was a pause and then Bock chuckled callously. "There. You see what I mean? He didn't even have the balls to take his own life."

"He had been stabbed with his own letter opener and there were signs of a struggle."

Bock gazed out at the city and, in the distance, the glistening water of Biscayne Bay, as a brightly lit party boat knifed through the gentle indigo swells. The water always made him think about his wife, but he was quickly snapped back into reality by the sound of the bathroom shower coming to life. "So he was murdered ... good riddance. What are you so freaked out about? The fact that someone got to him before us doesn't change anything."

Over the line, Bock could clearly hear the pandemonium of sirens and other street noises in the background as Williams tried to whisper over the racket.

"I just thought you would want to hear it from me directly instead of reading about it in the morning paper."

"Okay, consider me informed," Bock said, stifling another yawn. His companion had really earned her money tonight. "Speaking of the dead, Captain, what did you think of our little operation in California?"

"I assumed that was your doing," Williams admitted, "but I've been so damned busy trying to turn down the heat on the Waxman investigation, I haven't paid much attention to the news."

Bock grinned with pride. "Our crusade is picking up momentum, Captain, and, over the next few months, at least four more acquitted convicts will be dealt with."

"Well, let me know if there's anything else I can do..."

Bock never hesitated, his mind was like a powerful microchip, always plugged in and calculating. "As a matter of fact, Captain, I think there is something I need from you..."

"I'm listening."

"I think you need to wrap up this Sanborn situation as quickly and as quietly as possible. I don't have to tell you how the media gets when it gets its claws into something like this. Despite what I thought of him personally, Doctor Sanborn was still a prominent figure in the medical community. I want you to get into his office and scrutinize all of his files, destroying any you find pertaining to WDI. If you come across one you're not sure of, burn it anyway. I'm sure this incident will be the lead on tonight's local newscasts, but I don't want it dragging on any longer than it has to."

Williams had to raise his voice to be heard over a passing ambulance. "But I still have a killer at large."

"Play it down," Bock said calmly.

"How do you suggest I do that?"

Bock heard the shower shut off and the sound of wet feet padding around inside the bathroom. He closed his eyes and racked his brain; there had to be a way this could work to their advantage. Then, it came to him like a bolt out of the past—an idea that was so vivid, it almost took his breath away.

"I think I've just found Doctor Sanborn's killer for you, Captain."

"You're going to have to speak up. Did you say you know who killed Sanborn?"

"You know? Sometimes, I even amaze myself," Bock gloated as he reached over to the night stand to retrieve his eye patch. "Yes ... I believe I do."

"Who?"

Bock stretched the narrow elastic band around his head and covered his disfigured eye with the black patch. "Try to follow me on this, Captain," he said, condescendingly. "Sooner or later, Gabe Mitchell's in-laws were bound to start questioning his sudden disappearance, am I right?"

"Hold on a minute," Williams wondered, out loud. "What does Gabe Mitchell have to do with this?"

Bock's companion for the evening stepped out of the bathroom, toweling off her long dark hair, dressed in nothing more than one of Bock's own royal blue silk kimonos loosely tied with a golden sash. Bock gestured for her to mix him a drink by stirring his finger around in an imaginary glass. She shot him back a coy wink, untied the gold ribbon, and let the kimono seductively tumble to the floor. Bock rolled his eye as if to say, *Good God woman, what are you trying to do, kill me?* She lifted one of her firm breasts in each hand and wiggled her eyebrows lustfully at him. Bock covered the mouthpiece of the telephone with his hand and growled playfully back at her. As graceful and unabashed as she was insatiable, she seemed to float across the floor as she strode into the next room to fix his beverage.

"I believe we can kill two birds with one stone, so to speak," Bock said, turning his attention back to the very inopportune phone call.

Williams didn't get to his position of authority by not being able to read between the lines. "So, you want me to make it look like Gabe Mitchell killed Sanborn?"

"Why not? Think about it; the plan is foolproof! We couldn't have concocted a better script if we'd tried!" The excitement was rising in Bock's voice, as it did whenever he had a brainstorm. "Follow this scenario: we start with a terminal patient who, after growing despondent over the loss of his wife, daughter, and his partner, is at the frayed end of his emotional rope. Add to that dismissal from the force, the loss of his son to his in-laws in a messy custody battle, and then stir in his tragic diagnosis and prognosis ... and what have you've got? One volatile compound for murder."

"So you're saying..."

"What I'm proposing is that, when our desperate Mr. Mitchell couldn't take it any longer, he dove off the deep end and took out the doctor that broke the bad news to him. It's a no-lose situation for us. You get to put another notch in your belt by closing the case, and we tie up all our loose ends in one tidy little package."

"But then, what should I do about Sanborn's real killer?"

Bock gritted his teeth. "You hunt whoever it is down like a rabid dog, and we'll let Shayla handle them discreetly. No one gets away with murder on our watch."

"Okay, leave it to me."

"You've just got to keep your investigation into the real killer under wraps, Captain. After you make the announcement about Gabe, the Sanborn case should be officially closed."

There was silence on the line as Bock could tell Williams was considering his options.

"I think I can go on the news tonight and say that we apprehended Gabe a few miles away from the hospital, and there was a shootout. I think I know the ideal place..."

"I'm sure you do," Bock smirked.

"Now, all I need is a charred body from the morgue, and a burned up wreck from the impound yard, which shouldn't be much of a problem after last night's explosion. I think I can make all the pieces fit. I'll call in a few markers with the Medical Examiner's office and with a guy I know at the impound yard."

"Then get a move on," Bock instructed him. "I'm turning on the local news in a few minutes, and I expect to see your ugly mug plastered all over that television screen."

"Make sure to wave to me," Williams began to laugh.

"This is not a joking matter," Bock said, sternly.

"Of course it isn't. I was just wondering something else," Williams mused, before he hung up the phone. "I was just wondering how many times we're gonna have to kill Gabe Mitchell before he finally stays dead."

45

Bennett Chase and Nathan Waxman stared at the television set, their mouths agape in dumbstruck disbelief. A half-filled bottle of diet soda fell out of Chase's numbed hand and spilt its contents onto the carpet at their feet, but neither man paid any notice to the worsening stain. They both sat mesmerized by the late breaking bulletin that had just interrupted the 10 o'clock newscast.

"This just in," the anchorwoman dramatically read off her teleprompter, *"a shooting has been reported at Jackson Medical Center. Details are sketchy at this time, but Ken Garcia, who's over the scene in News Chopper Eight, might have some more information for us. Ken, are you there?"*

A jowly male face filled the television screen. *"This is Ken Garcia in News Chopper Eight, hovering over an abandoned lot a little over two miles away from Jackson Medical Center. The police have cordoned off this area to traffic, so anyone heading in this direction should seek alternate routes. Normally, this desolate neighborhood is a reputed refuge for drug addicts and prostitutes, but tonight, as you can see,"* he said, as the camera beneath the helicopter panned down through a smoky haze to a plume of orange fire that was being contained by a battalion of firefighters, *"it's been turned into a funeral pyre for the man police suspect killed a doctor earlier this evening in his office at Jackson Medical Center. We weren't notified until a few minutes ago about the shootout that occurred here, and, when we arrived on the scene, the car you see below was already engulfed in flames. I've just been told that Captain Leon Williams of the City of Miami Police Department is holding an impromptu press conference back at the medical center, and he might have some more details. So, from News Chopper Eight, high above the tragic aftermath of a deadly police pursuit, this is Ken Garcia for the News at 10. Now, to the hospital live..."*

"Was that your car?" Waxman was almost afraid to ask.

"How the hell should I know?" Chase snapped. "I couldn't tell. The damned thing was burning like a charcoal briquette."

"I've got a real bad feeling about this," Waxman said, as he noticed the soda spill for the first time and picked up the glass. "What a mess."

Chase had to press his hands between his thighs to stop them from shaking. "Screw the carpet," he seethed, "be quiet, so I can hear what they're saying."

Nathan Waxman wasn't used to being talked down to, but his pride was not at issue here and he did as he was told.

They watched and listened intently as Captain Leon Williams, surrounded by a swarm of reporters, fielded questions. Williams held up his hands for the crowd to back off, and they responded, as Waxman knew all too well, by closing ranks and besieging him with 50 questions at once.

"Please!" he pleaded angrily. "I'll try to answer all of your questions in turn, but you've got to give me some breathing room!"

Three uniformed patrolmen stepped in at their captain's request and corralled the media. Williams unruffled his overcoat, straightened his tie, and smoothed his mustache. Waxman knew a stalling tactic when he saw it.

"I've got a brief statement to make," he announced, trying to shift his face from camera to camera, "and then I'll answer some of your questions."

At approximately nine o'clock tonight, Dr. Kenneth Sanborn, a neurologist and surgeon on the staff here at Jackson Medical Center, was murdered while doing paperwork in his office. The suspect in this homicide was a former police detective named Gabe Mitchell, whom, as some of you may know, was under my command until just a few days ago."

"Well, I guess that answers that question," Waxman said, letting his body go limp on the couch.

"It can't be," the old man gritted his teeth. "I don't believe it."

"We received the 911 call within minutes of the actual murder," Williams continued on the screen. "We responded to the call immediately and pursued the fleeing suspect to an abandoned field a few miles northeast of here. Unfortunately, we found Detective Gabe armed and in a disturbed emotional state of mind. Shots were exchanged between the detective and two of my best officers, and the gas tank of Detective Gabe's vehicle was hit in the crossfire. Consequently, the vehicle exploded with Detective Gabe still inside. Firefighters are working as we speak to put out the blaze. Now, I'll take as many questions as I can..."

Chase stood up from the couch and began to pace chaotically. "I don't understand this. He only went to get some more medicine. How could this have happened?"

Waxman had his finger on the power button of the remote control and was about to shut off the television, but then thought better of it. "We'll probably never know, Bennett. I'm really sorry about this. In the brief time I knew him, Gabe seemed like a very decent fellow."

The old man clasped his hands over his ears, as though blocking out the sound would also drown out the sorrow.

"Captain Williams," one of the reporters yelled, "this was obviously not a random act of violence. Was there a relationship between Dr. Sanborn and Detective Gabe?"

Williams nodded. "Yes. Detective Gabe was a patient of Doctor Sanborn's. Over the past few weeks, Detective Gabe had not been feeling well on the job, displaying erratic behavior, and showing signs of mental stress and physical illness. A few days ago, he was diagnosed with an inoperable brain tumor and given a terminal prognosis."

"This is the same detective whose partner was killed last week?"

"Yes, but we believe her untimely death was only a contributing factor," he answered, pointing to another reporter in the back of the crowd.

"Can you give us any details about tonight's murder, Captain?"

"I can only tell you at this time that the doctor was stabbed to death."

"And Detective Gabe killed him because of his diagnosis? Doesn't that seem a bit drastic?"

Williams held up his hands. "We're only speculating as to the motive right now. But you have to realize that Detective Gabe had lost his wife and daughter in a car accident less than a year ago, and then his partner to a serial killer last week. Add the loss of his son to his in-laws in a messy custody battle, and then stir in his tragic diagnosis and prognosis, and you end up with quite a volatile mixture for murder."

"That's a load of crap," Chase protested, his eyes welling up with tears. "That's not Gabe Mitchell they're talking about."

Waxman pointed the remote control at the television set, lowering the volume. "You only knew him for a few short weeks, Bennett. Who's to say he didn't finally crack?"

Chase spun to face the ex-mayor who was staring at him unsympathetically. The old man's face was red and knotted as if some internal blaze was about to flame out through his eye sockets. "Cracked? How can you even consider those lies they're telling about him? Don't you have a shred of human decency in your body? Gabe Mitchell saved you from an assassination plot!"

Waxman knew there would be no consoling the old man, so he remained silent. Only the soft babble of the newscast droned on in the background. Waxman watched the old man wander aimlessly around the room, knowing firsthand how grief could affect people in different ways. In the case of his own wife's death, he had lost 30 pounds as his stomach literally shut down from the lament. On the other hand, his daughter handled the despair of her mother's passing much differently, even to the point of her breaking out in epidermal skin rashes. To each their own.

A pounding on the front door startled both men back to reality. They looked at each other apprehensively.

"What do you think?" Chase asked fearfully.

"They could have traced the license plates or vehicle identification number back to you," Waxman responded, rising slowly to his feet. "Damn, they work fast!"

The old man wrung his hands together. "What should I tell them?"

Waxman walked over and put his hand on Chase's shoulder. "Let me talk to them."

Chase's eyes widened. "Are you insane? You can't let them see you. You're supposed to be dead!"

Waxman squeezed the old man's shoulder reassuringly. "Well, I don't think that our little secret matters too much anymore, now does it?"

Chase pushed Waxman back toward the bedroom hallway. "Please, just let me handle this. Let me see who it is first. We might be getting all worked up over nothing."

Waxman stared curiously at the front door as the pounding renewed. "It's your house, so I'll respect your wishes, but, if there's any trouble, I'm coming back out."

"Fine," Chase agreed, waving his disheartened guest back into the darkness of the unlit hallway. "Just don't be a hero. The longevity of heroes isn't very long lately."

* * * * * *

Waiting until Waxman was out of sight, Chase moved timidly toward answering the door. "Who is it?" he called out from a few feet away, now regretting that he never bothered to install a security peephole.

"What do you mean?" came the response from outside. "Let me in, Bennett, I'm freezing my ass off out here!"

"Who is it?"

"For God's sake, Bennett," answered the voice. "What is this, some kind of joke? Let me in!"

There was a large, draped picture window that opened onto a magnificent view of his finely manicured front lawn, but it was still impossible to see anyone standing on the other side of the door through it. Chase pulled back the edge of his curtains and peered into the darkness of his front yard, but there was nothing to be seen out there. No car. Nothing. "Identify yourself," Chase yelled.

"Identify myself? What the hell is this, Alcatraz, all of a sudden? It's Gabe, for crying out loud. Let me in!"

46

Nathan Waxman heard the exchange from down the hallway and stepped back out into the light. "How is that possible? Let him in!"

Chase rushed for the door and yanked it open. It was true! Gabe Mitchell was standing there, quite alive in all of his shivering glory.

"Are you going to let me in?" Gabe grunted impatiently. "Or do I need some special password to get into this maximum security prison?"

Chase stepped forward and tied-up an overwhelmed Gabe Mitchell in a crushing bear hug. "God damn, son. They said you were dead, but I didn't believe it for a single minute."

"What are you talking about?" Gabe groaned, still locked in the old man's savage grip.

Nathan Waxman remained far across the room, stunned that Gabe Mitchell was actually standing there in the flesh.

"On the news," Chase started to explain. "They said..."

"Let go of him," Waxman called out. "Can't you see you're crushing the life out of him?"

Chase relinquished his vise-like hold, allowing Gabe to inhale a huge gasp of air.

"Hurry, come inside," the old man urged, closing and locking the door behind them. "Didn't I tell you it was a load of hooey, Nate? My boy Gabe here's got more lives than a freaking cat!"

Waxman was still skeptical. "What happened to you?"

Gabe stepped into the center of the living room. "I ran into a bit of trouble at the hospital," Gabe answered.

"Do ya think?" Waxman said, sarcastically.

* * * * * *

Gabe threw the two file folders on Chase's coffee table. They landed bloody side up. "Nothing I couldn't handle."

In unison, both men took a horrified step back.

"Oh jeez," Chase moaned.

"Is that Sanborn's blood?" Waxman asked, pointing at the folders.

Gabe looked at the ex-mayor like he had just pulled off some miraculous magic trick that defied logic. "How did you know about...?"

Waxman pointed at the newscast which was already recapping the story. Gabe moved slowly toward the television set as the highlights of the evening's events were recounted by his former captain. He watched the fiery spectacle through unblinking eyes and listened to the fabricated story through disbelieving ears.

Gabe rested his hands on the back of the couch, his entire body sagging under the invisible weight of betrayal. But at least now the puzzle was complete. Now he understood why Williams was the only officer to visit him at the hospital ... how Shayla Rand was waiting for him back at the motel after he tried to warn his trusted captain about the assassination plot ... the impeccable security credentials he was given at the marina. It all fit—and it all made him sick to his stomach. He looked up to find both men staring at him again. "Okay," he asked wearily. "Now, do you want to hear the truth?"

Gabe asked Bennett Chase if he would make him a pitcher of fresh tea, and all three men retired to the kitchen where they waited for the teapot to boil. Gabe sat across the kitchen table from both of them and began recapping his experiences of the past four hours in unabridged detail. When the whistle from the kettle interrupted Gabe's narrative, he asked Chase for some ice cubes, lemon juice, and plenty of sugar. The old man obliged and watched in fascination as Gabe downed glass after glass of iced tea.

"So," Chase said unsurely. "There is no brain tumor? You're not dying?"

Gabe reached across the table and took the old man's hand, embracing it gently. "I don't think so, Bennett."

"But those son-of-a-bitches made you think you were?"

"That was their plan."

Chase didn't know whether to sing for joy or spit for hatred. "What gives them the right to manipulate a person's life like that? It's … it's…" He couldn't find a word strong enough. "Despicable!"

* * * * * *

"You've been sitting there like a bump on a log during all of this, Mr. Mayor," Gabe said, turning his attention to Waxman. "What are your thoughts?"

Waxman leaned back and tugged on his ear. The side of his face still felt like it was being probed with pins and needles. "I'm just sitting here listening to your story, Gabe. You'll have to excuse me if I play the devil's advocate, but the level of corruption you're suggesting is staggering. Do you realize how fantastic this all sounds?"

Gabe calmly set down his glass of tea and slid his chair away from the table. Waxman watched as Gabe silently exited the kitchen. Seconds later, two manila folders came skidding across the kitchen table. The blood on the outside of one of them had turned to a sickening shade of brown.

Gabe stood in the doorway like a concrete monument. "Proof," he said, matter-of-factly.

Bennett Chase slid around the table so he could peruse the contents of the two files over Waxman's shoulder. Halfway through his reading, the old man looked up from the folder and winked proudly at Gabe.

"Digitoxin," Waxman looked up, keeping his finger pressed on the word. "This is the drug they supposedly poisoned you with?"

"I'm going to get my medical encyclopedia and see what it says about it," Chase said.

Gabe had to step out of the doorway to let the rotund old man squeeze by.

"And what's this all about?" Waxman asked, holding up the business card that had been attached to the inside of the second folder.

"That company's name doesn't sound familiar to you?" Gabe asked as he dumped three scoops of sugar into his beverage.

"No," Waxman said, turning the card over in his hand and examining the other side. "Should it?"

Gabe shrugged. "I guess not."

"Hey," Bennett Chase called out as he waddled back into the room. "I found it!"

"What does it say?" Waxman asked.

"I always keep this thing handy," the old man said as he skimmed his finger across the page. "With all the medicines I'm taking, I can't always trust my doctors to remember how one drug interacts with another."

Gabe took a long pull from his drink as Chase rifled through the pages of the thick book.

"Here it is," Chase announced. "Digitoxin: Other names: Lantoxin, Crystodigin, and Purodigin. A drug commonly used for treating heart failure, angina and blood pressure abnormalities. Tablet or liquid, Digitoxin can be given orally, intramuscularly or intravenously."

"What does it say about long-term usage?" Waxman asked, looking across the room at Gabe, who was leaning with his back against the sink.

The old man's finger crossed onto the next page of the book. "Umm ... let me see here ... An overdose ... I guess that's what we're talking about ... causes nausea, vomiting, diarrhea, blurred vision, and cardiac disturbances, such as tachycardia, pulmonary contractions, arterial fibrillation, and atrioventricular blocks ... whatever those things are."

"And what about the antidote?" Gabe asked. "Were the interns right?"

"Hmm ... Treatments," Chase read on. "The stomach must be flushed with tannic acid," he said, looking up and smiling at Gabe. "And the victim should remain lying down." Now he frowned at him. Gabe returned the old man's grimace with a guilty shrug.

"Stimulants should be given such as caffeine, ammonia or atrophine. If the pulse falls below 50 beats per minute, morphine is introduced. Wow..."

"Yeah," Gabe agreed. "I've got to remember to send those young doctors a thank you card when this is all over."

"'All over?'" Waxman griped. "What do you mean 'all over?' They tried to kill me once, and you twice! What makes you think the end to all of this is suddenly in sight?"

"So you're becoming a believer?" Chase asked, slamming the encyclopedia shut.

Waxman laid his hands flat on the table. "I'll concede that Gabe's account and these files seem to correlate, but I'm still not convinced that Leon Williams, one of the city's most decorated police officials, is in cahoots with August Bock. We may have worked for two different cities, but I've attended many a charitable function with the man, and, as far as I know, his reputation is beyond reproach."

Gabe turned to the stove and put on another kettle of water to boil. "I wonder if the Chief of Staff at Jackson Memorial would have had the same high praise for Kenneth Sanborn if he had seen those files..."

Waxman slumped back in his chair. "Okay, so what about this card?" he asked. "What do you think it has to do with all of this?"

Bennett Chase reached across the table and took the card. "Worldwide Dispatch Incorporated ... sounds like some kind of freight company. You know, I've still got some friends who work at the air freight terminal at Miami International Airport. Do you want me to make some calls to see what they can dig up?"

Gabe nodded gratefully. "Thanks Bennett; that would be a tremendous help."

The old man touched the card to his brow like he was doffing his cap and hurried out of the kitchen to make the phone call. It wasn't long before he returned with good news.

"Well, like I was saying," Chase said, walking over and handing back Gabe the business card. "I have an old buddy at Emery

Air Freight who's going to check into this Worldwide Dispatch Incorporated for us."

"So he's heard of the company?" Waxman asked.

"He sees so many damned freight companies come and go, he's not really sure."

"So, how much longer am I going to have to stay dead?" Waxman asked, as the teapot began to whistle again.

"It shouldn't be much longer," Gabe assured him, as he tended to the kettle. "The proverbial shit's about to hit the fan."

"Why do you say that?" Chase intervened, before the ex-Mayor could ask the same question.

"Because August Bock has finally made a very stupid mistake."

"What mistake was that?" Waxman asked.

Gabe dipped half a dozen small tea bags into the pitcher of steaming water. "You both saw it before I did. He had Leon Williams go on television and say that he killed me in that shootout."

"So?" Chase said.

Gabe poured half a cup of bottled lemon juice into the darkening brew. "By tomorrow morning, his forensics people are going to match my fingerprints to the letter opener they'll remove from Doctor Sanborn's abdomen, and just about every other stick of furniture in that office."

Waxman nodded knowingly. "So, Williams is going to know you weren't killed aboard *Mystique*!"

Gabe stirred the tea bags around in the pitcher. "And I'm willing to bet that, about three seconds after that, so will August Bock. They're going to have a real mess on their hands since they've supposedly roasted me in that bonfire they staged."

"Which they did in front of a national audience," Chase emphasized.

"You've got that right," Gabe said.

Waxman pounded his fist on the table. "So, why don't we just end this whole thing right here and now by going to one of the local television stations, or the *Miami Herald*, and showing them that we're both still alive?"

Gabe shook his head. "If I honestly thought that talking to the media could stop August Bock, I would've gone to them instead of Leon Williams. You and I rising from the ashes might get the captain put away for a while, but it won't get rid of August Bock. He'll just dig himself a hole and disappear until it's safe to surface somewhere else. Trust me: this guy's got the connections and the means to vanish like smoke ... and, believe me, he will."

"So what now?" Chase asked.

Gabe yawned. "Now? Now, we go to sleep. It's been a long night."

"Sleep?" Waxman bristled. "How can you possibly think about falling asleep at a time like this? What about Bock? What's he going to do when he learns you're still alive?"

"Probably the same thing I would do if I was in his place," Gabe said nonchalantly as he dumped the used tea bags into the garbage under the sink. "I'd send out my best man ... or woman in this case, and hunt me down and kill me. Only this time ... I'd make sure I stayed dead!"

47

The morning sun rose slowly over the Miami Beach skyline as if it were riding some unseen escalator. Still dressed in his plush maroon bathrobe, August Bock watched it ascend into the cloudless sky. Sitting at his glass breakfast table, he gazed misty-eyed over the waters of Biscayne Bay. The wind was blowing out of the north this morning, causing the sea to churn with a light chop. It wasn't an ideal day for sailing, but the windsurfers were out in force—their multi-colored sails tacking back and forth across the shimmering water. In the distance to the south, tall geysers of white steam bellowed from the funnels of the cruise ships lined up in the Port of Miami, their boilers being stoked in preparation for their weekly voyages.

It was in calm moments such as this that August Bock liked to contemplate what could have been. He envisioned himself jogging around the deck of one of those wonderful ships, his wife stretched out on a chaise lounge beside the pool, sipping a piña colada, without a care in the world. But just as quickly, with the shifting of the sun on a pane of window glass, a pitiable reflection became intelligible enough to shatter his daydream. Bock's transparent image was a cruel reminder to him that life was what happened to people while they were making other plans.

"Mimosa?" the dark-haired Asian woman asked.

Bock turned to look at the kimono-clad beauty, but his real focus was still on the nonexistent woman lying on the imaginary chaise lounge. "No thanks, Desiree, plain orange juice will be fine."

"You seem so distracted," she said, moving behind him with the pitcher of juice and making sure her breasts brushed against the back of his head. "You've hardly touched your eggs. Is there anything I can do to help?"

"Yes, pour," he said, holding up his empty glass.

"That's not what I had in..."

"Well, August," interrupted a familiar female voice. "I see you still have an eye for the tall, dark, slutty types."

Bock pressed the wand on the arm of his wheelchair and motored back from the table. "Shayla, I didn't hear you come in. Welcome back from California. Would you care to join me for some breakfast?"

Shayla Rand stood like a goddess across the adjoining living room. Between her long, nimble fingers, she twirled one of only three plastic keycards in existence which allowed access into Bock's private residence. She was dressed completely in white, with high heels, skin-tight leather pants, white turtleneck, and a matching leather overcoat. All this neutrality was set ablaze by her flaming red hair. She still sported a bandage to cover the stitches on her cheek, but this one was made of skin-toned plastic and was far less conspicuous.

"I already ate on the plane," she said in her soft Irish accent, as she sauntered with her stiletto heels clicking into the breakfast room, "but *I'd kill* for a cup of Earl Grey."

"Desiree, fix Shayla a cup of tea, please."

The woman in the kimono glared at Shayla like a cat who had just discovered another feline invading her territory. Desiree's expression was filled with venom, but Shayla's cold, merciless eyes were much more intimidating—like two jade stones behind her unblinking eyelids. "Anything for *you*, August."

"So, that's the flavor of the month?" Shayla huffed, as she walked over to the window and stared out at the water. "She's a bit broad in the beam compared to the others, August. You paying for them by the pound nowadays?"

Bock maneuvered his chair back to the table and started to butter himself a piece of raisin toast. "Don't take out your jet-lag on the hired help, Shayla. It doesn't become you."

Shayla slipped the keycard into the pocket of her vest and took a seat at the breakfast table. "I don't know why you continue to pay for something, August, that *I* would gladly supply you with for free."

"For free?" Bock's laugh boomed inside the cavernous glass walls. "Shayla, you've got to be the most expensive piece of ass in the world. Haven't you ever heard that mixing business with pleasure is a no-no?"

Shayla arched her eyebrows seductively. "Well, your flight engineer didn't think so. It didn't take much convincing on my part to make him an honorary member of the mile-high club."

Bock took a bite out of his toast. "I must leave myself a note to have the plane disinfected."

"I considered it a small bonus for a job well done," she said, stealing a piece of toast from Bock's platter.

"I thought you said you had already eaten on the plane?"

Shayla winked. "That was strictly a liquid diet."

"There are some things that an employee just shouldn't share with her boss," Bock said, shaking his head.

"What? I'm not allowed to unwind after a full day's work?"

"Of course not, especially when your work is successful."

Shayla looked up at the ceiling and laughed. "I should say so. They'll be picking bits of him out of the bunkers for months."

"Yes, I heard. Well done."

Desiree returned with Shayla's tea and set it down on the table. "Is there anything *else* I can get for you?" she asked, contemptuously.

"Don't take that tone, Desiree," Bock pleaded as he reached over and pulled out the chair beside him. "Please, sit down and have something to eat with us."

Desiree's resentful gaze never wavered from Shayla Rand. "No thank you, August. I've lost my appetite." She pointed to the bedroom. "I'm just going to get dressed, and I'll find my own way out."

"Not without leaving breadcrumbs," Shayla said, sarcastically, as she watched the curvaceous prostitute disappear into the bedroom.

Bock glared across the table at Shayla.

"What did I do?" she asked, pouring a few drops of milk into her tea. "I can't help it if that cow chooses *this* morning to try and shed some of those unwanted pounds. I wouldn't worry about her anyway; she looks like she could live off the land for quite a few days without much of a problem."

"Good God, Shayla," Bock said.

Shayla grabbed him by the arm. "Do you want me to apologize to her, love? I will if you ask me to."

"I don't think so, Shayla," Bock said, holding his hands up in mock surrender. "I think you've done enough damage for one morning, thank you. Let me handle it."

He was just about to back away from the table, when the telephone rang. He pointed to the portable phone lying on the kitchen counter, which Shayla retrieved for him. "Yes?"

The voice on the other end of the line was frantic. "*You're not going to believe what I have to tell you.*"

"You know, Captain," Bock lamented, "I don't give out my private number to just anyone, so why all of a sudden are you making me regret having ever given it to you?"

"*This is important.*"

"Twice in one day? It had better be."

"*After the discussion we had last night, I thought it best that I have my forensics team expedite their analysis of the crime scene ... you know, to get a lead on the real perp.*"

Bock put his hand over the mouthpiece of the receiver and whispered to Shayla. "If he wasn't so damned indispensable, I believe I'd have you make a house call."

"Just say the word," Shayla whispered back over the rim of her teacup.

"*Are you listening to me, August?*"

Bock took a sip of his orange juice. "I'm still here, Captain."

"*They came up with a positive identification from the prints on the letter opener, and a matching set on the doorknob to the office, and a third on a table lamp.*"

Through the panoramic window, Bock tracked a 747 jumbo jet as it soared across the horizon. How a plane that large could stay airborne had always been a mystery to him. The physics of flight were something that would never cease to amaze him. "And I suppose that these fingerprints should be significant to me because...?"

"*Significant enough that I had to double-check them myself.*"

"Okay," Bock said, swallowing the last sip of his juice, "tell me what you found before you have a stroke."

Williams said the name with the same cowering expectancy of a child experiencing the audible concussion of fireworks for the first time. "*Gabe Mitchell.*"

The glass paused on August Bock's lips as though it were suddenly glued there.

"...Come again?"

"*You heard me right, August. The prints we lifted from the crime scene match those in Gabe Mitchell's official police files. It took the computer all of 30 seconds to come up with the match.*"

Bock set the glass down on the table with an ominous clank. "I know you've been up all night, Captain. Perhaps you need some rest."

"*Rest my ass!*" Williams growled. "*You fucked up, August. Gabe Mitchell was at the hospital last night!*"

Bock cupped his hand over the receiver and pointed to a telephone jack on an inside wall. "Shayla, get me another phone; there's one in the next room with a speaker. You need to hear this."

Shayla Rand looked quizzically at her employer and reluctantly did as she was told. When she returned to the breakfast area, she plugged the second phone into the socket and set it down on the glass table.

"Captain Williams, Shayla Rand is here with me. I'm putting you on the speaker. I want her to hear what you've just told me."

Bock pressed a button on the speaker phone and hung up his portable unit. Williams' heavy breathing made the phone sound almost alive. "*What I told August was, that the prints we found in Kenneth Sanborn's office belong to Gabe Mitchell.*"

His words hung in the air like a storm cloud. Shayla's finger involuntarily moved up to her face, tracing the scar down the length of her cheek. "What you're saying is impossible! I saw him blown to pieces with my very own eyes."

"Fingerprints don't lie, bitch. I'd recommend an eye test too."

She looked over at Bock, who was looking at her skeptically. "Ask Damon, August ... he saw it too! No one could have survived that explosion!"

Bock toyed with his empty glass. "And there's no other way those finger prints could have gotten there, Captain? Say, on one of Gabe's previous visits?"

Shayla stared at the phone in disbelief, like she was seeing fire for the first time.

"The prints were all bloody. Sanborn's blood. There's no mistaking it. Gabe Mitchell is still alive."

Shayla slammed her fist down so hard on the glass table, Bock thought for sure it would shatter. "I told you, I should have killed that son-of-a-bitch back at the motel room when I had the chance. I don't know how he managed to survive that explosion, but if that bastard's still breathing, I swear I'll find him," she seethed, putting her fingers to her disfigured face, "and I'll kill him with my bare hands!"

Bock depressed the button on the phone.

"What the hell was all that about?" Williams demanded.

"Just a bit of steam being let off, Captain. Everything's under control."

There was a long pause on the line.

"It's easy for you to say that things are under control, August. You're sitting up there in your glass tower, while I'm the one who put his head in the noose by going on national television telling everyone that we killed Gabe Mitchell! By the way: what a brilliant idea that was! Now what happens if he decides to play Lazarus and tell his story to the press? What'll we do then? I'll promise you this, August: if I go down, I'm not going down alone ... and I'll guarantee you it's a long fall from where you're sitting."

Bock covered the microphone on the receiver with his finger. "The man's got all the qualities of a dog," he whispered to Shayla, "except loyalty."

"Don't worry, Captain," Bock assured, as he removed his finger. "If Gabe Mitchell *is* still alive, and he *were* planning on going to the press, he would have done it already. No, I think he has something else in mind."

"His medical records were missing from Sanborn's filing cabinet."

Shayla slammed her hands down on the table again as Bock tried futilely to mask his disappointment upon hearing the additional information. "Okay, this just means that he's probably already figured out that his future is not as bleak as we have led him to believe."

"How can you stay so damned relaxed about all this?" Williams cursed. *"Can't you read the writing on the wall? We're all going be spending the rest of our lives in prison!"*

Bock turned his chair to face the window. The streets below were coming to life as vendors unlocked and pushed back the iron gates that protected their shops at night. "As much as I appreciate your evaluation of our situation Captain," Bock said, "your pessimistic attitude disturbs me very much. I can assure you that nothing was ever accomplished by someone working in panic mode. I'm sure you've heard the expression, 'cooler heads always prevail?'"

"Well there's cool, and then there's inept. What happened out there on the water, anyway? I thought that bitch of yours was supposed to have been so thorough? Did she miss Gabe as he flew past her?"

"No one could have survived that explosion," Shayla snapped. "Gabe was on the yacht when it blew ... I saw him there."

"Well, unless someone found his dismembered hands, and then used them to kill Sanborn, I think you need to start wearing glasses."

"Please," Bock interjected. "This bickering is getting us nowhere. For now, we will have to go under the assumption that Gabe Mitchell is indeed still alive."

Shayla's anger bubbled like acid as she pushed herself away from the table. "Let me go, August. Let me track him down, and I swear I'll bring his head back to you in a sack." She walked over to the window and put her hands up on the glass. Not only had Gabe Mitchell humiliated her, but he had also left her with a permanent reminder of his deceit. Her marred reflection scowled back at Bock from the window

"So I take it you've already come up with another plan, August? It hope to hell it doesn't have anything to do with me going on television again."

Bock grinned like a shark. "As a matter of fact, Captain ... it does."

"You're kidding, right?"

Shayla turned from the window, disbelief filling her normally inscrutable features.

"You *will* be going on television again, Captain," Bock said, shrewdly. "And when you're through, we will no longer have to worry about tracking him down ... Gabe Mitchell will be coming to us!"

48

Gabe finally emerged from his bedroom around 1:30 the next afternoon. It wasn't like him to sleep this late, but it had taken nearly three hours of fitful tossing and turning for him to finally doze off last night. Standing out in the hallway, he stretched from side to side and scratched his scalp to get the blood circulating. He could hear the sound of a television somewhere in the house, but he didn't feel like making an appearance just yet, since he wasn't his most presentable right now, clad only in the pale blue hospital bottoms he had pilfered. Letting out a lion-like yawn, he shuffled down the hallway toward the bathroom, smacking his lips, which felt like they had been glazed with mucilage. Still, lethargy was his only ailment at the moment and a long, hot shower was just the remedy.

Flipping on the light in the bathroom, Gabe was surprised to see a neat stack of brand new clothes sitting on the edge of the basin. He lifted the items one piece at a time and held them up to himself in the mirror. Another pair of dungarees, a t-shirt, underwear, and a tan, long-sleeved dress shirt that he might have chosen for himself, if shopping wasn't one of his most dreaded things in life. It seemed that Bennett Chase had been a very busy man this morning.

Twenty minutes later, Gabe was showered, shaved, and refreshed, sitting on the edge of his bed in his new outfit, tying the laces on his tennis shoes, when he looked up to see Chase standing in the doorway.

"Another hour, and I was going to call for the paramedics. I'm glad to see you finally up and about."

Gabe twisted the lace around his finger and tugged on the bow to secure the knot. "Thanks for the new clothes, Bennett. When did you…"

"Oh, I don't sleep much these days," Chase brooded. "I figure there's going be plenty of that soon enough. I called a cab this morning and had it take me up to the store so I could get that stuff you're wearing, and then it dropped me off at a nearby car rental place. They stuck me in a Dodge … drives okay, I guess."

Gabe looked up. "Yeah, I'll bet it's not quite what you're accustomed to."

"Hey, I'll have you know that car's gotten me through some really hard times…"

"Yeah," Gabe snickered, "like the Civil War."

The old man put his fists on his corpulent hips. "Make jokes if you want, but I'm having that old car towed to the dealership as we speak, and they're going to whip it into shape."

Gabe stood up and straightened the cuffs on his jeans. "Why don't you see what the dealership will give you in trade for it, Bennett? Get into something a bit more modern, say … a Model T?"

Chase shot Gabe a sarcastic grimace. "I'm glad to see all that tea hasn't dampened your sense of humor. How many times did you have to get up during the night to pee?"

Gabe shrugged. "Never did. Slept right through the night."

The old man shook his head in disbelief. "What are you, a camel? You must have drunk five pitchers of tea last night. The caffeine alone would have had *me* climbing the walls. Wait till you reach my age, when the only way you can sleep at night is to keep a pillow in the bathroom."

When I reach his age, Gabe thought. That wasn't a prospect he had been able to consider lately. "If it puts your mind at ease, I pissed like Secretariat when I woke up."

Chase turned to walk out of the room. "Well, I'm glad to know you're half human. Come into the kitchen; I've fixed you a plate of food."

"Where's Nate?" Gabe asked.

The old man's voice faded down the hallway. "He's glued to the television set. I think he's gotten himself hooked on a soap opera."

"Thanks again for the clothes," Gabe shouted after him.

"Yeah, yeah..."

Gabe paused in the living room as he passed Nathan Waxman sitting on the couch in front of the television. "What are you watching, Nate?"

Waxman's head was propped up on his hand, his eyes transfixed on the screen. "How do people watch this drivel? In the two hours I've been watching this crap, I've seen one miscarriage, one case of amnesia, and a kid whose aunt is really his sister. Does someone actually get paid to write this junk?"

Gabe picked up the remote controller. "So why don't you just change the channel?"

Waxman snatched the clicker out of Gabe's hand. "What, and miss what happens next?"

Gabe did a double-take. "Well, not to change the subject, but did you catch anything more on the news today?"

Waxman lowered the audio, but his focus remained mesmerized on the picture. "As a matter of fact, I did. There was a perfunctory little piece on Sanborn's death, but they implied that, with your death, the case was now closed."

Gabe took a seat on the arm of the sofa. "Of course they would. They want everything having to do with last night dead and buried. There was nothing else?"

"What were you expecting?"

"I don't know. Panic maybe. Carelessness, hopefully. Believe me: when Leon Williams matches my prints, they're going to have to do something. I just don't know what ... yet. The waiting is going to be the hardest part."

Waxman fumbled with the remote, pointing it at the television, and the screen went totally silent. "That's what I need to talk to you about, Gabe ... the waiting. I don't think I can do it anymore."

Gabe slid down on the sofa next to the ex-mayor. "What are you trying to tell me?"

"Well, there was another side story on the news that I haven't told you about," Waxman said, gesturing toward the blank television.

Gabe sat sideways on the couch facing Waxman. "Okay, you've got my attention."

"They're holding a memorial service for me this evening at Temple Beth David on the beach. My daughter's going to be there."

Gabe let out a deep, commiserative sigh.

"I can't ... I won't ... let her go through that, Gabe. Just the emotional upheaval of both her mother and my deaths will probably have me paying for therapists for the rest of my life as it is. I can only imagine what's going to happen to my baby girl when I finally make my appearance."

Gabe ran his fingers over his freshly shaved chin. "So, what do you want to do?"

Waxman's expression turned grave as the phone rang and was quickly picked up somewhere else in the house. "It's real simple. I know you're not going to like this, but I'm coming out of hiding. I can't do this anymore." He reached out and put his hand on Gabe's shoulder. "I appreciate everything you've done for me, and, rest assured, I will do everything in my power to see that this conspiracy is nipped in the bud. But I can't just sit around here watching *General Hospital* and listening to old war stories while my daughter is walking past my casket. I just can't do it."

Gabe understood. He didn't like it, but he understood. He sat quietly for a long moment, trying to conjure up just the right words that would perhaps change Waxman's mind ... but in his heart of hearts, he knew it wouldn't matter. If the roles were reversed, and it was Casey sitting before *his* coffin, he would do anything to prevent that misery for his child. "You're right," Gabe said with resignation in his voice, as he stood up and slipped his hands into the front pockets of his jeans. "I don't have any right to hold you here."

"Thank you for understanding," Waxman said, looking up at Gabe.

"I'm not going to stand here and try to convince you to give me a chance. If I were in your shoes ... well, I guess I am kind of in your shoes, but no matter ... I still understand. I know firsthand how important your daughter is to you."

Waxman fidgeted uncomfortably on the couch. "I keep forgetting about your son."

"Don't worry about it," Gabe said, waving his hand. "The last time we saw each other, it wasn't a very happy meeting. I've really let the boy down. I was never there for him. I guess you could say I was a workaholic. Whenever I get," he corrected himself. "Whenever I got involved in a case, I was like a dog with a bone ... I just could never let it go."

"Like now."

Gabe nodded. "Yeah, I guess like now. I know that Leon Williams is going to get caught, that's a given as far as I'm concerned. I just can't live with the fact that..."

"...Bock might get away with it."

Gabe began to pace ferociously, like a penned up tiger. "I'd bet my life he is. Him and his team of assassins are going to feel the heat, and they're going bolt. Mark my words ... it may not be tomorrow, or even six months from now, but one day you're going to pick up the newspaper and read about another acquitted person having been killed in under mysterious circumstances."

Waxman's jaw dropped. "Oh my God."

Gabe turned to him. "What?"

The ex-mayor leaned over his side of the couch and grabbed the first section of the morning paper. He unfolded it, and threw it face up on the coffee table. The paper spun around so that the headlines were facing Gabe. "You don't suppose?"

Gabe quickly scanned the lead story. "Oh yeah, this is vintage Bock alright. This happened yesterday?"

Waxman nodded. "I still can't believe it. I actually met J.R. Jackson once, when he spoke at a fund raiser for the University of Miami's football program. He seemed like a real stand-up guy. I never believed he did those two horrible killings."

Gabe studied the photograph of a group of curious onlookers surrounding the giant brown hole in a sea of green Bermuda grass. To him, it looked like a meteor had impacted the desert. "Well Nate, you more than anyone should know it only matters what

August Bock thinks. The fact that this happened so soon after *your* assassination attempt tells me he's getting more aggressive."

Waxman stood up. "Why doesn't the F.B.I. or some other government agency do something about these killings? You don't think..."

Gabe shrugged. "I wouldn't bet against him doing work for them. They could very well be Bock's biggest client."

The ex-mayor ran his fingers through his hair. "Gabe, I'd like to help, I really would ... but my daughter means the world to me. I'm not cut out for..."

Gabe put his finger to his mouth. "No apologies necessary, Nate. I just need you to make me a promise."

"Name it."

Gabe turned introspective. "Whatever happens to me..."

"Gabe, nothing's going to..."

The phone suddenly rang twice and went silent.

"Whatever happens to me," Gabe asserted, "you've got to find this madman. No one's going to believe a word of your story, and you won't know who to trust. It'll be like trying to catch a shadow in a darkroom ... but he's got to be stopped."

Waxman frowned. "I thought you were going to ask me something easy, like taking care of your son."

Gabe shook his head. "That's a very kind gesture. But despite our differences, Casey's in pretty good hands with my in-laws. They're really good people when you cut away all the bitterness they still bear toward me."

Waxman put his hand on Gabe's shoulder. "Let's not have any more of this ominous talk, Gabe. Nothing's going to happen to you."

"You're wrong. As soon as Captain Williams gets those forensic results, I'm a dead man. I may have regained some of my strength, but I know what Bock has in store for me, and she's one tough kitty. I don't know whether I'll make it through round two."

"Then let me get you some protection."

"From whom ... anyone wearing a belt? I can't keep running for the rest of my life. There's got to be a showdown."

"But you don't even know how to find him."

"I think I can help in that area," Bennett Chase interjected, as he entered from the kitchen holding a notepad, a plate of food, and another large glass of iced tea for Gabe. "That was my buddy Daryl Blanding at Emery Air Freight on the phone. I think we might have struck pay dirt."

Gabe took the dish containing an egg salad sandwich and a handful of potato chips. "What did he find out?"

The old man flipped through his hastily written memos. "He had to do some deep digging, but according to Daryl, Worldwide Dispatch Incorporated is a licensed and bonded international freight carrier owned by August Bock."

"Very clever play on words, Worldwide *Dispatch*," Gabe snickered between ravenous munches. It felt good to have an appetite once again.

"It gets better," Chase added. "According to Daryl, WDI only has one helicopter and one private jet in their entire fleet, yet the company showed a net profit last year in excess of $238 million! You wanna tell me how that's possible?"

"Surely that kind of profit must've raised a red flag with the Interstate Commerce Commission," Waxman surmised. "They're supposed to regulate that industry."

"Not if you've got the right people in your pocket," Gabe observed between bites. "Don't forget August Bock is a former Federal Prosecutor, and if he's already got a well- respected police captain on his payroll, who's to say someone at the ICC isn't punching a WDI timecard as well?"

"Just how did your friend get all of this information?" Waxman asked of the old man, skeptically.

"He told me most of it's a matter of public record," Chase admitted. "I guess you've just got to know where to look."

"So what else did he find out?" Gabe asked as he washed down his sandwich with a long pull of tea.

"He says the plane and helicopter are housed in a private hangar at Opa-Locka Municipal Airport in North Miami. He reminded me that we've got a mutual friend, Eddie Chao, who still works the fuel pumps out there, and Eddie says he sees the plane all the time, but not so often the helicopter. Eddie even managed to get us an address for the company off one of the fuel bills. It's in downtown Miami," he said, handing the notepad over to Gabe.

Gabe licked his fingers clean of potato chip crumbs, took the pad, and recited the address. "Tower of the Americas, eh? So the son-of-a-bitch is right here in Miami. Well, that answers the question as to why they flew me off to that secluded island. Bock didn't want me to know that they pitched their tent right here in my own backyard."

"What are you going to do now, Gabe?" Chase asked.

Gabe turned to Waxman. "I know how anxious you are to get back to your daughter, but now that I've got this address, I'm going to ask your indulgence for just a while longer. The only thing I have going for me is the element of surprise, and, if you show up at that memorial service before they know I'm still alive..."

Suddenly, something on the television screen captured all three men's attention. There was a special news bulletin breaking into the afternoon soaps. Waxman pointed the remote control at the TV and raised the volume. The perfectly coifed male anchor from the evening news, Scott Newman, was shuffling a stack of papers at the news desk. *"There's been a strange twist to the murder of a doctor last night at Jackson Medical Center. For the latest on this late breaking story, we're going live to our correspondent Pam Wallace at the City of Miami Police department..."*

Waxman, Gabe and Chase all exchanged suspicious glances.

"They've matched the prints," Gabe muttered, grimly.

The camera was focused on a podium standing before a blue curtain, and, in the foreground, the heads of a congregation of reporters filled the bottom of the screen. Over the visual scene came the disembodied voice of the female reporter. *"This is Pam Wallace live at the City of Miami Police Department, where, in just a few seconds, Captain Leon Williams is about to give a press conference on a very bizarre development in the murder case of a prominent doctor last night at Jackson Medical Center. At this time, we don't know all the details, but we've been told ... uh, hold on a second ... Captain Williams has just entered the room, and it looks like this press conference is about to begin..."*

"Tape this," Chase directed Waxman.

The correct button on the remote was pressed, and the tape deck went to work.

Dignified as ever, but not looking well-rested, Leon Williams strolled to the podium and exchanged polite pleasantries with a few of the reporters in the crowd. He was followed into the room by two uniformed officers, who guided an older white couple to stand in the background by the blue curtain.

"Those bastards!" Gabe screamed, running up to the television screen.

"What's the matter, Gabe?" Chase pleaded, as he almost had to restrain his enraged friend.

"Those are my in-laws," Gabe said, pointing at the older couple flanking Leon Williams.

"I don't understand," Waxman said, leaning forward on the couch.

Gabe instinctively knew what the outcome of this press conference was going to be. He just couldn't believe August Bock would stoop to such a heinous tactic, but then he reminded himself of who he was dealing with.

The camera panned over to a young black man who held the door open for the entire entourage, and then remained cloistered in the wings. When the camera shifted back to the stage, Williams was removing a small bundle of index cards from the inside pocket of his impeccably tailored Italian wool suit, and was placing them neatly on top of the rostrum.

"Good afternoon ladies and gentlemen. My name is Leon Williams, and, for those of you who don't know me, I'm the Captain of Detectives for the City of Miami Police Department. I've called this press conference in the hope that *one particular person*," he emphasized the words, looking directly into the camera, "is viewing this broadcast."

Waxman and Chase both glanced over at Gabe.

"I'm speaking to the person who has kidnapped the grandson of Thomas and Edna Gibson, this courageous couple who stand here by my side." The camera panned back and forth over the faces of the distraught older couple. "Now, it's not normal department policy for someone like me to stand up here and make such a hateful crime a public spectacle, but there are extenuating circumstances in this case. You see, the Gibson's grandson is Casey Mitchell, the seven-year-old son of Detective Gabe Mitchell, whom all of you know by now murdered Dr. Kenneth Sanborn last night at Jackson Medical Center, and who in turn was apprehended and killed after a high-speed pursuit."

"They've got your son," Waxman said, appalled.

Gabe knelt in front of the screen. In his mother-in-law's grieved expression, he imagined he saw the face of his own wife, desperate to have her only child returned safely. "They're trying to flush me out."

"The other reason I'm personally involved in this case, besides having been Gabe's superior officer and a close friend..."

Gabe's hands knotted into fists.

"I was the one who received the ransom call, and, unfortunately, we were unable to trace its origin."

"*Why did you get the call?*" a female voice with an unmistakable Irish brogue shouted out from amid the audience of reporters.

Williams shook his head pathetically. "I don't know why I was chosen, but when the call came in, I contacted the family right away to confirm that their grandson was indeed missing."

"*Where were you at the time of the call?*" the same unforgettable Irish brogue called out.

"I was at a breakfast meeting on the fifteenth floor in the Tower of the Americas building in Downtown Miami," he underscored the location, "but I don't see the relevance of that question."

"What were the kidnapper's demands?" another reporter shouted out.

"I'm not at liberty to say at this time."

"But why are you going public with this situation? Aren't you worried about the boy's safety?"

Williams began to noticeably fidget behind the podium. "Suffice it to say, we're doing what needs to be done to ensure the safe return of Casey Mitchell to his grandparents. Again, I'm not at liberty to say anything else in this regard."

"*So there's another underlying reason for this press conference?*"

Williams looked directly into the camera once again. "I have no comment."

Another unfamiliar female voice rang out from the middle of the mob. "*Have you determined a motive for the kidnapping, Captain? Was this done as some sort of retaliation for Dr. Sanborn's death?*"

Williams shook his head regretfully. "I'm sorry, I can't say."

"*Then what is the reason for this press conference, Captain? Are you using this air time to send the kidnapper a message? Are you using this forum to respond to one of his demands?*"

"I have only one more thing to say," Williams announced as he removed his glasses and leaned in toward the camera. "I have given the family my personal assurance that by eight o'clock this evening," he once again emphasized, "we will have reached a favorable outcome in this matter. That's all I have to say for now. The family chose to be here in a show of support, but will not be answering any of your questions. Thank you very much."

The scene switched back to Scott Newman sitting at the news desk. "*Well, there you have it. A very determined Captain Leon Williams of the City of Miami Police Department obviously addressing, albeit cryptically, the kidnapper of seven-year-old Casey Mitchell, son of Gabe Mitchell—the detective who allegedly stabbed Dr. Kenneth Sanborn to death last night at Jackson Medical Center. We will continue to follow the events of this desperate story as it unfolds, and, hopefully, we'll have more details on Eyewitness News at five o'clock, so stay tuned. We're now going to return you to our regularly scheduled show in progress...*"

"Well, I guess that settles that," Gabe said, as Waxman once again lowered the volume on the television. "They want me there at eight o'clock tonight."

"Damn, those sons-of-bitches are devious," Chase groused. "I can't believe they took your boy."

"You've got to let me help you," Waxman said, rising to his feet. "You just can't go waltzing into their trap."

Gabe took the remote control from the ex-mayor's hand and rewound the tape. "I appreciate the gesture, Nate, but if I don't go in there alone, they'll kill Casey without so much as batting an eye. I don't have a choice."

"Hang on a minute," Chase said as he disappeared from the room, only to return seconds later carrying a wooden humidor. "Here, at least take this. I've been keeping it around here as a precaution, but it obviously doesn't matter anymore."

Gabe took the box and opened it. The stainless steel barrel of the Smith & Wesson .38 caliber revolver gleamed in the light. Gabe removed it from the velvet-lined box and swung open the cylinder. The gun was loaded, but had never been fired. "Are you sure, Bennett?"

"Are you kidding? I'm not going to need it anymore. I've even got an extra box of ammunition if you want."

Gabe reached out and shook Chase's hand. "Thank you, Bennett. I'm sorry I'll probably never get to repay all of your kindness."

The old man reached up and put his hand on Gabe's cheek. "Just get your boy back, and we'll call it even."

Gabe took the revolver and placed it gently back in its repository. "Would you two mind if I watch the tape again? I just want to make sure I didn't miss anything the first time."

"Of course not," Waxman said as he sat back down and stared intently at the screen. "Hand me the notepad, and I'll jot down anything that you tell me is important."

Gabe handed over the paper and pressed the button for the tape to start playing. It wasn't 15 seconds before he paused the tape, freezing the image of the young black man holding open the conference room door for Williams. "Damon Washington," Gabe said astutely. "I had a feeling that was him."

"Wait a minute," Waxman said, getting on his knees and moving closer to the screen. "You know that guy? I know that guy!"

Gabe looked down at the ex-mayor who was unceremoniously on all fours. "How would you know Damon Washington? Know him from where?"

Waxman winced as he strained to recall where he had seen that face before. "I don't *know* him by name, but I've *seen* him ... and on more than one occasion too ... at City Hall, I think."

"With Leon Williams?" Gabe probed.

Waxman shook his head. "No, the Police Plaza and City Hall are miles apart. Come on—think, Nate!" he chastised himself.

"And the name Damon Washington isn't familiar to you? He's August Bock's helicopter pilot, and I think he acts as his legs ... you know, his right hand man."

Waxman scratched his head in frustration. "Where the hell would I have seen him?"

Gabe released the pause button and the tape restarted. "Don't worry about it. It'll come to you. Here," Gabe said, handing Waxman a pencil off the desk, "Write this down: 15th floor, Tower of the Americas, eight o'clock. Boy, what I wouldn't give to get my hands on a blueprint of that office..."

Waxman jumped to his feet like he had been shocked with an electric cattle prod. "That's it! The office! I saw that guy coming out of..."

"Where?" Chase asked anxiously.

Waxman plopped back down on the couch as though all of his bones had suddenly been stolen along with his trust. "Umberto Espinoza ... that piece of ..." the ex-mayor exploded, as he fought off the urge to put his foot through the television screen.

"The deputy mayor?" Chase asked, surprised at the assumption.

"No," Waxman growled, his teeth clenched with anger, "now that I'm dead ... the newly appointed mayor!"

"Do you have any legitimate reason to believe that he would conspire to have you killed?" Gabe asked.

"Why else would Bock's man have been coming out of his office? Espinoza had every opportunity to drug me at my birthday party and then murder my wife."

Gabe put his glass of tea down on the coffee table. "I've got the badge numbers of two patrolmen who will probably be able to confirm that if it's true."

Bennett Chase reached across the coffee table and slipped a cork coaster under Gabe's glass. "Do you really think your deputy mayor was capable of having your wife killed?" he asked Waxman, sounding skeptical. "I mean, why not just run against you in the next election and try to win the office fair and square? Or better yet, and I mean no offense by this, why didn't he just have *you* killed?"

Waxman squirmed nervously at the speculation over his own demise. "Let me give you guys a brief history lesson on the intricacies of our local political system. First off, killing me would have only made my wife's ambition stronger. In the second place, Anna had a very dedicated political following for over 10 years, and everyone knew that I valued her input in every decision I made. Some political pundits went so far as to say that she was Eva to my Juan Peron—pulling my strings like I was her puppet."

Gabe remembered meeting Anna Waxman once while working security for one of her rallies. She was political dynamite incarnate.

"Anyone who knew my Anna," Waxman continued teary-eyed, "knew that she was a strong enough woman that, in the event of my death, she would have been immediately recruited to take over my office for the remainder of my term, and would have easily defeated *any* opponent in the next election. Killing my wife and framing me for her murder was the only way Umberto Espinoza would ever be able to find his way to the mayor's office over the next 20 years."

"Espinoza framed you so well, he convinced a lot of people you really *were* guilty ... including August Bock," Gabe conjectured. "He set you up so well, in fact, that you made it onto Bock's personal hit parade because you were acquitted. To be honest with you, before all this happened, I would have bet my pension that you really murdered her too."

"Yeah, you and about 10 million other people," Waxman added, as he put his hand on Gabe's shoulder. "You know the funny thing? Anna always warned me about letting that slime ball ride on my coattails, but I wouldn't listen to her. The city was ethnically divided, I told her. We needed the Latin vote. She always said that if it wasn't for me that incompetent cretin would still be bumping his nose into parked ambulances."

"Don't take this the wrong way," Gabe says, "but Espinoza seems pretty damned smart to have masterminded this coup d'état. I don't think you give him the credit he deserves."

"But thank goodness," Waxman said, letting out a grateful whistle, "a jury of my peers saw through his sham."

"And when they found you not guilty..." Chase interjected.

"Much to Umberto Espinoza's delight," the ex-mayor quipped, "August Bock sent Gabe to finish the job."

Gabe looked over his shoulder at Chase. "We were both swindled ... but tonight, it all ends."

Waxman held out his hand. "And you're sure there's nothing I can do for you, Detective?"

Gabe shook his hand appreciatively. "Thanks anyway, Your Honor. They've got my boy, and I'm going to get him back ... or die trying."

Waxman's hand tightened around Gabe's. "If it wasn't for you, Detective Gabe, I never would have discovered the truth."

Gabe stood up. "Well, I guess tonight we'll all be going our separate ways."

Waxman rose off the couch and stood between Gabe and the old man. One at a time, they placed their hands atop each other's in an unspoken musketeer's oath. To look at them, there was probably never such a diverse triumvirate of characters entering into such a symbolic covenant. "You know where you're headed?" Gabe asked them both.

"Well, my night's not going to be nearly as life altering as the both of yours promises to be," Bennett Chase said, enviously, "but I'll be here minding the mint if either of you should need me."

"And you?" Gabe asked Nathan Waxman.

"Me?" The mayor's eyes narrowed. "I've got a memorial service to attend."

49

The starless night fell like a wet blanket over downtown Miami. Ominous grey clouds drifted in over the city, urged on by an easterly sea breeze that smelled of a fresh storm on the horizon. But, as usual, the city would not heed their warning. There was a basketball game at the Arena tonight, and the streets were alive with music and life.

As the cab pulled to the curb in front of the Tower of the Americas, Gabe checked his gun one last time. He looked up to see the Cuban driver peering over the front seat, petrified at the sight of the weapon. "Don't worry, I'm a cop," Gabe said, trying to put the driver's mind at ease.

"Sí, señor," the driver said, knocking his knuckles on the glass partition that separated them. "I don't worry. This window is bulletproof anyway."

Gabe glanced at the meter and pulled out the only bill he had with him—a $20. It would be just enough, including a healthy tip for the driver.

"Muchas gracias, señor," the driver said, unlocking a small opening in the clear partition. "Do you wish me to wait for you? The building ... it looks empty."

Gabe slipped the gun into his waistband behind his back and pulled the University of Miami windbreaker Bennett Chase had given him up over it. "No thanks," Gabe said as he opened the door and spotted Shayla Rand's black Corvette parked just ahead of them by the curb. "I'm expected."

The taxi pulled away, leaving Gabe standing before two enormous glass doors. A security camera was positioned above the door and, when he stepped into its range, a small red light blinked on above the lens. Gabe took a step back and craned his head toward the sky. The sheer glass building seemed to rise to infinity when, in actuality, it was only 28 stories—but from his vantage point, it appeared to stretch forever.

Pedestrian traffic was light on this street. Unlike many metropolises, very few shops in downtown Miami stayed open past six o'clock. The few people that roamed the street this late at night appeared to be panhandlers or street vagrants settling into their makeshift roosts after a hot meal at the local soup kitchen. During his time on the force, this area had been very familiar to him, but now that felt like 100 lifetimes ago.

Checking his wristwatch, Gabe knew that he was a few minutes early. The air was cold enough so that, when he exhaled, his breath was clearly visible. There was no use showing up ahead of time; whatever waited for him on the 15th floor could hold on a few minutes longer. This might be the last chance he had to meditate on his life and he saw no reason to squander the opportunity.

Leaning against a "no parking" sign, his fists tucked tightly into his orange and green jacket pockets, Gabe reflected on what shambles he had made of his life. It was the same self-loathing lecture he gave himself every chance he got lately, and it never grew easier to hear. But now he had a chance to change it all. Even if he didn't make it out of this building alive, his son would always know that he came for him. This, more than anything else, was what he hoped to prove by walking into this obvious ambush.

Before he had left the house, Bennett Chase begged for Gabe to take him along or to take the rental car. But Gabe would have no part of it. He didn't want his friend involved. Chase tried to convince Gabe that dying at home wasn't what he wanted. He'd used the excuse that he didn't feel it was dignified enough for a combat pilot. He wanted to go out in a blaze of glory, and, while he was still strong enough to make the trip, perhaps he could run interference for him, or act as some kind of a decoy. If he couldn't die in the air, then meeting his maker while helping Gabe get his son back would be just as honorable a death. Chase had become so worked up during his frenzied argument that Gabe had to sit him down in a kitchen chair to let him catch his breath.

Gabe understood what his comrade meant, and if there had been any chance that Chase could have helped in this situation, Gabe would have enlisted him without hesitation ... but there wasn't. He knew what it meant to die with honor, and for a man and friend like Bennett Chase, the drawn out torment of cancer was not a fitting end. Gabe had seen the look in the old man's eyes when he handed over his gun. He knew it wasn't in the house for protection—it was there for when the pain became unbearable. To this end, Gabe was glad he had taken it from his friend.

His farewell to Nathan Waxman had been far less upsetting. The ex-mayor had been sincere in his thanks, but there was always something smarmy about a politician's gratitude. You always felt like you needed to scrub your hands after shaking theirs. Again, Waxman asked if there was anything he could do to help, but Gabe declined the offer. This had to be kept low key and by the book. Sending in the troops as Waxman proposed would only spell disaster for his son's safety.

The sound of screeching brakes echoed through the tall maze of concrete and glass buildings. The shrill noise was enough to jolt Gabe's mind back to reality. He checked his watch and saw that it was time. He had hoped to go into this thing a little better equipped, perhaps even with a schematic of the building's layout, but Bennett had been unsuccessful on his computer. Gabe shook his head wistfully. You could access the blueprints for manufacturing a pipe bomb on the Internet, but the design of a simple public building was off limits ... what a world!

Gabe walked up to the doors again, this time noticing that the camera was panning with him, following his movement. There was a digital keypad on the wall to his right, with a slot for sliding a card key for access. The light on the keypad was red, and when Gabe reached for the brass handles on the doors, they wouldn't budge.

Above him, the camera whirred and the lens grew longer. Gabe turned his face to the lens so whoever was monitoring the door could get a clear identification. Seconds later, the keypad buzzed and the light turned from red to green. Once again, Gabe pushed on the handles, and this time they gave way.

The lobby of the Tower of the Americas was cold, deserted and smelled from a fresh coat of floor wax. An information booth sat unattended in the middle of the vestibule, while flags from every country in the South and North American continents hung limply around the perimeter of the vast room. Gabe's wet rubber heels squeaked on the black marble floor as he made his way toward the bank of elevators just ahead of him. Again, a security camera mounted on the ceiling appeared to be tracking his every movement. Nearing the elevators, he noticed that none of the floor indicators were lit, but, as if on cue, a single lift came to life as he approached it. Then, like the gaping mouth of some ravenous beast, the mirrored doors hissed open and Gabe warily stepped inside.

One by one, the floors clicked by. The ride was only 15 seconds in its entirety, but seemed interminable to Gabe. His mind was a whirlwind of different thoughts as he stood in the back corner of the lift. His wife and daughter, his son, his partner—they all swirled before his eyes like a kaleidoscope of lost opportunities. Nothing had worked out as he planned. He had always been too preoccupied, too self-centered to notice that they had all slipped away.

Gabe tugged on the collar of his shirt, suddenly aware that he was sweating profusely. He was certain what lay beyond the mirrored doors, and his idealism had all but dissolved. How could he have thought that one man could make a stand against such overwhelming odds? All he could hope to do was negotiate for his son's life. What more could they take from him? He had cheated death one too many times, and now death, in the form of a red-haired Amazon, was about to even the score. Gabe's demeanor was detached. He had nothing left to lose.

The elevator lurched to a stop on the 15th floor, for a moment it hesitated, and then the doors slid open. Gabe exited the lift cautiously. Accompanied only by the sound of his own shallow breathing, Gabe stuck his head out and peered warily in both directions. He was in the outer lobby of Worldwide Dispatch Incorporated, and the room was uninhabited. A single beam of light from the ceiling illuminated what he figured to be the receptionist's desk. He surveyed the photo murals of the company trucks on the surrounding walls. The room was decorated with frescos of planes and trains that only existed to perpetuate the illusion of actual commerce. Two grand mahogany doors loomed before him as he made his way slowly across the office. He made sure one last time that his weapon was still in place before he reached for the handles.

"Ah, Mr. Mitchell," a voice boomed out, "punctual as well as intrepid. Do join us."

The inner office was cavernous. The entire rear wall was a picture window that looked out onto the city. Cutting across the horizon, a Metromover train streaked by on its monorail track, heading downtown.

"Dad!" young Casey Mitchell cried out. He was seated in the middle of the room, his ankles and wrists bound to a chair with plastic zip ties.

Gabe hadn't taken two steps into the spacious office before a pair of hands began to brusquely frisk him from behind. The hidden gun was quickly discovered and yanked out of his waistband. Gabe turned to see who was shaking him down and he wasn't surprised to find his ex-captain, Leon Williams, now brandishing the weapon.

Gabe shook loose of Williams' grip and ran to his son, kneeling before him. "Are you okay, Casey? Have they hurt you, son?"

Casey shook his head, his long hair flopping into his tear-filled eyes. "I'm alright, Dad, but you shouldn't have come."

Gabe brushed the hair out of his son's eyes. "You think I'd let anything happen to you, tiger?" he whispered into the boy's ear. "Just stay cool, and you'll be home before you know it. I love you, you know that, right?"

His son's lips were quivering. "I know it. I love you too, Dad."

Gabe wiped Casey's cheeks clean and kissed him gently on the forehead before he stood up. "Okay Bock, I got your message, and now I'm here ... so let my boy go. I'm the one you want; he's got nothing to do with this."

August Bock sat behind the largest, most ornately carved desk that Gabe had ever seen. The head of Worldwide Dispatch was flanked on one side by Damon Washington while Shayla Rand stood on the other. Bock was dressed in an Italian-cut, crimson blazer with a black shirt and matching tie. As he pushed his wheelchair away from the desk, he wore a toothy smile that Gabe had seen a thousand times before ... on criminals who were being shipped off for observation. "As much as I'd like to, Mr. Mitchell, I believe Master Casey knows a bit too much for his own good. I think it would be best for everyone concerned if he share your fate," he said, pointing to the Irish assassin. "But don't worry: unlike your death, Shayla has assured me that the boy's demise will be quick and painless."

"Dad?" Casey whimpered.

Gabe instinctively stepped between Bock and his son. "Don't worry, Casey. I'm not going to let anything happen to you."

Bock rolled from behind the desk with Damon Washington trailing close behind. Shayla Rand stood in place, motionless and unblinking, her eyes trained on Gabe. "Ah, the paternal instinct in full spectacle. How touching," she seethed.

Gabe put his hand on Casey's head and turned to Bock. "I thought killing an innocent child would be beneath you, but I guess I had you pegged wrong. You're not a champion of justice like you've convinced yourself you are. You're just a delusional mother..." Gabe caught himself in front of his son, "...spiffed up in a $1,000 suit."

Bock laughed. "I can't believe you would think killing your son would trouble me. Obviously you don't read the newspapers or watch television. I will do whatever it takes to carry on my work ... and neither you, nor your son, mean more to me than a minor distraction."

Gabe raised a curious eyebrow. "So why not pull the trigger yourself?"

"Excuse me?" Bock asked.

"If you believe killing me is so righteous, why don't you take the gun from this contemptible excuse for a police captain and kill us yourself? Why do you need someone else to do your dirty work? Your balls not functioning anymore either?"

"Insolent to the end, Mr. Mitchell," Bock laughed raucously. "I knew there was a reason I liked you. But to answer your question," his face turning to stone, "I wouldn't have the slightest qualm about putting a bullet into each of your brains, but I've promised that pleasure to someone who wants it even more than myself."

Gabe looked over at Shayla Rand, whose emerald green eyes seemed to suddenly sparkle in the light.

"I'm sorry that I'm not going to be able to stick around for the final curtain, Mr. Mitchell, as much as I would like to," Bock pouted, "but, thanks to you, it seems that my lease here has suddenly expired." He looked questioningly at Gabe. "I *am* assuming that Nathan Waxman is still alive and kicking as well?"

The corner of Gabe's mouth curled upward. "You bet your sweet ass he is."

"What a pity," Bock frowned. "Well, you know what they say: if at first you don't succeed…"

Gabe stepped to his right, blocking the path of Bock's wheelchair. "Whatever you do to me, I think you should reconsider putting Nathan Waxman's name back on the top of your hit parade."

"And why is that?" Bock asked.

Gabe made sure his words sunk in. "Because he didn't kill his wife."

"Come on, August," Washington urged from behind. "The plane's waiting. We're going to be late."

Bock grinned slyly. "And I'm sure Mayor Waxman has convinced you of that himself?"

Gabe shook his head. "He didn't have to convince me; I trust my instincts. But, if you don't believe me, why don't you ask your sidekick here?" he said, nodding toward Washington. "He knows the truth."

The man guiding the wheelchair fluffed off the question. "You're not taking any of this seriously, are you, August? This guy would say anything right now to save his son's skin. He's playing you."

Bock's good eye darted back and forth between his trusted pilot and Gabe. "I'm sure as a former prosecutor like myself, Nathan Waxman has made a persuasive case in his own behalf for you, Mr. Mitchell. But like you, I trust *my* instincts. I can't begin to count the number of convicted felons that have lived with treachery for so long that they themselves begin to believe them as the truth. I'm convinced this fantasy world is where Nathan Waxman now finds himself residing."

"The jury was convinced of his innocence," Gabe argued.

Bock grinned knowingly. "Robert Frost once said: a jury consists of 12 persons chosen to decide who has the better lawyer."

"So you've never even considered the possibility that he might not have committed the crime?"

Bock held up his right hand and examined his perfectly manicured nails. "I've studied the case files. Guilty as charged."

Gabe shook his head. "You're dead wrong this time. The man that had Waxman's wife killed now sits at the Mayor's desk, and your pal here knows it."

"He's babbling," Washington blurted out. "Why are we even listening to this bullshit? Let Shayla have her fun already and let's get out of here."

"I have to take my colleague's side on this matter, Mr. Mitchell. Damon has never been anything but loyal to me."

Washington was grinning behind Bock like a jack-o-lantern.

"You may as well have patches over both your eyes," Gabe said, regretfully. "You've been blinded by your own ambition."

Bock pointed toward the office door and Washington began to push him toward it. "Well, I must be off. My helicopter awaits on the roof, ready to shuttle me to my plane, and soon I shall be planting my roots elsewhere. Perhaps somewhere less humid, I should think. I haven't quite decided yet."

"And just like that, it's over?" Gabe asked.

Bock held up his hand for Washington to stop pushing. "Mr. Mitchell, regardless of Nathan Waxman's guilt or innocence, you and your son have become a liability to me, and must be dealt with accordingly." He paused. "I will make you a promise though: I promise to keep my eye on His Honor's situation, and should he prove to be innocent as you claim ... I promise to have an extra two dozen roses delivered to both you and your son's graves in a show of my heartfelt remorse, how's that?" He cocked his head back and began to laugh again.

Washington turned to Shayla Rand. "No fooling around with them this time. The chopper's already primed, and I want to lift off in less than five minutes."

Gabe looked over at his Captain who still had the pistol poised and ready. "Feeling good about yourself, Captain?" Gabe muttered under his breath.

"So long, Mr. Mitchell," Bock said, as Damon Washington escorted him out through the office doors. "You were a worthy adversary."

50

"Let's just get this over with quickly," Williams urged, "I don't want to miss our ride out of here."

Shayla Rand waited for the door to close before she stepped from behind the desk.

"If your finger even twitches on that trigger," she said to Williams, "it will be the last muscle you ever move. I have a score to settle," she said as she ran her hand along the jagged scar on her face, "and if you interfere with me, I'll kill you where you stand."

Gabe moved to his right to keep himself between the woman and his son. In any other venue, Shayla Rand would have been considered a perfect 10. Even with the hideous scar, she was as beautiful as she was lethal. Her hair was dyed bright crimson to match her skin-tight red leather jumpsuit and matching heels. Circling like a hungry predator, she oozed a deadly sensuality that she manipulated as easily as any other weapon.

"You don't need to protect your son, Gabe. Although killing him first would probably reduce you to a blob of quivering mush, I want you at your best. I want him to see you ripped limb from limb, and then I'll just snap his neck quickly ... like a dried twig."

"Dad!"

Gabe glanced over at Leon Williams. "Nice gang of characters you've climbed into bed with, Cap. I hope they're paying you well."

Williams lowered the gun to his side. "I didn't have much a future left here with you and Waxman rising from the dead. They're giving me a new identity and plenty of cash to live the good life overseas. So, I wouldn't worry too much about me, if I were you. I think you've got enough on your plate at the moment."

Gabe gritted his teeth. "Well, if I were you, Captain, I'd make sure to fasten my seatbelt on that chopper out of here. You're just as big a liability to these people as we are."

Gabe could see the hesitation on Williams' face, and it made him feel good to know he had struck a nerve. He didn't think he had much time left, but what little he had, Gabe decided to spend like Johnny Appleseed, planting seeds of doubt wherever they might have a chance of blossoming.

"Enough talk," Shayla shouted.

Her left heel shot up in a crimson blur, catching Gabe squarely on the side of his face, whipping his head savagely to the right.

"Dad!" Casey screamed.

"Shut your mouth, boy," Shayla growled at the youngster, "this is only the beginning."

Gabe was still reeling from the first blow, when Shayla caught him with a vicious roundhouse punch that knocked him backward over a glass coffee table. He was on his back, blood streaming from a gaping wound on his upper lip. The taste of his own blood was bitter, and he spit it out.

"Get up," Shayla yelled as she bounced on the balls of her feet in classic kickboxing style. "Get up or I'll kill your son like I killed your partner."

"Shayla," Williams interrupted, "I think we'd better hurry."

She turned to Williams with a glare that would have curdled milk. "Speak to me again, and you'll never leave this office alive!"

Gabe had to summon every ounce of strength to push himself up off the floor. It sounded like there were a billion wasps making a nest inside his head, and it felt like they were all stinging him at the same time.

"I told August I should have killed you in the alley when I had the opportunity," she announced to Gabe, who was staggering up from his knees. "I won't make the same mistake twice."

"You killed Joanne Hansen?" Gabe asked, wiping his mouth with the back of his hand.

"Of course I did ... with your gun after you collapsed. I killed that big galoot too. It was either him or us."

Too much information to absorb. "Just let my son go. He can't possibly do you any harm."

Shayla flexed her fists. "Where I come from, children spend their entire lives avenging the deaths of their parents. Do you really think I'd let that happen here?"

"Please..." Gabe begged.

"Dad!" Casey struggled, rocking his chair back and forth in an effort to free himself, but the plastic straps held firm, digging deep into the tender flesh of his wrists and ankles.

Shayla did a front-facing scissor kick, catching Gabe just beneath his chin. If he hadn't brought his left arm up to slightly deflect her foot, it might have taken off his head. Regardless, the power of her leg snapped his neck back with such force, he thought he felt his teeth rattle.

Gabe stumbled backward against Bock's desk with Shayla lunging toward him. He managed to roll to his left, but she still caught him with two of her razor-sharp nails across his right ear. Gabe had his back to her now, and she hit him with a fierce jab just above his kidney, sending nearly all the air out of his lungs. He was gasping for every breath as he searched frantically for anything he could defend himself with. His eyes were wide open, but he was practically blinded by the intense pain in his lower back and head. He groped across the top of the enormous desk and came away with a Lucite paperweight. With all the strength he could muster, Gabe brought the clear weight around in a sweeping arc. Shayla was too fast, too adroit, to be caught off guard by Gabe's slow-motion haymaker. Her arm shot out to block the punch, and the paperweight flew harmlessly across the office.

Shayla yanked Gabe off the desk, spun him around, and held him up by his collar. She pulled him so close; he could smell the leather and feel her hot breath on his face. Their eyes were mere inches apart as she reached up and dipped the tip of her finger in the blood that poured from the cut on his mouth. "This is what I wanted," she purred as she touched the bloody finger to her tongue. "Now I have your taste."

Gabe's left arm came out of nowhere, rising upward with all of his weight behind it, catching Shayla point blank in her midriff. The air blew out of her lungs in one shocked gust. She teetered backward, her face as red as her dress, and her eyes bulging. Gabe continued forward, keeping his head down, giving his opponent as small a target as possible. Shayla had been surprised by the uppercut, but hundreds of sit-ups a day had toughened her abdomen into a rock-hard slab of muscle. She winced a bit, rubbed her hand across the damaged area, and just as quickly was ready to retaliate.

Shayla stood her ground against the approaching onslaught, blocking every one of the feeble counterattacks, and landing her own powerful combinations to the sides of Gabe's head. Blood and spittle flew from Gabe's mouth with each new blow. His face was hideously swollen, the initial redness already fermenting into grisly purple and black bruises.

Casey was crying and screaming uncontrollably, no longer fearful of his own fate, but petrified of the unmerciful beating his father was taking. With each kick, with every punch, more blood sprayed from Gabe's disfigured mouth, hitting everything within a couple of feet of where he stood staggering. Casey was spattered head to toe, and, as much as he wrestled against his restraints, the young boy was helpless to do anything about his father's predicament.

With his legs powerless to support his own weight, Gabe finally collapsed to the floor, falling into a fetal heap at Shayla Rand's feet.

"If I were to break every bone in your body," she bristled, "it still wouldn't offset the pain and humiliation you have caused me." She walked over and picked up the paperweight that had landed across the room. "I will carry the mark of our encounter long after you're dead and buried, Mr. Mitchell. So what I want is for your son to hear you plead for me to spare your miserable life." She looked over at the boy. "If you grovel enough, then perhaps I'll just let Captain Williams put a bullet into your brain, saving your child the brief, but gruesome, memory of my bashing your skull into bone meal with this stupid curio."

"Enough!" Williams yelled. He had his gun raised and was pointing it at Shayla Rand. "This has gone far enough, Shayla. You've taken your pound of flesh, so what more do you want? Let me finish it now so we can get out of here."

Shayla juggled the paperweight in her hand, all the while never taking her eyes off Williams' weapon. "Most people end up regretting aiming a weapon in my direction, Captain."

Williams moved to his right, his pistol never wavering, his back now to the large window. "Lady, don't threaten me. All the kung-fu in the world ain't never stopped a .38 caliber bullet."

"Alright, Captain," Shayla said calmly, setting the glass block down on the desk and stepping away from Gabe's motionless form. "Since it seems you're holding all the cards, I see no real reason to prolong the inevitable any longer. Be my guest..."

51

As Williams lowered his gun to line the barrel up with Gabe's head, the room suddenly began to vibrate. It was a low, thumping bass sound that reverberated inside the office like a kettle drum. Seconds later, the room was filled with brilliant white light. Instantly diagnosing the situation, Shayla dove for cover, but Williams had turned to face the window and was frozen like a deer in the headlights of an oncoming truck.

Two helicopters slowly rose into position. They were painted white with black lettering on the side that read "*City of Miami Beach Police.*" A sharpshooter sat perched in each open doorway, an automatic rifle trained on the slightest movement inside the office. Instinctively, Williams raised his weapon hand to shield his eyes from the blinding glare. It was only a slight twitch of his arm, but an aggressive gesture nonetheless, and one that would be his last.

The window exploded into a million pieces. Williams never got a shot off as a hurricane of bullets and flying glass riddled his body. To his right, the wall of television screens Bock used to monitor his potential targets shattered and sparked like a Fourth of July fireworks display. The gun flew out of Williams' hand as he was catapulted across the room like he had wires attached to his back. He landed with a lifeless *thud*, his dead fingers clutching at the thousands of tiny slivers of glass that had impaled his face.

Shayla Rand was on all fours, scrambling for the protection of Bock's massive desk. Her hands and knees were bleeding freely from the broken glass scattered on the floor.

Gabe had opened one eye just as the pair of helicopters had come into view. This was one time he thanked God that Nathan Waxman hadn't listened to him. Just as the sharpshooters opened fire, Gabe reached over and yanked the legs out from under the chair Casey was strapped to. The boy crashed to the floor, but the minor injury to one of his shoulders would be nothing compared to what might have been.

A rush of cold wind roared into the office along with the deafening drone of the helicopters' engines. All the lights had been blown out in the room, leaving only the spotlights from the helicopters dancing across the office.

Once there was a break in the shooting, Shayla Rand was on the move. She sprinted across the office, her shoes crackling on the broken glass, a fresh stream of bullets trying to keep up with her. Like an Olympic gymnast, she vaulted over the back of a plush leather couch to safety, the bullets plugging harmlessly into the seat cushions.

"Are you alright, son?" Gabe screamed over the howling noise.

The youngster was dazed but seemed to be physically fine. "I ... I'm okay, Dad. But you..."

Gabe put his hand on his son's cheek. "Don't worry about me, tiger. As long as you're okay, that's all that matters."

"What happened, Dad?"

Even though it hurt like hell, Gabe still managed a faint smile. "It seems a good friend couldn't take *no* for an answer."

Casey didn't understand, but just seeing his father's grin was enough to settle his nerves.

"Now, son," Gabe said, trying unsuccessfully to loosen one of the straps on Casey's ankles, "it might take me a few minutes to find a way to cut you free."

Casey shook his head. "Go Dad. I'll be fine."

"Are you sure?"

The young boy gritted his teeth—a trait he had inherited from his father. "I said I'd be fine; now don't let that *bitch* escape!"

Gabe was visibly taken aback. "Do you kiss your grandparents with that mouth?"

Casey shifted his weight so that he was lying on his side facing his father. "Hey, you can punish me later, alright? Now, go!"

Gabe and his son turned to see Shayla trying to make her way toward the office door. "Those guys in the helicopters know we're the good guys, don't they, Dad?"

Gabe crossed his fingers. "I sure hope so, son."

The gale from the rotor wash was unrelenting. Loose papers swirled around the office like they were caught in a tornado. The steady tremor from the helicopters turbine-driven blades shook most of Bock's oriental sculptures free from their pedestals where they smashed into piles of stony rubble upon striking the marble floor. The offices of Worldwide Dispatch Incorporated had been turned into a war zone.

Shayla Rand peeked out from behind the couch and her eyes locked with Gabe's. There was no hint of fear in her expression, only cold calculation. To her, Gabe was merely one more obstacle blocking her path to the roof.

During the initial barrage, when Bennett Chase's pistol had been blasted out of Leon Williams' hand, the gun had skidded to rest halfway between the desk and the sofa. Gabe and Shayla both spotted the weapon at the same time. For what seemed like seconds frozen in time, they both stared at the gun. Gabe dove for it, but Shayla was quicker. Gabe rolled to his right, hiding behind a large pedestal in an effort to evade the shots he was expecting would surely follow ... but they never came. Instead, Shayla Rand was lying on her back, firing out the window at the helicopters. She was shooting sparingly into the light, until she heard the sound of shattering glass and half the office went dim. Gabe wasted no time using the shadows to crawl toward Leon Williams' lifeless corpse. Oblivious to the fragments of broken glass that were piercing his arms and legs, Gabe finally reached his captain's body and peeled open his blood-soaked jacket. Like any good cop, Williams always packed his service revolver. Gabe released the gun's cylinder and held it up in the meager light. Now he stood a chance.

52

The helicopters began to rise out of the line of fire. Electric sparks continued to arc and crackle from the wall of short-circuited television monitors, their brief flares of light creating a flashing strobe effect inside the darkened office. Shayla used the shadows to her advantage, just as Gabe had. Once she found a darken spot that concealed her, she raised her weapon in both hands and started to scan the office in 90-degree increments. As badly as she wanted Gabe Mitchell dead, she knew her window of opportunity was closing rapidly. Shortly, the building would be crawling with the local police, if it wasn't already. She had to make a decision. Was a washed up cop and a seven-year-old boy really worth her own freedom ... or possibly worse? For someone who had spent most of her adult life appreciating the rewards that her unique skills afforded her, the prospect of plastic utensils and cold concrete walls made her choice an easy one. "I'm afraid we're going to have to call this round a draw, Mr. Mitchell," she yelled, her voice echoing inside the enormous office. "But you know the old adage, '*She who fights and runs away...*'"

Shayla knew Gabe couldn't see her shrouded in the darkness, but he fired a single shot in the direction of her voice. The bullet sliced through the air, missing her by a good thirty feet. She heard him call out from behind the cover of the pedestal. "Give yourself up, Shayla. There's no place to run!"

"That's where you're wrong, Mr. Mitchell," she shouted, "my ride's waiting for me on the roof."

Grimacing at the glass wounds that etched her body, she quickly evaluated her situation the way a quarterback improvised on a broken play.

"Do you really think Bock's still up there with all those police choppers buzzing around?" Gabe continued. "Face it, Shayla, your boss is long gone. He's saved his own hide and left you behind."

Shayla inched along the far wall toward the office door, making sure she stayed in the shadows. She wanted to respond to Gabe, to tell him that he didn't know August Bock the way she did, but experience told her that the slightest sound would tip off her position. Shayla tore open the door and bolted for the roof as light flooded into the office.

53

Gabe was momentarily blinded, and, by the time his eyes had become acclimated, she was gone.

He pulled himself to his feet and limped clumsily toward the door. Every muscle in his body was working on overtime. With his hand on the doorknob, he suddenly paused. "Casey?"

"I'm okay, Dad."

Hearing the courage in his son's voice was reassuring. "You sure?"

"I'm fine. Don't let her get away!"

Gabe straightened up, his paternal pride working like a shot of adrenaline. "I love you, son."

"I love you too, Dad."

First left, then right, he pointed his weapon around the doorway to the outer office. No sign of her. The floor lamps above both elevators were out, which left her only one egress to the roof ... the stairwell. *How tall was this building?*

Gabe found the entrance to the stairs at the end of a small corridor, which also led to a pair of restrooms. Although he doubted Shayla would have chosen to hide there, he had no choice but to investigate them. His quick search ended up nothing more than a waste of valuable time.

Hobbling down the hallway, Gabe closed in on the metal fire door leading to the stairs. The door had a window in it, mounted just about eye level. He strained to see inside, but the opening was too small to give him much of an advantage. Just as he was about to push the door open, the hair on his neck bristled to attention. This had ambush written all over it.

Gabe kicked the door open, stayed low, and moving out onto the landing. A large, black number "15" was painted on the wall opposite him. Inching cautiously toward the stairs, he paused and listened, but heard nothing. If she was running up the stairs, he should have heard something. One at a time, Gabe began the long ascent upward, stopping every few steps to listen. Something wasn't right. He should have heard her.

A shot rang out, reverberating through the stairwell. At the same instant, the metal handrail sparked just ahead of Gabe, and a searing pain ripped through his left shoulder. He had been struck by a ricochet. He fell backward, a red smear appearing on the wall as he slid slowly to the ground. Gritting his teeth against the pain, Gabe pulled off one of his sneakers and yanked off his sock, stuffing the sock underneath his shirt to stem the flow of blood. From deep within some neglected well of courage and strength, Gabe dragged himself to his feet. With one arm hanging uselessly by his side, he wiggled his bare foot back into his shoe. Even in perfect health, Gabe would have had difficulty scaling these steps, but in his weakened condition and with blood pouring out of his shoulder, every step would be an endurance test.

Keeping his back pressed to the outer walls, Gabe braved onward. Reaching the next landing, he discovered how Shayla had been moving so stealthily. She had discarded her shoes and was now running barefoot. Carefully, Gabe stepped toward the railing and darted his eyes upward into the coil of stairs. He caught a flash of red and pulled the trigger, his shot errantly sparking off the landing three levels up.

Shayla leaned over the handrail to return Gabe's fire, and a running gun battle ensued that advanced unrelentingly up the 12 remaining flights of stairs to the roof.

* * * * * *

With her lungs on fire, and her leather skirt sticking to her overheated body like a second skin, Shayla burst through the final metal door and out onto the roof. In that crucial moment, when she ran out into the freezing wind, and only moonlight filled the empty helipad, Shayla Rand experienced an emotion she hadn't sampled in nearly 20 years—betrayal.

Now, with nowhere to run, and the pair of police helicopters hovering overhead, Shayla had to take refuge behind one of the two colossal air conditioning units that were positioned at opposite ends of the roof. Trying to stay out of the glare of the searchlights, she scampered across the roof, her feet getting torn up by the loose gravel that covered the roof's surface.

Moments later, Gabe crossed the open threshold, his weapon raised with his good arm, first pointing left, then to the right. A searchlight caught him in the doorway and followed his movement as he prowled guardedly across the roof.

The wind at this altitude, combined with the downdraft from the helicopters' rotor wash, buffeted Gabe with almost hurricane force velocity, at times making it nearly impossible for him just to stand his ground. As he rounded the corner of what appeared to be an air vent, a bullet struck the vent's metal housing and sent out a shower of sparks. Two more inches to the right, or one infinitesimal second later, and Gabe would have been dead on the spot.

Shayla was having no problem tracking Gabe's movements. Thanks to the searchlight, he was lit up like a movie star at a Hollywood premiere. Blood flowed freely from the shredded soles of her feet, but she never felt a drop of it. In her present state of heightened awareness, Shayla Rand was oblivious to pain. Trained from her youth, her brain had merely clicked into another mode of operation—one best described as *survival instinct*. Checking her gun, she knew she was running out of ammunition and needed to make every remaining shot count.

Having to keep her eyes shielded from the perpetual cloud of dust being whipped up by the helicopter blades, Shayla crept closer to the beam of light that silhouetted her target. She was so intent on narrowing the gap between herself and Gabe that she was uncharacteristically startled when she suddenly found herself ensnared in the second searchlight's beam. Staring up into the intense glare, she could just make out a flak-jacketed sharpshooter pointing his automatic rifle directly down at her. With ingrained accuracy, she fired a salvo of shots, the first hitting the exposed sharpshooter in the neck, two more rounds piercing the undercarriage of the fuselage. Black oil spewed from the belly of the helicopter as a trail of black smoke marked its spiraling nosedive to the street below. Only through his trust in a higher power and his expert proficiency did the pilot manage to land the burning craft safely on the sidewalk below.

* * * * * *

The floodlight from the remaining helicopter began to patrol the roof as Gabe bolted for the cover of another air vent. Flying gravel tore at his skin as the helicopter made a loud, sweeping pass directly overhead. Gabe protected his face with his good arm as he knelt down behind the second air conditioning unit. His breathing was coming in short, labored gasps, and he could feel his energy draining out through the hole in his shoulder. All he could do now was to hope and pray for one clean shot...

* * * * * *

Easily evading the focus of the lone searchlight, Shayla circled around the perimeter of the roof until she finally spotted Gabe. She found him cowering behind an air vent with his back to her. This was almost too easy. She could see that she must have hit her mark at least once already, from the telltale dark brown stain on the back of his windbreaker.

* * * * * *

Gabe never actually saw her slithering up from behind, but out of the corner of his eye, he caught the edge of a shadow ... then his cop's instinct took over. He fell to his left and fired what proved to be his last remaining round. Over and over again, his finger continued to pull the trigger, even though the hammer was clicking on an empty chamber.

Shayla Rand laughed as her hand came away from her thigh soaked in blood. "Not even close," she yelled, as she limped into point blank range and leveled her pistol at Gabe's forehead. Before she could fire the fatal shot, the roaming searchlight captured her again, temporarily blinding her. She covered her eyes with her hand and Gabe quickly seized the opening. He rolled for her legs, sending her sprawling to the rocky surface; her gun was jarred loose and swallowed in the shadows.

Knotted like lovers, Gabe and Shayla wrestled across the rough pavement with the hovering helicopter illuminating their struggle. Hanging out of the open hatch, the sharpshooter hesitated, unable to get off an unobstructed shot.

Trained in hand-to-hand combat and torture techniques from the time she was a young girl, Shayla twisted her thumb deep into Gabe's wound, making him wail in agony. With one arm absolutely useless, Gabe had to throw the Marquis of Queensberry rules out the window, kicking and clawing, and doing just about anything he could to inflict damage.

Closer to the precipitous ledge they battled, with Gabe never having the slightest misgivings about using his one good arm to pummel this good-looking woman to a pulp. Waiting for her opening, Shayla ducked low, using a sweeping leg kick to knock Gabe's legs out from under him. Falling awkwardly onto his back, Shayla moved in and straddled his body, wrapping her hands around his throat. Gabe struggled beneath her, his body bent backward, hanging halfway off the edge of the building. With both her hands digging into his neck, Gabe turned his head toward the sidewalk and spotted the shot-up helicopter 28 stories below, its blades still rotating. Shayla noticed it at the same exact moment and cackled wildly. "It may not happen tonight," she growled menacingly, applying even more pressure to his head, "but I want you to go to your grave knowing that, someday, I *will* be paying my respects to your son."

That was all Gabe had to hear. Suddenly, an untapped source of determination invigorated his bruised and battered features. And, for the first time since they had crossed paths, there was the definite hint of fear in Shayla Rand's steely green eyes.

"Respect *this*, bitch," Gabe growled, as he twisted in her grasp and snapped his neck forward, head-butting her face as hard as he could. With her nose broken and spouting blood like a geyser, Shayla's hands faltered around his throat. Gabe reached up, and, with all the energy he had left, grabbed the back of her jumpsuit collar, and yanked her over the ledge. Shayla Rand's horrified screams echoed into the night as she plummeted like a mannequin, 28 stories straight down, and into the whirling blades of the crippled helicopter.

54

Gabe waved off the helicopter on his way back inside the building to check on his son. He didn't know how he was going to ever repay Nathan Waxman for his timely reinforcements, but at least he'd have the rest of his life to try.

By the time Gabe stumbled back down to the 15th floor, the office had been secured by a special weapons and tactics squad, and a team of paramedics were already checking on Casey.

"Dad!" the boy yelled excitedly as Gabe staggered into the office.

Gabe fell to his knees and they hugged long and hard.

"I knew you'd come back, Dad. I just knew it!"

It felt so good to be holding his son; Gabe never even realized he was wincing in pain from his shoulder wound. "I love you, tiger."

Casey's head was pressed against his father's chest. It felt like a natural thing. "I love you too, Dad."

One of the paramedics who had been watching the tearful reunion politely separated father and child. "I've got to take a look at that wound," he smiled at Casey. "Why don't you go sit on that couch over there while I treat your father's shoulder?" he suggested.

Casey shook his small head adamantly. "Uh-uh. I'm staying right here with my Dad."

"You're incredibly lucky," the paramedic commented, as he removed the bloody sock from beneath Gabe's shirt. "It looks like the bullet passed clean through the soft tissue of your shoulder."

Casey grimaced as the paramedic slipped the bloody sock into a plastic bag.

"Listen, tiger," Gabe whispered to his son, "as soon as this man's finished dressing my wound, there's one more thing I've got to do."

Casey reached over and wiped a curl of sweat soaked hair away from his father's eyes and then sulked. "You have to go after that guy in the wheelchair, don't you?"

Gabe winced as the paramedic cleansed the wound with hydrogen peroxide. "You don't want him to get away, do you?"

Casey shook his head. "He's not going to shoot you too, is he?"

Gabe and the paramedic smiled at each other. "Hopefully not," Gabe moaned.

"I'm going to give you something for the pain," the paramedic told Gabe, "but you've got to get this looked at A.S.A.P."

"You don't have to tell me twice," Gabe said, letting the paramedic help him to his feet. Gabe wobbled in place for a second, feeling slightly lightheaded from the loss of blood. Slowly, as his equilibrium recovered, he managed his way across the office to Bock's desk and picked up the phone, only to learn that the line was dead. "Are any of you carrying a cell phone with you?" Gabe asked of any of the S.W.A.T. members or paramedics still lingering in the office.

"I've been told they're going want you for a debriefing as soon as you're up to it," the S.W.A.T. leader informed Gabe as he stepped forward and volunteered his portable phone.

"Who's *they*?" Gabe asked him, suspiciously.

"I don't know," the S.W.A.T. leader shrugged. "You don't know who *they* are?"

"I don't know who *anyone* is anymore," Gabe admitted, as he flipped open the receiver and proceeded to make the most fateful phone call of his entire life.

55

Across town, an evening memorial service was being held for the late Mayor of Miami Beach at Temple Beth David. He was being eulogized by friends and family for the great work he had performed as a civic leader and for his dedication as a caring father and a devoted husband. The somber hall was filled with dignitaries from national, state, and local government.

The newly appointed Mayor of Miami Beach, Umberto Espinoza, had arrived fashionably late by limousine, enjoying all of the pomp and circumstance of an office he had no chance of ever winning by the popular vote. Everything had worked out perfectly for him. Espinoza was in a win-win situation. If the ex-mayor had been convicted of his wife's murder, then he would have taken control of the city. When Waxman was acquitted (which to that day Espinoza couldn't understand, because the framing had been perfect), and all seemed lost then, out of the blue, like an angel sent to answer his prayers, he was approached by a representative from Worldwide Dispatch Incorporated. It was the best $8 million he had ever spent. He planned on making that investment back in no time, through his union connections and a few sizable zoning deals.

It was in the middle of Espinoza's stirring, if not well-rehearsed, tribute to his beloved predecessor that a murmur began to stir through the congregation. The microphone on the podium before him screeched from feedback as if to herald the unexpected guest's arrival. One pew at a time, the crowd slowly rose to its feet in stunned disbelief as the late Nathan Waxman, seemingly back from the dead, strutted triumphantly down the center aisle, accompanied by a handful of his city's finest.

56

"How much longer is this going to take?" Bock fumed, as he pounded his fist on the arm of his wheelchair. "First, the plane's not fueled up, and now this! It's been nearly an hour!"

Damon Washington stepped around the sleek beige wing of the private jet, running his hand along its leading edge. "These things happen, August. There was a problem with the fuel tanker's pump ... and now it's fixed and pumping. People do get sick ... and so they've sent us a replacement pilot. You've got to learn to roll with the punches. Everything's going to be just fine."

"People don't call in sick and stay on my payroll," Bock griped, as he rolled his chair onto the platform of the hydraulic lift. "This is cutting it much too fine for my taste. It was bad enough we had to leave Shayla back there to fend for herself."

The caustic smell of the jet fuel made Washington blow his nose. "We didn't have a choice, August—but you've got to look at the silver lining instead of the cloud; there's a reason for everything. If the jet had been fueled and the pilot was here, we wouldn't be able to give Shayla these extra few minutes to catch up to us."

Bock shook his head as he reached down and locked the brakes on his chair. "I don't know, Damon. Did you see all those patrol cars down on the street when we took off? How could she make it out of there?" He lowered his head. "I don't know how I'll ever be able to replace her. They'll never be another Shayla Rand in my life."

Washington glanced around the tarmac. This late at night, when the air was still, and Opa-Locka's executive runways were all but abandoned, hundreds of wild rabbits, which lived around the small municipal airport, would scramble out of their burrows, romp across the tarmac, and huddle around the blue, red, white, and green runway lights for warmth. It was an amazing thing to watch. "If anyone could make it out of there," Washington assured his boss, "you know as well as I do, it'd be Shayla Rand. I just hope..."

Bock turned his head. "You hope what?"

Washington shrugged as the fuel operator detached the fuel hose from the wing tank. "I just hope she forgives us for leaving her back there. You know the temper that girl's got when she gets pissed off!"

Bock held up his hand. "Don't you worry about her temper, Damon. If she makes it back here, we'll all be drowning in so much Irish whiskey by the time this plane leaves the ground, tonight will be nothing but a bad memory."

The tanker driver handed a clipboard to Washington and he signed for the fuel. "Well, I guess that's it," Washington said, tearing off a copy of the receipt and stuffing it into his pocket. "It looks like Shayla's not going to..."

From far across the airport grounds, the sound of squealing tires interrupted Washington. A pair of headlights loomed closer, and grew more intense along with the low rumble of a finely tuned engine. Washington turned to Bock, who was grinning ear to ear.

"I'd know the sound of her Corvette anywhere," Bock shouted jubilantly. "Damn, if she didn't make it. Yes! I believe it's almost time to break out the whiskey!"

The black Corvette came to a skidding stop alongside the jet. Washington was halfway to the car when he stopped dead in his tracks and pulled a pistol out of his waistband. Slowly, almost painfully, the driver's door opened and a single bloody sneaker stepped out onto the tarmac.

August Bock was more than a little surprised to see a battered and bleeding Gabe Mitchell step out of Shayla Rand's black Corvette.

"Where is Shayla?" Bock called out incredulously.

Gabe reached up and wiped dried blood from the corner of his mouth. "She went for a spin," he said, slamming the door shut behind him.

Washington eased closer to the car, the gun still trained on Gabe's forehead. When he got close enough, he moved around behind Gabe and began to frisk him down. "He's not carrying a weapon," he shouted.

"You're quite the little Energizer Bunny, Mr. Mitchell. So, what are you going to do, take me in?" Bock asked, casually folding his hands across his lap. He was desperately trying not to show the rage he was truly feeling, now that his worst expectations about Shayla Rand had become a grim reality.

Gabe walked like a zombie toward the aircraft, with Washington trailing him close behind. He had no idea what invisible force of nature was holding him up or keeping his legs moving in the correct sequence.

Bock's lips bent into a snarl. "You've proved to be much more resilient than we ever anticipated. Good for you, but you've only won this skirmish. Our crusade carries on."

"Not if I can help it," Gabe warned.

"Do you really think that I'm worried about you, Mr. Mitchell?" Bock asked, doubtfully. "No one's ever going to believe your preposterous stories of terminal patients being used as explosive weapons of justice." He pointed a gnarled finger at Gabe. "After all you've been through, and despite everything you've discovered, you still don't seem to have grasped the concept. Don't you see how absurd it all sounds? Skepticism is how my organization survives. It's simple human nature."

"It ends here; it ends now," Gabe groaned, his face expressionless.

"How?" Bock asked, shrugging his shoulders. "I've done work for some of the most influential people in the world. Read the newspapers. Listen to the radio. Watch television. This is a righteous fight I'm waging, and I've got a list of potential clients as long as that runway, all waiting for me to right a wrong for them. So don't stand there and bore me with your moral indignation! My twisted form will never cast a shadow on the inside of a prison wall."

From out of the opened cockpit window, the pilot reported that clearance had been granted, and that the plane was ready to go.

Seconds later, the twin jet engines whined to life, making shouting the only way to communicate.

"Our numbers are growing, Mr. Mitchell!" Bock yelled as Washington pressed the "*up*" button on the lift's control panel. "Think about how many times you've seen a guilty criminal set free, and berated yourself for not having done anything to prevent it! That same conversation goes on every night, around every dinner table across this deteriorating country of ours. I'm supplying the service," Bock said as he proudly thumbed his chest, "that everyone secretly wants done, but no one has the courage to carry out themselves!"

The engines' drone increased to a near deafening level.

"Go home, Mr. Mitchell," Bock encouraged, as his lift continued up the side of the plane. "Our business together is finished. There will be no retaliation on my part. This violent world is a far better place with men like you and me both patrolling it. So, go to your son, Mr. Mitchell, hold him close, and sleep well tonight knowing that, in one way or another, justice will always prevail."

Gabe took a step closer, but Washington backed him off with the threat of his pistol.

"Stop!" Gabe demanded feebly, over the steady howling of the jet's engines.

"I'm sorry, Mr. Mitchell," Bock cupped his hands around his mouth, "but you're just going to have to try better next time!"

The head of Worldwide Dispatch rolled himself into the cabin and waited while the specially designed hydraulic platform disappeared into the floor of the plane.

Down on the tarmac, Damon Washington politely tipped his gun barrel to his brow, and slowly backed up the stairs, careful not to divert his attention from Gabe. Once inside the cabin, Bock's assistant automatically retracted the stairs behind him, and closed and sealed the hatch. Through one of the small rectangular windows, August Bock waved victoriously as his private jet began to taxi out into the night.

"There ain't gonna be a next time," an exhausted Gabe Mitchell muttered, as he flashed a "thumbs up" toward the cockpit.

Bennett Chase acknowledged the signal and waved a final heartfelt farewell to his friend.

Don't miss it!

Also by Lyle Howard:

Mr. Sandman: A Thrilling Novel

Trouble in Paradise: A Thrilling Supernatural Mystery

Made in the USA
Columbia, SC
24 May 2021